The
Ugly Sisters

Danny King

The Ugly Sisters

Copyright © 2021 Danny King

ALL RIGHTS RESERVED

No part of this book may be reproduced in any form,
by photocopying or by any electronic or mechanical means,
including information storage or retrieval systems,
without permission in writing from the copyright owner.

All characters and events in this book are fictitious.
Any similarity to real persons, living or dead,
is coincidental and not intended by the author.

Cover design by the author
Glass slipper: AlexLMX licensed through shutterstock.com
Background image: Ashim D'Silva via unsplash.com
Chateau image: Bernardo Lorena Ponte via unsplash.com

ISBN: 979-850305978-6

19-05-21

CHAPTER ONE

IT WAS A FINE DAY for a stroll. The sun was shining, the gardens were in full bloom and the good people of Andovia were out in force.

Of those enjoying the air were two sisters, Marigold and Gardenia. Marigold was the older but Gardenia was the fairer. They never missed a Saturday afternoon stroll and, as ever, were dressed in the season's latest fashions — Marigold in strawberry pink, Gardenia in pineapple yellow — with corsets, crinolines and countless petticoats to buff up their outfits and hold it all together. Some might've argued they'd overdressed for the occasion, with more layers of satin and lace to lug around the park than most, but the sisters had a reputation to uphold as the best-dressed maidens in all of Andovia and they weren't about to let an Indian summer come between them and that.

"I say, 'tis frightfully clement for the time of day, 'tis it not, Marigold?" Gardenia observed, fanning herself relentlessly to make up for the lack of breeze.

"That it is, dear sister, but do save some air for the rest of us," Marigold replied, taking Gardenia's arm in an attempt to halt the constant wafting locomotion that had been following her since lunchtime.

Gardenia gave Marigold a withering glance and folded her fan away. She knew better than to argue with her sister. Besides Marigold was right. It wouldn't have been prudent to let the gentlefolk of their fair city suspect that her fine gown was causing her any sort of discomfort on this warm September afternoon. She would simply have to endure just as her beloved mother had always taught her to do. For appearance's sake. Because in Andovia, appearances, like reputations, were everything.

"Good afternoon, ladies," Monsieur Eames said, doffing his top hat as he passed by with his wife on his arm. Madame Eames was a client of Mother's. She'd bought five dresses from her to date and was putting the latest through its paces before recalling Mother for alterations.

"Good afternoon, Monsieur Eames. Madame," Marigold and Gardenia gleamed in unison, with Marigold adding, once they were out of earshot, "Such nice people the Eames. And their eldest comes out this autumn."

"Isabella is fifteen already?" Gardenia said.

"Just in time for the Prince's ball," Marigold confirmed.

"We must send the Eames a card to congratulate them on Isabella's debut," Gardenia suggested.

"Mother has them on the list," Marigold assured her.

They walked along the lakeshore and through the shade of the cherry tree groves but Gardenia found no relief from the heat that had built up between the hoops of her underskirt.

"If only I could air my ankles for a moment," she gasped in exasperation.

"And perhaps dip your buttocks in the duck pond while you're at it?" Marigold sympathised.

"Don't tempt me," grumbled Gardenia.

"Then be my guest," Marigold smiled. "Only do take care to weigh your knickers down with a rock when you kick them off as we wouldn't want them to blow across the park and cause a scene now, would we? Good afternoon Captain Durand."

Captain Durand came to attention with a snap of his heels to acknowledge the sisters' greeting. The handsome officer looked resplendent in his blue tunic with gold braiding and Gardenia couldn't help but notice that the colours matched his eyes and hair.

"I hear he's a favourite with the Prince," Marigold said with a covert backward glance. "Some say he'll make *Aide-de-*

camp when the Prince becomes King."

"How exciting," Gardenia cooed, overcome with the urge to start fanning herself once again. "What have you heard of his arrangements? Is he promised to anyone yet?" Captain Durand had the most exquisite features in all Andovia.

"Steady yourself, Gardenia. She who is too forward will more often than not finish last."

"Well, I think he looks very handsome in his uniform," Gardenia said.

"So does the messenger boy's mother, my dear, but we must be realistic. You are a pleasing girl but I fear the Captain may be beyond your reach and the stain of such a rejection will only further limit your options." Indeed, Gardenia was pleasant enough to look upon, with fair hair, a babyish round face and cheeks so rosy that they took several layers of foundation to tame. But there were fairer in the land. Fairer and from better families. As the elder sister, Marigold had already learned this bruising lesson the hard way. Gardenia still had it all to come. "Choose your target well. And never ask a question of a gentleman that you don't already know the answer to."

Gardenia recognised the words. They were the same ones their dear sweet mother had sung them in place of a lullaby when she'd tucked them to bed each night — over and over again — in preparation for things to come.

"Besides, Mother has an eye on Lieutenant Olivier for you. Do you not feel he would make an agreeable match?"

Gardenia kept her thoughts about Lieutenant Olivier to herself. He may have been more attainable — and the Grand Duke's youngest son to boot — but he was no Captain Durand. Not that Marigold would've understood. She, like their mother, followed her head rather than her heart when it came to the question of marriage. To them, love was like a chess match, not a waltz, and every maiden in Andovia was a

Grand Master. But this just depressed Gardenia even further. An advantageous union was all well and good but where was the romance? Where were the thrills and spills, the heady feelings of punching one's way through the clouds and leaping off sheer mountains and into the arms of your one true...

"Good afternoon, ladies!"

"Good afternoon to you, kind sir... urgh!" Gardenia grimaced when she turned and saw Andovia's filthiest tramp saluting them from his favourite park bench with a chicken bone he'd sucked almost translucent. Gardenia quickly looked away and hurried after Marigold before anyone saw her talking with *Dirty Didi*, as he was (less than) affectionately known around town.

Once again Marigold waited until they were out of earshot before delivering her verdict. "Shall I make enquiries as to his arrangements too?"

*

THE LINE AT STEFANO'S Ice Kiosk was always long on a Saturday afternoon but today the warm weather had stretched it halfway around the boating lake. Fortunately for Marigold and Gardenia, the lines in Andovia didn't work on a first-come-first-served basis. There was a protocol and everyone knew their rightful place.

"Good afternoon ladies," said the unaccompanied gentlemen at the very back of the line as they stepped aside for Marigold and Gardenia, doffing their hats as they passed by.

"Good afternoon to you, kind sirs," Marigold and Gardenia replied, making quick progress as they passed the lower ranks and up towards the business end of the line.

Once past the unaccompanied gentlemen, the sisters reached a cluster of couples — courting first and then married before them — who were also required to stand aside for two single ladies.

"Our compliments to your mother," Marigold and Gardenia were wished as they now passed these customers by.

"I would be pleased to pass it on," Marigold smiled with a bow, noting that the Perrins were three places in front of the Legrands this week, adding fuel to the fire that Monsieur Perrin was indeed in talks with the Grand Duke about supplying the army with beef this winter. Nothing had been officially announced, of course, but the line never lied. Marigold made a point of wishing Madame Perrin a "Good day" and nudged Gardenia to do likewise.

"So lovely to see you out and about again," Gardenia smiled, clearly getting Madame Perrin confused with Madame Perez who'd died three weeks earlier.

Marigold almost tripped over her own feet. Had anyone picked up on Gardenia's blunder or had it just been her? No one seemed to be recoiling in horror so it looked as though they'd got away with it but Marigold would need to have a word with her when they got home. A *faux pas* like that could derail a girl's prospects as effectively as a cold sore at Christmas. She had to learn to be more circumspect.

Finally Marigold and Gardenia arrived at the head of the line. Here there were no men, only girls, a couple of small boys and a few old widows who tried to stand their ground until Marigold's tut-tutting finally compelled them to step aside.

Five customers now stood between the sisters and Stefano's hallowed serving hatch. The Moreau boys were not yet ten but were only too keen to show how grown-up they were by letting the sisters in. The same, alas, could not be said of the Laurent girl. She and Marigold were approximately the same age. Their mothers both ran successful businesses and their fathers had both passed away. Yet Nina Laurent's father had been felled by smallpox whereas Marigold's had been felled by a musket ball at the Battle of Widows' Ridge, therefore no one could dispute whom should stand aside for whom. It was simply a matter of Nina Laurent acknowledging Marigold's superiority.

"Sweet Nina," Marigold smiled icily. "Your mother still has the bakery in the square?" Marigold didn't need to elaborate any further. The threat was clear and Nina stepped aside before she could heap any further shame upon her family's good name.

"Do please communicate my best wishes to her when you see her," Marigold cautioned, letting Nina off the hook but making a mental note to sign her next Christmas card "Season's greetings" rather than "Kindest regards" to put the jumped-up little brat back in her place.

Next came Claudia Ricci and Suzette Weiss. Claudia had just received her ice cone from Stefano and was out of contention but Suzette had yet to be served. She took one look at the approaching sisters and immediately stepped aside with a gracious smile.

"Sweet Marigold, dearest Gardenia, please after you."

But this time Gardenia made no mistake. She remained where she was and met Suzette's smile tooth for tooth.

"Oh no dearest Suzette, we insist, you first."

"Are you sure, sweet Gardenia? I don't mind waiting," Suzette parried, checking the younger sister's resolve.

"I'm still making up my mind. I would be curious to know which dessert you decide to have," Gardenia said, ending any lingering doubts in Suzette or anyone else's mind.

"You are too kind," Suzette simpered, touching Gardenia's hand to signal that the contest had been called.

Marigold breathed a sigh of relief. She'd stayed out of it because this had been Gardenia's clash but her sister had acquitted herself well and had paid Suzette the correct amount of respect. The line looked on with silent approval. The Weisses were an important family. Their grapes covered the slopes of their vast *Combien* vineyards. More importantly, their wines filled the cellars of a dozen noblemen and it was even said that the King himself had a few bottles put aside for informal occasions.

"A lemon sorbet, if you please, Monsieur Stefano," Suzette requested when she turned back to the hatch.

"An excellent choice, Mademoiselle," Monsieur Stefano said, snapping his fingers to relay the request back to Hans in the rear.

Marigold's heart began to flutter when Hans brought out a little dish of flavoured ice. He looked more rugged than ever, with his dark floppy hair, square jaw and emerald eyes. They lit up when they fell upon Marigold but she didn't return the compliment. She wasn't being rude or dismissive. She simply couldn't converse with Stefano's boy when he was at work. Or indeed, when he was not.

Marigold and Hans had known each other their whole lives and yet barely a dozen words had passed between them. Work and circumstance made meeting virtually impossible. Hans rose at 3am every morning to trek up to the summit of *Mont Magie* for the day's ice. The snow caps up there never thawed, even in the hottest of years, and once his barrels and panniers were full he would wrap them up to trap the cold and transport them back down the mountain to replenish the tubs of Stefano's ice room. It was gruelling work and desperately long hours but Stefano had no wife or child to leave his kiosk to. One day it would all belong to Hans and he'd have a boy to fetch the ice for him. And on that day, it would be deemed acceptable for a girl of Marigold's standing to speak with a boy of Hans's. But not before.

Gardenia knew nothing of Marigold's feelings. Nobody did. And after years of lecturing her younger sister on the importance of making a good match, it would've been impolitic to confess to longing after Stefano's bucket boy.

But it wasn't complete double standards by Marigold. Gardenia was fairer than her, after all. So much so that her comely charms had been turning heads since she'd bloomed a year earlier. Whether or not she had enough to bag a gentleman, this was to be seen, but this was the name of the game. And in Andovia everyone played it.

The sisters were now close enough to the serving hatch to feel the cooling breeze drifting out of Stefano's kiosk. It brought the tiniest breath of relief to Gardenia, who was sure she would melt if she didn't get a snow cone in the next sixty seconds but Suzette was in no hurry now that she'd got hers.

"Such wonderful gowns," she complimented, leaning back against the hatch as she licked sorbet from her silver spoon. "Your mother's designs I take it?"

"We are so lucky," Marigold confirmed, feeling Suzette's eyes running her up and down looking for loose threads. She would find none. "You still have yours made by Monsieur Vasseur?"

"His family has served mine for over a hundred years," Suzette replied to underline her pedigree.

Marigold smiled and looked Suzette's summer dress up and down. "I guess this is why he is such a genius at turning out such... traditional designs."

Suzette almost choked on her spoon but there was no coming back from that one. She'd walked into Marigold's trap and was now reeling from the suggestion that she was behind the times simply because she hadn't worn her Sunday best on Saturday afternoon. All eyes were now on Suzette. All eyes, that was, but Marigold's, who took the opportunity to steal a glance at Hans and was rewarded with the flicker of approval as it danced across his lips. No one messed with his girl and got away with it.

Suzette's humiliation was only cut short by the clatter of top hats being doffed as yet another thoroughbred filly rode her family name to the front of Stefano's line.

"Oh come on!" old widow Renard exclaimed as she was relegated back another place for the umpteenth time. She'd barely moved an inch since two o'clock despite Stefano running a roaring trade and was ready to give up on her lemon lolly altogether when she saw the latest eyeful sail past. The Moreau boys jumped so far back that they almost fell into the boating lake and Nina Laurent left the queue altogether. She had seen the face of the future and it didn't resemble hers in any way, shape or form.

Suzette, Marigold and Gardenia all stared at the girl before them and were dumbstruck at her beauty. Her eyes were like diamonds and her skin the pallor of milk. Her hair of pure gold had been tied back into a simple ponytail and her elfin-like features were unspoilt by greasepaint or powder. She was Marigold's height and yet had the waist of one of the Moreau boys — the younger one. Her clothes were fine but not too fine. They were elegant and unfussy and they enhanced her natural beauty without overshadowing it. Gardenia felt all at once overdressed and naked in this stranger's company and didn't know whether to step aside or go for her throat.

Suzette seized her chance and moved on to leave Marigold grappling over the issue of who should be served first. The line knew who they had their money on but Marigold wasn't about to be pushed aside by some mystery girl who had yet to realise she was a swan swimming in a duck pond.

Marigold threw down the gauntlet and dared this new girl to pick it up.

"Please, my dear, after you," she smiled, stepping aside to give her a clear view of Stefano's serving hatch.

"Thank you," said the girl with an unmistakable French accent, stepping forward to ask for two dozen sorbets in all different flavours before Marigold knew what had hit her.

"What's going on? What do we do?" Gardenia panicked as Marigold looked down the line for its reaction and didn't like what she saw.

Mother had not prepared her for situations like this.

Five minutes later and the sorbets were still coming, but none in Marigold or Gardenia's direction. Just how many puddings did this strange girl want anyway? Stefano plonked ice dishes onto the hatch until there was little room for any more.

"Two dozen, in all different flavours, as requested," Stefano finally said without asking why she should want so many.

The girl handed Stefano an unfamiliar gold coin and asked if it would cover the cost and Stefano confirmed that it would, after first biting it to check it wasn't chocolate.

Only now did Marigold understand when a huge crowd of street children appeared from out of nowhere and began leaping about with excitement as the girl passed out the desserts amongst them. There was even one for Didi, who licked his glass clean and handed it back with a sticky burp of satisfaction.

Gardenia was aghast and refused to let that particular glass out of her sight, horrified at the thought of getting her own dessert in the same.

With these actions, by definition, the girl had ranked all these scruffy urchins and, Didi too, as better than every lord, lady and gentlemen in Stefano's queue. It was nothing short of scandalous and yet no one batted an eyelid. Had the world gone mad? Did etiquette and protocol and all they'd grown up clinging to count for nothing if the face was pretty enough?

"Look at their joy. Have you ever seen anything so wonderful?" the girl asked, basking in the radiance of her own good deed.

"Simple pleasures. What more can one ask for?" Marigold echoed, wondering what more indeed. If a maiden's eligibility could elevate her prospects then who knew how high this girl could ascend. Of course, it all depended upon her family. Who was she? Where had she come from? Who was her father? And what did he do?

"Do you know these children?" Gardenia asked, lending her voice to the least of Marigold's questions.

"I do now," the strange girl smiled, handing Gardenia an empty dish before scampering off to cries of, "Who wants to go for a paddle?"

Gardenia dumped the empty dish on Stefano's hatch while Stefano complimented the sisters on their outfits and asked what he could get for them. But Gardenia no longer wanted anything and Marigold was not listening. She was watching Hans as he picked up the dishes that had been left on the grass, hoping to catch his eye. But Hans never turned around. He just kept looking over at the lake —

— and the heavenly figure slipping out of her shoes by the cool water's edge.

CHAPTER TWO

"MOTHER! MOTHER! There was a girl in the park who went paddling with the children," Gardenia said, the moment the sisters got home.

"Never mind about that. Get out of those dresses immediately. I want to take a look at them. How did they hold up? Who did you see?" Mother asked, dismissing Gardenia's red-hot news as inconsequential tittle-tattle as she turned her around and began unlacing her from behind.

"But Mother, she was in the lake. I saw everything, for Heaven's sake!" Gardenia exclaimed, scarcely able to believe what she'd witnessed. The girl had kicked off her shoes and waded into the shallows, hoisting up her skirt as she went. She'd shown the world her knees. It was unthinkable.

"What are you blathering about, child?" Mother asked, pulling Gardenia's yellow dress over her shoulders and pulling it down past her hips so that she might step out.

"A strange girl. In the park," Gardenia simply repeated, at a loss how else to describe what she'd seen.

Marigold confirmed all she said, adding that this girl was no farm girl taking in the sights. She was a girl of breeding with gold to spend and a face to acquire more.

"I will make enquiries," Mother reassured her girls. "But she sounds like a serving girl who's gone potty and made off with her Lordship's coins. Chances are she'll be wearing chains by the end of the day."

Mother hung Gardenia's dress on the dressmaker's dummy by her cutting bench and set to work helping Marigold out of hers.

"You saw anyone else while you were out? Besides Lady Godiva I mean?"

Marigold rattled off the names of those they'd passed, not forgetting to mention where the Perrins and Legrands had stood, but she couldn't help but feel that none of this was as significant as their final encounter. Their paths would cross again, of that she had no doubt. But the next time she would be ready.

The bell above their front door let out a telling tinkle. Mother helped Marigold step out of her dress and then headed through the curtains to greet this hour's caller.

"Madame Eames, what a pleasure it is to see you again. And what can I do for you?" Marigold heard Mother ask.

"Madame Roche, I saw your lovely daughters in the park a little earlier on and was quite taken with Gardenia's dress. Do you think you could manage something similar for my Isabella? She debuts at the Prince's ball next month and we so want her to make a good impression."

"It would be an honour, Madame Eames. I will call on Isabella first thing in the morning to take her measurements. And she shall be the belle of the ball."

Marigold hung her dress on a second dressmaker's dummy while Madame Eames went through a bundle of swatches with Mother. Mother's gowns were indeed the finest in all Andovia and her reputation was slowly spreading. She'd worked hard to get to where she was and Marigold and Gardenia had done their bit, not least of all on days like today, parading themselves around town in her latest designs like mannequins come to life. The sisters might not have liked it, and their poor father might've turned in his grave at the thought of his daughters reducing themselves to clothes horses, but every girl played the cards they were dealt.

Or at least, learned to cheat better than everyone else.

*

MOTHER'S OWN STORY had almost ended before it had begun. Abandoned on the steps of the cathedral when she was just a couple of days old, she was so tiny and frail that the Bishop saw no point in dispatching her off to the orphanage.

"This cherub will not survive the night," he solemnly predicted, thus becoming the first person to fall foul of Mother's legendary stubborn streak. For two days and two nights, she wailed in protest at being denied any form of nourishment (spiritual asides) before the Bishop finally relented.

"Her cries have so offended our Lord that He hath chosen not to take her unto His bosom. Remove her at once. And may God have mercy on thy keeper's soul."

Duly, the infant was delivered into the hands of the parish orphanage while the Bishop was delivered into the Lord's just two weeks later when he keeled over whilst pouring the communion wine.

Much has been written about the cruelty of orphanages: the terrible conditions, the appalling food, the filthy wretches that reside inside. But what is not considered is that every spoonful of oats that goes into an orphan's mouth must first come out of a rich man's pocket. Charity pays for food. Charity buys clothes. Charity repairs the roof when a storm blows through the Kingdom. And charity settles the doctor's bills when the children grow sick — or more usually the undertaker's. Without charity, there was no orphanage. Charity was life. And yet for so many in Andovia, charity began at home — for those who were lucky enough to have one. The orphanage did the best with what it had. Very few did more.

The first thing the superintendent gave its newest resident was a name: Catherine because she had been found on the steps of the Cathedral. And Petit, because she was so undernourished and frail.

In the years to come, Catherine would tell her daughters very little about her time in the orphanage. She felt it would've been ungracious of her to hold it to account for its shortcomings after all it had done for her. This hadn't been much, admittedly, but it had been more than her own mother had been prepared to do. Gruel, rags and a leaky roof: these basic requirements were all she had known until her twelfth birthday when the superintendent deemed Catherine old enough to fend for herself. The orphanage was overcrowded and underfunded. Beds were needed. Extra mouths were not. Catherine was given a pair of shoes, an old blanket, a hessian sack and an emotionless farewell. Her childhood was over.

The world was a dangerous place for a young girl in those days, particularly one left to fend for herself. Catherine may have been scrawny and undernourished from birth but she had an innocence that shone like a beacon in a world of long shadows. Many was the time she had to run for her life. Danger lurked around every corner. But Catherine was a fast learner. She lived by her wits: stole food, begged for pennies and evaded the authorities for two long years until one December night, three days before Christmas, her luck finally ran out…

*

"THIS WAY! THIS WAY! I see the little thief!"

Catherine could hear the cries of soldiers all around her. The entire army seemed to have taken up the chase, all for a couple of turnips. She knew these woods well but they had numbers on their side. Why hadn't she waited until after midnight like last time? Why had she taken such a risk?

Catherine hurried through the trees clutching the turnips inside her hessian sack as though they were gold. She hadn't eaten in three days and hunger had forced her hand. The night had been dark but her footprints in the snow had alerted the sentries to her larceny. Now there was no hiding from them. Whichever way she ran the fresh snows continued to betray her.

"Stop or we'll shoot!"

Catherine didn't stop. She didn't even pause. The punishment for looting from the army was death so what difference did it make if they shot her in the back or tied her to a stake in front of their flag?

She'd come the way she always came when pilfering their stores, through the slopes where the woods were at their most impenetrable. She was small and she was sprite and she could duck through brambles a field mouse would think twice about entering. She'd done it several times before, since the army had made its camp in her neck of the woods, but this time they'd been ready for her.

"I said stop!" CRACK! The sound of a musket shot made Catherine change direction.

A thorn scratched her cheek as she darted between two shrubs but the cold had numbed her face so that she barely winced. More painful were her feet. They were soaked through and frozen and the shoes the orphanage had given her were falling apart. She'd lost all sensation below the knees and could scarcely stay upright but she pushed herself on, through the snows, the woods and the pain.

"Go right! Cut off the flank!"

Another thicket, another gash, this time it took a chunk from her thigh. The shock knocked her into the snow and sat on her back while she screamed in silent agony. This was more than any girl could endure but there was simply no choice. She had to get up and move. The crunch of boots on snow got louder as her pursuers got closer and soon they were closing on all sides.

"In the bushes, there. Use your bayonets. Use your torches. Flush the little rat out!"

Catherine scrambled through the undergrowth and tumbled down a short slope. The mention of bayonets drove her on in spite of her injuries. At the bottom of the slope, she found a gulley and used it as cover but it only took her so far. Torches to the fore soon stopped her in her tracks. They fanned out left and right while others found the entrance to the gulley. She was surrounded on all sides and had nowhere to go.

Catherine reasoned she had one last chance and threw herself into a snowdrift. She kicked and burrowed in a last desperate attempt to conceal herself but it was too late. Before she knew it a hand had grabbed her ankle and she was dragged out to face the consequences of her desperation.

"Got ya, you little rat!" the soldier cackled from behind a flaming torch, but that was all Catherine heard. Panicked through with terror and bleeding from head to toe, her wits finally deserted her and she passed out where she lay.

CHAPTER THREE

ISABELLA LIKED THE PINK satin but Madame Eames liked the blue. And while the customer was usually right, Mother would let them have neither. Isabella had fabulous hazel eyes, she told Madame Eames upon their next housecall. It had to be apple green or nothing.

"Do you think so, Madame Roche?" Madame Eames asked, holding the swatches against her daughter's brow to contrast the colours.

"There are no second chances to debut, Madame Eames. If Isabella is to make a grand impression she must use what nature has so generously provided. And your daughter's eyes are surely the most beautiful in all the Kingdom."

Isabella giggled with delight and ran straight to her parlour mirror to scrutinise herself at length. She always suspected she had nice eyes but here was independent confirmation. They were not only nice eyes, they were beautiful eyes, nay the *most beautiful in all the Kingdom*. And if a person's eyes were the windows to their soul, then surely it followed that she must have possessed the most beautiful soul in all the Kingdom too.

Just as she also always suspected.

From this moment onwards she would always wear green. It would be her colour.

Gardenia flicked through the swatches.

"Purple's nice too," she said without thinking.

Mother snatched them out of her hand and sent her off to join Isabella at the mirror. It had taken her almost 45 minutes to settle their minds on green and she wasn't about to have Gardenia plant a seed of doubt now. Especially with that job lot of green satin she had taking up all the shelf space in their stockroom back home.

"I believe I have all the measurements I require for now," Mother said, rolling up her tape measure and dropping it back into her sewing kit. "I will send word when the garment is ready for Isabella's first fitting and arrange a time that is suitable for you and your daughter."

"And my husband too," Madame Eames insisted.

"Of course. That goes without saying," Mother said with a flicker of fatigue. Three critics were always harder to appease than two. And fathers generally offered more opinions than ideas when it came to their daughter's state of dress.

"Excellent. I shall look forward to seeing you then," Madame Eames smiled as she rose from her chaise lounge and walked towards the oak-panelled double doors that led out to the hallway. "Good day to you, Madame Roche."

There was no invitation to stay for tea. There never was at the Eames but that was just as well because the Eames were quite the most dreadful company imaginable. And that was saying something in a town where the competition for that particular accolade was exceptionally stiff.

"I will have my man help you with your bags," Madame Eames said, pulling a rope hanging next to the door to set a bell tinkling somewhere off in the depths of her château. "Hmm, now, whilst I have you here, would you be so good as to take a look at my lace trim. It snagged against the coach this morning and it seems to have lost a thread."

Madame Eames turned to show Mother her offending rear. This was the freebie. Whilst there was never tea at the Eames there was always a freebie. Madame had waited until she'd rung for the footman before asking for Mother's advice because Mother was now off the clock. It was an unwritten rule but those sorts of rules were often the most binding.

"I would be happy to do so, Madame," Mother said, popping open her sewing kit and kneeling behind Madame Eames with a long sharp needle in her hand. Oh, the temptation. But such an act of folly would've hurt Mother more than it would've hurt Madame Eames so she swallowed her pride and set to the work applying a few strategic stitches to the hem of her dress.

Of course, Madame Eames hadn't really torn her hem on the coach this morning. Madame Eames hadn't even left the house this morning. But she couldn't very well bring a torn dress down and ask Mother for a freebie on something that she wasn't already wearing, could she? That would've been premeditated. And you couldn't expect a professional dressmaker to apply her skills for free on something other than an incidental inconvenience.

"What a lovely ring," Madame Eames said, glancing down at Mother as she worked on her hem, eyeing the large opal ring on her left forefinger. "It is beautiful, Madame Roche. Where did you get it from, might I ask?"

"It was a gift," Mother replied without looking up.

"From a grateful customer, no doubt," Madame Eames fished. She had always desired a ring such as that. And it didn't matter that she had a dozen just like it and bigger in her jewellery box upstairs, it was the one on Mother's finger she now coveted. Tradespeople sometimes made gifts of their own possessions to help secure future business but Madame Eames would be disappointed today.

"From my late husband," Mother told her.

"It is so very beautiful," Madame Eames repeated, wondering just how attached to it Mother was.

"Thank you," Mother said, adding, "as was he."

Madame Eames took the hint but made up her mind there'd be no tip for Mother this Christmas. Not that there'd been one last year or the year before. But that was beside the point. Mother's attitude justified Madame Eames's fiscal prudence.

"Look at my eyes," Isabella said across the parlour, finally managing to tear her gaze away from herself and glare, unblinking, at Gardenia. "Do they not sparkle like magic?"

"They are most beautiful," Gardenia confirmed with a happy smile.

Gardenia liked Isabella. She was a sweet-natured girl but utterly self-absorbed. Many girls Isabella's age were and that was no one's fault of their own. After all, when a girl of breeding's only expectation was to be pretty and gay it was little wonder that most spent more time in front of the mirror than the bookcase. And now, with her big debut only a month away, Isabella's vanity had begun exerting such a powerful force on her that she was in danger of disappearing completely up her own prospects.

"Do you think Lord Hubert will notice my eyes?" Isabella said, fluttering her lashes at Gardenia in a clumsy first attempt at sexual semaphore.

"He would need to have lost his own not to," Gardenia reassured her, stifling a yawn and wondering how much longer they were going to be here. But this was Gardenia's job today. Mother took care of business while Gardenia bonded with the customers. Marigold had performed this role for many years but Gardenia was closer in age to Isabella, hence the mantle had been passed from one sister to the next today.

"I don't think I've ever seen anyone with eyes such as mine," Isabella said as she fluttered her heavy eyelashes, drawn once again to the sight of her own reflection.

The most depressing thing about the whole experience was that Gardenia recognised aspects of herself in Isabella. They were both young, they'd both been brought up to believe that they were pretty and they were both expected to make good matches. And while Gardenia had been urged to temper her own expectations, Isabella had not, buying wholesale into the notion that she was life's first prize in spite of all evidence to the contrary.

"I suppose you can never wear green because you do not have the eyes for it," Isabella told Gardenia, sounding almost sorry for her companion whilst simultaneously forgetting that Gardenia had worn green the last time they'd met only two weeks earlier. "So, what shall you wear to the ball, dearest Gardenia?"

The question caught Gardenia by surprise. Until now, Isabella had simply used Gardenia as though she were another mirror, so Gardenia hadn't expected to be asked about her own plans.

"I... I... I don't really know," Gardenia said, having been so busy helping Mother dress every girl in the land that she'd not really had time to consider herself. "I've not really thought about it," she confessed.

"How can you not have thought about it? What else is there to think about?" Isabella exclaimed, her mind in a spin at the very notion. She took Gardenia into a sisterly embrace. Gardenia, as ever, was wearing a delightful dress of cream and yellow. Mother had gone to great lengths this morning to ensure that she looked just right for their house call — fabulous and yet no threat to Isabella. It had taken a little extra thought but it had paid off with Isabella talking to Gardenia as though she were an equal while at the same time taking her under her wing.

"My dearest friend, you mustn't put off your preparations any longer. You have a pretty face, of sorts, and a cordial nature. You will surely find favour amongst many of the second-born gentlemen of court," Isabella reassured her, adding as a stark warning. "After all, you would not wish to end up like your sister now, would you? You have so much more to offer."

Poor Marigold, still single at 19 and how the good folks of Andovia knew it.

Mother finished her repairs on Madame Eames's hem just as the footman entered to carry her bags.

"There you go, Madame, as good as new," Mother said, climbing to her feet and closing her sewing kit once again.

"Oh, Madame Roche, you are a marvel," Madame Eames said, twisting her neck to stare at Mother's handiwork. "Now, do let me know the moment Isabella's dress is ready to be fitted, won't you?"

"Of course, Madame, I will give it my highest priority," Mother assured her.

"Thank you," Madame Eames beamed gratefully, checking her smile just a little to add; "And do pass on my warmest regards to your other daughter... er..."

"Marigold," Mother reminded her.

"Yes, that's it. Marigold," she said with a sad shake of the head. "Such a pity."

CHAPTER FOUR

MARIGOLD HAD NO USE FOR PITY. Unbeknown to most, she was already secretly betrothed. The only problem was that her secret was so closely guarded, she wasn't even sure if her intended was aware of their betrothal.

Marigold used the opportunity whilst Mother and Gardenia were out to rendezvous away from prying eyes. It meant an early start but the moment Mother and Gardenia left for the Eames's, Marigold threw off her summer dress and pulled on her riding leathers. They were dark and dowdy clothes, not the type Marigold was used to being seen out in, so she was confident she could slip out of town without being noticed.

Mother and Gardenia had taken their tap pulled by Queenie but that still left old Liquorice. He might not have been up to standing outside the houses of the great and the good anymore but he could still ride like the wind with Marigold at his reins.

Liquorice snorted with approval as Marigold strapped on his old cavalry saddle.

"Let's go," she whispered into his ear, giving his neck a loving pat and climbing onto his back in the most unladylike fashion possible. She ducked under the stable doorway as Liquorice set off at a canter and steered him around the back of the house, through the lanes and away from the town centre.

Andovia was the name of the city as well as the Kingdom, which left its citizens with the unsettling sense that no matter how far they strayed from the shadow of the King's grand palace, they were always in Andovia. It also made the street signs somewhat confusing for travellers with milestones for Andovia reading "30 miles" next to others which declared "Welcome to Andovia". But Marigold needed no milestones this morning. She knew exactly where she was heading and turned north, away from the cobblestones of Andovia and towards the windswept steps of *Mont Magie*, or *Magic Mountain* as it was otherwise known. Also in Andovia. But only just.

Once outside the city gates, the countryside opened up. Greys and browns of Andovia's thoroughfares gave way to greens and yellows of her fields and orchards. Wheat stems stirred in the morning's breeze, apple trees sagged against their heavy loads and wild berries seasoned the air with their sweet zests. Mother Nature was in full bloom, spurring Marigold on to her destination.

Without warning, Liquorice pulled up sharply, almost throwing Marigold from her saddle.

"Woah! What is it, boy?" she said, pulling back on his reins as she tried to settle her ride. In his cavalry heyday, Liquorice had seen seven kinds of hell so he wasn't the type of horse to startle easily.

Marigold heard them before she saw them. A low irritable buzzing barred their way. Wasps. They'd made their nest in the low branches of an old apple tree and were growing drunk and cantankerous on the fermenting fruit that lay all around them. Liquorice reared back and Marigold steered him away.

"We'll give them their space," Marigold whispered, patting his neck and leaving the wasps to their bounty.

After a couple more miles the dirt tracks turned to granite and the terrain started to slope. The mountains loomed large before her and the air grew frigid. Marigold pulled her cashmere scarf over her chin and gave thanks for the warm woollen lining inside her leather breeches. Liquorice didn't seem to mind the conditions though and soon worked up a sweat climbing the trails until they'd reached the northern pass. If she'd continued on her way she would've eventually reached the equally diminutive Kingdom of

Srendizi, a lawless backwater of ridges and canyons sandwiched between a frozen belt of inaccessible mountain ranges. But Marigold had no intention of going that far. No one in good conscience would. This was the point Marigold had set out to reach and she'd made it in good time. A second horse, this one with a cart, waited patiently by the side of the track for his rider to return and Liquorice greeted him with a snort.

Marigold jumped out of her saddle and looked towards the summit. All was still but for a few clouds rolling across the peaks. After a few minutes, a figure appeared on the horizon. He had three barrels with him and was rolling them down the slopes towards where Marigold was waiting. The figure stopped when he saw he had company and took a moment to assess the situation. Marigold pulled the scarf from her face and called up to him.

"I couldn't wait for my sorbet today so I thought I'd come and get it myself."

"Marigold?" Hans asked in bewilderment but otherwise happy to see her. "Is that you?"

Hans kicked his barrels packed with snow down the last hundred metres and pulled the dark goggles from his face to check his eyes were not deceiving him.

"You rode all this way?"

"No further than you come every day," Marigold replied.

"But you're a girl," he pointed out.

"Thank you for noticing."

Marigold wasn't offended by Hans's remark. The very pillars of their great Kingdom had been founded upon such expectations but it was one thing for the Eames and the Weisses of this world to underestimate her, it was another to let Hans do the same. Theirs had been an on-off-off-off-off relationship determined in part by Mother's own expectations for her daughters. But when Marigold had reached — and then quickly passed — the age of maturity without receiving a single proposal (honourable or otherwise) Mother's focus switched to Gardenia. Both girls had bloomed within a year of each other but Marigold's petals weren't quite as alluring as her sister's.

At least, not as far as the wealthy sons of Andovia were concerned. But there were some in this tiny Kingdom who thought otherwise.

"You are alone? No one is with you?" Hans asked, scarcely believing this was possible.

"For all I know we could be the last people on Earth," Marigold teased, making Hans's ruddy cheeks turn redder still.

"You are so bold," Hans said with a grin, "but clearly no tracker. Riders came through here this morning, from the north. You shouldn't be out here by yourself."

"I am not by myself. I am with you," Marigold said, taking a step towards him. Hans did not know how to behave. He'd spent so many years trying to bury his feelings that he was almost as frozen as the slopes they shared. He was a lowly bucket boy. Marigold was a lady of good name. He had no right to his desires even if they were all he had.

And yet still she was here and taking another step towards him when he instinctively backed away.

"No one will know," she said, finally cornering him between two boulders. She was close enough for Hans to feel her breath against his face. He trembled despite feeling unusually hot in his winter gear. Hans had no fear of wolf attacks or bandits or climbing sheer icy cliffs to reach sparkling icicles but his courage (and experience) faltered in the face of Marigold's boldness.

"My lady," Hans said, almost doffing his cap out of respect. "How shall I be? There is so much I want to say but I am afraid."

"Don't be. This morning is just for us."

Hans had no idea what this meant but before he was able to say so Marigold's ruby red lips were pressed against his. He squeaked in surprise but managed to go with the kiss despite cracking his head on an overhanging ledge. He had never been intimate with anyone before. He'd not even had a mother to kiss him goodnight or a dog to lick his face so Marigold's advance was both alien and Earthly all at once.

Their lips parted yet their bodies remained entwined.

"I've wanted to do that all my life," Marigold confided.

"Me too," said Hans, before unnecessarily adding, "with you."

Liquorice rasped his cheeks while Hans's own horse stayed wisely out of it. He had no opinion on the matter. He was just a horse, and a bucket boy's horse at that.

"I live for Saturday," Hans finally volunteered. "All I think about is that moment I see you coming for your dessert. That is my dessert. I always try to give you a little extra but not too much otherwise Monsieur Stefano might grow wise about my feelings for you."

"And what are your feelings for me?" Marigold asked, hoping they amounted to more than an extra spoonful of sorbet.

Hans pulled Marigold closer still, causing their winter leathers to squeak in their loving embrace.

"I feel for you as the moon feels for the sun. I am the wind and you are the mountain. We are two clouds drifting through an open sky," Hans recited, making the mistake of thinking Marigold was yearning to hear a weather report instead of the one word that had eluded her her whole life.

"Do you love me?" Marigold asked, silencing Hans before he'd had a chance to compare their relationship to rainbows, fog or blustery Tuesday afternoons.

"I... I... do, my lady..."

"Marigold," she said.

"Marigold," he smiled, as if the name brought pleasure

to his lips just saying it. "I want to shout your name from the top of the world."

"Then do so," she told him.

"And bring the mountain down on top of me?" Hans said, knowing full well the perils of making too much noise in avalanche country. "It might even be worth it."

They kissed again, though this time it was Hans who made the running. He'd kissed her a thousand times in his dreams but the reality was more wonderful than the fantasy. The feel, the smell and the taste of Marigold: these were the things his mind could not have imagined and these were the things he quickly found himself intoxicated by. He didn't want this kiss to end. He didn't want to go back to the cold realities of pretence and denial. Pandora's lid was off. How could things ever be the same between them again? But they had no choice. This was still Andovia, even all the way up here. And bucket boys and ladies of good name were not permitted to find happiness with each other.

Except on *Mont Magie*.

"I have to go before Mother returns," Marigold said, pained to tear herself from Hans.

"Will I see you again?" Hans asked, holding onto her gloved hand as she tried to pull away.

Marigold knew what Mother would say, and more importantly what Mother would do, if she learned of her eldest daughter's infatuation with Stefano's lowly assistant. She had no truck with her children's happiness but she was a pragmatist. Her iron heart had been forged in the fires of bitter experience. She meant well but she would've also tried to save Marigold from herself. And Marigold couldn't jeopardise her only regular contact with Hans, no matter how fleeting it might be.

"I'll see you on Saturday," she smiled sadly, climbing back onto Liquorice and leading him back down the stony trail and back to the lives they were expected to lead. Perhaps one day it would be different. Perhaps one day, when Mother had finally given up all hope of Marigold making a favourable match and Stefano had handed over his scoop to Hans, they might dare to dream of a life together. One day. But not today.

"And I shall see you," Hans called after her. "On Saturday. And I shall give you all the sorbet in the world, because I love you, Marigold Roche. I love you and I will always love you until the day I die."

The cold mountain winds prised the tears from Marigold's eyes as she made her way back home. She'd come here to check Hans still had feelings for her after Saturday's brush with the mystery girl. And while she'd at least managed to lay these doubts to rest, she had foolishly kindled her own fires only to come away with nothing to burn.

Mother had always warned her girls to guard their hearts. Mother, as ever, knew what was right, even when it felt so wrong.

"Marigold!" she heard Hans sing after her. "Marigold! Marigold! Marigold!" It was more of a whisper than a cry but she heard it all the same. He wasn't calling her back, simply rejoicing in the sound of her name, saying it as loudly as he dared —

— as though they were the last two people on Earth.

CHAPTER FIVE

THE FOOTMAN SHOWED MOTHER and Gardenia out, placing their bags in the back of Queenie's trap and helping both into their seats.

"You are most kind," Mother thanked the footman. She always made a note of thanking the staff. It wasn't customary. In fact, it was downright unusual in this town but it cost nothing and helped oil the gears. The aristocracy might've owned Andovia but it was their servants who ran it.

The footman bowed cordially then turned when he heard the crunch of footsteps approaching from behind. It was Madame Eames's gardener, Monsieur Samuel. He drew near with his cap in his hands and looked up at Mother and Gardenia in their seats.

"Madame Roche. I heard you were calling this morning and wanted to extend my respects," he said with due reverence, only too aware of the liberty he was taking but compelled to do so anyway.

Mother looked down at the gardener's disfigured face. A white scar cut through his top lip, exposing his crooked teeth and pulling his mouth into a permanent leer. Gardenia recoiled at the sight of him but Mother smiled and reached down to touch his broad shoulder.

"Monsieur Samuel. How are you, dear friend?"

Samuel's green eyes lit up upon hearing his name and he seemed to shed a couple of years.

"Honoured that you remember me after all these years," he said, looking from Mother to daughter and then back again.

"The honour is all mine," Mother replied. "You know my youngest?"

Samuel bowed to Gardenia and smiled in wonder.

"She is a credit to you, Madame. We are all so very

THE UGLY SISTERS

proud of her," he said, causing Gardenia to look at him in confusion.

Madame Eames appeared at the parlour window and caught sight of the impromptu reunion taking place on her front drive. The footman gave a cough to draw their attention to Madame Eames's disapproving gaze and Samuel reluctantly withdrew to let Mother and Gardenia go, not wishing to get them into bother with the mistress of the house.

"Wonderful to see you again, Madame Roche," he said, giving Mother one final bow. He thought for one moment and then whispered solemnly, "For *the King's men*".

"For *the King's men*," Mother replied with a veiled nod, jigging Queenie's reins to clatter their way down Madame Eames's pebble drive.

Gardenia looked back at the gardener as he replaced his cap and headed back to work.

"Who was that, Mother?" she asked as they passed through the gates and back out onto the main thoroughfare.

"Just an old friend," Mother said without telling her anything that she hadn't already gathered.

"I guessed that but how does he know me? And what did he mean they are all so very proud of me? Who's proud of me?"

"We are all proud of you, Gardenia. You should take it as a compliment and not make so much of a fuss about it," Mother deflected. Gardenia could tell she was deflecting and changed her tack.

"Who are *the King's men*?"

This time Mother said nothing and hoped not to have to but Gardenia pressed the matter.

"Mother?"

"I will tell you when you are older," Mother said, adding intrigue to Gardenia's growing curiosity.

"Tell me now."

"When you are older," Mother insisted.

32

"When's that?"

"Some time from now."

"Why not now?" Gardenia nagged.

"Because you are not yet blessed with the gift of circumspection," Mother replied as they passed Captain Durand leading a squadron of Guards towards the city gates. Mother welcomed the distraction but Gardenia wasn't put off for long.

"Does Marigold know about it?" she asked, trying to find a different route into the enigma.

"This is not a matter to be discussed with anyone, even your own sweet sister," Mother told her. "I mean it, Gardenia, I will tell you when you are ready to know but you must never mention a word of this to anyone. Do you promise me?"

"Why can't you tell me?" Gardenia said in frustration.

"Do you promise?"

"Ohhhh..." Gardenia groaned but she knew it was hopeless. "Okay, I promise," she finally relented, slumping into her seat to stew on her disappointment.

"Don't slouch," Mother said, denying Gardenia even her sulk.

They clip-clopped through the main square, past the cathedral and the Palace beyond. Gardenia stared up at the royal residence as they cantered past, with its turrets, balconies, parapets and keeps, and she wondered what it must be like to live in such a magnificent building. She'd never even set foot inside the Palace grounds but it had always been her dream. To tread the hallowed halls, even once, would've been a fairytale come true.

"Mother? Will I go to the ball?" Gardenia asked.

"Of course," Mother replied.

"As a guest?"

"Dear child, you know that is impossible."

"But as your attendant?" Gardenia said, still happy to know that she was going in some capacity.

"As a ladies' attendant," Mother corrected her.

Gardenia would attend many balls in the years to come but not the Prince's ball. That, like the handsome Captain Durand, was beyond her station and an invitation to the most eagerly anticipated event of the year was reserved for the daughters of ennobled fathers alone.

Gardenia accepted this and thought some more.

"What shall I wear, Mother?" Gardenia asked.

"I haven't decided yet," she replied.

"Shouldn't we start thinking about it?"

"One of the benefits of being a dressmaker is that you get to see what everyone else is wearing before you have to decide for yourself," Mother explained, steering Queenie around the Palace walls and towards the far end of town and home.

Gardenia felt reassured by the explanation but still wondered something.

"Should I wear green?" she asked, showing Mother her eyes as though she'd never seen them before.

"Certainly not," Mother replied with a snap of the reins. "Ghastly colour."

CHAPTER SIX

YOUNG CATHERINE PETIT awoke to unfamiliar surroundings. The night was dark but she could tell from the glow of a fire outside that she was in a large canvas tent. None of the fire's warmth managed to reach her though. Her body was frozen and her legs racked with pain. She tried to get up but found that she couldn't. Her ankles had been shackled. Suddenly the events of earlier came back to her. She let out a gasp of panic and began clawing at her shackles.

"Go get the Lieutenant. Tell him the prisoner's awake," Catherine heard a voice say.

A few minutes later the flap of the tent was pulled back and two soldiers looked in; one was clearly an officer with his starched blue tunic and an expression that matched while the other was a gruff-looking Sergeant with a trio of stripes to differentiate him from the rest of the cannon fodder.

"What a filthy beast!" the officer scowled in disgust. "Have your men form themselves up into a firing party immediately."

"Begging your pardon, sir, but do you think that's absolutely necessary?" the Sergeant ventured to ask.

The officer's tone ratcheted up a couple of octaves at the indignity of having to explain himself but he gave his reasons anyway, for he was a born leader, or so he had been born to believe.

"She was caught stealing from the King. The penalty for that offence is clear," the officer said, dropping the flap to indicate that the trial had come to its conclusion. Due process had been served.

Catherine felt her head spin in terror and yanked at the shackles with ever more determination to free herself but she was so weak from hunger she would've had trouble freeing herself from paper chains let alone iron ones.

"We don't actually know if she stole anything, sir. No food or provisions were found on her," the Sergeant said as he hurried after the Lieutenant.

"I understood from the Quartermaster that we are missing two turnips," the Lieutenant's silhouette said outside the side of the tent.

"That may be so, sir, but we can't prove she was the one who took them," the Sergeant said. "Might be wise to exercise prudence in this case, sir, just so there's no comeback, and prescribe a less punitive course?"

"What you mean like hanging?" the Lieutenant asked, just to check that he and the Sergeant were on the same page.

"Er no sir, I meant perhaps maybe a stiff word in her ear like, frighten the living daylights out of her and send her on her way," the Sergeant advised.

The Lieutenant could scarcely believe his ears. "Are you suggesting we simply let her go?" he screeched.

"We can't prove she did anything, sir. For all we know she was just lost in the woods when our sentries found her. It might be bad for morale if we start executing people for this, particularly little girls, sir," the Sergeant implored.

"Little girls!" the Lieutenant hollered. "She's nothing but a dirty stinking rat. Why on Earth should anyone even care about such a foul creature?"

"Why indeed, sir?" the Sergeant said, turning the question back on the Lieutenant as carefully as he could.

Catherine had been listening with her heart in her mouth but now it all went quiet while the Lieutenant sought a way out of the palaver without looking weak.

"She attempted to flee from your men, did she not?"

"Yes sir."

"Then that's noncompliance and resisting arrest. Two charges right there."

"Yes sir," the Sergeant reluctantly conceded. "And the punishment?"

The Lieutenant knew he couldn't prescribe death for every little misdemeanour otherwise he would've racked up more victims than the plague but an example had to be set nevertheless.

"A flogging. Fifty lashes, Sergeant," he ordered. "That's my final order."

"Again, begging your pardon but there's nothing to her. Fifty lashes would cut her in half, sir," the Sergeant argued.

"Twenty then!" the Lieutenant snapped in frustration.

"Five, might I suggest sir?"

"What?"

"Five of the best. And she'll wear the scars her whole miserable life, sir."

The Lieutenant wondered how on Earth they were still talking about this. For a feral child? It would've been better if she'd simply been bayoneted in the woods out of sight of the men and been done with it but she was here now and the Lieutenant would be damned if he was going to waste any more time on her.

"Ten!" he demanded, daring the Sergeant to try to barter with him further.

"Very good, sir. Ten it will be," the Sergeant agreed.

While pleased not to be facing a firing squad, Catherine shrunk at the thought of being beaten. The supervisors had wielded the cane freely in the orphanage and she'd found herself on the receiving end more than once but she had been a child then and treated as such. She was sure the army wouldn't make the same distinction now.

The tent flap was pulled back and the gruff-looking Sergeant poked his head inside.

"Best I could do for you,," he said with a genuine tinge of remorse. "Here." He handed her a bowl of steaming mush and a slab of stale bread. "Turnip stew. You're paying for it. You might as well eat it." And with that, he left Catherine to enjoy her first hot meal since leaving the orphanage.

CHAPTER SEVEN

THE MORNING GREW WARMER the further Marigold travelled down the mountain. By the time she had reached the flat plains of gold spun wheat, the sun was doing its utmost to boil her in her breeches. She stopped by the edge of the orchard and climbed off Liquorice to change her clothes. She needed to do so anyway. There would be more people about town to see her return than when she'd first left and if Mother caught sight of her in her cold-weather gear she would have some explaining to do.

Liquorice snorted and danced backwards and forwards. He remembered the wasps, Marigold told herself, and didn't want to stop here. Marigold patted his neck and told him it was okay, they'd come by another route but Liquorice was still jumpy.

Marigold got changed as quickly she could, out of her leathers and into the attractive blue riding habit she was expected to wear. She would also have to ride back into town the proper way, side-saddle, rather than the way men were permitted to ride. It felt less natural and a lot less comfortable but, then again, this was the age of corsets and crinolines: comfort wasn't a consideration when it came to the fairer sex.

"Almost done, just let me pull my boots on," Marigold told Liquorice as he stamped his feet and whinnied in a rush to get going.

Marigold was all but done and was just tying her laces when a black and brown coil sprang at her from a nearby thicket. Marigold leapt out of her skin but she didn't leap quick enough. She felt the bite in the back of her ankle and watched aghast as the snake slithered back into the undergrowth, its point having been made.

Her foot felt as though it was on fire so Marigold laced up her boot as tightly as she could and hobbled onto

Liquorice. He's tried to warn her. She saw that now but she had not listened. Her heart was pounding and her head began to spin. Marigold fought through the excruciating pain that was clawing its way up her leg to clamber onto Liquorice's back. Any thoughts of riding side-saddle were quickly forgotten. Speed was of the essence. She needed help. And fast. Or she would die.

"Home boy. Like the wind," she urged Liquorice, using the last of her strength to hang onto his neck as he took off like a cannonball.

Liquorice was an old campaign horse. He knew when his rider was in trouble and was trained to get them back to the surgeon's table as fast as possible. He now opened up through the meadows and bridleways as if in his prime again. Farmhands and foresters looked up as he thundered on by but Liquorice didn't stop for any of them. Marigold needed help and there was only one person to go to.

The gatekeeper at the city walls leapt out of the way as Liquorice bowled on through and people and ponies scattered in all directions as he ignored all highway etiquette to get Marigold back to Mother.

Mother and Gardenia had just arrived and were tethering Queenie up in the stables when Liquorice clattered across the cobblestones and into the stable courtyard.

"Mother, look!" Gardenia hollered, as Marigold slid from the saddle and into their arms.

"Snake…" Marigold just about managed to say before passing out.

Mother and Gardenia carried her inside and set her down on the sofa.

"Get the doctor quick!" Mother told Gardenia, having to snap at her to "Go!" when she failed to move, so distraught she was to see her beloved sister in such a perilous state.

Gardenia hurried out while Mother looked for the bite.

She found it beneath Marigold's boots and had to suppress her tears when she saw how purple and swollen her ankle had become. Mother ripped through her sewing kit until she found what she was looking for — a thick darning needle. Without a moment's hesitation, she drove it into the puncture marks making Marigold wake up with a scream.

"I have to do it! I'm sorry but I have to," Mother told her as she used her body weight to pin her down while working the needle in deeper. Marigold was so weak that she could scarcely breathe, let alone fend Mother off as she caused her more pain than she ever knew possible. Mother pulled the needle out of her swollen bite and a splash of blood shot out to pepper her dress.

Mother now grappled with Marigold to hold her down in order to stop her from kicking her in the face. She closed her mouth over the gaping wound and sucked to send Marigold into convulsions as fresh agonies swept over her.

"Please stop! Please..." Marigold begged, her head spinning and her body burning. But Mother kept on sucking, drawing out the poison and not relenting until she was sure she had accounted for every last drop.

Mother's mouth was full of blood and she realised she had nothing to spit it into. Under normal circumstances, she would've been appalled to see so much as a drop of tea land on the parlour carpet but now she didn't care, she spat Marigold's blood aside without so much as a second's thought.

Gardenia and the doctor arrived to find Marigold passed out and Mother tending to her.

"Stand aside, woman. Let me see her," Doctor Guillot said, urging Mother to desist before she sucked Marigold to a husk.

Gardenia began to weep when she saw how much her sister had deteriorated. Her skin had turned pale and her eyes deathly grey. The only colour about her was her inflamed ankle and the trickle of blood that rolled down her cheek from where she'd bitten her own lip.

Doctor Guillot held her wrist and closed his eyes to count.

"Her pulse is very weak," he said after careful consideration. "Weak but regular." He felt her sweaty forehead with his stumpy fingers and examined her ankle to see it was swollen beyond all recognition. "I will not give you false hope, Madame. All I will say is that you have done everything there is to do. Marigold's life is now in God's hands." And with that he climbed off his knees, handed Mother a small vial of brandy from his bag — "For the wound," he said unnecessarily — and saw himself out.

Mother set the brandy down and told Gardenia to hurry into the kitchen. "Fetch me some bread and milk; and lavender from the garden. I'll make a poultice," she said, damned if she was about to sit idle and let God assume responsibility for her daughter's life. Not after all He'd done for her and her family thus far.

Gardenia returned with the ingredients and watched Mother soak the bread in milk, mix it with the lavender and wrap it in gauze before shaping it around Marigold's ankle.

"What will that do?" Gardenia asked, desperate for even the smallest glimmer of hope.

"A sight more than the good doctor," Mother replied.

Lunchtime came and went without Marigold waking up or Gardenia or Mother eating. Several callers knocked but neither Mother nor Gardenia would leave Marigold's side to answer. Their shop would stay closed until further notice.

Eventually, the night drew in. Mother and Gardenia carried Marigold to her bed, undressed her and changed her poultice but Marigold did not wake.

"Find your bed. Get some sleep. I will stay with your sister," Mother told Gardenia as she leaned over Marigold and mopped her brow.

"I will not," Gardenia objected. "How can I rest when any one of these breaths might be her last?"

"And if none are, Marigold will need us in the morning. And we cannot look after her if we have not looked after ourselves. Please go. And I will trade places with you come the hour of two."

Gardenia saw that Mother was right. She was worn through with worry and hunger. And although she didn't feel like sleeping or eating she knew she would not be able to stay upright for much longer.

"Please call me if she needs me," Gardenia said, leaning in to give her sister one last kiss before withdrawing to the room next door.

Mother turned the lantern down to a flicker and pulled her chair close to the bed. Marigold looked so still in her repose that Mother listened closely to make sure she was still breathing. She was but only just. Marigold slept on the edge of the precipice that night. But where would she lie come the morning?

"Let me tell you about your father," Mother said softly, stroking her daughter's hair and allowing the tears to well up in her eyes now that Gardenia had left the room. "Your father was a wonderful man: a truly wonderful man. And he is here with you now," she whispered, taking an old army medal from her pocket and pinning it to Marigold's nightgown for luck. "He is always with you, Marigold, you and your sister. His strength shines in you both."

CHAPTER EIGHT

CATHERINE PETIT WAS TETHERED to a cold iron cannon and had her ragged shirt torn open at the back. There was a frost in the air but she was so cold already that she barely had any feeling in her goose-pimpled skin. That would soon change. The Lieutenant chose to personally oversee her punishment and had the whole camp turn out for what he thought was a morale-boosting exercise

"Ready when you are, Sergeant," he chirped gleefully, half wishing it could be him who meted out the pain.

The Sergeant picked up the strap, a large leather strip some ten centimetres wide and a metre in length. He'd sampled the strap himself in his younger army days and grimaced for the child before him at what she was about to endure. Catherine saw the strap as it unfurled in the Sergeant's grip. Part of the punishment was showing the offender the tools of their torment prior to use. Catherine closed her eyes and was fortunate that the Lieutenant didn't notice as he was standing at the business end of things. Best seats in the house and all that.

"Well Sergeant, you have your orders. Get on with it," the Lieutenant demanded, swishing his crop through the air and cracking it against his knee-high boots by way of a practical demonstration.

"Yes sir. Sorry sir," the Sergeant said, realising he had little choice but to go through with it. He might not have liked it but there was nothing he could do. If he refused to carry out the Lieutenant's order he would've been flogged himself and the Lieutenant would've found someone else to administer the punishment. At least this way he could try and go a little easier on the little wretch, in so far as he could while the Lieutenant cast his beady eye over the pair of them.

The company stared ahead as the Sergeant walked

around to the back of the cannon and took up his position behind Catherine. Not a man amongst them blinked nor made a sound. They stood impassive, witnesses to the persecution of a person of no account.

"This is what we do with the vermin we find sniffing around the King's camp," the Lieutenant declared for all to hear. "Be sure to scurry on back to the rest of your brood and tell them they'll find no crumbs at our table."

The Lieutenant then nodded and pulled a monocle from his tunic in order to enjoy the show to its fullest.

The sky was blue and the air was crisp. Nothing stirred on the parade ground except the breath of two hundred men as it drifted above their heads in the bright morning's light. It might have been a truly beautiful day, all things considered.

The Sergeant swung his arm and Catherine tensed. She heard the swish before she felt it but when she did the pain exploded across her back like a lightning bolt. But Catherine had no time to cry out, a second lash came hard on the heels of the first, grating her flesh just a hair's breadth from where the first had fallen.

The Lieutenant purred as he watched the strap swing. A flogging really had been a good idea. A shooting would have been far too quick: a short sharp shock and then instant release. In a way, the Lieutenant thought to himself, it would've done the rat a favour by shooting her. It would've put her out of her misery and that wouldn't have done at all.

Catherine finally hollered on the seventh lash, unable to hold in her cries any longer. The Sergeant hesitated on hearing Catherine's sobs but the Lieutenant just glared at him to continue. The Sergeant took a deep breath and told him himself there were only three more to go. The worst had been administered.

The Lieutenant smiled as Catherine's flogging resumed. No, it was better this way. This way she would get to enjoy her pain for weeks and her tattered back would serve as a constant reminder to others to respect the rule of law. God save the King, the Lieutenant told himself.

The Sergeant brought the last lash down on Catherine's bloodied back then went to untie her binds.

"What are you doing Sergeant?" the Lieutenant asked.

"Releasing the prisoner, sir," the Sergeant told him.

"Continue with the punishment," the Lieutenant demanded.

The Sergeant wondered if he'd heard right and reminded him, as respectfully as he could, "That was ten lashes, sir."

"I counted only eight," the Lieutenant smirked.

Catherine now forced herself to look around and into the eyes of her tormentor. There'd been hardly any light in the gloom of the tent last night. Now in the bright morning's sunshine she could see him clearly, even through the veil of tears that filled her eyes. She studied his face; committing it to memory in the event the day ever came when she had the opportunity to repay him in kind.

"Begging your pardon, sir, but it truly was ten," the Sergeant insisted.

"Are you saying I can't count!" the Lieutenant barked so sharply that his monocle almost fell out. "I say it was eight and it was eight. Now do your duty and carry out the punishment."

The Sergeant glanced towards the ranks and recognised an impossible situation when he saw one. The tiny creature before him had just about come through her ordeal but he wasn't sure how much more she could take. He wanted nothing more than to free her now but he couldn't. He was just a Sergeant. And he had his orders.

He stooped to pick up the strap again, wiping away the grit it had collected so as not to dirty her wounds, he then swung it twice more. Swish crack! Swish crack! Catherine howled, the Lieutenant purred again and the Sergeant fought the urge to turn the strap on his superior.

"How many was that, Sergeant?" the Lieutenant asked when the leather had finally stopped flying.

"Ten sir," the Sergeant said after a moment's thought.

"Are you sure?" the Lieutenant pressed with a malicious glint in his monocled eye.

The Sergeant wanted nothing more than for this whole sorry saga to be over so that he could help Catherine as best he could before sending her on her way but the Lieutenant was determined to make his point.

"Yes sir, ten lashes, sir," the Sergeant duly confirmed.

"Jolly good. As you were," the Lieutenant chirped, turning on his heels to head back to the officer's mess when a lone voice stopped him in his tracks.

"No sir!" someone shouted.

The Lieutenant turned back in surprise and saw the prisoner staring back at him.

"What did you say, little rat?" the Lieutenant said, daring this filthy scullion to give him an excuse to flog her some more. As it happened, that's exactly what she did.

"I said no sir, that was not ten, sir. That was only nine!" she gasped, her voice cracked and breathless and yet loud enough for the Lieutenant and the front few rows of the assembled troops to hear. The statuesque soldiers now began to stir as a whisper ripped through the ranks to spread Catherine's words to the furthest corners of the company.

The Lieutenant could scarcely believe his ears and snorted with laughter. "Did I hear you right, little rat?"

"It was only nine," she said through gritted teeth.

The Lieutenant grinned. "You heard the prisoner, Sergeant, that was only nine. Give her another."

The Sergeant was so stumped that he didn't know what to do but seeing as both the prisoner and his commanding officer seemed to want him to swing the strap again that's what he did. Another lash cut through the air and cracked across Catherine's back to make her yelp afresh.

"Satisfied now, little rat?" the Lieutenant asked, almost amused at this filthy little creature's fighting spirit.

Catherine fought hard to draw a breath after the last lash had knocked it out of her and replied once more.

"No sir. That's still only nine!" she shouted now louder than before.

The whisper that ran through the company now became a murmur and suddenly it was the Lieutenant's turn to not know what to do. The damn insolence! Just who did she think she was back-chatting an officer of the King?

"Give her another!" the Lieutenant bellowed, no longer smiling as he sought to crush the spirit that had amused him moments earlier. But like many before, he would come up short.

The Sergeant lashed Catherine again and urged her not to say anything else.

"You've made your point," he whispered but Catherine either didn't hear him and didn't care.

"Nine and a half," she now called out.

A sharp collective breath swept through the ranks on hearing these words and, in that moment, the company was impassive no longer.

"Give me that damn thing!" the Lieutenant yelled, snatching the strap from the Sergeant's hand and laying into Catherine with four or five angry strikes.

"What do you say now?" he screamed at the impudent little tyke.

Catherine could scarcely breathe; her body was paralysed with pain and her lungs were all but empty but she simply didn't know how to give in. She'd never done so before and she wasn't about to start now. When she finally found a breath with which to speak she croaked, barely audible but just about loud enough for the Lieutenant and Sergeant to hear: *"Nine and three quarters!"*

No one else in the company heard what she said but they didn't need to. The Lieutenant's reaction told them all they needed to know and suddenly all eyes were on him. And the Lieutenant felt every single one of them.

This was the feted King's Guards, seasoned campaign veterans who'd won battle honours in some of the bloodiest campaigns in living memory and yet not a man could ever recall seeing anything like this. This tiny waif of a girl, who was small even for a forest girl, had taken enough punishment to fell an oak and here she was defiantly inviting more. It defied belief and softened even the hardest of hearts to her cause. Almost.

"Stand to attention!" the Lieutenant snapped when he saw how order was dissolving in the ranks.

He now recognised the impossible situation he was in. He'd lost his own discipline and had let this little imp get the better of him. And yet if he continued to mete out the punishment she so surely deserved he would do himself a serious injury, let alone this worthless wretch. Was this her whole plan all along: to martyr herself at the expense of his authority? And what of his men? There were rumblings in the ranks already due to the lack of winter provisions. Some of the rabble-rousers would jump at any excuse to start trouble.

The Lieutenant thought on the dilemma. His men were watching him, the Sergeant was imploring him and Catherine was shivering against the cold steel of the company's field gun as she braced herself for more.

"She wants me to thrash her," the Lieutenant now saw. As inconceivable as it seemed, that's what she wanted. Well, the Lieutenant thought, she'd not make a monkey out of him.

"Dumb little rat! Can't even count," he declared, shoving the strap at the Sergeant and striding away as quickly as he could before the prisoner begged to differ.

The company waited for the Lieutenant to dismiss

them but it clearly slipped his mind and was left to the Sergeant to give the order once the Lieutenant was out of sight. The moment he did, a dozen men broke the Sergeant's way to assist him as he untied Catherine and hurried her back to his tent.

"Get me brandy and bandages," the Sergeant told his comrades as he laid Catherine onto her front and peeled her shirt away to inspect her angry wounds. Originally, he'd intended to simply patch her up and send her on her way but her injuries were now too severe for that. They would take time to scar over and eventually heal but they wouldn't do that out in the wilds in the depths of winter. This meant caring for her in the camp. The Lieutenant might not approve but he didn't need to know and the Sergeant was confident no one would tell him.

This little girl was something special. He couldn't just toss her back out into the cold. Whatever the dangers and whatever the cost, the Sergeant would look out for this lost child now. And not out of charity either.

But because a stubborn headed 'rat' such as this truly deserved to be saved.

CHAPTER NINE

THE FIRST THING MARIGOLD SAW when she opened her eyes was Gardenia smiling, her eyes sparkling with joy in dawn's first light.

"Mother! Mother! She's awake!" Gardenia cried, prompting the sounds of covers being thrown aside, vases being knocked over and doors slamming as Mother came running.

Marigold tried to sit up and ask what was going on but found she could do neither. Her joints had seized fast and her throat felt as though it was full of ashes.

Gardenia urged her to lay back and take it easy as she brought a glass to her lips. She sipped a little and sprayed the rest in Gardenia's face but what little of it she did manage to drink brought a soothing relief that swept over her like an ocean wave.

The door burst open and Mother hurried in still wearing her nightwear, which was most unusual. Marigold couldn't understand what all the fuss was about but little by little it soon came back. The mountain. The kiss. The wasps. The snake...

"Snake!" Marigold gasped, finally finding her voice.

"It's okay. You're okay. You're safe now," Mother reassured her, stroking the loose strands of hair from Marigold's eyes and looking down on her as if for the first time all over again.

Marigold had slept for two whole days and had burned red hot for most of it. Her temperature only finally broke the night before when, at last, her body learned how to fight the poison still in her veins. Mother and Gardenia had nursed her through it all, taking only short breaks to eat and sleep to maintain their energies for the task ahead but both were worn out, not so much from the physical exertions but from the remorseless and unending agony of seeing their sweet Marigold so close to the end. Too many times Gardenia had feared the worst when Marigold had sunk into complete silence, only for her to pull through with a gasp and go on breathing as before. Now she was awake, staring up at them and weeping with joy as all three of them fell into a euphoric embrace.

Marigold noticed the medal pinned to her nightgown.

"Your father was here too," Mother smiled.

"I'm famished," Marigold finally said.

"Me too," agreed Gardenia.

"Eggs. I will prepare some eggs," Mother said, rising from Marigold's bedside and heading towards the door. She stopped for a moment and looked back at her daughter before adding: "And then, perhaps you can tell me what was so important that it took you away from the shop whilst Gardenia and I were at the Eames?"

And with that, Mother headed next door to get dressed, leaving Marigold and Gardenia with the realisation that in Mother's eyes only death excused imprudent behaviour. Near-death, whilst unfortunate, mitigated nothing.

*

"THE ICE BUCKET BOY?" Mother said when Marigold confessed all. "You risked death and disgrace to see Stefano's ice bucket boy?"

Marigold wondered which Mother thought worse, death or disgrace, before concluding the latter.

Mother set her knife and fork aside and Gardenia gawped in shock, a forkful of scrambled eggs hanging in mid-air between her mouth and the plate.

"I'm sorry. We're friends, I just… I never get to speak to him because he's always at work and it would be unseemly of me to do so. Please don't be angry with me," Marigold said meekly, half-wishing the snake had finished her off because Mother was about to. Marigold hadn't even considered lying to Mother. Secrets were bad enough but lies were unthinkable.

Mother glared disapprovingly and wondered whether she should send Gardenia from the room. In the event, she decided she was old enough. She needed to hear what had been going on for herself.

"And what did you do when you saw him?" Mother scarcely dared to ask. "Did you… shame yourself?"

Marigold thought about this and decided she hadn't, one kiss and an exchange of feelings aside, their assignation had been about as proper as one could expect in sub-zero temperatures. As much as they secretly longed for each other, neither fancied taking off so much as a glove with that wind howling down the slopes.

"Hans never laid a finger on me," Marigold promised. Okay, some lies were probably called for and this was one of them.

"Oh, so it's Hans now is it!" Mother exclaimed with dramatic outrage.

"No, I think it's always been Hans," Marigold cheeked, making Gardenia choke on her eggs and Mother's eyes narrow just a little. Despite the years of careful tutoring, exposure to the finer things in life and the opportunities Mother had worked so hard to carve out for her, Marigold was still a Petit at heart. And nobody knew better than Mother how headstrong a Petit girl could be when backed into a corner. She chose her next few words carefully.

"Hans is a fine-looking boy, is he not?" she said.

Marigold did not know what to say. She had expected a fight, not a discourse. She reminded herself that whilst Mother had high hopes for her and Gardenia, she was first and foremost a loving parent and, as such, her highest hope of all was that her daughters find happiness.

"He is, Mother. He is most fine," Marigold agreed.

Gardenia had turned to stone. She could scarcely

believe the discussion they were having at the breakfast table and wondered if she should volunteer her esteem for Captain Durand while they were on the subject.

"He is admired by many young girls I shouldn't fancy," Mother then said, picking up just the tiniest morsel of egg with her fork and lifting it to her lips. She dabbed the corners of her mouth with her handkerchief and smiled warmly across the table at Marigold.

"I shouldn't fancy," Marigold once again agreed.

"Like a delicious strawberry ice cream on a hot summer's day," Mother winked.

Gardenia broke into a fit of giggles without quite knowing what she was giggling at but it all sounded delightfully scandalous all the same.

Marigold liked the analogy but tried not to show it. She always felt a flush of heat whenever she thought of Hans and started to blush a little now. Mother noticed and raised an eyebrow.

"Do you like ice cream, Marigold?" she asked.

Marigold was confused. Was this still an analogy or was Mother actually asking about ice cream?

"Ice cream," Mother confirmed. "Like the ones you might buy at Stefano's kiosk."

Marigold did like ice cream and saw no harm in admitting this. After all, who didn't like ice cream? Even Mother did. And as she and Mother were now on an even keel they were just two women enjoying an honest and open conversation. Well, two women and one silly sister who couldn't stop snorting her eggs through her nose anytime anyone said "ice cream".

"Tell me, which do you prefer, apples or ice cream?" Mother asked, smiling over at Marigold and ignoring Gardenia as she started turning a shade of scarlet.

"They're somewhat different," said Marigold.

"They are indeed different. But there would be no

choice to make if they were not," Mother replied assuredly.

Marigold gave this a little thought and said; "Ice cream I suppose," without sensing the trap she was walking into.

"And what of cabbage soup?" Mother now asked, continuing to delicately dissect her breakfast as she dissected her daughter.

"Oh, ice cream all day long," Gardenia blurted out, answering not only for her sister but the whole of mankind as far as cabbage soup went.

"And stew?"

"Ice cream," Gardenia said without hesitation.

"Wood pigeon?"

"Ice cream?"

"Salmon?"

"Ice cream."

"Toast?"

"Ice cream."

"And eggs? What about eggs?"

"Ice cream!" Gardenia laughed, mischievously pulling a face at her breakfast to make Marigold chortle but not Mother. This was something the girls would've been wise to notice. Mother sat calm and collected and looked from Marigold to Gardenia as they tittered like naïve schoolgirls delighting in the unexpected unshackling of their candour.

"Then we shall eat only ice cream from now on," Mother declared, setting her knife and fork down and touching her napkin to her lips to signal she'd finished breakfast.

Gardenia couldn't believe it. After years of guarded decorum, Mother had found her silly side. This was no doubt due to Marigold's brush with death but she had finally become playful.

"And cake! And chocolate! And sugar plums by the bucketload!" Gardenia enthused, now falling about the place with glee. This was in part relief at the ordeal they had come through and in part silliness but Gardenia couldn't remember the last time she'd felt so happy. And Mother's face was so straight, so controlled, that Gardenia would set herself off all over again just by looking at it.

But then Mother said, "I'm quite serious".

This had a sobering effect on Marigold. She stopped laughing and wondered if she'd heard right.

"I'm sorry?" she asked.

Mother rose from the table, taking her plate to the scraps bin and scraped the last of her eggs into it for Monsieur Thomas's pigs.

"I said I'm quite serious. From now on we shall eat only ice cream, morning, noon and night."

Gardenia still hadn't noticed it but the temperature in the kitchen had plunged a few degrees since Mother had risen from the table. Marigold finally sensed the trap and tried backing out of it but it was too late, it had already been sprung.

"I think that might be a little too much, Mother, even for me," she said, flashing her eyes at Gardenia in an effort to bring her back down to Earth.

"But you prefer ice cream to toast. To eggs. To cabbage soup," Mother reminded her, recapping the girls' admissions.

Marigold said nothing, taking the *least-said-soonest-mended* course of action, but she would not get off that lightly.

"Answer the question!" Mother snapped, finally stifling Gardenia's giggles out of her.

"I... I... I..." Marigold stammered, wondering how she could have been so stupid.

"Speak up, girl!" Mother demanded.

"I did," Marigold confirmed, looking down at the table in front of her rather than up at Mother who was glaring back with disappointment. Gardenia said nothing. She likewise stared straight ahead and sat stock-still, like a pheasant in the brush that had allowed a hunting party to approach to within an easy shot of her.

"Then if you like ice cream so much, why would you not want to eat it all day long?" Mother asked. Marigold sensed this wasn't a rhetorical question.

"Because it would not be good for me," Marigold said meekly.

"And why is that?" Mother said, determined to hear the words from her daughter's lips rather than her own.

"Because I would become stout," Marigold said.

"Fat!" Mother corrected her.

"Fat," Marigold repeated.

"And?"

"And... unattractive."

"And?"

"And... unwell."

"And?"

"And... unwise."

"And?"

"And... and...?" Marigold couldn't find the answer Mother was so clearly waiting to hear.

Gardenia thought she had it. "Smelly?"

"Quite possibly," Mother said, giving Gardenia points for trying before revealing the missing word. "Unmarried."

Gardenia shuddered. This was the word that she and her young friends feared the most. In fact, it was more than a mere word; it was a curse: to be left on the shelf, unwanted and all alone at a time when women's purses were primarily for show. The bulk of the Kingdom's money was still kept in its wallets and had been for hundreds of years. To the maidens of Andovia, *unmarried* didn't mean lonely and unloved. *Unmarried* meant cold and hungry: unwanted and unwelcome: in sickness and in health. Most spinsters turned their hands towards the few trades they could ply, most of which paid little and aged them prematurely. Mother had dozens of them on her books already, cutting, sewing, and embroidering the dresses she designed for the gentlewomen of this fair Kingdom. And while she paid better than most for this work, she'd rather hoped her daughters would stick to wearing dresses for themselves rather than hemming them for others.

"I suspect even your young fancy might think twice about you in such a light," Mother said. This was harsh but intentionally so. And it was for Marigold's own good.

"Yes Mother," was all her eldest daughter could say.

"Yes Mother," Gardenia echoed.

"But if ice cream is all we desire then why not indulge ourselves?"

Neither Marigold nor Gardenia replied this time. Each felt more crestfallen than the other. Mother was satisfied she'd made her point and let out a sigh. She loved her daughters and would've run through fire for either of them but one of a mother's less enviable tasks was to be cruel to be kind. Anything less would've been a betrayal of trust.

"So, if we can exercise self-restraint when it comes to ice cream, perhaps we can exercise self-restraint in other matters too. At least until these things are no longer a consideration."

And with that, Mother left the room. Marigold and Gardenia listened to her footsteps as she climbed the stairs and then the sound of her bedroom door as it closed behind her.

"What are you going to do?" Gardenia eventually asked when she figured it was safe enough to do so.

Marigold didn't know. She could tell that Mother's last remark about her waiting until these things were no longer a consideration was a comment on her age. She was, after all, nineteen and still without a ring. This wasn't unheard of in Andovia and girls did get married later on but their chances of landing a husband of substance lessened with every passing year. Mother had worked hard to forge the right connections and make the right introductions on Marigold's behalf and, to date, only Stefano's bucket boy had shown an interest. Hardly a stunning return on all her hopes and dreams.

Indeed, Hans might even scupper Marigold's hopes once and for all should word of her affections ever reach the ears — or worst still, the tongues — of those at court. This was Andovia, after all. Where reputations were everything.

Marigold rose from the table and took her plate to the scraps bucket. Despite not eating for several days she'd lost her appetite. She scraped her remaining eggs and toast into the bucket.

And resigned herself to avoiding ice cream for the foreseeable future.

CHAPTER TEN

WORD OF MARIGOLD'S BRUSH with death soon spread around town. The official story Mother put about was that she had gone out to pick wildflowers and most people seemed satisfied with that. A few young bucks desperate to prove their mettle went out into the grasslands and dispatched several dozen barley snakes, as they were known locally, much to the delight of Andovia's rat population, but it hardly avenged Marigold's honour.

In fact, the whole episode cost Mother and the sisters dearly with several valuable clients transferring their business to Monsieur Vasseur as soon as they heard the news. Marigold might've been at death's door but the Prince's ball was only three weeks away. And there was nothing more important than that. Their outfits, and those of their daughters, had to be ready in time.

But not everyone in Andovia was so uncaring. Marigold did receive a few thoughtful gifts from concerned well-wishers over the next few days, most notably a posy of Mountain Buttercups left anonymously on the front porch. Gardenia found them leaning up against the front door when she'd returned from her nightly bouquet-catching practice, as Mother had her do for twenty minutes each evening.

"Aren't they pretty," she said, showing Mother the flowers. "No note though. I wonder who they're from."

"I'll take those," Mother said, knowing all too well even without a note. "Not a word to your sister," she warned her.

Gardenia never saw the posy again.

The following morning a messenger boy delivered a note requesting the pleasure of Madame Roche's services from a hitherto unknown gentleman by the name of Beaufort.

"The château at the top of the hill on *Rue des Roses*. I

had no idea anyone had moved into the old place again," Mother said, intrigued but cautious. New business was welcome but it came with its own challenges. New clients liked to barter. No one ever wanted to pay the first price she set. She would be haggled down. People liked to think they were getting a bargain but if she named too high a price she could risk pricing herself out of a commission. Name too low a price and she ran the risk of not seeming select enough. It took a careful eye and a steady head to win new business. But if new business was a sapling, repeat business were the apples. And little by little Madame Roche was planting her orchard.

Mother, Marigold and Gardenia took Queenie and the trap through the town and out into the countryside to *Rue des Roses*. For years the old General had lived in the château at the top of the hill, tending to his garden and reliving his glory days through a fog of port and cigars until eventually, the bugler had sounded for him. He'd had no children, just some distant cousins who'd never visited the whole time he'd been on his feet and had no intention of doing so now that he wasn't, so the château had lain empty while they'd tried to find a buyer. This had taken several years. It was a draughty old pile, with tapestries and turrets and all manner of odd reinforcements the General had seen fit to shore the old place up with. As a home, it had less of a "wow" and more of a "what the hell" factor going for it but it did have potential — if nothing else.

Mother stopped at the gates and looked up at the dowdy and gothic château before them. The shutters had been removed from the windows and the gardens had been tamed. Several gardeners were going about their business at the side of the house and a maid could be seen polishing the windows in one of the upper bedrooms. Whoever had moved in had money for staff.

"Now remember girls, eyes open, tongues still. Let me

do the talking. And if he asks about your snakebite, leave your dress where it is. Even if he says he's a doctor," Mother said.

"Yes Mother," Marigold sighed, as if flashing her ankles to complete strangers was the sort of thing she would ever do. There were names for girls like that though Marigold's education was incomplete because Mother refused to tell her what they were.

"How do I look?" Marigold asked Gardenia, as they started up the driveway and towards the front steps. She was wearing one of Mother's very latest designs, a salmon pink dress with white lace trim and matching accessories; gloves, purse and parasol, and most importantly of all, a silk scarf to conceal her drawn neck. The last few days had taken its toll on Marigold and while she had made a valiant effort to regain her strength through soup and stew (no ice cream though) she was still a shadow of her former self.

"Wonderful," Gardenia reassured her although Mother felt that Marigold had gone mad with the facecake this morning. It was one thing to cover up the odd blemish but quite another to try to repaint one's features from scratch. But whatever her reservations she kept them to herself. Both her daughters tended to be a little heavy-handed when it came to making themselves up. Then again, what young girl wasn't?

Mother hadn't wanted Marigold to come. She still needed her rest and was prone to fits of wooziness but she had insisted. The sooner people saw her out and about again the sooner consumer confidence would be restored in their business. It wasn't so much that Marigold was irreplaceable; it was merely that people needed to be reassured that she wasn't about to kick the bucket and drag Mother into four weeks of mourning while their half-finished ballgowns gathered dust in the back room.

A footman greeted them at the front door and helped Mother and the sisters out of their seats.

"*Le Chevalier* is expecting you," the footman said. "If you'll be so good as to follow me."

Le Chevalier? Monsieur Beaufort was a nobleman? Mother had no idea but sensed a golden opportunity. Literally.

More staff busied themselves inside the house, sweeping, polishing and patching up the place to make it feel more like a home and less like a last stand. The furniture was upholstered and the floors were thick with rugs. Chandeliers hung from the ceilings instead of cobwebs and art from the walls instead of weaponry. The place had undoubtedly benefited from a woman's touch and yet no woman dwelt there, just a widower and his young daughter, both of whom awaiting them when they entered the parlour.

"Madame Roche, thank you so much for coming," said the master of the house with a welcoming smile. He was a distinguished looking gentleman, rugged and handsome, and yet well dressed and groomed, wearing a suit of royal blue over cream pantaloons and a few flecks of grey about his side whiskers.

"Monsieur *Le Chevalier*," Mother replied to give an approximation of his full title. "It is an honour to meet you." Mother then curtseyed so fully that she could've been accused of taking a seat before one was offered to her, but the gentleman said there was no need for such formalities.

"It is an old and redundant family title. Meaningless in this day and age," he said, brushing it off with a flick of the hand to make Mother wonder why the footman had even mentioned it then. "Please call me Monsieur."

"Of course," Mother said, excited to be on such terms with a true blue-blooded nobleman.

"Madame Roche, allow me to introduce my daughter, Ella."

A pretty blonde girl to his right now curtseyed on cue and said, "I am delighted to meet you, Madame Roche," before turning her radiant smile on Marigold and Gardenia. Neither responded. Both simply stood there and gawped. It was the girl from the park. They recognised her immediately, even with her shoes on. It was the girl from the pond with the ankles and knees.

"These are my girls, Monsieur, Marigold and Gardenia," Mother replied, turning to her daughters and sensing something was amiss. Marigold and Gardenia didn't move. They didn't even blink. They just stared at Ella in surprise. She was no peasant or serving girl who'd picked her master's pocket. She was a nobleman's daughter and the reason they'd been summoned here today.

"Girls! Girls!" Mother snapped to remind them of their place.

"Oh! forgive me!" Marigold said, curtseying especially low to make up for her lapse in manners.

"That's quite alright," Monsieur Beaufort excused before blustering; "My daughter has that effect on everyone." Mother could well believe it. Unlike her own fair daughters, this girl must've barely owned a face brush. Nature had already gifted her all she required.

Marigold tried to rise but the sudden crush of her corset took her breath away. She had felt alright earlier on but here and now, bent double and confined in the latest fashions, the room began to spin. Gardenia saw her sister turn pale even beneath several layers of cake but she was too slow to do anything about it. Marigold put out a hand to steady herself but found only empty air.

"Excuse me, I think I might have to sit…" she started to say, intending to ask for a chair but finding only the floor when it rushed up at her all at once.

"Marigold!" she heard Gardenia gasp but that was the last she knew. All at once, the world turned dark and still.

*

*

"MARIGOLD? MARIGOLD?"

Marigold had no idea where she was when she opened her eyes. A girl was leaning over and looking down at her. She looked strangely familiar and yet Marigold didn't know who she was.

"How do you feel?" the girl asked.

Confused would've been the appropriate answer.

Who was this girl? How did she know her? She had doll-like features and yet her eyes were full of life. They sparkled like diamonds, not sapphires, but diamonds of blue that suggested an ice-cold inner-strength. Her skin was flawless but for a sprinkling of freckles and her hair flowed like silk and shone in the sunshine that flooded in through the bay windows.

"Where am I?" Marigold asked groggily.

Before the girl had a chance to answer, Marigold heard a voice she did recognise. "Marigold? Are you all right? You gave us an awful shock."

Gardenia rushed to Marigold's side and helped her sit up. The room, the house and the girl now all came back to her and she felt mortified at having made a scene. However, this was nothing to how she felt next when she saw a maid on her hands and knees desperately scrubbing Monsieur *Le Chevalier*'s Persian rug to try to get Marigold's facecake out of it.

"Oh dear, I am sorry."

"Please do not give it a moment's thought. Your wellbeing is all that matters to us," Ella said, reaching for a glass of what Marigold assumed was water only to discover it was actually schnapps.

Marigold almost ended up on the rug again after taking a big swig and Ella and Gardenia had to take turns to slap her on the back for almost a minute before she could breathe again.

"Do you want some more?" Ella asked, offering Marigold the glass again at great personal risk to herself.

"I think she's had enough," Gardenia said, mopping her sister's brow with a wet cloth she'd found on the sideboard. It took most of her makeup off with it but made Marigold feel marginally better until the maid begged Gardenia's pardon and asked for her cleaning rag back.

"You're a big help," Marigold frowned.

The door at the far end of the parlour opened and Mother hurried in with Monsieur Beaufort.

"Is she awake? Marigold, are you well again?"

Marigold was awake but she looked far from well. She'd left most of her colour on the rug and her dress had split down one side on impact.

"Should I send for the doctor?" Monsieur Beaufort suggested but Mother didn't need two doctor's bills in one week, especially when he was inclined to simply refer most of his cases to The Almighty.

"No need for that Monsieur, she has a case of the vapours," Mother explained, which was a common ailment in young ladies of the age and which displayed a wide range of symptoms that included — but was not limited to — anything that couldn't be explained by medical science. Monsieur Beaufort sympathised and said that his own daughter suffered greatly from the vapours too and had often required confinement to either the attic or cellar, which sorted out the problem within a day or two.

"Ella, would you be so good as to find Marigold a change of clothes to wear? She cannot travel home with her dress in that state," Monsieur Beaufort said. Ella said she would be happy to and skipped off upstairs while Mother and Gardenia helped Marigold to the withdrawing-room to slip out of her tattered dress.

"I'm sorry Mother. What must Monsieur Beaufort think of me now?" Marigold said miserably as Mother unlaced her from behind.

"What Monsieur Beaufort thinks of you is neither here nor there. He is not the master of this household," Mother said to her daughters' great surprise.

"Who is then? Is there someone we haven't met yet?" Gardenia asked, failing to grasp what Mother meant.

"The girl," Mother replied. "Ella. She is queen of this particular castle."

Gardenia didn't understand but Marigold saw she was right. She knew it and yet hadn't known it until Mother had pointed it out. Now it was so obvious. In a house with no *Chevalière*, this young girl had assumed the role.

"His wife has been in the ground these past two years and he mourns her so. Ella is all he has and his life revolves around making her happy. This is his weakness and it is also Ella's strength. If we are to secure his custom it is not the monsieur of this household that we must win over but the mademoiselle."

Mother loosened the final lace of Marigold's dress and then lifted the whole lot over her head to leave her daughter naked but for her corset, crinoline, petticoats, pantalets and boots. There was a knock at the door and Gardenia hurried over to answer it.

"I found some clothes for Marigold," Mother heard Ella say. This was the perfect opportunity to start working on her. They had her all alone and while Marigold was undressed, Monsieur Beaufort wouldn't dream of entering.

"Do come on in," Mother called to her. Gardenia stepped aside to let Ella in.

"I hope these are alright. They were the best I could find," she said, bringing in a bundle of clothes and handing them to Mother.

Marigold crossed her arms across her chest. She felt uncomfortable to be standing in front of a virtual stranger with hardly anything on. And while they were all girls together and Ella had only shown her kindness thus far, she couldn't help but feel her new friend's sweet sticky smile contained just a hint of saccharine at her expense.

"You are too kind. I only hope that we can… oh!" Mother all but forgot herself when she saw what Ella had brought. It was a serving girl's outfit. And a rather matronly one at that.

"I fear none of my own wardrobe would've sat right on a girl of Marigold's frame," Ella smiled evermore sweetly than before. "But we have a housemaid who was thoughtful enough to lend Marigold the use of her spare uniform. I hope it fits okay. Not too snuggly."

Silence.

Nobody knew what to say. Gardenia just stood staring as though she was waiting for the punchline while Mother's eyes narrowed as she re-evaluated the girl before her. Ella's smile didn't waver. Not even for a second. Was she even aware of the offence she had just caused? She may have been new to Andovia but even so? Marigold saw that it was left to her to speak and took the clothes from Mother when she realised she wasn't about to.

"Please thank your housemaid for me. I am most grateful for her generosity," she said, sacrificing her own pride to defuse a difficult situation.

"I will tell her right away," Ella grinned, hurrying to the door and disappearing with a giggle of girly glee.

"Marigold, you can't!" Gardenia objected, a sentiment echoed by Mother, but Marigold just dropped the bundle of rags at her feet and began unbuttoning her crinoline.

"I have to, so help me."

It didn't really matter if Ella had meant the insult or not. It was an insult nevertheless but one that Marigold would have to suffer if they were to win the Beaufort's business which, from the looks of things, would not be inconsiderable. So she would suck it up and smile and not attempt to redress the offence for fear of causing her own — an unspeakable act in someone else's home let alone the house of a nobleman. And yet she felt humiliated all the same.

Some girls had big houses, noble titles, rich daddies and even servants to borrow pinnies from but others had only their reputations to regard. It might not have seemed like much to Ella but to Marigold, it was all she had.

So she would get changed, complete their house call and then climb into the back of the trap, hide under a blanket and stay hidden until they got home.

Because in Andovia, reputations were everything.

CHAPTER ELEVEN

IT WAS TWO DAYS BEFORE Catherine Petit could sit up without assistance. Two days of constant agony. The Sergeant dressed her wounds and brought her food but her recuperation was slow going. He even gave her a nip of brandy at night to help her sleep but it hardly touched the sides. The pain never left her, not for a minute, mot for a second or even a moment. After a time she learned to live with it and then, and only then, did it finally start to ebb.

The Sergeant would leave her to go about his duties during the day but return each night with hot soup and fresh bandages.

"There you go, Missy, get that down you."

He'd then sit on his sleeping mat across from her and watch with fascination as she tipped the whole lot into her face as quickly as she could. Any sense of civility had been chased out of this small girl after two hard winters in the wilds. She was more beast than child and it amused the Sergeant to observe her at close quarters, although he knew he would have to change her if he was to stand any chance of helping her in the long term.

"Spoon," the Sergeant said, holding up a wooden spoon for Catherine to examine. Catherine accepted it but simply clasped it in her hand as she went on chugging from the bowl. "*Spoon!*" the Sergeant repeated, this time a little more forcefully.

Belch! replied Catherine, wiping her face with her sleeve and dropping the empty bowl at the Sergeant's feet along with the still pristine spoon.

"Where did you learn manners like that? A pigsty?" he asked.

"Where did you learn yours? Scotland?" she cheeked back, momentarily shocking him into silence. A joke was a joke but there was such a thing as going too far. The Sergeant took a mental step back and tried to remember the sort of firebrand he was dealing with. The Lieutenant had failed to tame her with his big stick. Perhaps the Sergeant would have more luck with a carrot.

"I'm just trying to help you."

"Yeah, I can still feel your help all over my back," she sneered, unable to overlook who'd put the actual scars there.

"Would you sooner a bullet?"

"I never done nothing!" Catherine objected.

"Except nick two turnips," the Sergeant reminded her.

"I never. You said so yourself. You never found nothing on me."

"Oh didn't I?" he replied, pulling an old hessian sack from underneath his blanket and dumping it on the floor before Catherine. It was hers. She recognised it immediately. It was the one she carried her worldly goods in and which, for a time, had included two army surplus turnips.

"That's not mine," she lied, wary of the Sergeant and what he might want from her. There were no free lunches in Andovia, or so the saying went, and the Sergeant held quite a marker against her.

"Let's start again, shall we?" the Sergeant suggested, once more picking up the wooden spoon and holding it out for her to take. "Spoon."

Catherine eyed it grudgingly but felt herself in a corner. "Spoon," she repeated through gritted teeth, taking the utensil from the Sergeant if only to shut him up. Catherine had little need of spoons since leaving the orphanage. There wasn't much call for them out in the forest but she was hardly in a position to argue. Today, she would live by his rules but tomorrow or the next day, when she was well enough to leave, she would d what she had to do to survive once again.

"You're going to need to acquire a few table manners if you're to fit in around here, young Missy."

"I don't want to fit in around here. I want to get out of here and never see this stinking mud hole again," she said, her scars cracking painfully as she tensed her shoulders.

"Get out of here? And go where? Back to the woods? Back to the winter and no food, no people and no hope? What sort of plan is that?"

The Sergeant was no more than eight years older than Catherine but he'd aged considerably in the last few years. Soldiering could do that to a man, particularly in times of strife. Bum fluff was no match for powder burn nor innocence for the front line. The Sergeant and his comrades had seen many hardships but for all of it, they'd come through it together, stronger and more resilient.

Andovia was a small Kingdom surrounded by many greater ones. For much of its history, it had been forced to fight for its very existence. It was, for want of a better expression, a geographical runt. But the King and his ministers refused to accept that it was a runt and made as much noise as they could on the world stage to remind their neighbours of Andovian sovereignty. No treaty was signed without an Andovian signature added to the bottom and no battle fought without a detachment of the King's Guards scrapping around in a muddy corner of the carnage for the right to plant its flag. On whose side, the winners or losers, it rarely mattered, just so long as the King booked his place at the peace accord and continued to be regarded as the ruler of an independent state, on a par with his cousins in France, Spain, Austria and Britain.

"I was doing alright until you lot kidnapped me," Catherine said, making the Sergeant chuckle at just how boneheaded some people could be.

"How long have you been out there? How long have you been living like this?" the Sergeant asked but Catherine said nothing. This man opposite, with the nice smile and the warm food was not the friend he was pretending to be. He was the enemy. Everyone was the enemy. She only had herself to rely on and as soon as she was well enough she would steal everything from his kit bag and slip out under the wire to freedom again.

"Do you know what the future has in store for you?" the Sergeant said. "There aren't too many forest grannies out there in the wilds. Life for you is going to be brutal and it's going to be short. And the first time you put a foot wrong?" he snapped his fingers and left the rest of Catherine's imagination. "Which would be a pity, not least of all for you," he continued. "We're only here for a few more days, just until the Lieutenant's completed his winter manoeuvres, then we'll break camp and return to base. Come with us and you might stand a chance."

"I don't need nobody else," Catherine snarled.

"Everybody needs somebody, dummy," the Sergeant said. "Even you. Stop fighting the world and recognise a chance when one comes along."

"A chance to do what; be your slave? I'd rather be free and hungry," Catherine said, almost daring the Sergeant to slug her again now that she was armed with a spoon.

"Yes well, freedom is overrated, particularly when you're hungry," the Sergeant shrugged, lying back on his blanket and kicking off his boots. "Besides, who amongst us is truly free? I answer to the Lieutenant. The Lieutenant answers to the Captain. He answers to the Major and so on and so forth until we get to the King. And he's no freer than any of us what with all the conventions and traditions he has to live by. He just sleeps in a bigger tent, that's all."

"What rot!"

"You know what your problem is?" the Sergeant said, sliding his cap over his eyes to get some well-earned rest after another long day of duty.

"No, but I could tell you yours if you like," Catherine replied.

The Sergeant laughed into his cap but resisted the temptation to ask for the fuller explanation.

"Your problem is that you're still trying to fight the system. But you'll never win like that. Nobody does. Play the world at its own game, live and learn, it's the only way."

The Sergeant put his cap to one side and sat up on one elbow. He pulled a shiny brass medal from his top pocket that hung from a blue ribbon and held it out for Catherine to see. It glinted against the glow of the yellow lantern and she saw some words inscribed around the edge of it but she didn't know what they said. She couldn't yet read.

"This is the Medal of Valour. I got it at the Battle of Cedar Hill, or just before actually, for infiltrating the enemy camp and gathering vital intelligence. Pretty brave of me don't you think?" he said, lying back on his mat and dangling the medal over his eyes to watch it sparkle in the light of the lamp. "Now how do you think I did that? Did I go charging in with all guns blazing, swinging my sword and yelling blue bloody murder or did I simply swap coats with one of the prisoners we held and wander around the back of their lines, counting their guns and saluting their officers as if I was just another Austrian amongst thousands of the buggers? What would you have done?"

"I wouldn't have risked my life for some worthless chunk of metal, that's for sure," she said, refusing to be won over by the Sergeant's tale of heroism.

"I didn't do it for this," he said, slipping the medal back into his pocket. "I did it for the lads. We made our objective and lost only four men the next day. That's why I did it. That's what made the risk worthwhile."

Catherine found that harder to argue with but maintained that any amount of losses was still too many.

"At last, something we can finally agree on," the Sergeant said. "So you want to stick around? Give us a chance?"

"I'm not going to be your slave!" Catherine insisted.

"I'm not asking you to be. I'm a Sergeant. I've got half a dozen fellas to boss around already," he said.

"Then what?" Catherine asked warily.

The Sergeant sat up again and reached into his kit bag. What he pulled out now both alarmed and appalled Catherine. It was a comb and a pair of scissors.

"First thing's first, we're going to need to make you a boy."

"Stay away from me. I mean it. I scratch and I bite, just see if I don't," she said, rearing away from him despite the wave of fresh agonies that swept across her shoulders.

The Sergeant put the scissors and comb back into his bag. A strong breeze could've floored Catherine but he wasn't about to try cutting her hair if she didn't want him to. She had to believe in what he was trying to do for her otherwise it would've been pointless.

"You've seen the camp. Did you see any other girls out there? And what do you think the Lieutenant would say if he saw you wandering about the place again?"

"Just let him try," Catherine said, almost hoping he would.

"The Lieutenant? He wouldn't do anything. He'd have me do it. Or more likely, have someone else do it to us both. Haven't you learned anything yet? The officers don't get their hands dirty."

Catherine saw that this was true but just one more reason to put this place as far behind her as she could. A haircut wasn't about to save her from anything.

"No, but these just might," the Sergeant said, once more reaching into his kit bag and this time pulling out a couple of sticks.

"What are they?" Catherine asked, looking but not touching.

"Drumsticks," he said, tapping them together to make

them click. "There's a drum and a uniform too. Should be about your size. It's got one or two holes in it but nothing that can't be patched up."

"You want me to be a drummer boy?"

"I don't want anything. It's up to you. Do you want to go on running around out there scratching for scraps or do you want to try your luck on this side of the wire for a change? Which do you think will give you the better chance of making it through the winter?" Catherine said nothing and the Sergeant got fed up waiting for her to take the drumsticks so he tossed them to her and shrugged. "Look, the offer's there so think on it." And with that, he lay back on his mat, replaced his cap and resumed his slumber. Catherine examined the Sergeant's latest offerings and put them with her hessian sack and army-issue wooden spoon.

"Why are you doing this?" she asked, still suspicious of his motives.

"You looked like you could use a break," he said from inside his cap without stirring. Catherine still wasn't convinced. She'd had to fight for everything her whole life. No one had ever just given her something and not wanted something in return. Life wasn't like that. Or at least, it hadn't been for Catherine. She was still pondering these thoughts when the Sergeant said his final word on the matter.

"Oh, and by the way, Merry Christmas."

CHAPTER TWELVE

MARIGOLD'S TRAP RIDE HOME had been uncomfortable and undignified. Half a dozen urchins had chased their wheels as they'd left the Beaufort's château. No doubt they had been hanging around looking for more handouts from their new patron but no one who mattered had seen Marigold in a housemaid's outfit and that was the main thing.

What's more, it looked like it had all been worthwhile, with Monsieur Beaufort ordering a new dress for his daughter. A very very *very* expensive one at that. To be made from blue silk with a white lace trim, low off the shoulders, tiny at the waist and peppered with pearls and gemstones. The materials alone would cost a King's ransom but with the young Prince in attendance and shopping for a bride, that's just what every girl in the Kingdom was playing for.

"How can we afford silks and pearls?" Marigold asked when they got home.

"I have some savings and we will use a credit note to get the rest," Mother explained as she hurried inside to start on the designs.

Marigold and Gardenia stabled Queenie and followed Mother into the house. She was already busy clearing her cutting table and laying out paper and pencils to make the cutting patterns.

"We have much to do," she said. "Go and get changed. Gardenia, into something more suitable for work and Marigold… something slightly less so."

When the girls returned, she had already sketched a rough design out. It was the most beautiful and ambitious dress Marigold or Gardenia had ever seen.

"I will cut every cloth and sew every stitch. Nothing must be unexceptional. Only our finest work will do."

"All your work is the finest, Mother," Marigold reassured but Mother now had the bit between her teeth and was determined to take nothing for granted. This dress wouldn't be lovely. It wouldn't be eye-catching. It would be spectacular. "This opportunity demands nothing less."

The three of them worked for seven days straight, spurning all other business and burning the candle at both ends until, stitch-by-stitch, the dress started to take shape. It was indeed the most magnificent garment either Marigold or Gardenia had ever seen and it sparkled like a fairy princess's most treasured jewellery box.

At the end of the seventh day, Mother told Marigold to, "Find me a messenger boy and send word to the Monsieur Beaufort that we are ready for Ella's first fitting."

"Right away Mother," Marigold said, hurrying out.

Gardenia said nothing as she swept up the loose thread ends around the dress and Mother noted her silence.

"Speak Gardenia, while your sister is away."

Gardenia wasn't sure what to say. She wasn't entirely sure what was troubling her but something was up, even if she couldn't put her finger on it. She set her broom down and tried to explain.

"Why have you never made a dress like this for either Marigold or I?" she asked with a pout.

"Do you have the money for silk and pearls? Gold thread and Flemish lace?" Mother replied. She had expected such a complaint at some point from her daughters and her answers were ready and waiting.

"But if this is a dress to catch a Prince, then surely one of your own daughters should wear it and reap the rewards, should they not?"

It was a fair point and Mother could see it from Gardenia's side. She was a fair child, after all. But fair enough to catch a Prince's eye? His hand even? No, that would require something more, something special, and unfortunately, it was something neither Marigold nor Gardenia possessed. And never would.

That would require a name.

"I have a name," Gardenia insisted, failing to grasp the finer points of Andovian high society.

"Indeed you do. But your name is a pretty pink dress made from cotton and linen and picked out with shiny buttons. It is a lovely name. But it is the name of a dressmaker's daughter. And that is not enough for a King's son."

Gardenia looked disappointed but Mother told her not to lose heart.

"You will make a very fine match. Lieutenant Olivier perhaps? He is a fine man, is he not?"

Again with Lieutenant Olivier. This seemed to be Mother's one thought, seeing one of her daughters married off to Lieutenant Olivier. He might have been the Grand Duke's youngest son but he was a dire and disagreeable young man. Even the comfortable life he could've offered Gardenia wouldn't have been enough to cushion the blow that would have been derived from being Madame Olivier.

"Do I not deserve to be happy, Mother?"

"Does your happiness depend upon you wearing a crown?" Mother asked, handing her daughter the dustpan and brush instead of the reassurance she sought. Gardenia took them and finished sweeping up.

"Of course not," she replied.

"Then I will endeavour to do my part and leave the rest to you," Mother said, not entirely convincingly.

*

MONSIEUR BEAUFORT sent for them the next morning. It was normal to attend to wealthier clients in their own homes but Mother still felt nervous about travelling with such materials in her possession. She had ploughed all of her savings into this dress and tripled her investment with the use of credit notes and loans but it was worth it. Monsieur Beaufort was a man of means. He'd only been in Andovia for a month and already people were talking about him. He was going places. Or rather, his daughter was. And Mother had every intention of hitching a ride on the hem of Ella's fine dress.

In the week they'd been away, the château at the top of the hill on *Rue des Roses* had been transformed. Gone was the derelict fortress manned by a lonely old soldier and his ghostly battalions: in its place was a palace fit for a princess. Which, Mother presumed, was the general idea.

The footman greeted them at the front steps and showed them inside, summoning several smart servants with a snap of the fingers to carry their bags.

"Thank you," smiled Gardenia as one such servant took her bag.

Mother whispered to Gardenia that she wasn't required to thank the servants otherwise they'd be at it all day. It wasn't the done thing and it only made them feel uncomfortable anyway. Gardenia frowned. There was still so much to learn. "Sorry," she now said to the same servant, much to Mother's dismay.

Monsieur Beaufort and Ella were once again waiting in the parlour along with a dozen new oil paintings, several new busts and a magnificent tapestry that stretched across the whole of the back wall.

"Madame Roche," Monsieur Beaufort greeted. Ella curtseyed and Marigold and Gardenia remembered to do likewise. "I cannot tell you how much I am looking forward to seeing your creation."

"My dearest Marigold," Ella said, rushing forwards to take Marigold by the hands. "How do you feel? I trust you are recovered?"

"Quite so, thank you, Mademoiselle Beaufort," Marigold replied, grateful to be asked but sooner the whole episode was forgotten.

"You've clearly regained your appetite since you were last here. Hasn't she father?" Ella gleefully pointed out.

"She is looking most healthy," Monsieur Beaufort confirmed to make Marigold feel as though she'd swapped their housemaid's uniform for a horse's feedbag.

"You are too kind," Marigold said, none too convincingly.

"The dress? Shall we?" Monsieur Beaufort suggested, retiring from the room to let Ella get changed.

When Monsieur Beaufort returned he stopped dead in his tracks. The dress was more beautiful than anything he could've imagined. Surely they did not even have such things in France? Not even at le Palais?

"Madame Roche, you have outdone yourself," he declared.

Mother spat the pins from her mouth and thanked him on bended knees as she adjusted the hem of Ella's dress. It still required a nip and a tuck but it was already clear that Ella would not only be the belle of the ball but the tower and steeple too.

"Do you like it, father? Do you love it?" Ella asked.

"Your mother would have been so proud," he smiled.

After a few turns around the parlour, Ella's fitting was done. Mother left Marigold and Gardenia to help Ella out of the dress while she and Monsieur Beaufort went to his study to talk business.

"I know we agreed only half on first fitting but there is so little left to do that I insist I settle my account with you in full. After all, you must've had a great many expenses," Monsieur Beaufort said, opening a drawer in his writing desk and handing Mother a little pink purse heavy with gold. "I trust French coins are satisfactory? If not I shall summon a banker and have them changed into Andovian schillings at once."

"That won't be necessary, Monsieur Beaufort. Livres are quite acceptable," Mother smiled graciously, absolutely delighted with French gold and damned if she was about to swap them for Andovian coppers any time soon; particularly not at Monsieur Joly's exchange rate.

Their business concluded, the first fitting successful, Mother and the girls carefully repacked the dress and bid the Beauforts adieu. Once through the gates, Mother clutched the pink purse to her side and breathed a sigh of relief. Her gamble had paid off. She'd not only recouped her outlay, she'd made a tidy profit too, more than enough to justify all the business they'd turned away over the last eight days. Moreover her dress — nay her creation — would light up the Prince's ball in a few short weeks. People would be talking about it for years to come. She had upped the ante. And to whom would they turn when they wanted their own magnificent creations? She was quietly confident it would not be Monsieur Vasseur.

The city walls were only another two or three miles away when they heard the first thunder of hooves behind them. Marigold turned and gasped. Charging out of the woods and after them on horseback were four masked riders, each dressed in black and armed with crossbows.

"Oh no, go go go!" Mother yelled, cracking the reins and urging Queenie to race faster but three women in a trap were no match for four men on stallions. The ground between them was quickly closed until Marigold could see the whites of their assailants' eyes. Their faces may have been concealed but their intentions were not. They were plunderers, free-roaming bandits who lived by the sword and died by the rope. The countryside further north was rife with them but they rarely ventured this close to the city. Why now? Why today?

Mother could not let this happen. To surrender and lose all they had gained would be a disaster. The city walls were just beyond the next plain. If they kept their nerve and refused to stop they might just be able to make it. All bandits were cowards. They would've seen the three women as easy pickings but they'd not met anyone like Mother before. She'd come through worse.

"Go Queenie, go! And Marigold, the cushions!"

Marigold pulled a cushion out from beneath her bottom.

"Throw it," Mother told her.

Marigold did as she was told, hurling it behind them to startle the closest horse. The horse lost his footing and sent its rider headfirst into a shrub before ploughing into the horse immediately behind it. Two riders down, two remained, but the same trick failed to work a second time when Gardenia used her cushion. It bounced harmlessly on the track and lay there as the enemy's horses thundered straight past it.

What's more, they saw fit to respond in kind, firing their crossbows to make Queenie neigh and Marigold and Gardenia dive against the trap for cover. But Mother was no stranger to arrow fire. She cracked the reins harder still and rose in her seat, riding her buggy like a chariot as they swept around the last mountain pass and raced out into the open countryside. There in the distance was the city. Its towers and smokestacks sent tall shadows across the grasslands to guide Queenie home but they weren't there yet. Another bolt came through the seat of the trap and made Gardenia scream. Marigold answered with the last remaining cushion but it troubled their attackers about as much as a cushion could trouble armed marauders. Another bolt found their trap's left wheel and knocked out several spokes. Their ride began to shudder and this slowed the women further. After crashing across several hard ruts the wheel collapsed, driving the axel into the ground and throwing Mother and the sisters into the grasses.

The men were upon them before they had a chance to run, leaping from their mounts and dragging them out of sight. Their cries went unanswered. They were too far from the city walls for anyone to hear and even if they hadn't been, these bandits knew their business. They would be in the forest and gone long before anyone could arrive to help.

"Take your hands off me, scum. In the name of the King, I demand you unhand me," Mother hollered as she was bundled into the shadows of a thicket. The man who dragged her just laughed and brought his dagger up to her throat.

"I take no orders from an old hag like you," he cackled, his accent thick with Srendizian menace. Marigold and Gardenia were thrown to the ground and all three held at knifepoint as their assailants backed off.

"Please, don't hurt us!" Gardenia cried while Marigold turned white.

"Listen to me well, my daughters, you have nails and teeth. Use them if one of these cowards so much as lays a finger on you," Mother said, rolling back the years and recalling all she'd learnt from her days with the King's Guards.

Once again the bandits just laughed but neither tried anything. They simply stood guarding the women at arm's length and Mother now realised they were waiting for someone else to arrive. The thud of approaching hooves and a huge shadow that flashed between the gaps of the thicket told her that this same person had finally caught up with them. The rider dismounted, tethered his horse and pushed his way through the thicket until he stepped into view. If Gardenia had been fearful before, her terror was ratcheted three-fold when she saw the man who stood before her. He was a giant of a man, towering above his cohorts by a clear head and almost as wide as he was tall, with an enormous barrel chest, arms like tree trunks and hands the size of pitchforks. Unlike the others, he wore no mask. There would've been little point. He was so huge that he would've been instantly recognisable even with his grizzled face covered up. Besides, he was proud of his scars with his left eye sliced half shut and his top lip carved open. They terrified his victims more than any weapon could and the rope burns around his neck only confirmed his resilience.

For when it came to the crunch, not even the hangman was a match for Franz Grimaldi.

"It can't be true," Mother said, scarcely dared to believe it. Suddenly she saw the villains who'd ambushed them were no mere thugs. They served at the grace of the *Bandit King* himself.

"At your service, Madame," Grimaldi said, doffing his hat and bowing theatrically, only to spit an olive pip at her feet to the great delight of his lapdogs.

"When the Captain of the Guards finds out you've returned he will scour the countryside looking for you. You'll not escape the rope a second time."

"And whom, might I ask, is going to tell him? You Madame?" he asked, his opal blue eyes twinkling with menace.

"He'll smell you long before I need to."

Grimaldi popped another black olive between his cracked and cleft lips and considered the point.

"You have courage, Madame, I will give you that."

"I need no courage where you're concerned. I've kicked worse off my shoes," she snapped.

His men gasped but Grimaldi just spat out his olive with laughter. No one had talked to him like this in years, not since that Governor had come down from his ivory tower to taunt him as the noose had been placed around his neck. And who hadn't heard what had happened to him? It was a story that mothers packed their children off to bed with when they'd been especially naughty.

In a flash, the fiendish fugitive unsheathed his cutlass, a

murderous-looking curved blade a meter long that he'd prised from the cold dead hand of the last man to leave a mark on his face. Gardenia howled while Marigold scrambled into a tangle of brambles to get away. One of Grimaldi's lapdogs grabbed her by the ankles and started dragging her back.

"Get your hands off my daughters!" Mother shouted, a hint of fear finally shaking her voice, albeit not for her own sake. Grimaldi was satisfied to see he'd made his point and signalled his slathering jackal to let Marigold go.

The point of his razor-sharp sword now traced through the air and settled on Mother. Her jaw tensed as she readied herself to meet her maker but she didn't flinch. She'd never turned away from death in the past and she wasn't about to start now. Grimaldi's face contorted into a leer, which was about as close to a smile as his deformed features allowed.

"I like a woman with pluck, Madame, but you would do well to mind your manners. Bravery is one thing. Pigheadedness is another."

He swung his arm and sliced open her skirt to reveal the whites of her petticoats and the pink of Monsieur Beaufort's purse beneath, concealed as it was between the layers of her dress.

"Such a heavy load for such an upright woman. Allow me to relieve you of your burden," Grimaldi cackled, his taunts echoed by his toadying henchmen.

Mother clutched onto the purse to prevent him from taking it but Grimaldi once again allowed his sword to do the talking for him, moving to Marigold and then Gardenia before settling on Mother again. Mother instantly forgot the gold. As much as it represented, more than she'd ever known in her life, it was nothing compared to the lives of her daughters.

"Take it and go," she said, hurling it to Grimaldi. He caught it in his big hand and nodded approvingly when he felt its weight.

"A fine day's work, boys. Very gratifying indeed."

The purse went in his pocket but the sword remained free of its scabbard. It danced from chin to chin, taunting the woman for two or three terrible moments before Grimaldi finally spoke.

"You shall have a tale to tell. Think yourselves lucky. Few who've seen this face have lived to tell the tale. But you are an artisan, Madame, one of a kind. And in a world as ugly as this, beauty is queen, wouldn't you say?" he said, dropping his eyes to Mother's opal ring.

"That is mine," she told him, hiding it behind her back. "It is all I have left of my husband. You will not take it from me."

But Grimaldi just growled with amusement. "I have no wish to deprive you of such a precious artefact, for I know of rings such as this. I have seen several in my time. You are a most interesting woman, Madame. Most interesting indeed."

Mother said nothing and neither Marigold nor Gardenia knew what he was talking about. They simply clung on to the hope that they might live to tell the tale. They so wanted this to be true, to be free, to get away, and to never see Grimaldi's terrible face or his terrible sword again.

Grimaldi clicked his fingers and his men beat their retreat, hurrying through the thicket and back to their horses. Grimaldi finally sheathed his sword and reached into his pocket to pull out a little cotton bag.

"Olive?" he said, offering the bag of sour black fruits to Mother. She declined with a glare and Grimaldi found no takers amongst her daughters either. "They are an acquired taste," he conceded with a crooked smile. He helped himself to another then touched the brim of his hat.

"Good day to you, ladies. Do give my regards to the Captain of the Guards," he chuckled, pushing his way through the brush and taking to his horse. "Let's go," they heard him call and all at once the danger had passed.

The three women fell into a tearful embrace and Mother comforted Marigold and Gardenia until they were ready to move.

The sun was bright outside. The grasses swayed in the breeze and the birds soared and swooped, but all else was quiet. The city walls were less than a mile away. They might've made it had their wheel not given out. Close but not close enough.

Queenie stood tethered to the broken trap a short way away. She was anxious but unharmed. Marigold patted him on the neck while Mother searched for their bags. It had all been taken. Ella's dress, the extra silk, leftover lace, gold thread and spare pearls, it was all gone. Grimaldi and his men must've known what it was worth.

Mother was ruined. She'd gambled everything and lost. Well, not quite everything.

"Come on, girls, let us go home."

CHAPTER THIRTEEN

THE GREAT HALL in the royal palace reverberated with the clash of sabres. Steel met steel as two men jostled to show off their fighting skills: back and forth, cut and thrust, counter and parry. The Guards looked on but made no attempt to intervene. They were not here to stop the duel. They were simply here to observe.

Prince Carina liked to take the offensive. He wasn't one to sit back and invite his opponent on. A Prince needed to stamp his authority on every occasion, whether it was the battlefield or the ballroom, a leader was required to lead. He thrust at Captain Durand, forcing him onto the back foot, then followed up with a lunge. Captain Durand parried both attacks then countered, regaining the centre-ground and circling the Prince.

"You handle a weapon well, Captain," the Prince smiled.

"As indeed do you, Your Highness," Captain Durand replied.

"Would you care to double our wager?" the Prince suggested, feinting to strike but failing to provoke a reaction this time.

"I serve at Your Highness's pleasure," Captain Durand reminded him, which was true since the Prince had selected him personally for this plush appointment.

"Then it is agreed," the Prince declared with a wry smile. "I look forward to collecting."

The clatter of steel and big talk continued for another half an hour and was only stopped when the King poked his head in to demand what the hell was going on.

"There's an army of decorators out here waiting to get in and get the place ready for your ball. Can't you go outside and do that?" he shouted angrily.

"It's too hot out there. You know what my allergies are like at this time of the year," the Prince complained, looking around to discover the reason why his opponent had suddenly snapped to attention.

"Out! Everybody out!" the King shouted. Captain Durand and his men saluted and beat a quick retreat. The King desired a word with the Prince and this sort of thing was generally not done in front of the ranks.

The great oak door closed behind the last soldier with a dull thunk. The echo had barely finished reverberating around the vast ballroom when the King let loose with a torrent of exasperations.

"I don't want to hear about your wretched sniffles, boy. You're a Prince of the realm for Heaven's sake. Try acting like one."

"I do not need to act, Papa. I am one. Therefore anything I do is Princely, is it not?"

"It is not!" the King exploded. He had a terrible temper. It came with the job. But nothing drove him into a rage more than the Prince's arrogance. "A Prince sets an example. A Prince leads."

"As indeed I do," the Prince replied, sticking the end of his sabre into the floor and twirling the handle in little circles using just one finger.

"Stop that immediately, you'll mark the floor!" the King barked.

"Then get one of the decorators to fix it," he shrugged. He could sense his father's blood boiling and did what he could to turn up the heat.

"You shouldn't even be playing with that thing anyway. What have I told you before about indulging in this foolishness?" the King said, striding across the room to snatch the sabre from the Prince's hand. "Give me that!"

"I am a soldier," the Prince said, raising his chin and brushing a spec of imaginary dust from his jacket. "And as a soldier, I am a fighting man by nature."

"On the battlefield, boy, not in the ballroom. Like I did at Cedar Hill and the Grand Duke did at Widows' Ridge. That's proper soldiering, my lad. Not poncing around in your tights playing with my Guardsmen."

The King's hand shook with frustration as he clenched the Prince's sweaty sabre. He could still remember the heady thrills and spills of open warfare. He had served as a Colonel in the King's Guards when his father had been on the throne and he'd not disappointed him. His sword had tasted blood on the battlefield and he'd returned home with a chest full of medals and a gut full of glory. All he ever wanted for his son was the same, to uphold the family honour and fill the royal cribs with more Princes of Andovia. Fulfil his duty and he could fart around with the lads as much as he liked.

"Duelling is a noble art," the Prince said but he knew the King wouldn't understand. It was futile trying to explain anything to his father. He was a dinosaur. A relic of a dying age when all a Prince was expected to do was stick his sword into a few prisoners and propagate with some Rubenesque Princess to create more Princes. What was the point!

"And what if you had marked your face swishing these damn things around? What would your future Princess say about that? She wouldn't thank you or your silly playmates for being saddled with a disfigured husband for the rest of her life, would she?" the King shouted, half-tempting to give him a duelling scar just to teach him a lesson.

"Oh Papa. I could take a hammer to this face and drink myself stupid every night of the year and still have every 'lady' in the Kingdom throwing herself at my feet," he said, taking a none-too-subtle riposte at the King's penchant for Port. "It is this place they desire, not I. The maidens of Andovia do not say their prayers and go to sleep dreaming of one day being Mrs Carina. No, they wish for one thing and one thing only, to become a Princess. The Prince himself is merely an incidental inconvenience."

"That may be but you have a responsibility. Your role is to lead. To inspire. To reassure your people that all is well and bring stability to their lives."

"And what's in it for me?" the Prince moaned, having failed to appreciate that duty was its own reward.

"What's in it for you? You live in a castle, boy. You have servants waiting on you hand and foot. You don't even dress yourself most mornings and your breakfast, lunch and dinner appear in front of you as if by magic. You dress in the finest furs, the most expensive silks and the latest French fashions. You sleep in a bed bigger than most commoners' homes and your future is guaranteed. You will never know hunger or hardship. Ever! And what's more, your children's future and your children's children's future is already secure without you having to lift so much as a finger. It has all been handed to you on a plate, much like your breakfast, and all that is required of you is that you conduct yourself with dignity and continue the family line. These are the basic tenets that most people do without expecting some kind of additional incentive. Indeed, some people even aspire to such ideals."

"I am not like most people," the Prince smarted. It was something both he and the King could agree on.

"This ball is for your benefit. Do try to remember that. The cream of society is coming here with their fairest daughters and you are being given first pick. There are no treaties to be signed, no alliances to be forged, for the first time in over a hundred years, a Prince of Andovia is free to marry whomever he desires… within reason," the King explained, although he could still scarcely believe it himself. His own marriage had been used to ratify a peace plan while his brothers, sisters, uncles and aunts had all been used as bargaining chips in the Royal cattle markets of Europe. It was just how things were. But then suddenly they weren't. For one unique moment in history, the political stars had aligned in such a way that it didn't matter whom the Prince married. The third daughter of the Belgium King? The second cousin of the Ottoman Emperor? The fourth sister of the Duke of Burgundy's fifth wife? There was little to be gained from any of these alliances and everything to be gambled, for every alliance forged stirred hostilities in other quarters. There was really only one way out of it. The Prince was required to marry an Andovian girl of good name to save upsetting the foreign apple carts. This meant that suddenly anyone of noble birth, no matter how minor, had a chance of bagging a ticket to the top table. And that was something every Andovian aristocrat wanted 'for his daughter'.

"It's so tedious having such expectations placed upon my shoulders. I'm not ready to get married just yet. I've still got things to do," the Prince whined.

"Then do them. No one's going to stop you, least of all any future wife. Most of them will be so grateful that you've placed a crown upon their head that they'll let you do anything you want. So if you want a compliant wife, pick a compliant girl. If you want a meek wife, pick a meek girl. It matters not, just so long as you pick someone, preferably someone pretty. Someone the people can look up to."

"And what if I don't like any of them?" the Prince asked.

"Then, my boy, you and I shall have a problem."

And with that, the King flung the Prince's sabre across the room and took his leave, signalling to the decorators outside that the room was now theirs.

CHAPTER FOURTEEN

"THE FRANZ GRIMALDI!" Marigold heard Lieutenant Olivier yell through closed doors. She, Gardenia and Ella sat in the hallway outside the parlour while Mother explained to Monsieur Beaufort and the young Lieutenant what had befallen them earlier that day.

Gardenia wondered if this was an opportune moment to catch Lieutenant Olivier's eye but more angry words rocked the oak doors between them so Gardenia decided it could probably wait.

Marigold had said nothing since arriving back at the Beaufort's château. Gardenia neither. Both had experienced a nasty shock but were wise enough to realise that they weren't the only victims here. Monsieur Beaufort had lost his money and Ella had lost her dress. Mother would no doubt have to compensate them both but this did little for anyone in the short-term, what with the Prince's ball just a week away.

The three girls sat in silence, Marigold and Gardenia on one bench, Ella across from them on another. Gardenia reached out to take Marigold's hand. This was a habit from childhood, the need to hold her big sister's hand in times of distress, although she'd not done it for several years. Ella glanced over at them but said nothing. Too many voices were already saying too many things. This day needed fewer words, not more.

The door was flung open and Lieutenant Olivier strode out. Marigold, Gardenia and Ella all jumped to their feet but the Lieutenant barely noticed them. He was still barking his disdain at what he viewed was a scurrilous plot to deceive.

"Franz Grimaldi wouldn't dare set foot outside of Srendizi, not with a dozen death sentences hanging over his head on this side of the Alps."

"But Lieutenant Olivier, I assure you..." Mother tried

to say but Lieutenant Olivier was having none of it.

"I will not be a party to this charade, Madame. You are a liar and a thief. As if Franz Grimaldi would risk all for a dress and a handful of coins!"

"But it's true, he's back," Marigold insisted, remembering what Hans had told her about seeing riders in the Northern Pass just a few weeks earlier.

"Indeed, robbed you blind you say?" Lieutenant Olivier scoffed, giving Mother's large opal ring a stiff look. Mother realised what he was getting at but it would do no use to argue. Franz Grimaldi rarely left his victims alive, let alone with jewellery on their fingers. She should have hidden it before reporting the crime. Why hadn't this occurred to her? Her honesty had been her undoing. "That you would attempt to implicate a Lieutenant of the Guards in this fraud is bad enough, Madame, but to recruit your own daughters is unforgivable. I should clap you in irons this very day. All three of you."

Marigold turned white at the suggestion and Gardenia put her hand to her mouth to stop herself from crying out.

"There is no need for that, Lieutenant," Monsieur Beaufort said. "I should like to deal with this matter discreetly if you don't mind."

Fortunately for all, Lieutenant Olivier was a reasonable man. Not so much as far as criminals were concerned but he saw that the real victims of this crime, Monsieur *Le Chevalier* Beaufort and his beautiful daughter Ella, would stand no chance of making good on their losses if the Roches were tossed into the dungeons.

"As you wish, Monsieur *Le Chevalier*. You know my feelings but if you wish to handle this shameful business differently then you are, of course, free to do so. Just know that you can rely upon my support should you fail to receive satisfaction," he said, only too eager to assist a nobleman in the quashing of such a villainous plot.

A thought raced through Gardenia's mind and didn't stop until it reached her tongue.

"Please Lieutenant, in the name of *the King's men*, you have to believe we're speaking the truth."

Mother and Marigold gasped. The Lieutenant just stared in astonishment. Had he heard right? Had this girl really just said what he thought she'd said?

"Say that again!" he demanded, his face a torrent of anger and outrage.

"I… I… I… didn't say anything," she fudged, looking around the hallway and frightened by the look on Mother's face. Gardenia was young but she was no fool. She immediately saw that she'd said something wrong and now tried to bluster her way out of it.

"I… just said we were speaking the truth," she giggled nervously, hoping to throw the Lieutenant off the scent with a display of empty-headedness — which, coincidentally, was normally her seduction strategy too.

"The words you used. About *the King's men*. Say them again!" the Lieutenant shouted, taking a menacing step towards Gardenia and ready to slap her across the face should she lie to him again.

"Lieutenant please, my daughter doesn't know what she's saying. She's a simpleton. It's a burden we have had to carry for many years," Mother insisted, not necessarily scuppering Gardenia's chances with the Lieutenant but seriously denting them nevertheless.

"She knows perfectly well what she said and so do I," the Lieutenant growled, not buying it for one second. "Those words are a direct attack against my family and the King and we will not stand for it."

But try as he might, the Lieutenant could not get Gardenia to repeat the phrase and no one would corroborate his suspicions, not even Monsieur Beaufort, who claimed his hearing had not been the same since the Battle of Villafranca.

The Lieutenant had no choice but to drop the matter but with the sternest of warnings.

"Listen well, if I ever hear such sedition again I won't clap you in irons, I'll exhibit your heads on pikes outside the Guardhouse gates." And with a click of his heels, the good Lieutenant saw himself out, leaving Mother, Marigold and Gardenia to face a few awkward questions from their far-from-satisfied customer.

And thus, Mother lost the business she'd spent years building up. Monsieur Beaufort kept his word and never told a soul. But that didn't matter. Word spread like wildfire all on its own without the Beauforts fanning the flames. Butlers talked to footmen, footmen talked to maids and maids talked to mistresses. Within just a few short hours of losing every penny, Mother's reputation followed suit. When her creditors heard the news there was an outcry. Mother barricaded the front door and waited for the storm to pass. She would pay everyone whatever she owed: Monsieur Beaufort, the silk merchants and the jewellers who held credit notes against her. She was a woman of her word after all — but she needed time.

Her first move was to sell most of their furniture and their picturesque townhouse and downsize to something... well, less so.

*

"IT'LL LOOK OKAY ONCE we've given it a clean," Mother said, none-too-convincingly. Their new home was a hovel. There were no other words for it. It wasn't even a house, just a one-room brick shack on the outskirts of the city that had previously been used to store horse manure. Good stuff for the garden. Less so for the home.

"Oh Mother, I don't think I can even go inside. It hurts the senses so," Gardenia complained, holding her nose against her new home's overpowering odour.

"We have no choice, daughters. Our backs are against

the wall. But we have made good on much of our debt," Mother said, no longer wearing her precious large opal ring. She hadn't sold it. It was one of the few possessions she had retained but she no longer wore it. The time for that would come again but for now, it remained out of sight. "At least we'll get no more creditors at our doors."

"They wouldn't dare," Marigold replied, wafting away the flies.

Liquorice stood waiting with what was left of the Roche's possessions tied to his back. He didn't understand what the problem was. His new home smelled fine to him although he missed Queenie. She, with great reluctance, had been sold to help settle Mother's debts. It had been a terrible wrench having to let her go but they'd simply had no choice. They couldn't afford to keep both horses. Liquorice might have gone the same way had he been younger but these days he was worth more to a butcher than a horse trader so economies were made and Liquorice was spared. Family came first.

"We're going to need to make a fire for hot water. And rose petals too. Lots of them," Mother said, arming herself with a bucket and a broom and turning the front door handle to let battle commence.

The women worked day and night for three solid days. After their first day's efforts, they could enter their new home without retching. After the second, they'd swept the chimney and got a fire going to dry out the underlying damp that seeped through every beam. And after the third, they'd repaired the thatched roof, whitewashed the walls and cleaned the windows to let in a few rays of light again. It was still a hovel but at least it was now a picturesque little hovel for minimalistic open-plan living to match the claims made in the sales brochure.

CHAPTER FIFTEEN

"WHAT IF SOMEONE ASKS us for money?" Gardenia fretted as Mother laced her up from behind.

"On the street? In broad daylight? Unthinkable," Mother said, tying a final knot and tucking the loose ends out of sight.

"But what if they do?" Gardenia insisted.

"Daughter, the only person likely to ask you for money will be Stefano, when you buy a sorbet from him. In which case I would advise you pay him."

And with that Mother handed Marigold, who was ready and waiting, a little silk purse of schillings and opened the door for both. This would be their first stroll out since slipping from grace. Mother had dressed them stylishly yet modestly. Their dresses were beautifully designed without being too gaudy. It would not be prudent to flaunt silks while they still owed silver.

"I don't want to go," Gardenia said.

"I don't care," Mother replied, closing the door to keep them out.

Marigold and Gardenia steeled themselves for the gauntlet ahead. They might've fallen on hard times but they couldn't hide from the world forever. They had to put on a brave face — several layers, in fact — to show their friends and neighbours that they might've been down but they most certainly weren't out. Their futures depended upon it.

It was an unfamiliar route into town from their new home, taking them down the side streets and back alleyways to keep them off the main drag. Gardenia seemed almost relieved when they reached the park. They'd not encountered anyone of note since setting out and although this was the purpose of their stroll, to continue to exhibit Mother's wares, she would've rather worn a magic cloak of invisibility.

In the park, however, there was no hiding place. The sun was out and so were the crowds. Gardenia almost baulked when she saw the Eames heading their way, not just Madame and Monsieur, but Isabella too.

"Easy," Marigold whispered to her. "Nothing to worry about. Just be polite."

As they passed the Eames, Marigold and Gardenia smiled cordially but the gesture went unreturned. Monsieur and Madame Eames simply looked the other way. And despite possessing the most amazing eyes in the whole of the Kingdom, Isabella failed to spot them.

"That went better than expected," Marigold told her ashen-faced sister.

More snubs followed as they promenaded past the pagoda, meandered along the menagerie and finally slunk through the esplanade. By the time they reached the queue for Stefano's Ice Cream Kiosk, Gardenia had come to the conclusion that she didn't need to wish for a magic cloak of invisibility. She was already wearing one.

Marigold and Gardenia joined the back of the queue and not a person gave way for them, married or otherwise, young or old, rich or poor. Marigold tried coughing to remind young Monsieur Vipond, the undertaker's son, of proper protocol but he refused to budge.

"If that cough keeps up I expect my father will be seeing you soon," he said with a smirk, not even deigning to remove his hands from his pockets. Six places forward, the old spinster Mademoiselle Renard looked back and laughed but no one else acknowledged them. Marigold had never felt so humiliated in all her life.

But few situations are so terrible that things can't go from bad to worse if the stars decree it. Marigold heard Gardenia gasp and followed her eye. Approaching Stefano's line from across the park was Dirty Didi, the filthiest tramp in all Andovia.

"Oh my God," said Gardenia, already grasping the implications of his approach. Clutched in his hand was a shiny little copper coin he'd fished out of the wishing well, which was something Didi from time to time did when he fancied eating something that hadn't come from the bin. But there were no sausage vendors in this part of the park. And no pretzel peddlers either. There was only the line for Stefano's Ice Cream Kiosk. And Didi was heading right for it.

Gardenia tried to bolt — the thought of being compelled to stand aside for Didi was more than she could bear — but Marigold grabbed her wrist. "If we go now there will be no coming back from this shame," she whispered. "We must endure the unendurable if we are to ever walk tall again."

Gardenia didn't see how but she bowed to her sister's judgement. She didn't have to like it or even agree with it but it was generally accepted that Marigold was wiser in most matters. Besides, deferring to someone else always gave her the "I told you so" option, the most famous example of which was the Martial brothers' execution, when Enzo and Rafael kept up the blame game all the way off the block and into the basket. They had been lucky. Their end had come swiftly with an expert swing of the sword. But when the town learned of the Roche girls' latest and greatest humiliation, their demise would last considerably longer. And be infinitely more painful.

By now the entire line had spotted Didi approaching and turned to see the sisters' reaction. Most expected them to run, which would have been akin to them accepting they were now on a lower rung than a man who went to the toilet in his own shoes. But Marigold and Gardenia stood their ground. They were going to joust it out with Didi — etiquette-wise. This just got better and better.

Of course, they didn't stand a chance. Even if Didi joined the back of the queue and chose to wait his turn, it wasn't his decision to make. The queue was a living, breathing barometer of one's standing in society. It decided who stood where and nobody ahead of Marigold and Gardenia was about to forfeit this golden opportunity to put the sisters in their place.

Didi arrived with a huge sticky smile on his face. He'd been filling his face with flat beer and bacon rinds all morning courtesy of the inn keeper's slops buckets and now he fancied something refreshing to take the edge off his crippling gut rot. An iced fancy and a sleep in the bushes would do just nicely but he could tell something was amiss when he got to the line. Didi may not have known what month or year it was but he wasn't as ignorant as most people thought. Lots of faces up and down the line were looking at him in glee. They weren't usually pleased to see him but today they were. What was so different about today? It was then that he noticed the Roche sisters standing at the very back and not in their usual place. Didi couldn't know what had happened but he could tell from their position that they'd tumbled from grace.

"And now," Didi thought to himself, "the others are looking to me to ice their cake for them."

Marigold and Gardenia could feel themselves burning up while Didi remained a few steps back deliberating. All eyes were on them and pressure was already being brought to bear but Marigold couldn't move. It wasn't that she was refusing to do so — that would've been unthinkable, even more so than licking ice cream from Didi's beard — but she was simply caught between the devil and the deep blue sea and her legs refused to comply.

Monsieur Vipond now let out the first of several disapproving coughs and Mademoiselle Renard echoed this with a tut. But Didi hadn't yet joined the line and until he had, the sisters were within their rights not to move aside. Or acknowledge him. Or breathe.

Gardenia wanted to die. Nothing could be so bad as this, to make way for a tramp and, try as she might, she failed to suppress a weep.

Didi's face softened as he studied the wretched girls before him. Having successfully retreated from polite society some thirty years earlier their's was a misery he could scarcely remember, let alone understand. But misery was misery in whatever form it came and he was no merchant of the stuff. He pulled the wet centime from his pocket and flipped it in the air with a fat dirty thumb, catching it and slapping it on the back of his hand for all to see.

"Tails," he said with a mock sigh. "Looks like I'll get myself a candy cane instead."

And with that, he turned and trudged away, warmed to the ulcers at the thought of the sisters' relief and the mob's unrequited malice. Gardenia could not stop trembling but Marigold was too startled to remain shaken. She watched Didi wander off, her heart buoyed with relief and just a tinge of inner disappointment. She'd barely acknowledged Didi in her life, passing him by until now as if he were nothing but a bundle of old rags, and yet he'd shown her more compassion than she felt worthy of. It was a lesson she would never forget.

Gardenia felt less inclined to such introspection. She was just grateful to have dodged a cannonball and pulled at Marigold's arm, urging her to: "Come on please, let's get out of here before he comes back."

"He won't come back," Marigold reassured her but Gardenia wasn't listening.

"I don't care. I don't want a sorbet. I just want to go home."

"I don't want a sorbet either," Marigold replied, as indeed she didn't. She'd come to see Hans and with Mother's blessing to boot. This was her own particular silver lining to their predicament and the reason she'd dragged Gardenia halfway across town for their usual Saturday sabbatical. Given that her standing was now somewhere between Didi and an unswept pile of horse droppings, Hans was an acceptable catch for a girl of Marigold's advancing years and she had every intention of capitalising upon this mixed blessing.

And so Marigold and Gardenia waited. They waited and waited and waited, occasionally stepping aside for their betters, which now included the Moreau boys, much to Gardenia's shame, but Marigold didn't care. She ignored the disdainful looks from her former friends and acquaintances because none of it meant anything to her anymore. She had been released from the shackles of society and was now free to be with whomever she wanted.

Her heart fluttered as the queue grew shorter. Hans was in the back working the scoop as Stefano chatted amicably with those he was serving. Hans glanced in her direction but looked away again before she could catch his eye. She read nothing into that. He was right to remain guarded but when it happened again she began to notice. Gone was the long lingering looks she'd clung on to these last few years. Absent too was the knowing smile that Hans always wore when she was in the queue. In their place instead, on the few occasions Hans actually looked up, was an expression of pure embarrassment. Hans tried to hide it but hiding your feelings from an Andovian girl was like trying to hide sausages from a dog. The more he avoided her gaze, the more Marigold feared the worst.

Eventually, after more than an hour, they reached the front of the queue. At least, they reached the serving hatch. The queue technically no longer existed because Marigold and Gardenia were all that remained of it. Stefano dropped the need for pleasantries and simply asked what they wanted.

"Two lemon sorbets, if you please, Monsieur Stefano," Marigold replied, looking over his shoulder in an effort to relay an unspoken message to Hans. But neither he nor

Stefano could bring themselves to look Marigold in the eye.

Two sorbets were produced and placed on the hatch and Stefano took their money. Marigold had almost expected him to ask to see the money upfront but they'd been humiliated enough for one afternoon and no one was of a mind to heap any more onto them. Especially with what was to come.

"I must close up for five minutes. If you would please?" Stefano asked, inviting Marigold and Gardenia to step away from the serving hatch so that he could close the shutters.

Marigold couldn't have felt more depressed had she been facing the executioner with nothing smaller than a thousand schilling note. But then her hopes were raised a moment later when the side door opened and Hans stepped out.

"Mademoiselle Roche, might I speak with you in private?" he asked nervously, prompting Marigold to wonder if she'd got it all wrong. Had Hans been avoiding her gaze not because of her new-found status but because of a question that had been burning a hole in his heart since the last time they'd met? Gardenia came to the same conclusion and gawped in excitement before remembering she was surplus to requirements.

"Oh, er… yes, I'll just be over here if you need me," she said, scurrying out of earshot but only just.

"Mademoiselle Roche," Hans stammered, whipping off his apron and wringing it in his hands.

"Marigold," she reminded him but Hans shook his head and her heart sunk all over again.

"I wanted to apologise for any misunderstanding that may have occurred between us," he said carefully, taking his time over each individual word, almost as if he had been coached. "I may have overstated my feelings for you and wish now to make clear that, although I regard you in the highest of esteems, my heart belongs to another."

Hans went on to explain in some laboured detail about how Stefano had introduced him to his niece and how they'd formed an attachment, presumably with the help of clouds drifting through the sky, the Earth and the moon, wind and mountains and all the rest of it. Cynthia and Hans would take charge of Stefano's Ice Kiosk, keeping the name and paying Stefano a pension until that great scoop in the sky came down for him, at which point they would inherit the business, buckets and all.

Marigold turned colder than the sorbet she was holding. Some strange girl had come in at the eleventh hour and pipped her to her fantasy. Stefano hadn't given Hans a choice: his niece and the ice cream kiosk or Marigold and nothing? It was a painful decision but what hurt Marigold most of all was that Hans hadn't even the decency to lie that this was all about money.

"My lady…" he said when Marigold turned in tears.

"I am not your lady!" she snapped at him, throwing her glass dish at the side of Stefano's hut to plaster sorbet all up the wall. "And I wouldn't be, not even if we were indeed the last two people on Earth."

"I have hurt you. I can see that now," Hans said, clumsily trampling all over Marigold's pride now that he'd finished with her heart.

"Hurt me?" Marigold shouted to draw stares from far and wide. "You're not capable of hurting me. You're a bucket boy. And that's all you'll ever be."

Gardenia was shocked to find she was still within earshot despite stepping away and saw Marigold storm past without stopping. Gardenia raced after her, finally catching her at the bandstand, only to realise she was still holding a bowl of sorbet.

"What do I do with this?" Gardenia asked.

Marigold looked at it and had an idea. She took it from

Gardenia and went hurrying through the park, looking this way and that until she found the one person she was looking for. There, under an old oak tree, was Didi, sheltering from the sun and licking the stripes from a sticky red and white candy cane. Marigold approached him, not caring a damn who saw her and held out the dish.

"Please, Monsieur Didi, I would consider it an honour if you would accept this from me, as a token of my esteem." Didi could not have been more surprised had the Angel Gabriel himself had appeared before him to offer him a pudding.

"Mademoiselle!" he blinked in confusion, remembering just in time to yank off his hat to reveal a shock of grey hair. "I thank you kindly but the honour is mine," he said, accepting the sorbet with a wary look and a sniff.

Gardenia stood at a distance and struggled to understand why Marigold could have done such a thing. In broad daylight. After all they had been through. The shock of recent events had clearly told on her sister.

Marigold took Gardenia's arm and only added to her confusion when she led her away with these final words.

"That man is the finest gentleman in the whole of Andovia."

CHAPTER SIXTEEN

A FEW HOURS LATER, Mother, Marigold and Gardenia were sitting down to an unusually quiet evening meal when there came a knock at the door. The three women looked at each other and froze. Who could be calling upon them at this hour? Indeed, who would dare call upon them ever again after Marigold's moment of madness with Didi? Gardenia hadn't dared tell Mother about what had happened in the park but she would find out soon enough. Word would not take long to reach her ears.

Gardenia held her breath as Mother opened the door. Their visitor turned out to be even more unlikely than anyone Gardenia could have imagined.

"Monsieur Vasseur!" Mother said, neglecting to conceal the surprise in her voice.

The old dressmaker removed his tricorn hat and bowed courteously. He was an impossibly thin man who walked with a permanent stoop, caused by spending half his life on his knees for one reason or another. He always dressed simply and yet immaculately, in a full-length navy blue frock coat, with matching weskit and breeches. His stockings, neck stock and wig were snow white and his eyes deep blue, just like the freshly-cut crocus pinned to his lapel.

"Madame Roche. My apologies for calling upon you so late but might I speak with you in private about a somewhat delicate matter?" he asked tentatively.

"I have no secrets from my daughters," Mother told him, which wasn't exactly true seeing as she still hadn't explained to Gardenia what or who *the King's men* were. Some things were never to spoken of.

"I am more than happy to say what I have come to say in front of your daughters," Monsieur Vasseur said, making Mother realise he was actually fishing for an invitation inside, something she'd never thought to do with her chief competitor.

"Very well. Come on in," she reluctantly said, stepping aside to let Monsieur Vasseur enter. He'd barely taken four steps across the threshold before he found himself on the other side of the room. It was dark but the glow from the small hearth threw enough light out for him to see how his arch-rival was now living. There were two beds on one side of the room; a small single for Mother and a double that wasn't much bigger than the single for her daughters. Pots and pans hung from the walls and clothes hung in the roof space to keep them dry and free from lice, as the wood smoke that collected in the rafters acted as a natural pesticide. A table and three chairs dominated most of the room and it was to here Monsieur Vasseur was directed. Monsieur Vasseur wouldn't hear of unseating Marigold or Gardenia during their evening meal but the girls were only too happy to set their cabbage soup aside and give Liquorice his hay.

"Now, Monsieur Vasseur, what can I do for you?" Mother asked when the girls had left.

It is said in life that for every loser there is a winner reaping the benefits. Monsieur Vasseur had never known such a surge in business like it. He'd already had a healthy order book with the Prince's ball coming up but now he could scarcely cope. He'd hired all the seamstresses that Mother had been forced to let go but still it hadn't been enough. Demand had not so much outstripped supply as left her for dead in a ditch by the side of the road.

"Would you consider it an insult if I were to offer you employment, Madame Roche?" Monsieur Vasseur asked with his hat in his hands, both literally and metaphorically.

"I have my pride, Monsieur Vasseur, but I am not proud. I have debts to settle and food to buy. I will accept your kind offer, of course, and thank you."

Mother had little choice. No one else was about to

offer her work and Monsieur Vasseur had her over a barrel. This wasn't so much the hostile takeover as the meek capitulation.

"You are not worried my reputation will taint yours?" Mother asked, damned with etiquette and reaching for her own cabbage soup before it got cold. Or rather, colder.

"The only reputation I am concerned with is yours as a seamstress. Yours is the finest work in the whole of Andovia, superior even to mine," Monsieur Vasseur said to Mother's surprise. "When you first began all those years ago I'd never seen anything quite like it. Your needlework and attention to detail took my breath away. And your designs? What an eye! You worried me, Madame. No, that's not actually quite true. You terrified me. There wasn't a day that I didn't pray you'd make some mistake and encounter some misfortunate but you never did. Until this moment."

Mother set down her spoon. She'd been too quick to accept his offer of charity. He hadn't come here to throw her a lifeline but to gloat. At least that's how it sounded. Monsieur Vasseur saw the change in Mother's face and realised this too.

"Forgive me please, Madame. I meant no offence," he said jumping to his feet when Mother left the table and poured her soup back into the pot strung over the fire.

"You meant no offence and you intended no insult," Mother said, turning her back on Monsieur Vasseur in disdain. "And yet you made gifts of both."

Monsieur Vasseur was mortified. He was a dressmaker, a designer of beautiful clothes but he'd stitched his words together with five thumbs. He had to make Mother see what he was trying to say.

"All I meant was, in order to maintain my own business you forced me to improve the quality of my own work. I tried new techniques and new designs. You opened my eyes to new ideas. I learned so much from you, so much more than I might've done otherwise. For this alone, I will always be grateful."

Mother grimaced. Monsieur Vasseur had been trying to pay tribute to her and she'd done him a disservice. How the Sergeant would've laughed. She finally had a home to match her manners.

"Monsieur Vasseur, please forgive me. I spoke in haste," she said, turning around to her guest to find a smile where she expected to see a glare.

"It is quite alright, Madame," he said. "You speak with your hands. That is the only language I truly understand."

Mother had known Monsieur Vasseur for almost ten years but this was the most they'd ever truly spoken. She'd never cared to before now, the usual courtesies aside. He was the competition, after all, the enemy, to be routed and crushed. It was all she knew or understood.

"Andovia needs you, Madame. I need you. I am less without you. And it is my fervent wish that we might one day lock horns across the ballroom again — in mutually-assured-creation."

The fire crackled, the soup bubbled and the door creaked where Gardenia leant too heavy an ear against it.

"*Get back! Get back!*" they heard the girls whisper outside amid fleeing footsteps.

"Please forgive them. They are only concerned with my wellbeing," Mother said but there was no need. Monsieur Vasseur had spent half a lifetime around excitable daughters. It went with the territory.

Monsieur Vasseur promised to drop round several rolls of satin and two designs in the morning and Mother promised to have them both ready by Thursday.

"But that is just four days from now," Monsieur Vasseur said in surprise.

"You'll need time to attend to their first fittings and return the garments to me. You'll be far too busy to do this on Friday and the ball itself is on Saturday. I cannot attend the fittings myself, as you well know. You must safeguard your reputation, Monsieur Vasseur."

"And you must rebuild yours, Madame Roche," said Monsieur Vasseur. "And this ball gives you your best opportunity."

CHAPTER SEVENTEEN

THE DAY OF THE PRINCE'S BALL did not so much arrive in Andovia as engulf the tiny Kingdom. To the daughters who were about to debut it felt like the end of days itself. A lifetime of preparation had brought them to this point, now destiny was but a dance away. But to the parents and relatives of these conjugal competitors, this was not about one night. This was a Heaven-sent opportunity to establish their family names for generations to come.

The Prince was the ultimate prize, of course, but he was not the only ticket in town. Every eligible aristocrat in Andovia would be in attendance, from the sons of Lords and Ladies to the unmarried brothers, nephews and uncles of anyone with even a flicker of influence. If a girl missed out tonight she might as well pack it in and hightail it to the nearest nunnery. All future history would lead back to this day. The Prince's ball was to be a cornerstone event.

The invitation said eight o'clock sharp but the first guests were determined not to arrive until after ten. No one wanted to be first. You couldn't stage a grand entrance without a grand audience. And when the runners and riders did finally set off, most got caught in the huge traffic jam of carriages that choked the streets approaching the Palace. The street shovelers could scarcely keep up. The roses would grow tall in Andovia next season.

The Prince cruised the Great Hall in a garish gold frock coat, smiling politely and making small talk with various Viscounts he passed but overall the first part of the much anticipated Prince's ball was deader than the Kings that stared down upon him from their canvases upon high. The orchestra played, the waiters waited and the King paced the veranda outside the front windows, pulling his hair out and wondering if he'd written down the wrong date in his diary.

A few buoyant bachelors were trumpeted through the doors only to wonder what sort of party they'd been invited to but the Prince seemed unconcerned.

"The less time I have to be squawked at by a bunch of silly girls the better," he told the Grand Duke, who'd been charged with chaperoning the Prince away from the champagne and towards the dance floor this evening.

"I'm sure it'll all be worthwhile, Your Highness," the Grand Duke said, inwardly praying that tonight would not be a total disaster. Or, if it was, that the King wouldn't remember whose idea it had been in the first place.

The Prince was far from convinced and growing wearier by the second. He despised royal functions at the best of times. All the pomp and ceremony and court jiggery-pokery. It was gilded nonsense as far as he was concerned. He was a man's man, a fighting man, a soldier, a man of action, a warrior, a… a… a man of… limited synonyms.

The Prince looked around himself and felt his shoulders sag. He so desperately didn't want to be here but he felt trapped; trapped by destiny, trapped by history and ancestry but without the strength of his father to bear the responsibility. He snapped his fingers to summon a servant, handed him his crystal champagne flute and cursed his father for being King.

"I'm going to step out a while. If Papa asks after me, tell him I've gone to consort with my chamberpot," he told the Grand Duke, slipping behind a giant historical tapestry on the far wall to take advantage of the private doorway concealed within and slammed the door to deter the Grand Duke from following.

It was now half-past nine and still the only maidens present were those circling the guests with trays of champagne. Well almost. For there were two cosmetically-corresponding young ladies lurking in the wings anxiously awaiting their moment.

Marigold and Gardenia had resolved to stay out of sight for the time being, dressed as they were in Mother's newest designs. They were elegant, fashionable and beautiful and yet the dresses they wore were not partywear. They were not here to enjoy themselves. They were not guests. Their mother was a widow and their blood ran red rather than blue so they were unlikely to have made the guest list even without the help of recent events. Instead, they were here in service. A royal ball can be a bit like a battlefield. Hundreds of people in their finest and tightest court clothes bowing, curtseying and dancing. Seams can split, trains can snag, buttons can be lost. A small army of seamstresses must be on hand to patch up the casualties and get them back into the fray. Amongst them was Mother, sat fiddling with her ring in a small side room just off the Great Hall. Monsieur Vasseur had gone out on a limb for her. This wasn't because of the quality of her work, which was beyond reproach, but because the old dressmaker thought such a platform might help set the wheels of redemption in motion.

Any tear, even to one's character, must be mended one stitch at a time.

Marigold and Gardenia's role would be to circle the hall and discreetly guide whichever ladies needed a running repair to the seamstresses behind the curtains. Gardenia worried that they would be spurned after recent events but Mother had reassured her that quite the opposite would be true.

"You will be in service to some of your former friends tonight. Expect to be busy."

Gardenia had always dreamed of seeing the Palace and although she would have rather seen it in a different capacity, she was here all the same. She might not have been a guest but she was an attendant, to the great and the good, and as such Mother fashioned her and Marigold in outfits to reflect this cachet, choosing materials and cuts that trod a fine line between refinement and reverence. Their dresses were royal blue, the same shade as that worn by the King's Guards, and she'd raised their hemlines and used only half-sized panniers to give them a freedom of movement that would set them apart from the legions of gilt-edged ladies they would pass between.

At least, they would when the ladies finally got here.

"Where is everyone?" Marigold said in bewilderment as she hung back behind the great curtains at the rear of the Great Hall. Like the Prince, she and Gardenia were stuck. They were permitted, indeed encouraged, to mingle with the guests but couldn't do so until some ladies had actually arrived. They couldn't run the risk of being mistaken for a guest and having some uninitiated gentleman embarrass himself by attempting an introduction. The fall-out from such a faux pas would haunt all concerned until their dying days but once the ladies of court had arrived the distinction would be clear, even to the drunkest of Lords.

"Where's who?" Gardenia replied, only half listening. She'd been distracted since first setting foot in the Palace three hours earlier. She didn't care if she was here as an attendant, an aide or a ruffle fluffer. All she cared about was that she was here, on these hallowed grounds tonight — and so was *he*.

"You're not still looking for Captain Durand, are you?" Marigold realised.

"I saw him earlier, talking with the Prince. Did you see the way his buttons sparkled?" Gardenia whispered back, barely able to suppress her glee.

"If he'd had one missing I might've noticed. Otherwise, the Captain's sparkles are no concern of mine. Now do try to contain yourself. We are here at the behest of Monsieur Vasseur. Our first and foremost concern is with the gentlewomen of this great occasion."

"What gentlewomen? Nobody's here yet."

"The King, the Prince and the Grand Duke are

nobody? What impossible standards you have," Marigold scoffed.

Gardenia pulled a face behind Marigold's back.

"If the wind changes you'll stay like that and what chance would you have with the good Captain then?" Marigold said instinctively. She knew her sister almost as well as she knew herself.

"We've been stuck in here for ages. I'm dying of boredom."

"We are not here to enjoy the festivities, Gardenia, please try to remember that. What would you think if you heard a waitress complaining of being bored?"

"I'd probably agree with her," Gardenia replied.

"Just do as Mother says for once and remember your duties," Marigold said, returning her gaze to the half-empty hall and a cluster of distinguished gentlemen jockeying for position by the foot of the stairs.

Gardenia chewed her lip and tapped her feet impatiently. The Captain was out there somewhere and after everything else that had happened over the last few weeks, a Captain could prove their salvation. But only if she could get to him first. Later on, when Gardenia would be attending to her duties, she would have no hope of cornering him. But now, in the calm before the storm, when both she and the Captain had been engaged in an official capacity, she had a chance.

It was all about picking her moment. And when she caught a glimpse of the Captain heading out of the hall and away from the other guests she knew that her moment had finally come.

"Tell Mother I've gone to powder my nose," Gardenia said, attempting to dash out after the Captain. Marigold grabbed her by the arm and yanked her back before anyone could see.

"Have we not suffered enough scandal for one

lifetime?" Marigold asked, trying to look her sister in the eye but finding only the back of her head.

"Please, Marigold. I'll be discreet. Let me go."

"No, I won't. Your nose has all the powder it can support. Gardenia, stop twisting my arm or you'll bust a stitch."

"I know what I'm doing. If I don't act now I might lose him forever. Please, you of all people must understand that. The Captain and I are written in the stars," Gardenia said, attempting to prise her wrist from Marigold's iron grip.

"The stars write more nonsense than a poet full of port," Marigold said, her own recent altercation with destiny still fresh in her mind.

"Please, let me go," Gardenia said.

"No, you are staying here where I can see you. These were Mother's instructions," Marigold insisted, trying to steer Gardenia back towards the sewing room. They spoke in whispers so as not to draw attention to themselves but one or two gentlemen's eyes were still drawn to the red velvet curtain as it swished and bulged like a prelude to a Punch & Judy show.

"I pity you, dear sister, I really do. You had your chance and couldn't even hang onto Stefano's bucket boy. But now it's mine and I have no intention of ending up like you," Gardenia said, cutting her sister to the quick. Marigold was taken aback by the viciousness of Gardenia's words but only because they were true. Marigold had attended several balls when she'd been Gardenia's age. None anywhere near as lavish as this but she'd debuted nevertheless. And not as an attendant either but as an invited guest when Mother's star had shone at its brightest. She still remembered the overwhelming sense of excitement she had felt when she'd first arrived at her debut. And the overwhelming despair that hung over her when she left with an unblemished dance card and the most rested feet of the evening. More events and disappointments had followed until almost overnight the invitations dried up. It seemed Marigold was good enough to be invited but not quite good enough to be asked to dance. Soon everyone was keen to spare poor Marigold's blushes. At least, this was what they told themselves. Perhaps she would find a nice country boy to settle down with. Or maybe a lonely old widower. She had much to offer. Looks weren't everything. Poor Marigold. Such a pity.

And thus, the mantle was passed onto her younger sister, whom all expected to make a favourable match. But then came her Mother's spectacular fall from grace and suddenly Gardenia's prospects of being invited anywhere except the occasional haystack were gone in the blink of an eye. Such was the way in Andovia.

"Come on, we're going to see Mother," Marigold said, pulling Gardenia by the wrist and digging her nails in when her sister resisted. Gardenia reacted instinctively, shoving Marigold away but popping several stitches and causing her cleavage to tear open. Marigold grabbed herself with both hands before she could lose the last of her dignity and gasped: "How could you?"

But Gardenia took the opportunity to fly. "I'm sorry. I'm so sorry," she said contritely, dashing out from behind the curtains safe in the knowledge that her sister could not give chase. At least, not without endangering every monocle in Andovia.

Few gentlemen noticed Gardenia as she hurried on by. She caught no man's eye, glanced in nobody's direction and stopped for no one. The loyal Captain had trailed the Prince through the secret door concealed behind the moth-eaten tapestry and that was where she was going. She wasn't sure what she was going to do when she finally caught up with him but hopefully she would think of something. Perhaps she could faint or twist her ankle or something. Something that would allow the Captain to do what gentlemen do, dash to her aid, take her in his arms and tell her everything was going to be alright.

Gardenia slipped behind the tapestry and tried the door handle. It was unlocked so she stepped through before anyone could ask what business she had to be going in there. Wherever there was.

*

MARIGOLD HELD HER TOP in place while she hurried through the sewing room. Several seamstresses raised an eyebrow as she went past with one whispering to her friend, "The beasts. The sooner a few proper ladies arrive the better".

Mother looked up in concern and asked Marigold what happened.

"It was Gardenia. It was an accident but she's gone off after the Captain."

"You should've stopped her," Mother said in alarm.

"I would've stopped the orchestra if I'd gone out there like this but I'm not sure I could've stopped Gardenia," Marigold replied.

"Stand up straight. I will repair this quickly then you must bring her back. We have a duty to Monsieur Vasseur," Mother said, threading a needle and whipping off an arm's length of cotton with great urgency.

*

ON FIRST INSPECTION, the hidden door looked as though it led to a small dark service corridor and yet all was quiet. None of the torches were lit and no one was here to bark at Gardenia to get out of the way as they hurried past with trays. Whatever this passageway was used for, it wasn't on the tour.

She noticed several steps against one of the walls and climbed up to find a small flap set into an oak-panel. She opened it and saw eyes painted onto the flap and two holes it had concealed. She peered out of the holes and saw the Great

Hall, only from an angle of elevation. The orchestra continued to play, the waiters continued to wait and so did the guests. Gardenia felt positively sinful spying on so many handsome young men, almost to the point of forgetting what had brought her here in the first place, but a voice in her head reminded her of her mission, so she closed the flap and continued on her way, down the passage and in search of the Captain. And the destiny she'd spent a lifetime dreaming of.

The long winding tunnel headed down several stone steps and then ran beneath the Great Hall, opening up into a subterranean cellar. Thousands of bottles of wine sat gathering dust in the darkness as they awaited their ultimate uncorking. Hundreds of barrels of brandy were piled up likewise and an uncountable number of spiders sat guarding the lot from the webs that crisscrossed the joists. The floorboards overhead creaked and fine slithers of light glinted through to give the dank basement a subterranean feel.

Another doorway led off the cellar opposite the one Gardenia had entered by but she didn't take it. A movement in the darkest corner of the furthest aisle caught her eye. It was the Captain. She heard his voice and saw a flash of blue caught in the half-light and her heart missed a beat. She tiptoed through the maze of wine racks and wondered how she might explain her presence or indeed whether she would even need to. The Captain was a handsome man and she, by all accounts, was a young girl. Surely Mother Nature would spare them their deceits.

But then she heard him again. His voice was soft, his words affectionate and amused. He was with someone already. Someone dear to him. She could hear them kissing, giggling, purring. Her heart sank. She'd stolen a chance but had been beaten to the punch. But how and with whom?

"Not a serving girl. Please, anything but that," Gardenia said to herself, sneaking past a row of the Weiss's reds to see for herself.

But nothing could have prepared Gardenia for the sight that greeted her now. The Captain paused his smooching and, in that moment, Gardenia saw them clearly — both of them — panting, smiling and breathless. It was the Prince. The Captain had been kissing the Prince. On the mouth. With his own?

Gardenia was so confused that she forgot to stay quiet. The Captain heard her gasp and looked around to see her peering through the Pinot Noir wearing an expression of consternation. It was an expression both he and the Prince now adopted.

CHAPTER EIGHTEEN

CATHERINE PETIT EXAMINED the drummer boy tunic she'd been given. It did indeed sport a few holes in the back, acquired at the Battle of Petites Collines, which was coincidentally where the regiment had acquired the vacancy for a new drummer boy.

The breeches felt strange. Catherine had never worn anything but a dress her whole life. And pretty much the same one at that. But the rest of the uniform fitted well and for the first time since leaving the orphanage, she felt as though she was a part of civilisation. This wasn't an altogether good thing seeing as civilisation hadn't treated her brilliantly up until now but it was a start and it gave her something to build upon.

Catherine looked at herself in the Sergeant's tin mirror. She barely recognised the girl who stared back at her. The orphanage had no mirrors to speak of and the windows were so filthy that they scarcely admitted light, let alone reflections. She'd seen herself in ponds and rivers whilst living in the forest but these weren't places to linger with one's guard down. Either way, the girl she'd once known was gone. In her place, a young soldier boy with clipped brown hair and watery features stared back at her. It was an unsettling experience to know that she'd not only changed her clothes but her gender too. It would take some getting used to.

Two days after Christmas, Catherine took her first few faltering steps outside the tent and expected to be challenged the moment she was spotted, but no one raised an eyebrow at her, let alone their voice. A few soldiers patrolled the perimeter but most of the men were sat huddled around the wood-fired braziers that were set at the ends of each row of tents, drinking hot coffee and sucking on clay pipes in an effort to keep the chill from their bones.

The Sergeant looked up from one such group as Catherine wandered by.

"Drummer boy. Over here," he called to her. "Have some coffee."

Catherine accepted a steaming tin from him and almost dropped it again, it was so hot. She used her sleeves to protect her fingers and then simply held it to her ribs, enjoying the tingles it brought as it defrosted her innards. There were six men with the Sergeant, each uglier than the last, with whiskers and scars to sully their faces but none of them showed any hostility towards Catherine. Indeed, most regarded her with a twinkle of curiosity.

"You're well enough to walk then?" the Sergeant said.

Her wounds were far from healed and the scabs had started to make her skin itchy but she was at least able to stand again without wincing.

"Good," said the Sergeant, gulping his own coffee and grimacing as it scalded his throat. "If you're well enough to walk then you're well enough to work. Fire's going out. Go get some wood."

Catherine didn't like being told what to do. She wasn't used to it. But as luck would have it, she already had some wood about her person and pulled the drumsticks the Sergeant had given her from her pocket and held them over the brazier.

"Will these do?" she asked in an effort to bait her sponsor.

She half-expected the Sergeant to jump from his seat and snatch them from her hand but he didn't flinch. And neither did any of his men. He just went on drinking his coffee and hugging the brazier to keep warm. What would he do if she dropped them in, Catherine wondered? She decided not to find out. It was one thing to bait a person, quite another to pull them from the water.

She slipped the drumsticks back into her pocket and

trudged towards the camp gate with a sigh.

"I'm sorry but I didn't hear you. That's, *yes Sergeant. Right away, Sergeant!*" the Sergeant yelled after her as she crossed a sea of muddy ice. A couple of his comrades now let out a hoot, not least of all when he explained; "He's new. It's a lot to remember."

A huge sentry in a trenchcoat, boots and gloves stood between Catherine and the gate with a musket slung over his shoulder. He looked at Catherine as she approached but didn't move.

Catherine stopped and shivered as she waited for the sentry to step aside. It occurred to her that on the other side of the camp gate was the forest and freedom. Since being caught all those nights ago she'd been held against her will, tied up and flogged. And yet she had come through the whole ordeal almost intact only to find herself standing at the steps of salvation once more. The Sergeant had unwittingly given her the perfect opportunity to abscond.

"And where do you think you're going, young drummer boy?" the sentry said, pulling down his scarf to be heard.

"To get firewood," Catherine replied, which was true to a point.

"One, that's *to get firewood, Corporal.* And two, let's discuss your plan, shall we?" the sentry suggested.

"What plan?" Catherine asked, through chattering teeth as she willed him to let her by.

"Exactly," the sentry said instructively. He reached into the guard box for a large overcoat and a fur hat. "Unless you'd rather freeze to death, of course," he said, shoving them at Catherine.

The coat swamped Catherine and the hat fell over her eyes but both felt wonderfully warm. The sentry also gave her a small hatchet and a length of rope to tie up her firewood into a bundle for easier transportation.

"The surrounding area's been picked clean already. You

might have to head deeper into the forest unless you like smoke. We don't," the sentry advised. Living wood gave off smoke. Dead wood and fallen branches burned cleaner. Catherine nodded like she understood but that was just for show. She had no intention of collecting anything for anyone but herself. The moment the sentry let her out she would head into the forest and wouldn't look back. The hat, coat and hatchet she would accept as a payoff for her time in the army and if the sentry cared to let her have his musket, she'd find a tall tree overlooking the camp and repay the Lieutenant for his charity too.

The sentry finally opened the gate and Catherine almost knocked him over rushing through.

"Hold it," he said, stopping her in her tracks before she was two steps out of the camp.

Catherine froze. Had the sentry read her mind? Had she seemed too eager? She felt uneasy, as if her intentions were etched all over her face, but when she turned back she found not a musket pointed at her but a small picnic wrapped in a handkerchief.

"Take some biscuits with you. Just in case you get caught out in a storm. This weather can change without warning."

"Thank you... er... Corporal," Catherine said, accepting the bundle and tucking them into her pocket. She was genuinely touched by the sentry's unexpected kindness. The only other time when she'd ever been given anything was when she'd left the orphanage. But unlike that time, the army was rather hoping she might return. Fat chance.

"Now, if it's dark when you come back, I'll shout, *who goes there, friend or foe?* To which you reply...?" the sentry said, leaving Catherine to fill in the blank for herself.

"Friend?" she guessed, figuring it had to be one or the other.

"Welcome to the army," the sentry said, retaking his

post just inside the gate.

"What happens if I shout foe?" Catherine asked out of curiosity.

The sentry thought about that for a moment and stuck out a lip. "I don't know. It's never come up," he said, shutting the gate to draw a line under Catherine's short and yet illustrious military career.

*

THE FOREST WAS STILL. Nothing stirred. Not even a breeze. Fresh snow blanketed the trails, yet tracks had been made recently. Catherine couldn't tell whether they'd been made by soldiers or scavengers. Or indeed, if there was any difference between the two.

She followed the trails for some distance, hoping to lose the Sergeant should he decide to come after her, before heading into deeper woods and rougher country.

The snow grew deeper and progress was slow away from the trails. Catherine wasn't sure where she was going. There were several towns further south and the weather was milder across the border but she was now wearing a uniform and the penalty for desertion was death. She would need new clothes before she could risk going near a town.

She emerged from the forest to find herself on the bank of a large partially frozen lake. The shore was solid ice but this gave way to open water a little further out. Catherine saw a small cluster of forest children on the ice, some younger than her, a couple older. One or two laid on their bellies by the edge of the ice trying in vain to tempt fish into their makeshift nets while others were huddled around a fire further along the shore, awaiting a supper that was never going to come. No one saw Catherine. She could've slipped back into the trees and they would have been none the wiser but instead, she sat in the shadows and watched for a while. There was one girl, her own age, who looked more like her than her own reflection currently did. Watching her was like having an out-of-body experience and Catherine wondered where she'd come from. And more importantly, where she was going.

The girl walked out towards the water to see how the fishing was going but she misjudged the thickness of the ice. She panicked as it cracked beneath and tried to run but the ice broke apart and a moment later she was gone.

The girl emerged from the ice hole screaming for help and her friends ran to save her but the ice refused to let them near, cracking and splintering before they could get to within reach of her. She went under again but came up a moment later. The lake was deep enough to go over her head but shallow enough for her to kick up from the bottom. But she wouldn't last long. The cold was sapping her strength and her legs were almost frozen.

The children were trying to make a human chain but the ice simply would not hold them. Their friend would die and there was nothing they could do about it.

But then they saw someone come racing out of the forest, half running, half sliding across the ice and towards where they lay. He looked like a soldier, only in miniature.

Catherine shed the heavy coat and had taken only what she needed. Speed was everything. She ran most of the way and then scrambled the last few metres on her belly to spread her weight. She tied one end of her rope to the handle of her hatchet and threw the other to the girl.

"Everyone pull!" Catherine shouted, planting the hatchet into the ice to act as an anchor. The girl's friends came scrabbling as quickly as they could and pulled with all of their might. The ice was slippery and their friend was heavy in her waterlogged clothing but working together they soon hauled her free.

She was as white as a lily and scarcely able to move so they helped her back to the shore and Catherine wrapped her greatcoat around her while the fire dried her clothes.

"Biscuits?" she asked, pulling the handkerchief bundle from her pocket like a magician pulling a rabbit from a hat. The children couldn't believe their eyes and almost took Catherine's hand off. She forwent any biscuits herself but set an extra one aside for the girl who'd fallen through the ice.

They sat and chatted for a time, sharing similar hard luck stories and cautionary tales of where to avoid, until the girl's clothes were finally dry. Catherine took back her greatcoat while the girl got dressed and decided to get going before it got too dark.

"You're going?" the girl asked in surprise.

"I'm sorry, I have to," Catherine replied, buttoning up her coat against the cold.

"But why? Stay with us," some of them pleaded but looking around at their desperate faces Catherine knew that she couldn't. This chance encounter had shown her all too clearly where she had come from. And where she would be heading if she elected to stay. The winters in this part of the world were harsh. Only the most resourceful would survive and those that didn't would drag the others down with them. Life out here was tough. And so were the choices you had to make.

"Good luck," she said, knowing it would take more than this if any of them were to see the spring.

As she moved into the forest the warmth of the fire was soon forgotten and all grew bleak and cold once more. But a spark had been lit within Catherine and now she knew what she had to do.

*

"WHO GOES THERE, FRIEND OR FOE?"

"Friend," Catherine called back.

"Then approach friend and be recognised."

Catherine stepped out of the shadows and into the open. The forest was draped in night but the ground leading up to the camp was bathed in moonlight that reflected off the snow.

The sentry recognised Catherine and lowered his musket.

"You took your sweet time," he said, unlocking the gate. "I was about to send out a search party for you."

"Really?" Catherine said, struggling into the camp under the weight of the wood bundle on her back.

"Yeah, but only to get my hatchet back."

The Sergeant was also waiting to greet Catherine on her triumphant return, sat in the same place by the brazier as he'd been when she'd left. She wondered if he'd moved all day but decided not to ask. Instead, she dumped her wood bundle by the side of the brazier and warmed her frozen hands over the flames.

"You needn't have bothered. It's almost summer," the Sergeant said, to the amusement of his cronies.

"I got lost," Catherine replied without looking up.

"In a forest you've been roaming for the last two years?" he asked.

The fire crackled, orange sparks drifted up into the starlit sky and all eyes turned to Catherine but she didn't answer. And she didn't need to.

"If I send you out there tomorrow, do you think you'll get lost again?" the Sergeant asked.

Catherine looked up from the fire and over at the Sergeant who was watching her carefully.

"No," she replied, then added almost as an afterthought, "Sergeant".

CHAPTER NINETEEN

GARDENIA TURNED AND RAN. She didn't know what else to do.

"Stop! Stop right there!" the Captain shouted but Gardenia didn't look back. She had to get as far away from this place as she could.

"For God's sake, get after her!" she heard the Prince say, followed by the sounds of bottles smashing and footsteps slapping across granite flagstones but she was already out of the wine cellar and running as fast as she could.

"Wait, I want to talk to you. Come back!" the Captain called out, words Gardenia had longed to hear only moments earlier but now she was scared. She'd seen something she should've never seen and the notion of what they might do to her genuinely terrified her. She heard laughter through the walls. The guests were so close, oblivious to all that had been going on right beneath their feet. What would they say if they knew? More pertinently, what would they do?

"Halt! I order you to halt!" the Captain now tried, charging up the passageway behind Gardenia, but Gardenia had a sizeable head-start over the Captain and wasn't about to halt for anyone, least of all someone who used words like "Halt". She passed the peephole and knew the door to the Great Hall was just a few short strides away but suddenly a figure reared up at her out of the darkness and Gardenia ran straight into it.

Both she and her assailant went over in the darkness and Gardenia was about to aim a kick at their funny parts when she recognised their voice.

"What the hell are you doing? Mother's bloody furious," Marigold said, despairing to discover her cleavage had popped out again.

Gardenia jumped to her feet and hauled her sister up.

"Run!" she shouted, bundling them both towards the exit and looking over her shoulder to see the Captain a short lunge away. They got to the door and yanked it open.

"Wait!" Marigold said, desperately trying to stuff herself back in before her sister could push her out half-naked in front of every nobleman in Andovia, which coincidentally, had been a recurring nightmare of hers.

The Captain made one last desperate lunge in a futile attempt to grab Gardenia before she got away but he succeeded only in making an even bigger spectacle of her arrest by tumbling out on top of the two women in full view of everyone nearby. And those further away were not to be denied either. For in trying to arrest her fall, Marigold grabbed a handful of tapestry and managed to yank the whole thing off the wall, bringing it down on top of her and her sister with a crash, as a cloud of dust bowled into the astonished faces of every invited guest.

Mother could only look on in horror as Marigold and Gardenia punched their way through four hundred years of history and into the arms of the King's Guards.

"What have you done? How has this happened?" the Grand Duke demanded, aghast at the scale of the sisters' destruction, not only to this historic handwoven antiquity but also his historic ball.

"Don't listen to her, she's a liar," the Captain shouted from somewhere beneath the tapestry before Gardenia had even said a word.

"I demand an explanation!" the King bellowed, fighting his way through the crowd to tear the culprits in two. Gardenia could barely speak. Her head was so crammed full of etiquette and protocol that nothing seemed appropriate for this situation. She attempted to curtsey, but the King just screamed at her even more. "Never mind all of that! What the bloody hell have you done?" he raged, blood vessels popping out across his temple.

"It was the Prince…" Gardenia managed to whimper. Given any other choice, she would've gladly lied and pretended she'd seen nothing but this was the King. She could not lie to him. "The Prince and the Captain…"

As if on cue the Prince appeared at the now not-so-secret doorway and stared out in horror at the disaster before him.

"Papa!" he pleaded, causing the King to turn from red to white as though someone had flicked a switch on the back of his head. A horrific realisation now came over the King. Something terrible had happened. And something even worse was about to unless he took drastic action.

"Everybody out!" the King shouted. "The ball is off. The Prince has the mumps!"

It was the best excuse he could come up with at short notice but it did the trick, obliging the guests to leave, especially when the Grand Duke summoned in the rest of the King's Guards to herd everyone out post-haste.

Marigold and Gardenia attempted to join the exodus but the Grand Duke snapped his fingers and suddenly they found themselves facing drawn swords. "I think we might have you two stay for a while longer," he sneered, his voice measured and yet menacing. "You too," he said, pointing a finger at the Captain when he tried to slip away.

Marigold didn't have a clue what was going on but she knew from the King's reaction and Gardenia's comportment that it was something unspeakable. But what? What had Gardenia done with the Prince and the Captain? Her mind scarcely dared to boggle.

When all the guests were all gone the Grand Duke waved a hand and it was the servants and the Guards turn to withdraw.

"Leave that. Clear it up later," he had to tell several maids who lacked the willpower to walk away from the mess and the King's own Valet, who needed to be chased from the

Hall when he failed to comprehend that the order applied to him also.

When the doors were finally locked only Marigold, Gardenia, the King, the Grand Duke, the Prince and Captain Durand remained. It was inconceivable that two sisters from such modest stock should be granted an audience such as this. Neither looked up from the floor and neither dared speak. They simply stood with their heads bowed holding each other's hands.

Gardenia was trembling like a leaf. Without knowing what had happened, Marigold tried to reassure her sister with a squeeze of the hand but Gardenia was too petrified to respond. She'd really done it this time. She'd placed herself and her beloved sister in terrible danger simply through her own selfish folly. Were the King to summon Franz Grimaldi himself to deal with them she couldn't have been more terrified.

"What did you do?" the King demanded.

Gardenia tried to find her voice but the question hadn't been put to her. It had been put to the Prince.

"I didn't do anything, Papa. I swear on all that I hold dear," the Prince lied with such blatancy that he sent the King into a rage all over again.

"You hold nothing dear but yourself, you vain, feckless, stupid little boy!"

Marigold was shocked. To hear the Prince, of all people, spoken to in such a way was almost as impossible to comprehend as being granted a private audience with the King himself. Today would definitely go in her diary when she got home. If indeed, she ever did.

The King now turned an accusatory finger on the Captain.

"You. Speak now and if you dare lie I will have your head on a pike!" he said, snatching an ornamental lance from the nearest freestanding suit of armour to send the rest clattering to the ground.

The Captain dropped to his knees and stared at the gleaming lance and the impossible position he found himself in. If he lied he was dead. If he spoke the truth he was dead. If he did nothing he was dead. Whatever he did he was dead. And the Captain didn't want to be dead. He liked being alive. Very much, in fact.

"I… I…" he stammered but little else sprang to mind.

Marigold had been watching closely and had somehow pieced it all together. She wasn't as naive as people liked to think and she had noticed the Prince and Captain together. As scandalous as it would be viewed, they had some sort of special connection, something beyond mere friendship. Gardenia must have seen them together and panicked. And they, in turn, had seen her. Marigold now saw the bind everyone was in. This secret was bigger than all of them, even than the King himself. News of this could not be allowed to reach the people. And yet tongues would already be wagging. Left unchecked, the rumours would spread like wildfire across the Kingdom and then the borders beyond.

And nobody had a clue how to stop it. Not the Prince, the Grand Duke, not even the King.

But Marigold had an idea where they might start. And one that might just save them all.

"The Captain, he tried to accost us. The Prince was only defending our honour, Your Majesty," Marigold said, catching everyone by surprise and stopping the King in his tracks before he could run the snivelling Captain through.

"What?" the Captain objected, looking up from his knees.

Gardenia was about to put Marigold straight when she felt her fingers crushed in Marigold's grip. As much as it pained her to defame the good Captain, this was a lie that might be regarded more favourably than actual facts. What's more, it not only spared the Prince, it cast him in a positively heroic light. He was the gallant knight in shining armour while the Captain was a back-alley cad. If the Kingdom was to be fed a story, the least they could do was sugarcoat it.

"That's right," Gardenia echoed, realising that this lie could save everyone, including the Captain. "He tried to kiss me. He had me pinned to the wall but then the Prince pulled him off," she said, forgetting to address the King by his proper title but fortunately the King and the Grand Duke were so busy doing the maths that neither noticed.

The King liked the sound of this version very much. The Prince liked it even more. The Grand Duke liked it best of all. But the incorrigible Captain didn't care for it, regardless of its obvious merits.

"The very idea," he objected, failing to see the advantages of playing along. As far as he was concerned, he'd been accused of one of the most heinous crimes an officer and a gentleman could ever be accused of — impropriety. With a common serving girl, to boot! "As if I'd ever lay a finger on you. You or your *ugly sister*!"

But the King had heard all he needed to hear.

"You will be silent or I will silence you myself!" he roared into the Captain's face, half-tempted to do it anyway but stopped in his tracks by the Grand Duke when he wrestled the lance from his hand.

"The Captain needs to corroborate all that the er… uhum, young ladies have said. After which time he can be dealt with in the appropriate manner," the Grand Duke advised, escorting the King to a quiet corner to thrash out the finer details.

A deathly hush settled over the Great Hall. The King and Grand Duke whispered to one another but no one else said anything. Nobody dared. Marigold and Gardenia averted their eyes while the Prince and Captain continued to swap anxious glances, although it was starting to feel like one-way traffic to the Captain.

The King and Grand Duke returned from their deliberations to deliver their verdict and make sure everyone else was willing to sing from the same hymn sheet.

"And so, this is what happened, is it?" the King asked the Prince. "The Captain tried to impose his favours upon this maid."

Ladies' Attendant, Marigold thought inwardly, although she decided against correcting the King on this point.

The Captain looked to the Prince, pleading with him to speak up in his defence. Sure, they needed to agree upon a story but why this one? This one might save their necks but it would mean disgrace and ruin for him. But the Prince refused to meet the Captain's eye. He had his own problems to contend with and considerably further to fall. This might have meant the end for the poor Captain but there were lots of other Captains in the Kingdom whereas there was only one Prince.

"It is, Papa. I'm sorry for the resulting fracas but I could not stand by while the Captain dishonoured this lady."

The Grand Duke's eyes narrowed a little. It was one thing to buy into a conspiracy, quite another to ham it up.

"And you," the King now said, turning to Marigold and Gardenia attempting to look them in the eye, although he would've had to have lain at their feet to have managed it. "Are you prepared to place your hand upon the good book and swear to all you have said?"

Marigold rather hoped it wouldn't come to that but what choice did she have? The water was hot enough already. There was no sense turning up the heat just to avoid getting on the wrong side of the Almighty too. Besides, the King never specified which book he was talking about. There were lots of good books. Hundred even. She could work with that.

"I am, Your Majesty. The Captain chased Gardenia and I through the tunnels and attempted to apprehend us while His Highness, the Prince, chased the Captain, in what I can only assume was an attempt to stop him. I swear this upon my honour as a lady."

The King frowned. He was looking for a little more collateral to pin his continuing dynasty upon than a serving girl's honour but it would have to do.

"Very well," the King said, turning to the final piece of the jigsaw. "You sir, are a scoundrel and a disgrace." He grabbed the Captain's epaulettes and half-ripped them from his shoulders, before giving up when it became clear they'd been sewn on too well. "I'll see you in chains before this night is out. Grand Duke, he is your responsibility now."

And with that, the King grabbed his son and dragged him away, out of the Great Hall and out the mire he'd landed everyone in.

The Captain turned from frantic to furious when he saw how things had gone but it wasn't the King or even the Prince who earned his most caustic scorn. "I will have my vengeance upon you," he hissed at the stoic sisters who'd just saved his neck. Literally and metaphorically.

Normal protocol for a woman in service when replying to a gentleman of the Captain's standing would have been to have respectfully submitted to his grace. But Marigold felt they were a little beyond that point by now and besides, the Captain wasn't standing and hadn't done so for some considerable time. He was on his knees while she and Gardenia remained on their feet. Once more, both literally and metaphorically.

"You're welcome," she simply replied, turning to the Captain and returning his glare until he looked away.

*

OUTSIDE IN THE STREETS, all routes to and from the Palace were gridlocked with coaches now coming and going. Those turning up late to make a grand entrance could scarcely believe the ball was already over at this early hour but when word of the Prince's blight leapt from driver to driver, somewhere along the line the word "mumps" was supplemented by "plague" and panic set in. Women screamed, gentlemen fled and carriages crashed into each other as their drivers cracked the whips to get away. The King and Prince could only look out from the Palace windows and wonder if they were witnessing the end of the world. Or their world at least.

Marigold and Gardenia walked home through the crowds, the chaos and the confusion. They didn't stop to put anyone straight. They simply hurried on by wearing black shawls and black expressions in the hope that nobody recognised them as perpetrators of this panic. This had been their first Royal ball and it occurred to Marigold that Mother was right. It had been a night she would never forget.

In the pandemonium that followed, nobody noticed the jewel-encrusted carriage on the very fringes of the fracas. Most simply ran straight past it, fleeing for home in order to pack up and quit the city now that the Black Death had returned. But if they had've stopped and looked, they would've seen that it was a carriage like no other in a Kingdom of grand carriages. Gloriously gilt-edged and glittering like a treasure chest on wheels, it was a ride fit for a princess. A none-too-subtle hint, perhaps.

The driver saw the agitation and knocked on the roof to alert his passenger. The lace curtain inside was pulled aside and the scene surveyed.

"What do you want to do, mademoiselle?" the driver asked.

"Home," she replied and, as magically as it had appeared, the white and gold carriage backed away into the shadows and disappeared into the night.

CHAPTER TWENTY

MOTHER WASN'T SO MUCH waiting up for Marigold and Gardenia when they got home as preparing to bust them out of the stocks.

"You're back? How are you back? What in Jupiter's name happened?"

Marigold and Gardenia had been sworn to secrecy. But Mother was family and scarier even than the King so they confessed all and braced themselves for her fiery reaction.

Strangely, it did not come.

"Fate has entrusted you with a powerful secret. One that could bring the King himself down. It must never leave this house," Mother said warily. "Swear it."

"We already did," Gardenia replied, sagging her shoulders as if to demonstrate she knew that already.

"Swear it to me," Mother insisted. "You must never talk of this to anyone, not your friends, not each other, not even to the priest in confession."

"I wouldn't tell that gossipy old dirt-peddler anything anyway," Marigold said, earning a rebuke from Mother when she slapped the table to remind her that this was a lecture, not a discussion.

"Swear it!"

"I swear it," Marigold said, a sentiment that was echoed in unison by Gardenia.

A chill now ran through both girls. The fire in the grate was dead and the hour was late. Only a single oil lamp burned with its wick set low. Marigold couldn't see Mother's expression in the gloom but she could hear it in her words. She was not angry. She was afraid.

"This secret does not mean privilege and opportunity. It means danger. Guard it well and never try to prosper from it. It can only do us harm."

Marigold and Gardenia swore once more and helped Mother unpack some of the belongings she had been packing to flee with. Not all of them, just some.

"We might have to go yet. Be ready to go at a moment's notice. And trust no one."

*

THE GRAND DUKE took charge of the cleanup operation the next morning and personally selected the newly appointed *Captain* Olivier to help him with this task. The Duke's trusted son was dispatched to drag the Prince from his slumber, throw a blanket over him and hurry him from the castle via the back gate. A coach was waiting, instructions were given to the driver at the last moment and the Prince was spirited away to the furthest corner of the Kingdom before he could do said Kingdom any more damage.

Once he was out of the way, the rumour machine was cranked into operation. No official proclamation could be made about the events of the previous evening but enough clues were scattered about the city for the people to work out what had happened. Or at least, what the Duke wanted them to think had happened. The Prince was reported to have been taken ill while his tunic was sent for repairs with several stitches popped. Next, the disgraced Captain Durand was seen driven through the streets by the newly promoted Captain Olivier (back and forth several times to make sure no one missed him) with his tunic torn and his ankles in shackles. Then an odd whisper started circulating amongst the Guards that the Captain had been arrested for striking out at "someone of great importance". And finally, it was reported that the King had been seen escorting a couple of 'ladies' to a royal carriage to be driven home the next morning. This had actually happened too. Marigold and Gardenia had been whisked back to the Palace under a blanket and the whole thing staged under the Grand Duke's direction for the benefit of a few handpicked eye-witnesses.

And finally, and just to make absolutely sure that no one was in any doubt as to what happened, Father André was sought for his advice, in the strictest of confidence, so that by lunchtime there wasn't a soul in the Kingdom who didn't know what had transpired.

The unofficial story? The Prince had injured himself in the defence of a maiden, risking his big night and his future happiness in an act of unrivalled chivalry. But who was this mysterious maiden whom the Prince had seemingly sacrificed everything for? That was the question on everybody's lips. Who was his damsel in distress?

The answer could scarcely be believed.

*

MARIGOLD AND GARDENIA were repairing the dresses they'd worn the night before (and once again for this morning's re-enactment) when somebody thumped loudly against their front door. They'd been hauled away once already today and they feared the Guards' return. What subterfuge would the Duke have them play a part in now? And for whose benefit? Mother knew the fickle whims of the aristocracy only too well and reasoned there was only so many times the girls would be allowed to walk free.

"I'll buy you some time," she whispered. "Slip out the back and head for the woods. I'll meet you there presently."

It was a classic plan, but unfortunately for the sisters, there was no back way to speak of but a small slat window that half-opened up onto an alleyway so narrow that light could barely squeeze down it, let alone a detachment of Guardsmen in full uniform. This would give them the advantage.

Mother continued to stall for time while Marigold inflicted no end of suffering upon her little sister as she attempted to stuff her through the opening.

"Just be a moment. I am an old woman. I don't move as quickly as I used to," Mother called, halving her voice and seasoning it with splutters for the benefit of her caller.

Gardenia dropped out of the window, scuffing her back on the windowsill, before repaying Marigold in kind when she yanked on her ankles to now pull her through.

"Just looking for my keys," Mother called, dropping a big bunch of keys on the floor and then grinding them in the lock, despite the door being unlocked. "Almost there," she reassured whoever was outside. She was fully prepared to stand there all afternoon jangling keys and rattling doorknobs had the person outside not finally spoken up.

"Forgive me, Madame Roche. I had no wish to put you to so much trouble. I will call another time," Monsieur Beaufort said, turning to leave with his hat in his hand.

Mother recognised his voice and yanked open the door before he could make it off the WELCOME mat. Monsieur Beaufort? It was Monsieur Beaufort? In person. Not the odious Monsieur Joly or the newly promoted Captain Olivier but Monsieur Beaufort himself. To say Mother was surprised was an understatement.

She still owed him a considerable sum of money, at least half the price of the dress, which he'd insisted on paying upfront and which now nestled in Franz Grimaldi's pockets. If only he'd settled his account on delivery as agreed Mother might've been left ragged but not ruined.

"Monsieur Beaufort. This is an unexpected honour," Mother said, a little unsure of herself. The proper thing would've been to invite him inside but Mother felt ashamed of how they were now living and was conscious of the fact that her home served as a reminder of her downfall. As indeed did the man before her. "I was about to water the garden. Would you care to join me?"

Mother stepped out and closed the door behind herself without waiting for Monsieur Beaufort to answer, but in the event, he seemed quite amenable to the idea. "Do lead on."

Mother escorted him to a little patch of dirt that had

been turned at the side of her home and doused it with a can of rainwater, not because it needed watering, but simply for something to do.

"What are you growing, Madame. Roses? Lilies?" Monsieur Beaufort asked. It was difficult to tell from the wet mud at his feet.

"Winter vegetables, Monsieur *Le Chevalier*. They are more use to me than lilies and roses these days."

"Of course. Forgive me," Monsieur Beaufort said, nodding to acknowledge his own thoughtlessness. "Which brings me to the reason for my visit."

"Monsieur Beaufort, I can only apologise. I am sure you have heard by now that the ball last night was cut unexpectedly short. I did not receive my salary for the evening, therefore, I have not been able to…"

But Monsieur Beaufort held up a hand and urged Mother to say no more.

"Please, you misunderstand me. I am not here to seek payment," he said, with a semi-regal shake of the hand. The very idea. As if a man of *Le Chevalier*'s standing would knock on a lady's door and ask for money? Especially a dungheap like this. Monsieur Beaufort took the watering can from Mother and placed his hand on hers.

"The whole Kingdom this morning is talking about how the Prince came to the defence of Mademoiselle Gardenia's honour. That the very highest of the high should take it upon themselves to stand up for the lowest of the low is an example to us all," Monsieur Beaufort said without thinking his sentiment through.

"Madame Roche," he continued, "I wish to follow the Prince's example and waive the debt you owe me. You have repaid me too much already."

Mother could not believe her ears. Had she heard him right? Was he really offering to write off a small fortune in gold Livres? "I beg your pardon?" she asked, looking up into his gentle brown eyes and wondering if this was some sort of abominable jape, dreamt up for his own amusement.

"I have wronged you. I allowed you to think that it was from you that the bandit Franz Grimaldi stole that day but it was not. He took from us both and I am ashamed to have denied you this simple truth until now. Please forgive me," Monsieur Beaufort said, dropping to his knees to make Mother almost reach for the water can again. He'd clearly lost his marbles and there was no telling what he might try next.

"Please Monsieur, get up before somebody sees you. Think of your reputation," Mother urged him, dragging him to his feet and brushing some of the mud from his cream breeches but only as far as his stocking tops.

"My reputation is nothing compared to my integrity and it is this that I wish to redress," he said, his face a montage of majesty and melancholy.

"Your generosity overwhelms me but I cannot accept. The debt is mine and mine alone and I will repay it, every Livre," Mother assured him. It was the only way to restore her honour and reputation. Absolution could only ease her burden in the short term. Besides, if Gardenia's honour was now thought of as something that was worthy of defending — by the Prince himself — perhaps they were on the brink of a change of fortune.

But Monsieur Beaufort was having none of it.

"No Madame, I cannot rest knowing that I have reduced you to this," he said, glaring contemptuously at the little stone shack he wouldn't have dreamt of keeping his dung in — let alone his horse's!

"I have known worse, Monsieur," Mother told him, which was an understatement, to say the least.

"I will not take no for an answer, Madame," he insisted.

"Then I fear you face a great disappointment, Monsieur Beaufort," Mother replied flatly. She was all grace but no emotion. A battering ram could not have dented her resolve.

"Is there nothing I can do to make you change your mind, Madame?" Monsieur Beaufort asked, stumped by Mother's obstinance.

"I am, as ever, your humble servant," Mother curtseyed, a clear indicator that their conversation was now at an end. Some people might have argued that Mother was cutting off her nose to spite her face but there was a logic to her pride. This was Andovia. And in Andovia reputations were everything. Her name and that of her daughters had taken a battering. The simply could not take any more scandal and she feared that if her chief creditor waived all his debts simply out of 'the kindness of his heart', tongues would wag and the rest of the Kingdom would not show her, or more importantly her daughters, the same level of charity.

Monsieur Beaufort wasn't so much disappointed by Mother's reaction as flummoxed. It hadn't occurred to him that she might refuse his offer and now that she had he found himself on the horns of a rather tricky dilemma. He wanted to earn her trust but his offer had given her cause for concern. She was a cautious woman and had every reason to be after what had happened. But he could not allow such doubts to linger. He had to show her that she could trust him, implicitly. There was more at stake than mere money. With this in mind, he elected to up the ante. Considerably.

"Madame Roche, I completely understand your reluctance to accept my offer. I am a stranger to you. And we live in... complicated times. Perhaps then, I might put an alternative offer to you? One that I hope will put to rest any fears you have as to my intentions." Monsieur Beaufort once more took Mother by the hand and composed himself. "Would you, Madame Roche, deign to consider becoming *Mon Chevalière?*"

"I beg your pardon?" Mother said, her steely resolve suddenly cracked.

"Will you be my wife?"

Mother was stunned. She'd been surprised when he'd pulled his previous offer out of his hat. Where precisely he'd pulled this one from was anyone's guess. Was he serious? Was Monsieur Beaufort really asking her to become Madame Beaufort? And a noblewoman at that? It was a twist of fate so incomprehensible that she couldn't believe it was true.

"Let me explain," Monsieur Beaufort said when he saw her reaction. "May I?"

Monsieur Beaufort rose and led Mother across to a rickety old bench. There they sat and talked, never once letting go of each other's hands.

"I am a wealthy man. But since the passing of Ella's mother, I have been lonely. We came to Andovia to make a new start but our loneliness followed us from France. Our house is too big for us. We have more rooms than we need and all are empty but for sticks of furniture. I need a companion. Ella needs a mother. Our house needs a family to become a home."

Mother listened without comment. Monsieur Beaufort had a reassuring way about him: kind eyes, a soft voice and a gentle smile. He was charming without being brash, a rare quality in a man of his pedigree. And yet, so far, all he'd spoken of were his needs. He needed a wife. His daughter needed a mother. His house needed people. What about her? What about her daughters? Were they just more sticks of furniture to buy?

Monsieur Beaufort sensed her misgivings and changed his tack to address them.

"I have known you but a few short weeks, Madame Roche, but in this time I have come to admire you greatly. The way you conduct yourself, your strength and your resolve, you are a woman like no other. And your refusal to accept my charity shows that you are a woman of honour too. I would like such a woman by my side as I approach the autumn years of my life."

"Late summer," Mother suggested.

"Late summer," he conceded with a smile, adding, "with perhaps the first flakes of snow," as he brushed his greying sideburns with the backs of his fingers.

Mother liked that. Despite being in the business of beauty she had no time for petty vanity, particularly in men. It was to Monsieur Beaufort's credit that he could see himself as he was and be comfortable with that.

"I know what I am asking has probably come as something of a shock. I am not expecting an immediate answer. Only that you consider my proposal. Speak with your daughters. They should have a say in this matter. They are fine girls and would make wonderful sisters for Ella. Just know that this offer is from my heart."

After listening to all he had to say, Mother felt that Monsieur Beaufort was sincere but the mention of her daughters saw her jumping from the bench and hurrying to the corner of the house. She looked down the narrow alleyway and sure enough, there were Marigold and Gardenia caught between a rock and a hard place. Literally.

"Are they gone?" Gardenia asked with a grunt, attempting to move but stuck fast in mid-flight.

Monsieur Beaufort now stared in bewilderment down the narrow cranny at the girls he saw floundering there.

"Monsieur Beaufort!" Marigold exclaimed in surprise. "Do pardon us." She and Gardenia barely had enough room to smile let alone curtsey but they attempted both, successfully wedging themselves even deeper into the tapering fissure that had snagged them so securely.

"What are they doing?" Monsieur Beaufort asked, unsure whether this was something he should be seeing but unable to tear his eyes away.

"Disproving the land agent's claims," Mother said with a sigh. "It appears our rear thoroughfare is not quite so adroitly proportioned as he would've had us believe."

CHAPTER TWENTY-ONE

THE WEDDING WASN'T SO MUCH a small affair as positively clandestine. They married just two weeks later on the lawn of Monsieur Beaufort's own home with only their immediate families and the Beaufort's staff in attendance. Father André officiated the service and the couple's three daughters acted as bridesmaids. It was the second time around for both the bride and the groom and there'd been no time to form any sort of an attachment so that their union was not so much a marriage of convenience as one of utility. Happily, it was an arrangement that suited both parties.

Mother had made her own dress as well as those of her bridesmaids. She wore lavender and her bridesmaids wore blue. Their dresses were simple and yet elegant, designed to reflect the low-key nature of the occasion, but Ella hadn't worn hers. She had not refused when Mother first suggested it. She'd simply come out of the house shortly before the wedding wearing a different dress entirely, leaving the dress Mother had spent many hours making hanging in her wardrobe untouched.

Marigold hurried over to Ella and told her to get back upstairs and get changed before Mother came out but Ella wouldn't hear of it.

"This was my own beloved mother's favourite dress. It was her dying gift to me," she replied, twisting from side to side to make her glittery pink outfit sparkle in the soft golden rays of this perfect autumn morning. "Would you have me wear something else on my father's wedding day?"

Marigold was dumbfounded and Gardenia incensed but the moment Monsieur Beaufort turned and saw his daughter he announced: "My darling Ella, you are a vision. How proud your mother would have been," and that was that, there was nothing more the sisters could do about it.

Besides, it was too late anyway. The gardener squeezed out a few bars of Bach on his accordion to signal the arrival of the bride and Father André invited everyone to take their places. The wedding was about to start.

*

MOTHER SAID NOTHING about Ella's dress and shot Marigold a look when she tried bringing the subject up. This was a day for harmony, not acrimony. They were a family now and it would take some getting used to. But Mother was keen for them to start off on the right foot and Marigold was keen not to spoil the day.

Mother looked beautiful in her wedding dress, more beautiful than either Marigold or Gardenia could ever remember. She'd had a hard life and the stresses and strains had taken their toll on her appearance. She'd been a skinny girl in her youth and found it impossible to fill out in later life, making her look bony and austere. But today she had blossomed. The years had fallen away and her sparkle had returned, albeit thanks to a few yards of satin and a strategic application of rouge. But the smile was all hers and she wore it magnificently.

"To my new wife," Monsieur Beaufort said, raising a glass to toast Madame Beaufort (née Roche). The staff did likewise, raising the glass of champagne they'd been allowed for the occasion before being ushered back to work. Gardenia felt terribly grown-up trying her first sip of champagne but the promise failed to live up to the expectation. It was sharp, bitter and the bubbles went up her nose, much to Ella's amusement.

Mother and Monsieur Beaufort cut a small fruit cake and handed out a slice to each of the girls.

"Thank you, Monsieur Beaufort," Marigold said automatically with a little formal curtsey.

"Please, call me Father," Monsieur Beaufort smiled.

It hadn't occurred to Marigold until this moment that

she would be required to think of him this way. She'd never known her real father, or at least, she'd had only the haziest half-memory of him before he was taken from her. And as Mother had never remarried or formed any other attachments, in Marigold's eyes, it was not a role that had stood vacant but one that had simply ceased to exist.

"Thank you... er, Father," she said with a little effort. It was an unfamiliar word and felt odd on the tongue.

The cake was delicious, much more to the sisters' liking than the champagne, and they finished it with relish right down to the last crumb. But Gardenia saw something and nudged Marigold. Ella hadn't eaten hers. She hadn't even touched it. She'd simply wrapped it in a napkin and handed it to the footman to take inside.

"Did you not like the cake?" Marigold asked when she saw what Ella was doing.

"I loved it," Ella replied. "That is why I wish to keep it as a treasured memento of this special day. I could never eat it."

Monsieur Beaufort swept Ella up in a loving embrace and told her how happy she made him feel while Marigold and Gardenia stood clutching empty plates that had been licked clean. Ella looked over Father's shoulder and gave her new sisters a wink.

Today was the first day of the rest of their lives. And didn't they just know it.

*

AFTER THE SERVICE, Mother and Monsieur Beaufort retired to discuss their new living arrangements. Monsieur Beaufort had refused to see his bride-to-be and her daughters live in their "barnacle on the city walls" another moment so he had invited them to stay in his guest quarters until the wedding, a comfortable little cottage behind the stables. But now they were a family and as such, entitled to move into the main château. It was more than they could've ever imagined.

THE UGLY SISTERS

Marigold and Gardenia looked around their new bedroom in wonder. Just this one room alone was bigger than their last home and it was airy and light, with enormous south-facing windows and nary a dropping in sight.

Their beds were enormous and soft, so big in fact that Gardenia could scarcely reach the edges when she laid in the middle and stretched out her arms and legs to the sides.

"Waiting for anyone in particular?" Ella asked, breezing into the room as though she owned the place, which indeed she did — or at least had until now.

Gardenia jumped off the bed and straightened herself up while Marigold turned to face Ella as she circled the room glancing over the girls' bags.

"I hope you're happy in this room. It used to be mine," Ella said with a heavy heart.

"Remind me again how long have you been living here?" Marigold asked, knowing full well she'd been here barely two months.

Ella smiled but didn't answer.

"Where's your bedroom now?" Gardenia asked.

"In the attic," Ella shrugged, adding; "where it's cold and draughty."

"Would you like to share ours? We have more than enough room," Marigold offered, safe in the knowledge that Ella wouldn't dream of doing so. Especially not when there were two empty rooms on either side of this one. And yet still she had moved into a cold and draughty attic? How curious.

"Thank you, dear Marigold. That is most kind of you but I am afraid I am a very light sleeper and fear I should get very little rest if I were to muck in with you two chatterboxes."

Gardenia denied she or her sister were "chatterboxes" but Marigold was more intrigued by the word "muck", which she refused to believe had been a mere slip of the tongue.

"Then perhaps we can help you draught-proof your room. I'm sure we could make it snug for you in time for winter," Gardenia offered, having recently gained invaluable experience turning the most unlikely of dwellings into a home.

"My room is private," Ella said instantly before softening her stance just a little. "Forgive me, sweet Gardenia, but it is my little sanctuary, somewhere just for me, and I'd prefer to keep it that way. Just while we get to know each other. I hope you understand."

"Of course, dear Ella," Gardenia said, almost feeling like she should apologise for making the offer before deciding against it. "We have no wish to intrude."

Ella noticed the way Gardenia and Marigold spoke. They often referred to themselves as "us" and "we", but rarely "I" and "me". She'd not noticed it before but now that she had she couldn't stop hearing it.

Marigold began hanging her clothes in the mahogany wardrobe opposite her bed. She'd brought a few dresses with her this morning in order to have something to change into after the wedding. The Beaufort's footman would bring the rest up later on.

"We have servants for that sort of thing, you know," Ella said, watching with a quizzical eye as Marigold unpacked.

"It's no trouble," Marigold assured her but that was not what Ella meant.

"It's not the behaviour of a lady to attend to such tasks oneself. And the servants get terribly upset when they feel they're not needed," Ella said, hanging off the bedpost at the end of Marigold's bed. "We have a duty of care towards our staff so please, if you don't mind, you're no longer a serving girl."

Marigold's eyes narrowed. She and Gardenia had been in service to Monsieur Vasseur for a grand total of two hours and they'd done precious little in that short time except to wreck the place. She wondered how long this serving girl tag would follow them around. As long as Ella could make it stick, she quickly concluded.

Marigold dropped the dress she was holding and stopped unpacking but only for Ella's benefit. She'd hang the last of her clothes up once Ella had gone, damned if she was going to ask a servant to do something she'd happily managed to do for most of her life. No matter how unladylike her new stepsister thought it.

"Tell me, because I've been dying to ask," Ella said, flopping onto Gardenia's bed and resting her head in her hands. "What was he like? The Prince? Was he handsome? Was he dashing? Was he everything they say he is?"

"And so much more," Marigold replied, without a word of a lie.

"Everyone is very jealous of you," Ella told Gardenia, catching her by surprise.

"Are they?" Gardenia asked.

"Of course," Ella said, rolling onto her back and gazing dreamily up at the ornate ceiling. "What girl would not wish such an honour? Songs will be sung about you. Poems will be penned. You will be remembered for centuries to come as Andovia's damsel in distress. The humble maiden whose virtue the Prince risked his Kingdom for."

This was news to Gardenia. She'd agreed to the cover story because she'd feared for her life but it had never occurred to her how she might be regarded afterwards. She and Marigold hadn't ventured into town since the night of the ball. Neither had dared show their faces after what had happened so it came as something of a surprise to hear that the pendulum of public opinion had swung in their favour once more.

"What was he like?" Ella persisted, rolling over and looking up at Gardenia in excitement. "Tell me everything. Omit nothing, no matter how trivial."

Ella may have been family but that didn't mean they had to share everything with her, particularly when she had a 'Keep Out' sign hanging from the handle of her own bedroom door. Marigold shot Gardenia a look but there was no need. Gardenia was happy to go with the official version of events, more so now than ever.

"He was… the perfect gentleman," Gardenia confirmed.

"How disappointing," Ella winked, catching Gardenia off-guard and making her blush. Marigold had never heard anything so shameless. What would Mother have said about such a comment? This was Marigold's first thought. With her second thought, she wondered why this was always her first thought.

"Do you have any experience of boys?" Ella asked. "The Captain asides, I mean?"

"Certainly not," Gardenia replied haughtily. "My honour is unblemished."

Ella sat up and smiled. "Don't go believing your own publicity," she advised.

"How about you? How many boys have you kissed?" Marigold asked, turning the tables on their bold new stepsister.

"More than you I would wager," Ella said with no hint of shame. "Then again, that's to be expected. You are the ugly sister, I suppose."

"What?" Marigold gasped, outraged at such an insult. But Ella held up her hands and insisted they weren't her words.

"That's what they're saying in town," she gleefully reported, looking Marigold up and down as if to make a judgement of her own.

"Who's saying that?" Marigold demanded. "Who?"

Ella got up from the bed and looked out towards the distant spires of Andovia, just about visible from their bedroom window.

"They are. Everyone. Well that's what the Captain had said, wasn't it? *'I brought great shame upon myself with Mademoiselle Gardenia but I never laid a finger on her ugly sister.'*"

Ella let these awful words hang in the air while Marigold and Gardenia came to grips with them. Where had they come from? Why had they been uttered? The Captain had said something to this effect and both Marigold and Gardenia had heard him say it. But to have had these words turned and twisted in such a way so that they became part of the official story was beyond the pale. Why had the Grand Duke done this? What possible purpose could this have served other than to have added a splash of colour to an otherwise black and white story?

And all at the expense of Marigold's good name.

Ella watched Marigold closely. Her mask had slipped to reveal the edges of something deeper. Just as Ella had suspected. There was more to this story than met the eye but getting to the truth was going to prove harder than she thought. All three of them were now sisters and sisters shouldn't keep secrets from each other. But two of the sisters were closer than the other.

What, Ella wondered, was she to do?

CHAPTER TWENTY-TWO

SEVERAL MILES AWAY, beneath the towering spires of the Beaufort's magnificent view, the King and Grand Duke were holding another round of crisis talks. The doors were locked, the staff dismissed and the Great Throne Room was theirs. For the time being.

All efforts until this point had been focussed on damage limitation and rumour control. The Duke's cover story of the Prince needlessly injuring himself on his big day in the defence of a lowly serving girl had been swallowed hook, line and sinker, helped in no small part by a series of official denials from the Palace, which always added fuel to the fire. The Prince's sudden disappearance also added credibility. It was rumoured that he was convalescing in the countryside and had been so gravely injured in the fight that it could be weeks before he was seen in public again. Other speculation included a rumour that he would renounce his succession in order to marry the serving girl whose honour he'd saved. While one or two of the more extreme rumours had him either joining a religious order after being visited by an angel and/or fighting a snow beast who'd been spotted in the north of the Kingdom. It was all wonderfully diverting and the Grand Duke could not have been happier at the fog he'd created but one of the more outlandish rumours to circulate turned out to be true.

The Roche girl, who it was rumoured, had been at the centre of the incident, had disappeared from her grotty little shack outside the city walls and was now living at the home of a new-to-town French aristocrat. What's more, he was said to have married her widowed Mother and adopted both daughters as his legal heirs. But how had this happened? Only days earlier no one would've even acknowledged them in the street. Now it seemed they were to be counted amongst the ranks of minor nobility. It was a strange turn of events indeed.

"The Prince's touch seems to have cleansed them, Your Majesty," the Duke surmised in flowery terms. "Their sins forgiven, the girl's purity reborn."

"And this wily old cockerel has bagged her as some sort of trophy daughter, you say?" the King said.

"A cunning move for someone looking to elevate his social standing in short order," the Duke agreed, almost in admiration at Monsieur Beaufort's audacity.

"I don't like it. I don't like it at all," the King said, circling the throne room like a tiger with his tail up. "What if she talks?"

"She and her sister have benefited a great deal from this incident, Your Majesty. More than they could have ever hoped for. I think it highly unlikely that they should feel inclined to look such a gift horse in the mouth," the Duke said, marvelling at how calculating some people could be. The Roches were clearly cut from his kind of cloth. He was glad he'd decided to spare them, although he would keep a close eye on them from now on.

"But the man's a Frenchy? We have enemies abroad, you know," the King growled.

"We have far more at home, sire, and your position has become increasingly vulnerable of late. We must stop reacting to events and take charge of the narrative," the Duke said, speaking down to the King — literally — as he stood on the stage next to the royal throne. Made from gold and silver and bedecked with a myriad of sparkling jewels, the throne was surely the most magnificent seat in all the land. And possibly quite the most uncomfortable too. For both the occupant's backside and brow.

The King continued to pace, wearing a hole in the carpet with his worries. "What do you think we've been doing all this time? Writing our names in the snow?"

"Sire, your son must be recalled to the city, married forthwith and produce an heir. Until such a time as he does, your line will not be secure. If we can arrange this, all your other problems will disappear," the Grand Duke said, laying a hand upon the throne's ornate crest in order to draw the King's attention to what mattered most.

"Ha, fat chance of that! The boy's a left-hander for heaven's sake. He admitted as much himself. Blubbed at my feet he did. Get a hold of yourself, I told him, we all get these urges. I was in the army too, you know, but we have to fight them, I said. Take long walks and cold showers and do what's right for your Kingdom. That's what I did."

The Grand Duke thought about this and agreed with the King in principle without feeling the need to contest some of his less salient points. "Indeed, sire," he said, wondering if this was why the King always looked so refreshed and exercised.

"So we're stumped. Twenty-four years old and still unmarried. People are beginning to talk, you know."

"There's always a way, sire. Have faith," the Grand Duke said surreptitiously. The King stopped pacing when he noticed the Duke's hand lingering on the crest of his throne.

"What are you getting at? What are you suggesting?"

"I am merely saying, your Highness, that we must be practical and accept the Prince's limitation. But there are alternatives," the Duke told him.

"Suggesting yourself as next in line when the Prince fails to produce an heir?" the King said in a sudden fury.

"Of course not, sire. The thought never entered my head," the Grand Duke said, snatching his hand from the throne as if it had suddenly turned red hot.

"Codswallop it didn't. That's your game, isn't it? I should've known," the King thundered, hurrying to the oak-panelled wall and snatching down a sword. The Duke baulked and dashed around the back of the throne, determined to keep it between him and that sword while the King was in this sort of mood.

"I assure you, Your Highness, I am your humble servant," the Grand Duke said. "I serve at your discretion," which was true. The Grand Duke had lived to see three Kings come and two go in his lifetime and they'd all been the same, paranoid to the point of madness that everyone was after their job. And to be fair to them all, past and present monarchs included, they'd not been wrong. If there was one thing a royal throne commanded more than adoration, it was avarice.

But the Duke had no such inclinations. He was a man of modest ambitions and happy enough with the third-largest Palace in the Kingdom, the second-highest income and more land than he could point to without the help of a map. Not to mention unfettered access to the King, whose greatest attribute was to take the blame for everything and the credit for nothing. He had no desire to overstep the mark and spend the rest of his days looking over his shoulder in an effort to keep the crown on his head. That was a game for knaves and glory-seekers. The real power lay behind the throne.

"Just whose idea was it to have this blasted ball anyway? Yours if I remember rightly. You must've known what the Prince was up to. You planned to have him make a spectacle of himself in front of everyone, didn't you?" the King roared, taking a swipe at the Duke but missing by a mile. The swipe, much like the sword, was purely ceremonial but the Duke ducked all the same just out of deference.

"Your Majesty, please, I had no idea the Prince was anything other than your worthy successor," the Duke insisted, backing away from the King as they stalked across the room.

"Are you saying he's not my worthy successor?" the King growled, seizing upon the Duke's words as evidence of high-treason.

"Not a bit of it, My Lord. He shall follow you as surely as night follows day," the Duke said with a gracious bow, taking care not to bow too low in case the King tried his luck.

"Oh indeed, making plans for when I'm not around, are you?" the King barked. "Knight takes King and checkmate, is it?"

"Of course not, sire, you are my one and only sovereign Lord, Your Majesty."

"And I expect that's what you told the last fella too, didn't you!" the King thundered, raising his sword to take another strike at this snake in the grass.

There are times in a person's life when appeasement seems to cause more trouble than effrontery and this was one of them. The Grand Duke finally snapped, snatching the sword from the King's hand as one might a toy from a tantruming child.

"The last fella was your father, for pity's sake!" the Duke said, slinging the sword aside and glaring his sternest glare at the King. "And I used to get quite enough of this from him."

The King didn't know how to react. He'd never been talked to this way before. Certainly not since becoming King. The last person to raise his voice to him had been his own father — and a bad-tempered old coot he was too — so the King was more confused than anything else. He should've probably called in the Guards and had the Grand Duke thrown in the dungeons alongside Captain Durand but that would've left the King having to face his problems all by himself. And that wasn't something that held much appeal for the King, or indeed, he'd had much practice with.

Besides, the King didn't really suspect the Grand Duke of conspiring against him. He was just blowing off steam at the only person he could. Wasn't that what Grand Dukes were for?

"Yes well… we'll say no more about it," the King

blustered, feeling contrite but not quite understanding the emotion. He trudged across the room and flopped into his magnificent gold throne as though the party was over and his balloons had been popped.

It never failed to astonish the Grand Duke how the King could switch from volcanic rage to desolate despair within the blink of an eye. It was just as well the King was the King and not an ordinary citizen as he wouldn't have lasted five minutes out there in the real world… thought the man with the third-largest palace in the Kingdom.

"Your Highness, I have a plan," the Grand Duke announced.

"You have?" said the King in hope.

"We must scotch any rumours before they have a chance to take seed and forge ahead with an ironclad strategy that will secure both your legacy and your lineage for generations to come."

"Yes?" said the King, buoyed by his chief advisor's steely rhetoric.

"I propose we delay no further. We must grasp the nettle and remind the Kingdom of your greatness with the most lavish event the world has ever seen."

"Yes! Yes!" the King agreed, thankful that he'd shown his old friend mercy and not lopped off his head.

"I propose…" the Duke said, with great aplomb.

"Yes! Yes! Yes!" the King said, now on the edge of his throne.

"I propose… another grand ball."

Silence descended over the throne room. Neither man stirred. The Duke waited for the King to say something but the King seemed lost for words. This was either a good sign or a very bad one.

The King blinked a few times to order his thoughts and finally found his voice.

"Guards!" he roared.

CHAPTER TWENTY-THREE

ELLA STOOD AT THE WINDOW of the parlour watching Gardenia play catch in the garden outside. This was a strange enough activity for a 'lady' to be engaged in but the spectacle was stranger still because Gardenia was not playing with a ball. Instead, she was pitching and catching a small bouquet of flowers. She'd press-ganged the elderly gardener into her game and now he was tossing the bouquet at her from all angles, forcing her to leap, dive and pirouette to snatch it from the air before it hit the grass.

Marigold joined Ella at the window.

"She's practising," Marigold said, answering Ella's unasked question. "Catching the bridal bouquet."

Ella nodded, recognising — if not quite understanding — what her new stepsister was doing.

"Why aren't you out there too? Don't you wish to catch a husband also?" Ella asked.

"Sure," Marigold shrugged, adding; "If I find the right man."

"Well, aren't you particular," Ella said with great amusement, leaving Marigold to read into that whatever she liked.

"I suppose some of us must be, yes," Marigold replied with a shrug.

Ella's composure cracked a little before she patched it up with a giggle. "Aren't we a wicked pair? So, tell me, dear Marigold, while we're on the subject of all things wicked, what exactly did the Captain do to our dear sweet sister in the catacombs? I promise, on mine honour as your sister, your secret will stay safe with me."

"Gardenia's secret," Marigold reminded Ella.

"Gardenia's secret, your secret, my secret. We are all

sisters, there are no secrets between us. What's mine is yours. I hope you feel the same."

"Of course, sweet Ella," Marigold simpered through gritted teeth. "But I'm afraid I couldn't say."

"You were there?" Ella said, feeling around the edges of Marigold's resolve with delicate fingers.

"I didn't witness the incident myself. I happened to find Gardenia in the passageway after it had happened," Marigold said, which was more or less true.

"But your sister would have told you, surely?" Ella pressed, no longer watching Gardenia rolling around on the lawns outside, her attention now focussed solely on Marigold. "If only to ask her older sister about something she might not have fully understood. She is so young, so innocent, dear Gardenia. We must help her to understand these things."

Marigold agreed with Ella's assessment but she was still unwilling to furnish her with specifics. It wasn't her place to do so or Ella's place to ask. And either way, the more specifics she invented the more pits she dug for her herself.

"I'm not entirely sure this is a fitting conversation for ladies," Marigold said, using one of Mother's favoured techniques to deflect Ella's line of inquiry. But Ella was not to be put off and seemed to enjoy weeding out every salacious detail from Marigold, in spite of her obvious discomfort.

"Forewarned is forearmed, my dear. We are mere girls, after all. We have but our wits to defend ourselves with," Ella said darkly. "And some of us have more to defend than others."

"With fewer wits too," Marigold agreed.

Ella glowered at Marigold. Either could've walked away but neither wanted to give the other the satisfaction. They may have been living in a huge château surrounded by gardens that ran off in all directions as far as the eye could see but neither could avoid the other indefinitely. Besides, the girls were family now, all three of them, and for better or for worse, they needed to try to reach a tolerable understanding.

But not at any cost.

"How do we even know Gardenia's telling the truth?" Ella postulated, twirling her golden locks. "I mean, how do we even know the Captain actually did anything?"

Marigold feigned shock.

"Of course he did. Gardenia would not condemn a man for no reason. How could you think such a thing?"

"An absence of facts makes the mind wander," Ella said, then smiled at a sudden scandalous thought. "What if it wasn't the Captain at all? What if it was the Prince?"

Marigold had already used her 'shocked look' so it felt forced using it again so soon afterwards but what choice did she have?

"The Prince? Are you mad? That's treason to even suggest such a thing," Marigold hissed, looking around to make sure no one was eavesdropping or if they were, that they saw her vehemently denying Ella's accusation.

Ella took a moment to read Marigold's expression and saw something in her face that shouldn't have been there. Fear. It ran through Marigold like a watermark. And Ella had just held her to the light.

"Treason? This is simply girl talk. You'd be surprised by the sorts of things the girls in Paris talk about," Ella said, in an effort to remind Marigold how sophisticated she was. Or rather, how unsophisticated Andovian girls were. "Like I say, Gardenia is young and naive. Perhaps she misunderstood certain... hmm," Ella searched for a suitable word before finding just the right one, "... compliments," she said with a smile.

"Compliments?" Marigold repeated.

"Compliments of attention," Ella explained. "But if she'd had no such experience she might have panicked and fled, the poor thing."

Marigold stayed silent while Ella elaborated in ever

greater detail just what the Prince "might have done" to Gardenia. If this was truly what the girls in Paris talked about, Marigold thought to herself, then no wonder that place was such a mess. Ella continued.

"And then there's the ignoble Captain Durand. Naturally, being a loyal officer of the crown, he would've had no hesitation but to sacrifice himself to save the Prince. What Guardsman wouldn't? It is their solemn duty, after all."

Marigold realised that she couldn't go on rebutting Ella's theories forever. She'd not let up since the day of the wedding and was clearly intent on digging until she'd got to the bottom. Marigold had tried to seek solace in Mother's wisdom but every time she'd tried to speak with her, Monsieur Beaufort was there by her side. For the first time in her life, Marigold felt all alone despite being surrounded by more people than she'd ever known.

"Of course, a Prince is not just a Prince, but a man of flesh and blood," Ella speculated, continuing with her favourite parlour game. "And while it is expected that a Prince should favour the finest wines served in the most exquisite of crystal flutes, a flagon of something frothy can occasionally quench a thirst too, wouldn't you say?"

Marigold wouldn't. And she didn't. Instead, she decided to turn the tables on Ella and ask a few questions herself.

"So is this why you came to Andovia? To quench the royal thirst?"

"You know full well that I was unable to attend the ball due, in no small part, to you and your mother's... supply difficulties."

"Whose mother?" Marigold asked with a raised eyebrow.

Ella smiled. "Of course. *Our* mother. Not that I bear any malice. I had no desire to attend the ball anyway."

Marigold considered this at the same time as recalling all the silk and pearls and gold thread they'd spent hours stitching together and thought she caught a glimpse of Ella's own watermark.

"You had no desire to attend the ball?" Marigold asked sceptically. "So it was just a happy coincidence you moved to Andovia within weeks of the invitations going out?"

Ella stopped playing with her locks and narrowed her eyes at Marigold's suggestion.

"I reiterate, I was unable to attend the ball, thanks to you."

"Ella, everyone was unable to attend the ball, thanks to me, but that doesn't mean they didn't want to. Besides, I'm sure you could've found something to wear if you'd put your mind to it," Marigold said, looking down at Ella's dress. She seemed to have a different dress for each day of the week. Marigold couldn't remember seeing her wearing the same thing twice. And while some of her dresses were practical and some were simple, others were anything but, her current gown of silk and silver being a case in point.

"If you don't believe in coincidences how can you possibly believe in magic?" Ella said with a sad shake of the head. This was a good question. It was just a shame Marigold had been looking for a good answer.

"Then why did you come here?" She pressed, just as Ella had pressed her earlier.

"As I've said, we wanted to make a new start when my mother passed away," Ella explained with more than a hint of irritation now audible in her voice.

"That's a reason to leave somewhere, not to come somewhere," Marigold said. "Why Andovia?"

"Why not?"

"That's not an answer either."

"Then perhaps you should ask my Father. Or do you suppose it was my idea to move to this…hmm, darling little Kingdom?"

Finally, it was Marigold's turn to treat her sister to a

smile. "Well I guess we both have our little secrets, don't we?" she said, turning to leave with her head held high.

Marigold headed for the door, unable to stand the starchy air a moment longer. But then Ella called to her before she disappeared.

"You know, I have a shawl that would work well with that dress," she said, catching Marigold by surprise.

"I beg your pardon?" Marigold asked, wary of Ella's latest trap to make her look foolish; the stable master's filthiest horse blanket perhaps or a string of freshly laid lawn sausages courtesy of gardener's untrainable dachshund.

"In the back of the cellar, in an old trunk marked shawls, I have a several from England including a lace wrap from Nottingham that would look lovely with your dress. You are welcome to it or anything else you find in there if you wish to take a look."

Marigold was unmoved. Ella gave a little shrug and said; "Think of it as a gift between sisters," before turning back to watch Gardenia outside attempting to field her own dreams.

CHAPTER TWENTY-FOUR

LUNCH WAS ON THE VERANDA and the family ate together. The food was wonderful, the service impeccable and the atmosphere convivial. Ella read poetry from a book she'd found in the library, Monsieur Beaufort looked on with pride, Mother listened politely and Marigold successfully masked her astonishment that Ella could read. The only member of the family not present was Gardenia. She was presumably still upstairs getting changed and picking the grass seeds from her hair.

The weather was warm, the skies were blue and the setting could not have been more picturesque. The gardens were immaculate. An entire army of gardeners had ensured no blade of grass had been left unmanicured. The château had been restored to its former glory with its original fixtures and fittings fixed and refitted by the finest workmen in the land. And there was a full detachment of household staff to oversee the running of the household and wait on the family's every need.

It was a lifestyle to which many would aspire. And yet Marigold was not content. She wasn't used to sitting idle while others did the work. She liked having an occupation. She liked to keep busy. She liked helping Mother with her business. But Mother's business was no more, on the insistence of Monsieur Beaufort. No wife of his could be permitted to work. Daughters neither. Such a thing would've been unheard of for a man of his standing. And this was a great blow for Marigold because she liked working with Mother. She liked cutting and sewing her new designs. She liked the process of creating beauty. She even liked getting dressed up and parading their new gowns around town. Not for vanity's sake. But because it gave her a sense of purpose and a sense of pride. It made her feel valued on a genuine level. But here they were not even allowed to pull out their own chairs. The Beauforts (of which she was now one) had people for that sort of thing. They had people for everything; cooking, cleaning, tidying, laundering, gardening, fetching, carrying, dressing, grooming and just plain standing around looking regal. They had just about every base covered, every base, that was, except for companionship. For that and that alone, they only had each other.

Of course, Ella and Monsieur Beaufort had only arrived in the Kingdom a few short months earlier and that should have been enough time to introduce themselves to Andovian society. Anyone who was anyone was welcome on the circuit and a widowed French aristocrat and his beautiful unattached daughter would have been regarded as manna from heaven by some of the town's more meddlesome matchmakers. But much to Marigold's surprise, the Beauforts seemed content to steer clear of the town, spurn all invitations and live the type of idyllic country lives that are enough to drive most people mad after only a few short weeks.

She didn't get it. After all they had been through? After their lives had been turned upside down, thrown in the gutter and then plucked out again, only to find themselves reborn into a family of noble birth with their reputations intact? This should have been their big chance to step into high society. Instead, she and Gardenia might as well have been walled up in an attic or cast away in a nunnery. How were they meant to make a match if they never left the château? Monsieur Beaufort might have enjoyed the quiet life but Marigold could not remain a prisoner of luxury forever.

And what of Ella? Ella never expressed an interest in anything one way or the other. She seemed content to spend her days roaming the château like a ghost, haunting her sisters at every turn and watching them wherever they went. Sometimes she amused herself by taking leftover buns to the ragtag pack of urchins that lingered beyond the gates but other than that, she seemed to want nothing more from life.

Except...

To know about the Prince.

She had never met him but her new sisters had. And she wanted to know everything. Her appetite for tittle-tattle knew no bounds.

Their existence was tedium turned into a fine art. And neither Marigold nor Gardenia could see an end to it.

Marigold had tried to escape the boredom by grooming and tending to Liquorice but Monsieur Beaufort soon took on one of the urchins as a stable boy and suddenly she had even less on her plate than before, exquisite as her plate might've been.

"Bravo," Monsieur Beaufort said when Ella came to the end of her recital. Mother clapped politely which woke Marigold up and prompted her to do the same. Ella smiled graciously but her eyes lingered on Marigold. She'd failed to take up Ella's kind offer and accept one of her shawls but neither commented on the fact. It simply hung in the air like an unspoken misunderstanding and flavoured the rest of their day's conversation. Or at least, what little of it they attempted.

"Where has that girl got to?" Mother asked out loud, staring at Gardenia's empty chair.

"Would you like me to go and fetch her?" Marigold offered, eager to leave the table.

"Oh no, please sit. We have people for that sort of thing," Monsieur Beaufort replied nonchalantly, snapping his fingers and summoning a footman.

The footman leaned in but before Monsieur Beaufort had got the words out, a screeching from the house caught everyone's attention as a maid came tearing out in hysterics.

"Come quick! Come quick! It's in the house. Monsieur Beaufort! It's in the house!"

The footman moved to intercept the overwrought young lady before she could inflict her wailing on the Master but Monsieur Beaufort, not to mention Mother and Marigold, were by this point more than a little curious to know what was in the house.

"A snake! A horrible black and brown thing. It went right for me."

Marigold gave a shudder as the memory of her last encounter came snapping back to her. She didn't like the thought of a snake being on the loose in her new home. Monsieur Beaufort was already rounding up a posse of gardeners with pitchforks and shovels to go in and tackle the beast but Marigold was adamant that she wouldn't set foot in there or sleep a wink until it was caught.

Across the table, Ella was oddly unconcerned. She continued eating as if nothing had happened and avoided all eyes. Marigold thought nothing of it until Monsieur Beaufort asked the maid where she'd seen the vile serpent.

"In the cellar, Monsieur. I went down there to fetch a bottle of wine and it slithered right by me, past the bottom step and into the log store."

A second shudder ran down Marigold's spine when she thought about how close she had come to going down there to investigate Ella's trunk of shawls. It was just as well that she and Ella were…

"Oh no!" Marigold gasped, jumping to her feet to send her chair clattering back onto the stones.

"What is it?" Mother said, immediately concerned by her eldest daughter's reaction.

"Gardenia!" Marigold said, dashing from the table and running for the house.

"Stop! Marigold, no!" Mother shouted and several of the gardeners tried to make a grab for her but Marigold was too quick for them. She hurried past and in through the French doors, running along the corridor to the cellar entrance under the stairs.

"Don't go down there!" they shouted at her but Marigold didn't hesitate. Her fears were forgotten in an instant and all she could fixate upon was the conversation she'd had with her sister just before lunch about Ella's blasted shawls.

The cellar was dark and the lamps unlit. There, at the bottom of the stairs, was a brass candle holder, dropped in a panic and left to burn where it had fallen by the hysterical maid.

Marigold picked it up and looked around. The flickering pall of yellow light barely penetrated the darkness down here. Shadows stretched to all corners of the dank cellar. The snake could be lurking anywhere.

"Marigold! For God's sake, come out of there!" Monsieur Beaufort called to her from upstairs but she couldn't. The terrible dread she felt in the pit of her stomach compelled her to go on, into the darkness and the winding passageways beyond without a thought for her own regard.

"Gardenia! Gardenia, are you down here?" she called, hoping and praying to hear her sister reply. But the only responses she got were the anxious echoes of her own desperate entreaties.

Boots came thumping down the stairs, accompanied by the clanking of steel on stone, as her would-be reinforcements clattered their shovels against the walls in an attempt to dissuade the enemy from striking. "Come back to us. Come here girl, now!" But Marigold refused to wait and hurried through the shadows towards the furthest corner of the cellar, to where Ella had said her trunk lay. She'd not been down here before but she had described its exact location to Gardenia. And when she rounded the corner and kicked something lying on the floor, she realised her fears had not been groundless.

It was a second brass candle holder. This one missing

its candle.

Marigold was now almost paralysed in fear but necessity pushed her on. She raised her candle to send a pall of light across the floor in front of her and let out a wail.

"Gardenia!"

There on the ground next to Ella's open trunk lay her sister, crumpled and lifeless but for a strange stirring that seemed to ripple across her face. It was a barley snake, black and brown, same as the one that had left its mark on her all those weeks ago, only this one much bigger.

Marigold screamed, not in terror but in anger at the loathsome serpent that had attacked her sister. She grabbed a mop from a nearby bucket and lunged it at the snake's head. The snake took a bite at it but only succeeded in getting its fangs caught in the mop head. Marigold was able to sweep it away from her sister, into the corner of the cellar and keep it pressed against the wall until help arrived.

As the gardeners meted out swift and merciless justice with their iron shovels, Marigold scrambled across to her sister and checked for signs of life. Gardenia was still breathing but only just. The colour had drained from her face and her lips had turned black.

"Mother!" Marigold cried out in anguish before collapsing in tears by Gardenia's side.

CHAPTER TWENTY-FIVE

CATHERINE PETIT'S FIRST TASTE of real soldiering came with the early thaws of spring. A company of King's Guards headed for the mountains and the borderlands with Srendizi. They'd received reports of bandits raiding several smallholdings in the north and this sort of unchecked plundering could not be allowed to go unanswered.

Catherine (or rather Calvin, as the Sergeant had renamed her) marched with her drum and sticks but was advised not to bang them while traversing the northern passes. A whole winter's worth of snow lay on the slopes above them and the slightest rat-a-tat-tat could shake it loose. Besides, the company was now on a battle footing and it rather spoiled the surprise if you banged *Here Comes The King's Guards* all the way to the enemy's front door. Therefore, Catherine's campaign duties would be confined to distributing ammunition, running messages and applying bandages, should any need distributing, running or applying.

It was a two-day march to the border then scouts were sent across to locate the enemy while the rest of the company pitched camp. Catherine's nerves were jangling. She had no idea what to expect but she knew it would be dangerous. The Sergeant reassured her that rounding up bandits was more like sweeping up ants than charging into battle.

"You have over a hundred brothers at your side. The enemy is probably less than twenty and they don't know we're coming. In a way, I almost feel sorry for them," the Sergeant said, as they hunkered around a crackling fire in the shadow of *Mont Magie*.

"Do you really?" Catherine replied in surprise. She knew the Sergeant was a good man but had no idea his humanity extended to his enemy too.

"Of course, until I remember what these twenty people

did to the five they found sleeping peacefully at the Rousseau place last month," he said, taking a moment to dwell on the images that seeped through his mind. He brushed them aside again and reached for his bayonet, affixing the razor-sharp spearpoint to the barrel of his musket with a twist. "Then I'm very much at one with what has to be done."

Catherine asked no more. And there was no time anyway. The scouts returned. The enemy camp had been located and the company was put on standby.

"We attack at dawn."

*

CATHERINE BARELY SLEPT THAT NIGHT. The cold crunched her bones and fear jangled her nerves. But she was very much in the minority. Most of the company slept like babies and had to be roused a few hours before daybreak with coffee and kicks.

Everyone knew what they were doing and the company broke camp and moved out with barely a word being spoken. On the march across the border, Catherine brought up the rear. This wasn't to protect her — the Sergeant was considerate but not that considerate — this was to protect everyone else. Only the most experienced soldiers led the advance, out of the mountains and into the tangled valleys of Srendizi beyond. Surprise was everything.

They marched and marched, downhill and through the melting snows. Spring was on the way and once through the mountains, everything turned from hard and frozen to cold and wet. It was hard going and a hundred men fully ladened with equipment made slow progress but the order to halt came as the skies above them were turning orange. The peaks to their rear were basking in the first rays of dawn but down here on the forested slopes, the new day was still a good hour away.

The Lieutenant, whom Catherine had successfully managed to avoid until now, directed his company to fan out, with half his men going east and half going west. The enemy lay directly before them in a small cluster of winter cabins on the edge of the forest. They had no idea the King's Guards were coming and by the time they did, it would be too late.

Catherine was beckoned forwards and planted behind a rocky outcrop by the Sergeant.

"Stay here. And try not to get your head blown off," the Sergeant told her. Catherine wasn't sure if that was advice or an order. Either way, she was determined not to disobey him.

The Sergeant now joined a forward party, leaving Catherine to guard the supplies, presumably with her drumsticks. Several others took up positions around her, including the Surgeon, the Quartermaster and the Lieutenant, who bagged the best seat in the house and now awaited the last of his men to get into position before starting the show.

Catherine peeked over the top of the snow-dusted boulders and saw a group of log cabins blanketed in snow and bathed in night. All was quiet in the camp but the slopes on either side of the clearing stirred as the company took up their positions.

The Lieutenant raised his lantern and swung it from side to side to give the order. Yellow flames ignited rags doused in paraffin and these flickering lights were hurled against the enemy's doors.

The fires burned unchecked for almost five minutes. No one attempted to flee and or put the blaze out. Catherine wondered if the enemy had already left but a gunshot from one of the windows soon answered that question.

A hundred muskets of the King's Guards replied as one to pepper the burning cabins with lead. All at once, the enemy knew they were in a fight and began shooting from the doors and windows in all directions as the forest around them exploded with noise. Catherine looked to the shallow slopes above but the Quartermaster told her it was fine. No chance of an avalanche in this neck of the woods. They could let the whole of Srendizi know they were here if they wanted to. Which, in fact, was precisely what they had set out to achieve.

A musket ball cracked past Catherine's left ear to make her duck. It sounded as though it had passed within an inch of her head but the Quartermaster, who hadn't flinched, assured her they could get a lot closer than that.

"It's the ones you don't hear that you want to worry about," he smiled.

Still, the fires burned and the fighting continued. A man ran from one of the cabins, his clothes smoking from the heat, but he didn't get more than a couple of steps before he pitched headfirst into the snow. Catherine expected him to start rolling around in an effort to put out his smouldering clothes but he didn't move and all at once the snows around him turned red. Catherine turned away, horrified at what she saw.

"You'd better get used to it. There'll be a lot more of that before this mornings out, young Calvin" the Quartermaster told her. "You're in the army now."

A new noise caught Catherine's attention. It was the sound of horses whinnying in fright. She looked out from her vantage point and saw a large wooden stable set back from the burning cabins. The sounds of musket fire had obviously startled the horses inside and now they were trapped and panicking as all hell broke loose.

"You boy!" the Lieutenant shouted but it took Catherine a few moments to realise he was talking to her. "Come here now."

Catherine hurried over to the Lieutenant, keeping low to avoid the scattergun fire cracking all around her. She almost fell on top of him as she stumbled the last few steps, landing at the feet of the man who'd had her flogged her some three months earlier.

Not a flicker of recognition registered in his

expression. She was nothing to him. Just another pawn on his board. And he was only too happy to sacrifice her.

"Reporting for duty, sir," she said with a salute, just as the Sergeant had taught her to do.

"Take this message to first squad and be quick about it," he snapped, handing her a slip of paper with the Sergeant's name scribbled on it.

"Yes sir," she said, taking the message and stuffing it into her tunic.

She hurried away as quickly as possible, keen to give the Lieutenant as little time as possible to linger on her face, and skirted along the line, past men crouched in the trees firing and reloading as far as the eye could see. The noise was relentless and in amongst the musket fire were the sounds of shouted orders.

A young rifleman lay on his back gasping for breath. Catherine recognised him but didn't know his name. He'd been shot in the shoulder and looked too startled to register the pain. Catherine looked around but no one else seemed to see him. She knew she had to go but she lingered just long enough to pull one of the bandages from her kit bag, stuffed it into his tunic and tied it in place.

"I'll be back," she promised him, hurrying on with the Lieutenant's message burning a hole in her pocket.

First Squad were on the right flank and the Sergeant was at the fore. The gunfire increased in intensity the nearer Catherine drew to the front line until eventually, her only option was to crawl on all fours.

"Where the blazes are you going?" Corporal Jacques barked at Catherine as she squirmed past the tree he was hunkered behind reloading.

"To see the Sergeant," she replied, now soaking wet and frozen to the skin as the Corporal lobbed a shot in the enemy's direction.

"Well, tell him from me he's a horse's ass!"

"Will do," Catherine promised, now the carrier of two important messages.

Besides musket balls and general cordiality, the air was thick with smoke. The cabins were now ablaze and the acrid stench of cordite filled the forest with no breeze to blow it away. Catherine looked around but visibility was down to just a few metres. She couldn't see the Sergeant but she knew he was close.

"Sergeant!" she called.

"Over here!" a reply came back.

Catherine slithered the rest of the way until she found herself at the Sergeant's boots. He was taking cover behind a thick pine tree and picking the enemy off one-by-one as they tried to make a run for it. No need to risk a frontal assault. The fire was their ally and only too happy to do their work for them.

"Message from the Lieutenant," Catherine said, holding out the damp and crinkled piece of paper for the Sergeant. He took it, carefully unpeeled it and frowned at what was written inside.

"Damn it!" he said, screwing up the message and throwing it aside.

"What's the matter?" Catherine asked.

"Never you mind," the Sergeant replied tersely, jerking his head back as pine bark splintered just a hair's breadth from where he'd been peering out.

"Hey, I just risked my life to bring you that message. The least you can do is tell me what was written inside."

The Sergeant looked down at Catherine as she lay shivering by his feet, hugging the ground and trying to squeeze in behind the same tree as death cracked past in all directions.

"We've run out of apple strudel. I need to amend my lunch order," he said with a glower. "Happy now?"

Not entirely, was Catherine's first thought but she didn't

get a chance to express it because at that moment there came a desperate crashing from the direction of the enemy camp. The fires had spread to the nearby hayloft and the horses were hammering against the doors in a desperate attempt to escape the approaching flames.

"The horses!" Catherine said, looking out at the smoking stables as the doors and walls were kicked from the inside.

"There's nothing we can do for them," the Sergeant said, taking aim and letting off a shot before ducking to reload.

"But they'll die," Catherine implored.

"Better them than me," the Sergeant said, pouring powder into his barrel and dropping a musket ball in after it.

But Catherine couldn't leave it at that. The horses were innocent in all of this and about to suffer the worst of fates. The warring sides needed to realise this and call a truce so that someone could free them but if the Sergeant didn't care, what chance did Catherine have of convincing anyone else?

"Please," she tried again, hugging the Sergeant's pine tree as musket fire continued to rake the forests around them to shower her in bark splinters and pine needles.

"Get back to the Lieutenant before you get hurt," the Sergeant replied, taking a quick aim and knocking a musket from the shoulder of a fleeing bandit.

Incensed that the Sergeant was unwilling to help, Catherine lost all sense of self-preservation and resolved to free the horses herself. So when the next musket volley fizzed harmlessly by, she leapt out from behind her forest shelter, initially slipping on the wet snows to land flat on her face, then scrambled to her feet and ran hell for leather for the burning stable's doors.

"What the hell! Get back here!" the Sergeant called after her but Catherine was only going in one direction, much like the enemy's fire. The sight of a uniformed drummer boy sprinting across open ground was too generous a gift to refuse and a dozen muskets trailed her every step, firing one after the other to chalk up an easy kill.

But Catherine was small and quicker than most and proved frustratingly hard to bag. She was a bird on the wing and ran in zig-zags rather than straight lines, evading their shots and proving impossible to predict. More than one shot skimmed her scalp but none could claim it outright as she ran through the eye of the storm and out the other side with only a few more scratches than she'd started with.

Musket balls whipped by with a crack and several kicked snow in her face but the Sergeant had been right about one thing; she was part of a family now and her hundred big and overly protective brothers found a renewed accuracy with their own aims as the enemy popped up their heads from behind the parapet. The Sergeant knocked off two hats in quick succession to help Catherine on her way whilst the Lieutenant commented that at least someone under his command had balls, even if no one else did.

Catherine crashed into the stable doors at full pelt and almost knocked herself flat again. She grabbed onto the large wooden latch and after a little effort yanked it free to swing the doors back.

The horses bolted immediately, knocking the doors open and bowling Catherine over by way of a thank you. Several thundering hooves almost did what no musket ball had managed but Catherine curled up when she hit the ground and the horses leapt over her, out of the hell's fire and into the crisp air of salvation. Once free they didn't stop for anything; they swept from the camp in an indignant fury and stampeded through the lines without looking back. A couple of Guardsmen attempted to stop them but they just ended up rolling in the snow as Catherine had.

The musket fire crackled to a halt with the departure of the horses. The enemy realised that their last hopes had bolted with their rides and to fight on was futile. Several muskets were tossed from the windows and men appeared in the smoking doorway with their hands raised. Mercy was as good as they could expect.

The Sergeant was relieved. Some foes preferred to fight on to the bitter end rather than let themselves be taken, which wouldn't have pleased the Lieutenant at all. His earlier message, the one that Catherine had run the gauntlet to deliver, had been abridged into a single angry word:

"PRISONERS!!!"

Always a challenge when facing someone from the death or dishonour school of warfare. But Catherine's actions had taken the wind out of the enemy's sails and spared further casualties. On either side. First Squad broke cover and moved in to take the surrender while the Lieutenant hurried down to grab the glory.

The Sergeant allowed himself a moment of pride in his young protege before marching across the camp to where she still lay, battered and bruised, to tear several strips from her.

"What the hell do you think you're playing at? This isn't a game. You could've got yourself killed for the sake of a few mangy horses or, worse still, let the enemy grab you and use you as leverage. This is the army, not the bloody orphanage, and there's a way to do things and a way not to do things and THAT WAS NOT HOW WE DO THINGS! Do you hear me?"

Catherine, on balance, preferred the horses' reaction. At least it had been one she could understand. But rather than take the Sergeant on and risk further reproach she resolved to take it on the chin and stick to her duties for the rest of the campaign.

"Well, what have you got to say for yourself, Private?" the Sergeant demanded of Catherine.

Catherine picked herself up and winced in pain as she stood to attention.

"There was a second message, Sergeant. From Corporal Jacques," she said.

"Oh yes? And what did it say?" he asked.

This message, unlike the Lieutenant's, contained four words rather than just the one and Catherine was happy to deliver it in its entirety.

CHAPTER TWENTY-SIX

MOTHER CUT AND DRAINED Gardenia's swollen forearm where she lay. Speed was of the essence and there simply wasn't enough time to get her upstairs and comfortable just for propriety's sake. The serpent's poison was winding its way through her veins and taking Gardenia's life with it inch by inch.

Marigold was distraught. How could lightning strike twice in the space of as many months? It beggared belief and shook her faith in a benign Almighty.

"Milk and honey," one of the Beaufort's gardeners was saying whilst another insisted on applying strong vinegar and garlic to the afflicted area. These country labourers knew about bites and each had their own homespun remedies but none had the sort of firsthand experience of Mother. She took charge of the situation and began making preparations to administer her own antivenom whilst her new husband, the ignoble Monsieur Beaufort, stood at the back looking ashen-faced at the drama unfolding before him.

"Get me a clean bottle and a syringe of some kind. And a strap. Also a sharp knife and a bowl and some boiling water, and make sure it's boiling," Mother demanded, adding: "MOVE YOURSELF!" when the Beaufort's staff tried to furnish her with questions rather than equipment. Mother now turned to her eldest daughter. "Marigold! Marigold darling!"

It took Marigold a few seconds to shake out of her daze but eventually, she looked up.

"What?" she asked, too numb to answer with etiquette.

"What would you do to save your sister?"

Marigold didn't understand the question and failed to answer.

"Tell me now. What would you be willing to do?"

Mother repeated.

"Anything," Marigold replied, ready to give all that she had but unable to understand how she could help when more experienced hands couldn't. But Mother spared her the details and instead turned to her husband and told him to run and fetch his most medicinal brandy.

"Of course," he croaked, glad to finally have a role to play and hurrying away to do the one thing he had any experience in.

"Please Mother, don't let her die," Marigold cried, holding her sister's hand as tightly as she could, unwilling to let it go.

"I will try my utmost Marigold but I need your help. You can save your sister but you must trust me," Mother said in an attempt to prepare her for what was to come.

"Of course, Mother. I'll do anything, anything at all," Marigold promised. "But how?"

Mother took a deep breath and embraced her eldest daughter. "By being stronger than you've ever been before."

Monsieur Beaufort returned with a suitably dusty bottle of brandy followed soon after by his staff, bringing with them the provisions Mother had dispatched them to find.

"Drink this," she told Marigold, handing her a glass of brandy that would've given the old General pause for thought. Marigold gagged at her first taste of brandy and she didn't much care for her second either. "All of it. Quickly. Time is slipping away from us." The spirit burnt the back of her throat and wracked her stomach with aches but she managed to drain the whole lot only to find the glass immediately refilled. "Go on," Mother urged her.

Several of the Beaufort's staff cast each other curious looks but no one said anything. Mother seemed to know what she was doing even if nobody else did.

By the time Marigold emptied her second glass her tummy had stopped turning only for the basement to start.

"I don't feel at all well," she said, feeling the sudden urge to lie down on the cold hard flagstones next to her sister.

"Give me the strap," Mother demanded, tearing Marigold's sleeve open and loosely fixing the strap to her upper arm.

"What's that for?" Marigold asked, looking at Mother and then the sea of quizzical faces that surrounded her. The only face absent was Ella's. It could've been argued that this was no place for a lady but then again it could've been equally argued that the only two people actually doing anything were both ladies, one through attending to Gardenia's wounds, the other by getting pie-faced.

Mother used some of the remaining alcohol to wipe down Marigold's arm and the other pieces of equipment and then looked her in the eye.

"Now hold still," Mother advised her, "because this is going to hurt a lot."

Mother wasn't in the habit of lying to her daughters and she hadn't started now. Marigold felt the knife before she saw it. A sharp relentless pain pressed into her soft skin and cut a crease along her slender forearm. Marigold yelped and tried to pull her arm away but she was held fast by two burly gardeners.

"Keep her still!" Mother demanded and the gardeners piled on the pressure forcing Marigold to endure the worst agony she'd ever known, certainly since the last time she had been bitten. But it hadn't been her who'd been bitten this time. Why was Mother doing this?

"Stop!" she pleaded and at last Mother complied, but only because she'd finished what she needed to do. She set down the knife and placed the sterilised bowl beneath Marigold's arm to catch the trickling blood. It flowed out quickly and soon filled the shallow bowl. When she had all that she needed Mother tightened the strap and covered Marigold's wound in clean bandages, instructing her to keep her arm bent until the bleeding had stopped.

Marigold was still none the wiser how this could help her sister but she watched as Mother now took the syringe, which had been soaking in the boiling water, held the needle to the bowl and pulled back the plunger to suck up the blood.

"Now hold Gardenia still," she told the gardeners and they switched their attention from Marigold to her sister despite her being near devoid of life.

Mother took the syringe and pushed it into Gardenia's wound. Gardenia jerked but the Beaufort's men held her fast while Mother pumped one sister's blood directly into the other.

Once she was done she removed the syringe and bandaged the wound.

"Now, only time will tell," she solemnly declared.

Gardenia was moved upstairs and put to rest in her own bed. Mother and Marigold watched over her, sometimes together and sometimes taking it in turns so that the other could grab some food and rest. It was unnerving for Marigold to see this same ordeal from the other side. Until this moment, she'd had no idea what her sister and Mother must've been through during her own dance with death. And for Mother to endure it twice? What a terrible toll it must have taken on her.

Marigold took her father's medal and pinned it to Gardenia's nightgown. He'd been there for Marigold when she had needed him most. Now his intervention was called upon again.

"He watches over you now, sister," Marigold whispered, giving Gardenia a little kiss on her forehead.

*

LATE THE FOLLOWING EVENING, while Mother was sitting up with Gardenia, Marigold went to the kitchen to fetch some soup that had been left out on the stove for them. They'd not taken their meals with Father or Ella, nor had they been expected to do so. Consequently, Marigold had seen precious little of her stepsister since Gardenia had been taken ill. But suddenly there she was, waiting for her at the foot of the stairs when Marigold emerged from the kitchen with a small tray of supper.

"Oh my dear Marigold, you shouldn't be carrying that. We have people for that sort of thing." This was the first thing to come to Ella's mind.

Marigold was tempted to show Ella what she thought about that but she was loathed to waste two bowls of perfectly good soup. Instead, she merely smiled and thanked her for her concern, adding, "Please don't let me keep you up."

"Oh, but I can't sleep knowing that our dear sister's life hangs in the balance. I was up all last night with worry and had no one to turn to," Ella fretted, looking as fresh as a daisy all things considered.

"We are each of us alone with our grief," Marigold replied, taking to the stairs but getting no further than the first step before she felt Ella at her elbow again.

"We do not have to be, sweet sister. I am here for you," she promised, holding onto her arm to ensure she remained so for as long as possible, whether Marigold liked it or not.

The normally bustling house was dark and quiet. All the servants had turned in for the night and Monsieur Beaufort had gone into town so there was no one left in this part of the house to overhear their exchange. Marigold wondered if Ella had planned this on purpose, for this very reason, then wondered if that sounded paranoid.

"Thank you... Ella, you are most kind. And I know where to find you should I wish to speak to someone," Marigold said, dislodging her arm from Ella's clutches to head upstairs.

Ella came with her every step of the way, unwilling to relinquish their precious moment together.

"It is as though fate has brought us here," she declared in wonder. "That I should be with you in your hour of need. And that, should the unthinkable happen, God be praised that it doesn't, I would be honoured if you would think of me as you do Gardenia."

Marigold stopped for one moment to think of her sister lying upstairs burning with fever and at death's door and agreed she would be happy to think of Ella this way.

"Now, if you'll forgive me, I must get back to Mother," Marigold said, hurrying up the last few steps and on to her bedroom where she knew Ella wouldn't venture.

"I will remember Gardenia in my prayers," Ella called after her. "And Father has gone to the Palace to inform the Prince. He will no doubt wish to hear of Gardenia's condition."

Marigold didn't reply or look back. She simply headed into the bedroom and pushed the door behind her, relieved to be away from one 'sister' and back with the other. Mother was asleep in her chair, her head rested on Gardenia's bed. Fatigue had caught up with her and Marigold made as little noise as possible so as not to disturb her.

Marigold sipped her soup and nibbled her bread but she tasted neither, her mind was too preoccupied with Ella's words. She had spoken as though Gardenia was already dead, readily volunteering to fill the void in Marigold's heart as though this could be filled as easily as hiring a new housemaid.

"It is as though fate has brought us here..." she had said. Marigold's toes curled at the thought.

Of course, some people are naturally inept at dishing out sympathy and few things freeze the brain more than death and disaster. At the old King's funeral some thirty years ago, the new town Burgermeister had apparently tried to console his young son by telling him that his father had been a "great King, the likes of which we will not see again in our lifetime" before realising he was talking to the new King. Needless to say, that was the last official act the town Burgermeister carried out and thirty years later he'd become known to most simply as Didi — or *Dirty Didi*, to give him his full name.

But Ella wasn't one of these people, at least not in Marigold's assessment. She was sharp. Razor-sharp at times. And beautiful. And rich. What more could any girl wish for?

What more indeed?

*

MARIGOLD WASN'T SURE what time it was when she awoke but it was either very late or very early. The candle by Gardenia's bed had burned out and when she lit a new one she found her mother and sister sleeping peacefully together. Mother must have been exhausted. Marigold too was worn through but something had woken her. She listened carefully but there were no sounds.

She opened the bedroom door and hung her head out onto the landing. The house was draped in shadows and deathly quiet but for the distant echo of faraway voices.

"… … … far enough …"

"… … … do it or else …"

The words came in waves, muffled by a howling gale and any number of walls they were having to pass through.

Marigold crept along the hallway scarcely breathing so that she might make out the voices. She listened at the top of the stairs but the voices didn't seem to be coming from below.

"… … … in too deep now …"

"… … … get us both hanged …"

And they were too far away to be coming from one of the bedrooms on this floor, which left only one other place.

Ella's cold and draughty attic bedroom.

Marigold tiptoed along the hallway until she reached the attic door. It was closed but on turning the door handle she found for once that it wasn't locked. Beyond the door was a winding staircase that led up the attic room in the easternmost turret.

The voices became clearer the moment she opened the door and she thought she recognised them. One was clearly Ella while the other was Monsieur Beaufort. The subtext also became clear. An argument was taking place but about what, Marigold couldn't make out. Either way, she was staggered to hear an eighteen-year-old girl talking to her father as she was.

"… important information and we must leave nothing to chance."

"… never agreed to this …"

"… you knew what you were getting into …"

This exchange was followed by some inaudible mutterings bordering on pleading.

"… … then perhaps you should tell him yourself?"

CREAK!

The creak came from Marigold. Or rather the step she had just stood on. She had climbed half a dozen steps in order to hear what Ella and her father were saying but suddenly they weren't saying anything. The attic had fallen silent.

As quickly and as quietly as she could, Marigold hurried back the way she'd come, down the stairs, through the doorway at the bottom, along the hallway and into her bedroom, making it with just moments to spare.

She closed the door behind her and put an eye to the keyhole. Sure enough, several seconds later, someone passed by on the other side. Marigold could see nothing more than shadows and shapes out there but when her view turned black she knew that whoever was roaming the hall had stopped right outside her door. The handle began to turn and the door inched open.

Slowly and silently, someone now peered in.

Marigold didn't see who it was because she had jumped into the chair next to Gardenia and was now feigning sleep.

The prowler studied the three women, looking for any signs of movement but none of them stirred and Marigold herself barely breathed.

Marigold waited and waited and eventually heard the click as the door closed. She waited further still, eventually daring to open one eye.

Whoever had checked on them was gone and hopefully none the wiser. Marigold breathed a sigh of relief and then looked to her Mother and sister, still blissfully asleep. Only then did she notice the telltale candle next to Gardenia's bedside; standing tall and burning brightly, having clearly only been lit a few minutes earlier.

CHAPTER TWENTY-SEVEN

AFTER THE FIGHTING WAS DONE and the enemy had surrendered, the King's Guards counted seven bandits killed and thirteen prisoners taken for only two of their own wounded, neither mortally.

The prisoners looked wretched in defeat: black and blue, tired and frightened. What fate awaited them? Each man could only imagine. On the other hand, the Lieutenant was ecstatic. It had been a textbook operation, which was where he'd learned how to command his troops.

Mission accomplished, the enemy camp would now be razed to the ground and the prisoners marched back to Andovia, where they would be put on trial and punished for what they had done to the Rousseau family.

The King's Guards would get a new battle honour to inscribe into their annals; the Major would get a new ribbon, the Captain a new medal and the Lieutenant a new pip, while the troops who'd done the actual fighting would get an extra schilling in their pay packets at the end of the month; a token of appreciation from their glorious King, which they would be expected to spend in one of the King's own hostelries whilst toasting his honour.

Catherine Petit walked along a line of prisoners who sat in the snow before her and studied them carefully. Some were young and some were old. Some were big and some were small. Some were fair and some were... well, frankly not, but none were the bogeymen of folklore that supposedly prowled the black forests of Srendizi. Most simply looked lost, humbled and humiliated. Well almost.

"Boo!" one of the grizzled prisoners snapped, making Catherine jump in surprise. A couple of his cohorts snorted at her expense but all that changed when the Sergeant approached.

"Don't worry," the Sergeant told Catherine, helping her to her feet. "Watch this." He turned to the prisoner who'd startled Catherine and ordered him to: "Try that again".

The prisoner scowled but refused to play along so the Sergeant instructed the rifleman nearest to shoot him for failing to comply. The prisoner panicked and blurted out "Boo" again but it was a hollow echo of his first effort and Catherine didn't even flinch.

"One *Boo* and he's all used up," the Sergeant said. "Now you say it."

"What?" Catherine said.

"Say *Boo*. To him," the Sergeant told her.

Catherine looked at the prisoner and quietly said "Boo". The prisoner didn't baulk but he looked genuinely frightened nevertheless and Catherine realised the Sergeant was right; she had nothing to fear from this man while he had everything to fear from her. And with good reason too.

As if to further prove the Sergeant's point, the Lieutenant suddenly ordered one of the prisoners out of the line. The prisoner refused at first, keeping his head low and gesturing that he didn't speak the language, so the Lieutenant had a couple of his men drag him out and haul him to his feet. The prisoner was old beyond his years, with hollowed-out eyes and a long shaggy beard. He looked like an archetypal Srendizian outlaw and Catherine didn't hold out much expectation when the Lieutenant told him to, "Stand to attention!"

But much to Catherine's surprise, the prisoner obeyed, albeit reluctantly, bringing his heels together and standing daffodil straight, if not quite ramrod.

"I always wondered if our paths would ever cross again, Private Xavier. How happy I am that they have."

"Sir, honest, I didn't do…"

"SILENCE!" the Lieutenant barked. "I will not tolerate any lies from the likes of you. You are a deserter and a thief and you shall not slip justice a moment longer."

The Lieutenant turned to the Quartermaster and demanded he fetched up a length of rope. In her naivety, Catherine imagined the Lieutenant was planning on tying Private Xavier up to prevent him from escaping. But Private Xavier's race was now run. And in this snowy corner of Srendizi, he would remain forever.

"No, please..." he pleaded, dropping to his knees when he saw the Quartermaster return. He handed the rope to a young fearsome-looking soldier with a hideous scar, by the name of Corporal Samuel, who slung one end of it up into a skeletal tree and then looped the other around its trunk.

"The prisoner will stand to attention," the Lieutenant demanded, instructing Private Xavier to be hauled to his feet when it became clear he was unwilling or unable to do so under his own steam. The Lieutenant glared contemptuously at the blackguard he saw before him. It was a look Catherine knew only too well. "Private Xavier, I find you guilty of desertion whilst in service of the King, theft of government property and collusion with the enemy. And by the powers divested in me, I hereby sentence you to death. Sentence to be carried out immediately."

"No!" Private Xavier hollered but it was no use. A clutch of burly riflemen dragged him through the cold snows and tied his hands behind his back.

"Let me go! Let me go or I'll kill you! I'll kill the lot of you," Private Xavier ranted despite posing less of a threat to them than the prisoner who liked to say *"Boo"*.

And now the Lieutenant had that oh so familiar look in his eye and this time he wasn't to be denied.

"Drummer boy?" he barked, but Catherine failed to register he was talking to her, too mesmerised was she by what she was about to witness. "DRUMMER BOY!"

This time she did hear the Lieutenant and hurried over to his side to snap to a crisp salute. Today wasn't the day to get on the wrong side of the Lieutenant. Was there ever?

"Sir?"

"Drum roll," he ordered, as Private Xavier was heaved atop a wooden crate, still struggling every inch of the way.

Catherine panicked. She didn't have her drum with her and had to run back to the rear to go and retrieve it which gave Private Xavier time to rethink his defence strategy.

"Wait, you can't do this! I didn't desert. I'm on a secret mission for the General. Please ask him. I know where Grimaldi is! I know where his hideout is!"

Catherine found her drum on the other side of the camp. She slipped the strap over her head just as Private Xavier was having a noose slipped over his and ran back to rejoin the fray.

"Has the condemned any last words?" the Lieutenant asked, holding out a hand to silence Catherine before she could start drumming.

Private Xavier did but little of it went beyond what he'd already spent the last two minutes pleading. "I didn't do nothing… I tried to stop them… I can give you Grimaldi… Let me go and I can make you all rich…" etc.

Corporal Samuel, who Catherine later learned was the designated company executioner, pull on the rope to take up the slack and tied off the other end with a hitch. The Lieutenant now instructed Catherine to begin her drum roll and Catherine duly began to play as though her own life depended upon it.

Private Xavier yelped like a stricken animal as a sack was placed over his head to obscure his view on the world for the final time. The Lieutenant gestured for Catherine's drum roll to end but Catherine couldn't stop playing. The Lieutenant gestured again but still she couldn't stop because she knew the moment she did, Corporal Samuel would kick the crate away and Private Xavier would drop to his death. In essence, the poor man's life was in her hands. Her drum roll kept on rolling, faster and faster as the tears rolled down her cheeks. The Lieutenant turned to glare at her in a fury for ruining his carefully choreographed execution and even Private Xavier looked at her from inside his flour sack, surprised to find himself still on the side of the living but Catherine continued to play.

"Drummer boy!" the Lieutenant barked. "Desist!"

But she couldn't, her sticks simply wouldn't stop rolling and Private Xavier's final waltz would've no doubt continued late into the night had the Sergeant not grabbed them from her to signal Corporal Samuel to do his duty.

The crate was kicked out and the rope snapped tight. Catherine looked away, fearful at what she might see but the Lieutenant demanded she bore witness.

"Eyes front!" he yelled, determined that Private Xavier's example should not go to waste. This was what happened to deserters, turncoats and thieves. Private Xavier might have once marched with the King's Guards and even carried the regimental colours on campaign. He might have seen action at Cedar Hill and Petites Collines and counted many of the men present as friends, including Corporal Samuel, whose life he had saved at Petites Collines. But the moment he had slipped the wire in the dead of night last October, taking with him half a dozen maps and a crate full of muskets, none of that counted for anything. He was a traitor and a Judas. And as such, destined to share that treacherous disciple's fate.

Despite all of this, Catherine couldn't look. She stared at the snows beyond Private Xavier's feet and when they, at last, stopped twitching, the Lieutenant murmured with approval.

"Should I cut him down now, sir?" Corporal Samuel asked.

"No, leave him for the wolves. They need to eat too," was the Lieutenant's considered judgement before delivering another. He lashed Catherine in the face with the back of his hand when she was least expecting it to send her sprawling in the dirty, wet snow.

"And the next time you think of disobeying an order, drummer boy, I'll have you dance a jig of your own, just like Private Xavier here. No coin for this one, Quartermaster." And with that he strode away to oversee the finer points of his triumphant return to Andovia, leaving Catherine to spill blood for her country, whilst lying facedown in another.

And not for the last time either.

CHAPTER TWENTY-EIGHT

JUST LIKE MARIGOLD, Gardenia opened her eyes on the morning of the third day, dazed but responsive. It took another hour or so before she found her voice but when she did she uttered one single word.

"Snap."

The tears of relief spilled down Marigold's cheeks as she hugged her sister and refused to let go until Gardenia's pillow was wet through.

"Snap," Marigold finally replied, unable to stop crying and laughing and doing neither particularly well. Mother checked Gardenia's pulse and smiled without saying anything more. The worst had passed and she had come through the longest of nights.

Father's medal had worked its magic again. Gardenia unpinned it and returned it to Mother but Mother insisted it was theirs now, he would want his daughters to have it, so Marigold took it for safekeeping, reluctant to leave something so precious lying around with Ella wandering the house.

Monsieur Beaufort heard Marigold's cries of joy from the other end of the château and sprinted along the corridors and up the stairs to investigate, followed hard on his heels by Ella. Neither could mask their astonishment at the sight of Gardenia sitting up in bed, seemingly back from the dead and looking happy again. Ella quickly remembered herself and found a big smile before launching into an overly gushing eulogy in Gardenia's honour.

"Sweet sister, the heavens be praised, it is a miracle. Our prayers have been answered and the demon snake smote. The Good Lord has seen fit to deliver you back into our hands," Ella said, causing Monsieur Beaufort to glance in her direction, as though this might not necessarily have been the most prudent thing to do.

"I too am much relieved for your safe return, dear daughter. It is truly a miracle," Monsieur Beaufort agreed, stepping forward to reveal an expression not only etched with relief but also shaded with fear.

"The heavens be praised indeed," Mother echoed, "but the Good Lord had nothing to do with Gardenia's deliverance. That was all Marigold."

Ella looked confused.

"You heard, presumably, of Marigold's similar experience some months ago?"

"Two sisters, both of whom fell foul of serpents? It's as though a curse lingered over them," Ella said, sounding like someone with a hankering to start just such a rumour.

"Indeed, and yet it turned out to be more of a blessing," Mother said to Ella's confusion. "What doesn't kill you only makes you stronger, or so they say, which in the case of certain venoms is true. Marigold survived, for whatever reason, perhaps because she was bitten by a juvenile animal or perhaps because it failed to strike her properly but in doing so, her body created its own medicine. Without this, Gardenia would have surely died."

Monsieur Beaufort remembered the procedure that Mother had carried out in the cellar and suddenly, it all made sense.

"Marigold's blood was Gardenia's salvation," he said in wonder.

Marigold and Gardenia regarded each other lovingly and could barely bring themselves to look away, two sisters now closer than ever.

"Then, if that is not a miracle," Monsieur Beaufort surmised, "I don't know what is."

Ella went to great lengths to agree.

"We are so very lucky," she said with an unconstrained smile of happiness.

"Yes," Marigold replied with a smile of her own,

though one not so boundless. "Aren't *we*."

Monsieur Beaufort made his excuses and withdrew, sensing the sisters' desire for privacy, but Ella was either oblivious or indifferent to the room temperature and stayed for another hour, chattering away at them almost non-stop until Gardenia passed out through sheer exhaustion.

"I think we'd better leave her to rest," Mother suggested, ushering Ella from the room before she put them all on their backs.

Once Ella was gone, Gardenia woke again and Marigold finally got the chance to ask her what had happened. Gardenia was hazy on some of the details but clear on one thing; the snake had been hiding in Ella's trunk of shawls, hence the reason she'd been bitten on the forearm.

"It must've snuck in there to hibernate," Gardenia reasoned.

"And how did it get in the trunk in the first place?" Marigold asked. "Was the lid already open when you got there?"

Gardenia couldn't remember but Marigold couldn't believe it was.

"Who leaves the lid of a linen trunk open in a damp and dirty cellar?" she said.

"What are you suggesting? That someone put the snake in there on purpose?" Mother asked. It sounded mad, paranoid even, and Marigold had no proof to back up her suspicions, just a growing sense of unease.

"I don't know what I'm suggesting," Marigold said, reluctant to speak ill of Ella or Monsieur Beaufort for fear of incurring Mother's wrath. "It just seems odd, that's all."

Mother considered this point and much to Marigold's surprise, agreed, it did indeed seem odd. Mother tip-toed to the door and looked out onto the landing to make sure no eavesdroppers were lingering at the keyhole, before returning to Gardenia's bedside.

"Trust your instincts," she told her daughters, "but keep your own counsel. Do not do or say anything to alert Monsieur Beaufort or his daughter to your misgivings."

"In case we are wrong?" Gardenia asked.

"No child," Mother said with a look of concern. "In case you are right."

Mother admitted to finding Ella a trifle overbearing but hadn't noticed anything sinister in her before now. Monsieur Beaufort neither. He was aloof and uptight but no more than any other aristocrat she'd ever met. Under normal circumstances, Mother might have dismissed her daughters' suspicions as nothing more than step-sibling rivalries, the likes of which second marriages were prone to. But these were not normal circumstances, as Gardenia's lily-white pallor could testify. However improbable it might have sounded, Mother could not be sure that Marigold wasn't right. And until her fears were allayed, nothing short of constant vigilance would do.

"After all, do we really know what happened to Monsieur Beaufort's first wife?" Mother speculated.

The three women resolved not to let Ella or her father get too close or stray too far until they'd established how that snake had come to be in the trunk but almost immediately they failed in their second task. Just hours after Gardenia had regained consciousness, Monsieur Beaufort began packing to leave. He claimed he was needed in France on urgent business and promised to come back as soon as possible but Ella refused to let him go, almost as though she knew he had no intention of returning.

"No Father, you can't go. Remember your oath to Mother, that you would never leave me," she said, all but dragging him out of the saddle as he attempted to climb onto his horse.

"It is only for a few short weeks, Ella darling," he insisted. "And I will be back before you know it."

"But I need you," she insisted, taking the reins from the stable boy and holding onto them to prevent him from departing.

"Look to your new mother while I am away. She will take care of you," he said, peeling her fingers from the reins.

Mother and Ella's stepsisters watched from the front steps as Ella made a scene. It seemed like she had about as much desire to be left alone with her new family as they with her and any pretence to the contrary was forgotten.

"Winter is coming. The roads will soon be impassable," she said.

"That is why I must go now," Monsieur Beaufort replied, half-tempted to use his boot to get on his way before thinking better of it. "Please Ella, you must let me go."

"Some harm may come to you," she warned, which sounded more like a threat than a premonition and Marigold wondered just how many snakes Ella had at her disposal.

"I shall bring you back a present, my sweet child. Anything you desire," Monsieur Beaufort promised, finally yanking his reins free and thundering away before she could tell him what that might be. "Bye. I love you," he cried over his shoulder without looking back, either at Ella or his new family.

Ella watched Father disappear with a scowl before turning to glare at Mother, Marigold and Gardenia, each watching her with a bemused smile on the front doorsteps. They seemed far happier about Monsieur Beaufort's departure than she did. And why not? For their part, this was a marriage of convenience, nothing more. Mother had married Monsieur Beaufort to get out of a bind — and a bind of his making at that — and give her daughters a second chance. She needed only his money and his title for that. Monsieur Beaufort was surplus to requirements. This may have seemed a little mercenary but the incident with the barley snake had unsettled Mother and she felt safer with her new husband out of the way. If only for a time.

"Would you care to join us in the library?" Mother asked. "We thought we might recite a little poetry this afternoon."

Ella didn't answer. She simply stormed into the house without a word, hurrying to her attic room and locking herself away for the rest of the day. Mother raised an eyebrow and the sisters smiled. For a few short weeks, the château would be all theirs.

CHAPTER TWENTY-NINE

AS THINGS TURNED OUT, Ella had been right to worry about her father's trip. Captain Olivier arrived at the château two days later with his hat in his hands and a face full of sympathy.

"I regret to inform you, Madame Beaufort, that your husband has befallen a misfortune," he told her in the quiet privacy of the drawing-room. It was an odd turn of phrase, particularly considering that the misfortune in question had been a sword to the head just two miles short of the border.

"Neither his horse nor his personal belongings were found alongside him. We can therefore only conclude that Monsieur Beaufort was accosted by... outlaws."

Mother noticed Captain Olivier's deliberate avoidance of the word "bandits", perhaps because this word was associated with one bandit in particular. A bandit with whom they'd had prior dealings.

"I see," Mother replied, staggered at just how accurate Ella's premonition had been but trying hard not to show it. *Some harm may come to you*, Ella had warned her father and she'd been right. Had she genuinely foreseen his death or had she simply done what all girls do when their loved ones embark on a long journey? Only Ella would know.

"On behalf of the King, my father the Grand Duke, and the people of Andovia, I offer you my deepest sympathies," Captain Olivier said formally, as though this was all that was required of him. But Mother was not about to let him off the hook that easily.

"What do you intend to do about it, Captain? Have you mobilised your men? Have your scouts picked up these outlaws' tracks?" Mother asked, sensing an opportunity to clear her name and that of her daughters at the hands of her arch-accuser.

"We have conducted a search of the area, Madame, but the perpetrators were long gone by the time we arrived," Captain Olivier said with an impotent shake of the head.

"Then I suggest you go after them. Ride into Srendizi and root them out in their own backyards," Mother said, having had some experience of this sort of thing in her earlier days.

"Srendizi?" Captain Olivier said in surprise. "Why on Earth should we ride into Srendizi?"

"Because that is where you will find Franz Grimaldi," Mother said, equally surprised by Captain Olivier's reaction.

"Monsieur Beaufort was not found anywhere near to Srendizi. He was ambushed fifty miles south, just short of the border with Genoa."

Genoa? But Monsieur Beaufort had said he was returning to France? Genoa was in the opposite direction. Where was he going? And why would he lie?

"I seriously doubt we would find Franz Grimaldi anywhere near the Genoese border. That is too far from home for his liking," the Captain said.

"I seem to recall you claiming something similar last month and yet here we are," Mother scolded.

"Are you suggesting the two incidents are related?" Captain Olivier fizzed.

"Are you proposing they are not?" Mother replied.

Captain Olivier side-stepped that question and stuck to the script.

"We accompanied Monsieur *Le Chevalier* back to Andovia and brought him directly to the Viponds rather than bring him here. I hope that was agreeable to you. And might I suggest that you opt for a closed casket, if only to spare his young daughter the ordeal of seeing her father…" Captain Olivier thought for a moment, choosing his words carefully. "… not at his best."

Mother understood. She'd seen first hand the sort of

damage a sword could do and this wasn't the way Monsieur Beaufort would have wanted to be remembered, particularly not by Ella, whom Mother would have the difficult duty of informing once the Captain had left.

Captain Olivier clicked his heels and bowed with as little accord as possible in order to precipitate his leave. It didn't sit right with him that this woman and her daughters were set to inherit everything from the late Monsieur *Le Chevalier* after all that had gone before. It seemed a little too... convenient. Marriage might have wiped Madame Roche's slate clean in most eyes but not the Captain's. He knew what sort of people the Roches... or rather the *Beauforts* as they were now called — were. They were weeds; invasive and ingratiating creepers who grew where they weren't supposed to and came back stronger each time you cut them away.

But were they assassins too?

The Captain decided to keep any misgivings to himself. It was dangerous to speculate without proof, especially since the Prince had shown such favours towards the younger girl. And his own father, the Grand Duke, had made it clear that both she and her sister were beyond reproach. A commoner? Beyond reproach? For that was how Captain Olivier still saw them. Three weeks of marriage did not a noblewoman make. So the Captain decided to keep a close eye on the Roches from now on, if only as a duty to watch over Monsieur *Le Chevalier*'s true daughter, whose wellbeing was now his first concern. There was something he didn't like about the other two. He couldn't put his finger on what but they just weren't as goodly as their stepsister. Any fool could see that.

"Madame Beaufort, fair day to you," he said, turning his back and only too pleased to show himself out.

He passed Marigold and Gardenia in the hallway but didn't acknowledge either despite their formal curtsy. It was only when he encountered Ella at the front door, coming in from the garden with a basket of wildflowers, that he stopped to extend his most heartfelt respects.

"Mademoiselle, I am your humble servant. You must call upon me day or night for whatever reason. My men and I are at your service."

Gardenia, suspended in mid-curtsey, whispered to Marigold: "He has eyes for Ella."

Marigold agreed. "He's welcome to her," she said, before finally lifting her eyes and unbending her legs when she heard the front door shut. Ella watched her stepsisters with a coy smile and curtseyed in reply to their unanswered curtsey but suddenly Mother was at the drawing-room door looking grave.

"Ella, would you step in here for a moment?" she beckoned.

"Of course, Mother," Ella replied, then noticed Mother's demeanour. "Is everything alright?"

"If you'll come with me, all will be explained," was all Mother would say.

Ella set her basket down by the front door and followed Mother into the drawing-room. The door closed behind her. And Marigold and Gardenia were left alone to wonder what message the Captain had brought.

*

MOTHER HAD SEEN MANY funerals in her time. Some were grandiose affairs, with psalms, eulogies, flowers and mourners while others were a hole in the ground in a forgotten corner of a foreign field, but it made little difference to the object of the exercise. They rarely complained and the trappings were entirely for the living.

Monsieur *Le Chevalier* Beaufort's funeral was an understated affair. He had known few people in Andovia so his funeral more or less mirrored his wedding with only Mother, their three daughters and a smattering of staff present to mourn him.

Ella cried, as to be expected, and Marigold and

Gardenia moved to comfort her by the graveside. She seemed so small and pathetic that their suspicions were soon forgotten at the sight of her anguish.

She held out a rose, with ruby red petals and a long straight stem, and dropped it into the hole on top of her father's casket.

"Goodbye…" she just about managed to croak through a veil of tears. She turned to Gardenia and accepted her warm embrace on a cold, dark day before burying her face into her shoulder and sobbing without restraint.

"Come, let us go home," Gardenia said, leading her away by the hand, just as Marigold did for her when she needed comforting.

Marigold may have previously doubted Ella's sincerity but she could not doubt her pain. She was a little girl lost in a land of long shadows. She had tried desperately to prevent her father from leaving and now he was never coming back. Where did she go from here? Whom did she turn to when the only other people in her life seemed to mistrust her? Despise her even?

It gave Marigold pause for thought and made her think of all the mistakes she had made in the past. As terrible a day as this was, perhaps it was also a day for new beginnings.

Marigold could not have known how right she was. Because on returning to the château, Mother began going though Monsieur Beaufort's papers, as was her right as his next of kin, only to discover a terrible truth.

And one that no person could have foreseen. Not even Ella.

*

"WHAT DO YOU MEAN he's broke?" Marigold said in disbelief.

"Exactly that. There is no money in his accounts and he has hardly any assets to his name. This house and a few pieces of furniture are all that he owned. The rest is leased.

And outstanding."

Mother had gathered Marigold, Gardenia and Ella into Monsieur Beaufort's office to give them the shocking news, that they weren't quite as wealthy as they had been led to believe. In fact, they were dirt poor again. And growing dirtier and poorer with every passing day thanks to Monsieur Beaufort's spectacularly reckless mismanagement of his accounts.

"It's going to be difficult but we are all going to have to make sacrifices if we are to avoid ruination," Mother said, noticing that Ella was wearing yet another new string of pearls to go with her wonderfully stylish funeral dress. Just how many jewels could one girl have? "I'm afraid that means all of us, Ella."

Ella sensed what Mother was getting at and unclipped her necklace with a heavy heart. It was a beautiful piece of jewellery but as Mother had said, they all need to make sacrifices.

"It's okay," she said magnanimously as she handed it over. "I've got plenty of others."

If they hadn't just attended her father's funeral Marigold might have laughed. Instead, she just looked away and chewed her lip while Gardenia wondered if Ella was serious. Mother decided not to pop Ella's bubble just yet and thanked her for her understanding.

"We'd better start on our outgoings."

The staff were the first to go. Most were aghast to discover that there was no money in the kitty with which to pay them but Mother saw that none left her service empty-handed. Ella's overflowing wardrobe came to the rescue, while those few bits of furniture that weren't leased were used to settle the accounts for the furniture that was. The portraits were removed and sold, the chandeliers sent back and the stables emptied of every animal but Liquorice. Even the urchins beyond the gates drifted away. They must've sensed that the party was over and the free hand-outs were gone. The Beauforts could barely afford to feed themselves all of a sudden, let alone anyone else. Mother's only hope was to pawn the ring Monsieur Beaufort had given her on the day of their wedding. She had no more use for it and, in its place, she wore her large opal ring instead; the one from her first marriage. And with that small gesture, it was as though Monsieur Beaufort had never existed at all. Almost, but not quite.

For when all was said and done, the old château stood empty but for the odd table and chair and a lumpy bed for each. But this was still more than the sisters had had when they'd been living in a hovel outside the city gates with mud for a garden and a reputation to match. Now they had a new home, a new name and a new start.

And a new sister to boot.

CHAPTER THIRTY

NOW THAT ELLA NO LONGER had "people to do that for her" she found herself more lost than ever. Until now, she had barely known where the kitchen was, let alone her way around it, something Marigold and Gardenia were more than adept at. They'd been happy to look after their wilting stepsister at first in the mistaken belief that they were helping her through her period of mourning but on the third day, Mother decided to bestow the gift of self-reliance upon Ella.

Which she accepted most ungraciously.

"What? Me? You want me to make the breakfast?" she said indignantly, wondering if she'd heard Mother right.

"You don't have to lay the eggs, my dear, just fetch them from the hen house and scramble them in a pan," Mother replied without looking up from her darning by the fireside. Winter was drawing in and the château was growing cold. In order to preserve wood and keep themselves warm, most chores were undertaken in the kitchen.

Ella looked dumbstruck. She'd come down for her breakfast and pulled out her usual chair only to find that she was the one who was expected to provide it. "Like a common scullery maid?"

"Cooks cook food. Scullery maids wash dishes," Marigold corrected her. "More about which you'll learn after breakfast."

Gardenia shifted uncomfortably in her seat. She and Marigold were under strict instructions not to lift a finger to help Ella today otherwise she would continue to rely on them for everything and never learn how to do anything for herself.

"I don't cook food," Ella explained. "I am the mistress of the house."

"We are all mistresses of this house, Ella. And we must all do our bit," Mother told her, shooting Gardenia a cautionary glance to stop her from jumping to her feet and telling Ella not to worry about it today.

"I have a title," Ella reminded them. "I am the daughter of a nobleman," horrified at the thought of what might happen if other people were to hear she had been forced to toil over a hot oven.

"Eggs are scrambled on a stovetop. Pies go in an oven," Marigold corrected her again, only too happy to help Ella out with advice on her first day of work.

Ella screwed up her face and implored them to try to understand, she simply wasn't up to the task. "My father died only last week."

"Grief is no forgiver of indolence, stepdaughter. Only the occupation of your hands will release your mind from its suffering," Mother explained with a tone of compassion.

But Ella failed to appreciate the redemptive powers of household chores. All she could see was her shrew-like stepmother and lazy stepsisters sitting around on their fat backsides waiting to be handed their nosebags. It failed to occur to her that both Marigold and Gardenia had cooked and cleaned for her the day before, and the day before that. In fact, they'd done everything since Mother let the staff go three days earlier. But the contradiction never crossed Ella's mind. She was the lady of the house. Other people cooked and cleaned. It was as simple as that. How else did the world go around?

"My father would be very unhappy to know what is being asked of me," Ella said, reminding Mother of the reason she had a magnificent château to call her home rather than a dung-heap boil on the backside of the city. But Mother would not be blackmailed, emotionally or otherwise, particularly not by a novice like Ella.

"Your father is gone. Get used to that fact. We are your family now and it is up to you to abide by our rules."

"Rules?" Ella jumped to her feet to send her chair

crashing to the floor. She was quite prepared to go without food rather than be dictated to by a lowly seamstress. "Don't talk to me about rules. Who on Earth do you think you are?"

"As of this week, your legal guardian," Mother told her in no uncertain terms. "Unless of course, you'd rather seek refuge in the town orphanage?"

Mother knew full well that at eighteen, Ella was too old for the orphanage but her point was made: until Ella turned twenty-one she had no rights of her own. And as this was the eighteenth century and she had been born a girl, she would get precious few even after that.

"I'm not hungry anymore. I think I'll get some air," Ella announced, stomping across the flagstones but stopping at the door. "Unless you'd like me to fetch you some of that too?"

She didn't wait to hear the answer. Ella slammed the door in her wake and headed out into the garden, or more particularly, the apple tree at the end of it. But she was in for a shock. The apples had all been picked two days earlier and preserved to see them through the coming months. All the nuts and wild berries in the vicinity too. Marigold and Gardenia had been busy raiding nature's larder to fill their own while Mother took a thorough stocktake of their provisions. They wouldn't go hungry this winter but they weren't likely to grow fat either, particularly not on nuts and apples.

*

ELLA STAYED OUT for most of the day, returning only later that evening when the light had begun to fade. Marigold was grooming Liquorice in the stables after dinner when she saw her crossing the fields towards the rear of the house. Where had she been all day? The city was in the opposite direction and too far to walk, particularly in the sort of dainty shoes Ella chose to wear.

Had she had anything to eat all day?

She must have been starving. Marigold watched her go into the château, then finished up with Liquorice, throwing a horse blanket over his back and wishing him goodnight before locking up the stables and following Ella inside.

She entered to the sounds of shouting. It was Ella. Of course. Who else could it have been?

Marigold followed her indignant commentary through the winding hallways and towards the kitchen but suddenly it all went quiet. Marigold reached for the door handle but the kitchen door was yanked back from within and Ella came rushing out.

"You're nothing but a bunch of trogs," she shouted, running upstairs and slamming the door to her attic room.

Marigold entered the kitchen. It was warm and welcoming in here, with a fire flickering in the grate and a small portion of pumpkin stew bubbling in a pan on top of the stove. Mother and the girls had already eaten but they'd set a little aside for Ella. This had been the cause of her outrage. It didn't matter that they'd offered her a hot meal that she didn't deserve. And it didn't matter either that for the fourth day in a row she was being asked to eat *peasant food*. No, what really mattered to Ella was that she was being offered a panful of leftovers. At least, that's how she saw it.

"She'll come around when she gets hungry," Mother predicted, as she mended an old skirt in her chair by the fireside. "The head may be strong, but the tummy is king."

CHAPTER THIRTY-ONE

ANOTHER WHO COULD'VE TESTIFIED to that fact was Captain Durand. Or rather, simply Durand as he was now known. He'd been languishing in the King's deepest, darkest dungeon ever since the Prince's ball and enjoying a starvation diet of bread and water — and very little of either, at that. Such deprivations had reduced this once proud man to someone who would've happily eaten another's leftovers even if they'd been dropped in mud and he'd had to fight off a pack of rats for the privilege.

It was a spectacular fall from grace and yet deep down, Durand knew that it wasn't entirely undeserved. His affections for the Prince were no more genuine than the Prince's for his people. Durand had simply seen his opportunity and taken it, recognising the King's son for what he was the first time he'd laid eyes on him. How no one else had was beyond Durand, but that had been their hard luck and his gilt-edged chance to rise up the ranks quicker than he might well have done otherwise. At 25, he'd become the youngest Captain of the Guards in Andovia's history, younger even that half the men in his company, and yet Durand wasn't content to stop there. He had big plans for himself and with the idiot Prince in his pocket, nothing had seemed beyond his reach. Until now.

The sounds of someone howling in despair at the other end of the tunnel rocked Durand from his slumber. He felt groggy and delirious and it took him a moment to realise where he was. When he did, he wished for delirium again.

How was this fair, he thought to himself? All he'd done was what every eligible maiden in the Kingdom had hoped to do and bag the Prince. The only difference was he'd got there first. And of course, he was more to the Prince's tastes than the rest of the field.

Durand suppressed a sob and rattled his chains. How could this be? How could this be?

In some respects, Durand had got off lightly. If the King had had his way, the Captain would not have been thrown in the dungeons, he would've been stuck on the parapet. Or at least, his head would've. But the Grand Duke urged the King to exercise discretion. If only so that their story held up. The punishment had to fit the crime. Executions were well and good for treason and treachery, but for slap and tickle, it seemed a tad excessive. Even if the Prince had got a fist in the face into the bargain — which was also part of the official story.

No, disgrace, imprisonment and eventual banishment to the most desolate corner of the Kingdom would suffice. The only problem was that one day this meant releasing Durand. So the Grand Duke saw fit to first break him. He would be manacled, malnourished and maltreated until his body was so ravaged by hunger that he would hardly be able to sit straight, let alone stand. No daylight would touch his eyes. No warmth would touch his skin. He would rot down here, alone and forgotten until he could no longer remember his own name. Then — and only then — the Duke would start to rebuild him. A biscuit here, an apple there. Perhaps even a whole cooked partridge, if only to watch with scientific detachment through the bars of his cell door at what primal savagery looked like.

Then the possibility of release would be dangled before him. It would be snatched away again, then offered and snatched away, offered and snatched away until Durand had been driven beyond his wits. Imprisonment can crush a man but nothing comes quite as close to destroying one's will as hope — or rather the loss of it.

After that, Durand would do or say anything that the Grand Duke asked of him, even if that meant standing on a wooden crate in the middle of the town square to describe in excruciating detail to an audience made up entirely of his own extended family how he'd dragged their great name through the mud. All with a big smile on his face.

Only then would the Prince's reputation be safe. And with it, the King's.

But the Grand Duke's plan had one crucial flaw. It took for granted that no one on the outside would be willing to come to Durand's aid.

"Oi! You in there! You awake?"

Durand opened his eyes. A flaming torch was hanging through the bars to throw a flicker of light across his dank home for the first time since he'd moved in. He turned away sharply. The light hurt his eyes.

"Look 'ere. What's your name?" the stranger whispered, moving the torch from side to side to get a better look at Durand's face.

Durand didn't know how to answer. Was this another of the Duke games? If he gave the wrong answer, would he be horribly punished again, either by having his pitiful rations reduced further still or by being doused with freezing water and left to flounder in a pit that never dried out? But what was the right answer? Was there even one? Or was this all part of his suffering?

"Prisoner, tell me your name and be quick about it, 'afore the guards come back."

"Durand," Durand croaked miserably, shielding his eyes and waiting for the inevitable.

Until now, a malicious cackle had preceded every torment but nothing prepared him for what came next. A bundle was shoved through the bars and dropped at his feet.

"You ain't alone. The Prince be thinking of you. Get ready," the man told him before withdrawing and hurrying away to plunge Durand into darkness once again.

He felt for the bundle and quickly unwrapped it. Inside, to his astonishment, was food: an apple, some parsnips and even a small side of bacon. There were shoes too, something he'd been denied since his incarceration, and the blanket was enough to take the chill from his shoulders for the first time in weeks. But the most precious thing the man had brought was the message itself. He wasn't alone. The Prince was still with him.

Durand ate half the food and hid the blanket and shoes when the guards came with his stale bread and water. He acted as though nothing had changed and tore into his rations like a man possessed. And so he was. With hope. But not the false hope the Grand Duke liked to feed him. But the real undeniable hope of a man with friends on the outside, albeit that chump of a Prince he had duped into loving him. But Durand could not afford to think of the Prince that way with salvation so close to hand. He may have despised the royal brat before his incarceration and burned with a hatred for him ever since, but if there was even the slenderest of chances of getting out of here, Durand would need to play him like a harp.

The old man with the torch did not come back for two whole days but Durand had no concept of time. The late autumn sky did not reach his cell and bread and water came when his jailers remembered to bring it. He'd begun to wonder if the whole thing had been a cruel hoax to drive him to despair or if the Prince had changed his mind, but then one night he awoke to the sounds of clanking.

A small yellow flame flickered outside his cell door and someone was grinding metal on metal on the other side.

Durand crawled over to the door and tried to look out but the manacles around his ankles stopped him from reaching the window.

"Who's that?" Durand whispered.

"Quiet," came back the reply from the man grinding metal on metal. The lock made plenty of noise but refused to budge so the man pulled his makeshift key out and filed away at its teeth for a few seconds before trying again.

The key still would not turn and the noise was excruciating. Every clatter and clunk seemed to rise in volume as it raced away down the long stone corridors.

"For the love of God, man, keep it down," Durand implored his potential rescuer but the man was unperturbed. He carried on rattling his homemade key inside the great iron lock until something gave and the key finally turned.

"What's going on down there?" came a distant cry but the man didn't hesitate. He twisted the key a few more turns using both his hands and all of his strength before putting his shoulder to the door.

Durand gathered his shoes and the last of his provisions but he could not yet escape. He was still manacled to the floor but the old man had a key for that too. Sort of.

"Shift 'em!" he said, hoisting a huge great axe he'd brought with him for the job, only to hit the ceiling when he misjudged his initial swing.

"Are you sure about this?" Durand baulked, urging him to slow down. His ankles were barely a loaf of bread apart and held together by sturdy iron manacles that didn't look like they'd come off with gunpowder. If indeed, it was even the manacles the old man was aiming to lop off?

"Watch your toes," was all he said as he swung the axe at the second attempt, striking the central link between Durand's ankles to set him free. Durand breathed a sigh of relief but the noise the old man had made was enough to wake the dead and sure enough, the sound of footsteps soon reverberated through the catacombs.

"*This way. It came from the lower passage!*" Durant heard someone shout so the old man told him to put his shoes on and follow.

"We go down," he said, leading Durand out of his cell and along a narrow passageway that seemed to slope deep underground. The man kept a hand cupped around his candle flame and Durand could barely see where he was going, scraping his head on the low-hanging ceiling more than once.

"What is this place?" Durand asked, struggling to keep up with the old man as he scurried with ease half-running and half-stooped through a labyrinth of dank tunnels.

"And spoil the surprise?" his liberator chuckled.

After a while, the passageways opened out into a much larger chamber and Durand almost turned back in shock. Piled in great twisted heaps were thousands upon thousands of old bones. There was no order to the stacks: leg bones, thigh bones, ribs and skulls, the place was a dumping ground for the dead.

"Not everyone's as lucky as you, boy," the man said with a knowing leer. "Some folks gets in but they never gets out."

Until now, Durand had imagined death as the ultimate punishment. Now he knew that wasn't true. To be cast away and left to crumble to dust down here would've been infinitely worse than the brief painful flashing of a sword. It was a fate beyond his wildest nightmares.

"Not far now," said the old man, leading him past the damned until they came to a small black underground lake. Here the catacombs ended. There seemed no other way out and for a moment, Durand thought he had been tricked.

"What is the meaning of this? I thought you were taking me to the Prince?"

"What did you expect, a red carpet?" the man cackled.

Durand now studied his rescuer fearing the worst. With the candlelight settled upon his face, he looked like no sort of man the Prince would ever know. He looked fifty going on ninety with sunken eyes, pale skin and wooden teeth, all splintered, rotten and caked with the remnants of dinners gone by to leave him with breath you could grow mushrooms on.

"Who are you?" Durand demanded, despite being in no

position to demand anything.

"Folks call me Hooky," the old man said, despite not possessing any hooks Durand could see. "I run this 'ere underworld."

"You're a guard?" Durand exclaimed.

Hooky hooted with laughter to give Durand a full blast of his poisonous breath. "I've been here longer than any snot-nosed guard. This is my world. They is here at my discretion."

None of this made any sense to Durand but he figured he'd take it at face value rather than waste any more time arguing the toss with this filthy wretch. He was out of his cell and free of his chains. But how did he get out of the dungeons?

"Hold that," Hooky said, handing Durand the candle.

Durand watched as Hooky lay on his belly at the lake's edge and reached into the water without bothering to roll up his sleeves. He felt around for several seconds before finding what he was looking for and hauled out one end of a length of rope.

"Cold that is," was Hooky's assessment. "Goes right through to your bones."

He took the candle back from Durand and handed him the slimy wet rope.

"Tie it to your wrist otherwise you're liable to lose it halfway through," Hooky advised ominously.

"Halfway through?" Durand asked, not liking the sound of that one little bit.

But Hooky didn't elaborate. He just helped Durand loop and knot the rope around one of his wrists and then tugged on it three times.

"*Bon voyage,*" Hooky winked. "Deep breath now."

And with that, the slack began to run and before Durand knew what was happening he was yanked into the lake and dragged underwater. What little breath he'd managed to snatch was knocked straight out of him by the icy coldness. Hooky had been right about that. He'd never known an agony like it. It wracked every inch of his body and made him want to scream out in pain, but to do so would've been to suffer an even worse agony.

Deeper and deeper he plunged, away from the light and into the bottomless blackness. With what little coherent thought Durand could muster, he now knew he'd been tricked. Had this all been the Grand Duke's plan all along? To tie him up and throw him into a watery grave so that he would never be found? To have him simply disappear?

But just as all hope started to fade, he felt himself change direction. He seemed to be travelling sideways now, through a gap in the slippery rocks and bumping and scraping through an underwater tunnel as the rope dragged him faster and faster towards the unknown.

His lungs were empty and he yearned to breathe. He knew to do so would mean death but he didn't have the strength to resist. He was so weak and so tired, his mind swam with stars and his ears felt as though they'd been hammered with spikes but still the rope pulled him through the silent abyss.

"En garde, Your Highness," a faraway voice whispered into his ear and then all at once he saw a speck of light. It was way off in the distance but clear as day. He was racing towards it, spinning and twirling as he went, drawing closer and closer to that irresistible glow until suddenly the water around him began to churn. The rope went slack, something grabbed him and noise and confusion flooded his senses as he broke through the surface.

He was dragged bodily, passed from hand to hand and dumped onto the soft bank.

He tried to rise, coughing, spluttering, heaving and retching as he rolled over onto his front, gasping for breath but unable to breathe. Someone cut the rope from his wrist and jumped onto his back to pump the water from him. Once they were done, he was rolled over and several flaming torches shone in his face. The light burned his eyes but he felt no warmth. He was too numb for that and too delirious to think.

He knew only two things. One: he was alive. And two: he was free. And he was wrong about one of those things straight away.

"Nice to meet you, Captain," said an unseen voice. "We have much to talk about."

Durand heard something land in the mud beside his face. It was an olive pip. And now the huge shadow standing over him leaned in to reveal the twisted features of his face.

"Franz Grimaldi!" Durand gasped in horror, before blacking out through dread and exhaustion.

CHAPTER THIRTY-TWO

IT HAD TAKEN ALL OF the Grand Duke's persuasive powers to convince the King to hold another *grand ball*. His neck was on the line should anything go wrong but the Duke saw no way around it. He'd reviewed the alternatives and realised it was their only option. It would help quash any doubts about the Prince's conduct (should they surface) and allow them to right the wrongs of their first attempt.

But the King was still far from convinced. If the Prince married an Andovian girl from one of the great families and word got out about his proclivities, it could trigger a rebellion amongst the King's own nobility. It wasn't so much that the act itself was objectionable. It was all a matter of blood. As next in line to the throne, there could be no doubt whatsoever as to the lineage of any heirs he might produce. Which there surely would be should his future princess fall pregnant and word got out that he preferred the company of men.

"I know all this, damn it!" the King had raged. "We did this once already and look at the mess we got in."

But the Grand Duke wasn't looking to repeat past mistakes. He had a masterstroke, something so ingenious that he couldn't believe he hadn't thought of it before. For the next Prince's ball, they wouldn't just invite the usual aristocrats. They would invite *everyone*.

"Everyone? What do you mean everyone?" the King demanded.

"I mean, we shall invite every eligible maiden in the Kingdom, regardless of family, title, name or pedigree. We shall invite," he paused for dramatic effect, "everyone."

At this, the King's brain melted. He couldn't take in such a concept but the Duke's idea had something rather special going for it, namely that it would cause such excitement amongst his people that the prior debacle would be completely wiped from the pages of history. Or at least, be reduced to a footnote.

"And then, there's the question of the bride," the Grand Duke had said. "Just think about it; an opportunity to be the next Princess of Andovia. A Lord prepares his daughter for such a possibility all her life and therefore has certain... expectations."

"Expectations?" asked the King.

"Both the Lord and his daughter," the Duke clarified. "But the daughter of an innkeeper?"

"An innkeeper's daughter?" the King baulked.

"Or a farmer?"

"A farmer's daughter!" the King repeated.

"Or a cheesemaker?"

"Cheesemakers have daughters too?" the King gasped.

"Or perhaps even a daughter of no one at all, from the orphanage, of Andovia herself?"

"Andovia?" the King muttered, still waiting for the punchline.

"A girl with no family to turn to for advice, no name and no account. What would a girl like this do if she were offered the chance to be plucked from the gutter and held up to the stars?"

This was no mere rhetorical question but it took the King several seconds to realise this. "I don't know, what?" he eventually asked.

"Anything *we* want," came the answer.

"My son won't like this," the King said, pointing out a rather obvious flaw in the Grand Duke's plan.

"I don't doubt it, sire," the Grand Duke replied. "But he will get used to the idea once the benefits become apparent."

But the issue wasn't settled with this one discussion. The King and Grand Duke locked horns over the issue all week. His son was a Prince. Not a very good one, admittedly, but a Prince nonetheless. He could not marry a commoner. The King clung to custom, heritage and tradition whereas the Duke championed pageantry, pantomime and magic. And they might have been stuck there forever, fighting their respective corners until the end of time had it not been for one thing. The Prince's own meteoric recalcitrance.

He had not stopped sulking over his treatment for weeks, imagining his fate to be on a par with that of Durand's while confined to the King's luxurious country retreat. He spent days in bed, taking most of his meals in his pyjamas and refusing to acknowledge another living soul, not even to lift his head while they attempted to fluff his pillow.

The King and Grand Duke rode out to consult him and couldn't believe the sight that greeted them. Or rather didn't. The sun was shining, the deer were frolicking, the fish were spawning, the geese were flying and yet the Prince was nowhere to be seen. He was still in bed, drunk, unshaven, unwashed and stinking out the place to high heaven. His valet had tried to dress him in preparation for his father's arrival, his maids had tried to wash him and his cooks had attempted to get some breakfast down him but all to no avail. He wanted nothing to do with anything. His father could go to hell, so could the Grand Duke and the throne itself. He'd never asked to be born and just wanted to be left alone (except when he was hungry and needed cakes being brought up to him and his bedpan taken away).

The King refused to be kept waiting and stormed upstairs, bursting in on the Prince to find him cowering beneath the sheets.

"What on Earth is going on with you, boy?" the King demanded.

"I'm not coming out," the Prince replied a tad ironically.

"Show yourself this instant!" the King said, snatching

at the covers and dragging them off the enormous four-poster bed to reveal a dishevelled tramp that he'd been assured was his son.

"I hate you!" the Prince shouted which would have been regarded as treason in anyone else, but in the Prince, it was just his usual morning greeting. He stayed where he was, curled up in a foetal position in the centre of the bed, with his back to the King and his bottom sticking out of his nightgown. The Grand Duke couldn't keep track of how many breaks from protocol this represented and gave up trying.

"The Duke and I have something to discuss with you," the King announced, sending the Prince's valet and a serving maid from the room so that they might have some privacy.

"I'm not discussing anything with you. You've ruined my life," the Prince moped, wracked with guilt at having to throw Durand to the wolves to save himself. He'd had weeks to dwell on his conduct and his anger at the King had swelled like a cyst — all whilst not enquiring after the Captain or his wellbeing once.

"For Heaven's sake boy, get over it. We're not asking you to charge the guns at Widows' Ridge; just get married, that's all," the King exclaimed.

"To some chubby little ugly Duchess who hates me on sight and I her? I'd rather die," the Prince snorted, causing the King to flash scarlet before exploding in a rage.

"We'll all end up with our heads on spikes if you don't snap out of it! It doesn't take much for the Barons to sense weakness. And if we do, I'll see yours is put on upside down!" he screamed, ready to end three hundred years of dynastic rule with his own bare hands if the Prince kept this up.

"Please allow me," said the Grand Duke, stepping in and addressing the Prince in more measured tones. "What would you have us tell the people, your Highness? Help us to help you."

"That's *your* problem. Go help yourselves," the Prince replied, jumping up to grab his bed covers and drag them over himself once more.

The King had always known his son was prone to mood swings but he had no idea he was self-destructive too. But even self-destruction would have been fine. What he could not allow the Prince to destroy was the family name. It had been entrusted to the King by the ghosts of Carinas past.

"You will come to heel," was the King's parting shot before following the Duke out of the room and trudging down the stairs feeling every one of his fifty-eight years. The King arrived at the bottom step and said nothing for the longest time. He simply stared at the flecks of dust that hung in the air and thought about dancing, the dancing he'd enjoyed with his own sweet Queen on their wedding day and the dancing he'd hoped to see the Prince do with a Princess of his own. Was that such an unreasonable ambition?

"And you are sure we'll be able to control her?" the King simply asked, catching the Grand Duke off-guard.

"The commoner? By all means, Your Majesty. Most have known only deference and servitude their whole lives anyway. She will be our puppet," he promised.

"And we will hold the strings?" the King demanded.

"Indeed. And when the time comes, I shall cut them too," the Grand Duke told him most assuredly.

"Very well then," the King reluctantly agreed. "Find him a cheesemaker's daughter if you can. That is, if a cheesemaker's daughter would lower herself to take that wretch for a husband because personally I have my doubts."

The Grand Duke smiled the smile of a man one step ahead of the game. "Actually, I already have someone in mind," he purred.

"You know a cheesemaker?" the King said in surprise.

But the Duke just shook his head. "Cheesemakers? No. But a seamstress? Perhaps."

CHAPTER THIRTY-THREE

THE SISTERS HAD BARELY SEEN Ella all week. She'd shut herself away in her attic tower just as the Prince had done in his ivory equivalent, and not for dissimilar reasons either. But unlike Prince Carina, Ella had no one to bring her food or take it away so how was she managing?

The first ill winds of what was to come began to bite. A false winter, as it was known in these parts, as the weather patterns shifted to blow snow and ice off the mountains before the real winter set in. A frost at the start of the week had turned the countryside to sugar and sucked every breath of warmth from their threadbare château. For two days, Marigold got up only to feed and water Liquorice before returning to bed. It was the best place for them. She and Gardenia had few chores to do and Mother told them it would conserve their dwindling reserves of firewood for harsher days to come. Marigold wondered how Ella must've been coping in her "cold and draughty" attic. It must've been bitter up there, even more so than in the rest of the house. But Ella never emerged. She avoided her family as she avoided her chores. And the door leading up to her room remained permanently locked.

On Wednesday, the clouds parted and the sun came out. The air retained a sting but the day was glorious. Marigold and Gardenia emerged from their temporary hibernations, got dressed and went out to explore the gardens.

Mother warned them not to wander too far but there was little chance of that. A fresh blanket of snow lay ankle-deep in all directions and, but for a few rabbit tracks, was utterly unbroken. The land was so white and the skies were so blue that it almost hurt Marigold's eyes to look out across the fields.

"Shall we have a snowball fight?" Gardenia suggested.
"Mother wouldn't like that," Marigold replied.
"She doesn't have to join in," Gardenia shrugged.

But Marigold was in no mood for horseplay. Why was this Gardenia's first thought whenever she saw snow, to throw it in her sister's face? She was the same with autumn leaves. And hay. And grass cuttings. It was like a compulsion with her. Marigold was only thankful it was she who cleaned out Liquorice's stables and not the pair of them together.

"Winter's coming early this year," Gardenia said as they crunched across the crisp white front lawn. It was only October and the Kingdom didn't normally get snow until Christmas so Marigold figured it would either melt away again or... or...

"Or?" Gardenia asked.

"Or we could be in trouble," Marigold replied, mentally stock-taking their meagre provisions.

"I guess things could be worse. We could be ice cream vendors," Gardenia said without thinking. Marigold agreed and thought of Hans, albeit with a shrug of sadness.

The girls' prospects had taken yet another spectacular reversal of fortunes with the death of Monsieur Beaufort. Yes, it was true that Mother was now free to accept any invitation on behalf of her daughters that they might receive but once word of their financial straits became widespread, the invitations dried up as quickly as their coffers.

Marigold resigned herself to the situation with as much quiet dignity as she could muster. She had long since concluded that the people of Andovia must surely be the worst in the world but it was harder on Gardenia. For one so young to have had her hopes raised and dashed so many times in such quick succession was almost unbearable. It should have left her bitter and twisted. It should've. But it hadn't. And this just made Gardenia's benevolence and eternal gentle will all the more remarkable.

"We should check on Ella," Gardenia said in hope, looking up to the turret which stuck out on top of the east wing. It seemed an appropriate place for Ella's bedroom, almost as though the room itself didn't want to be a part of the main house. But it was utterly exposed to the elements and must have been freezing up there. How could she stand it?

"I worry about her," Gardenia admitted. "We're all she's got now."

Marigold was mulling these thoughts over when a bird appeared in the east. It crossed the opal blue sky and flew straight towards Ella's bedroom, landing on a ledge before disappearing from sight. Marigold kept on watching but the bird failed to reemerge. Had it gone inside? Was her window open? In this weather? Like Gardenia, Marigold was suddenly worried about Ella. She was headstrong and intensely unlikeable but she was still a member of their family and needed looking after, even from herself. Stubbornness was a streak Marigold knew only too well but Ella seemed to have taken it to a whole new level. Some people cut their noses off to spite their face. Marigold thought Ella was capable of cutting off her whole head if she thought it would get back at her hair for not doing what she wanted it to do.

The girls headed back to the house, stamping their feet outside the front door to shed a layer of snow before heading inside. They swapped their boots for shoes and coats for shawls but for all intents and purposes remained wrapped up in as many layers as they could carry.

They headed to the kitchen at the back of the house and were kissed by a warm peppery smell of broth when they got there. Mother had made a fresh batch and handed them both stoneware mugs to thaw out their frozen fingers. Marigold sipped hers gratefully. It was only now, once she'd come in from the cold that she realised how truly cold she was.

Behind her, Gardenia took a third mug, filled it with broth and covered it with a saucer. Mother saw this and raised an eyebrow.

"I thought… I'd take some up to Ella, in case she was hungry too," Gardenia smiled apologetically. She waited for Mother to take the broth from her and damn her weakness but Mother barely blanched.

"Very well," she said turning back to attend to the cloth patterns she'd lain across the kitchen table. "But come straight down once you've seen her. We have much to do today."

Marigold quickly knocked back her broth and hurried after Gardenia, surprised to have received Mother's blessing and aching with curiosity to see how Ella was faring. The sisters scurried along the hallways and up the stairs, almost fearing Mother would change her mind and call them down again, before arriving at Ella's door — or at least the first of Ella's doors. Beyond this one lay a winding wooden staircase that led up to Ella's inner sanctum. The sisters had long speculated on what they might find up there should Ella ever go out and leave her doors unlocked. Now Marigold feared it might be Ella herself, frozen solid and covered in starlings.

She tried the handle. The door was locked. As always. Marigold knocked.

Nothing.

She knocked again, this time louder. She thought she could hear movement but it was difficult to tell with Gardenia asking her what she could hear every three seconds. Was that Ella moving about up there or was it an enormous crow jumping from side to side and flapping its wings in order to shoo some of the smaller birds away from Ella's prized morsels?

"What is it?" asked Gardenia once more. "What can you hear?"

After a little more flapping there was a click and a clunk

and then a clip-clop-clip as Marigold heard the unmistakable sounds of footsteps approaching. The footsteps stopped on the other side of the door, there was the sound of a key turning in the lock, then the door cracked open and Ella looked out.

"What is it?" she asked, as though half-expecting some urgent news.

"We've brought you a little hot broth," Gardenia said to Ella's obvious disappointment. At least until she held it up for her to inspect. There it hung halfway between them, all steaming and savoury and warm, to the point where Ella found it impossible to rebuff.

"Erm… thank you," she said, opening the door a little to accept the gift. Unlike the sisters, Ella was not bundled in swaddles of old clothing. She was relatively undressed, wearing only a simple frock and a headscarf to protect her from the elements. Marigold was confused. But then she looked closer and noticed Ella was also wearing streaks of grime about her face and knees. This was most unlike Ella, who was quite particular about her appearance. But the closer Marigold looked, the more she realised what these marks were.

"You have cinders on your face," she said in astonishment.

Ella tried to wipe them away but it was too late, Marigold and Gardenia had seen them and they were under no illusion as to what they signified.

She had a fire upstairs.

Suddenly, Marigold remembered their stocks of firewood. It hadn't occurred to her until now but they seemed to be going through a great deal more wood than she could reason, hence their long days in bed as they tried to ration it out. Marigold had assumed that this was because of the château's size, that a place like this simply burned more fuel than most houses but now she realised it was because they were burning two fires; the stove in the kitchen and Ella's secret hearth in the attic. And no doubt one of these was blazing around the clock in an attempt to defrost the month of October.

"Thank you for the broth," Ella said, quickly closing the door before Marigold could say anything more.

They heard her hurrying away upstairs and slamming the upper door before it all went quiet again, save for the occasional bird noise. They must've got into the rafters somehow.

Gardenia now turned to Marigold.

"She was covered in cinders."

"Yes."

"She must have a fire in her bedroom."

"Yes."

"She must be sleeping right on top of it to get that dirty."

"Pretty much," Marigold agreed.

Gardenia thought on this revelation some more.

"You know what we should call her from now on?" she suggested.

"Yes," Marigold agreed. "A thieving little cow."

Marigold went straight back downstairs and started hiding some of their winter provisions. Mother asked what they were doing and Marigold had no hesitation in telling her.

"There is a simpler solution," Mother said, heading upstairs to fit a bolt to Ella's door. If their precious stepsister wanted to remain in the attic behind a locked door then that was just fine with them. But the lock would be on their side from now on.

That night, Marigold was awoken by the sounds of Ella's fury. She hammered against the door and cursed them for their duplicity, promising all sorts of unspeakable consequences unless they let her out.

"Open this door! Open it now! I know you can hear

me! I know you're out there! Open this door or you'll be sorry you ever met me!"

Marigold turned over on her pillow and looked up at Gardenia in the half-light of the moon. She was sat up in bed and chewing her fingernails as she listened to Ella's angry tirade but Marigold told her not to lose any sleep over it.

"Just how much sorrier could we possibly be?"

CHAPTER THIRTY-FOUR

WHILST MOST IN THE KINGDOM continued to go about their business wrapped up and hunkered down against the unseasonal cold, few people noticed the appearance of a lone adjutant as he emerged from the Palace and pinned an official proclamation to the bulletin board in the town square.

When the proclamation was finally noticed, the first few people to read it thought it a hoax. It had to be. The very notion was absurd. But word quickly spread and gradually more and more people gathered in the square to read it for themselves — or in the case of most, have it read to them. As such, it decreed:

"... that every eligible maiden in the Kingdom, being no younger than sixteen years of age and no older than nineteen, are hereby and formally invited to attend the Palace this coming Saturday, where His Royal Highness, the Crown Prince of Andovia, shall select from amongst his own people, his bride and future Princess."

There was some additional small print about the Prince's decision being final and terms and conditions applying etc but on the whole, the message was clear. The Prince was to select a bride (again) but this time everyone had a chance of bagging him, lady and laywoman alike.

Within an hour of the proclamation being pinned up, the entire city had ground to a halt. Most ordinary girls had never even seen the Prince, save for a blur that occasionally thundered by on horseback whenever he rode out to the countryside, so the idea that they were to attend a ball in his presence, never mind the possibility that they might end up a Princess, was mind-blowing. Amélie in the hat shop burst into tears when she heard the news and didn't stop crying for almost four days, while Raina, a milk maiden on the Keller's farm, refused to touch another udder again, believing it her destiny to become a Princess after all these years of sitting around under cows fantasising about just such an event.

By and large, the reaction was positive. There was jubilation on the streets and a renewed outpouring of love for the Prince, just as the Grand Duke had predicted. But this was strictly limited to the people, as numerous as they were. In the aristocracy, the story was quite different. Most were appalled. Was the Prince really proposing to take a bride from amongst the great unwashed?

A delegation of indignant dignitaries descended upon the Grand Duke and demanded an explanation, only to discover it was no hoax; the Prince would indeed choose a bride from amongst the whole of his people and not just the great and the good.

"But this is an outrage!" thundered Baron Weiss, turning redder in the face than one of his vintage merlots. "Do you really expect my beloved Suzette to rub shoulders with the… with the… the rabble?"

"I expect nothing of the kind, Your Lordship. It is an invitation, not a subpoena," the Grand Duke replied from behind his huge ornate desk. He'd had the delegation wait outside for over an hour to remind them of their place and now he kept them on their feet while he reclined in his official chair and showed them his soles.

"Does the King intentionally insult us, Your Grace?" Lord Ricci asked, flocking to Baron Weiss's banner of righteous indignation. "This goes against everything we stand for. It impugns the honour of our daughters no less."

The Grand Duke dropped his feet off his desk and leaned forwards.

"Are you telling me, in all seriousness, Lord Ricci, that Prince Carina might overlook young Claudia should a few comely farm girls attend the ball also? Or you, Baron Weiss, that your Suzette could not hold so much as a candle to a lowly candlemaker's daughter? And what of you, Monsieur Eames, is your young Isabella so unappealing that the mere presence of a peasant girl would entice the Prince's favours?" the Grand Duke scoffed. "In which case, perhaps I should bar my chambermaid from attending too. I mean, we wouldn't want to make the competition too stiff, now would we."

The Lord and Barons didn't know whether to be insulted or incensed but the fact remained, as popular as it might prove with the plebs, to raffle away the Prince's hand in such a manner would cause huge resentment amongst the aristocracy and it was they who held sway in the Kingdom. Not the riffraff.

The Grand Duke allowed Lord Ricci to vent his anger before smiling mendaciously.

"As if I would allow it to come to that," he said with a Cheshire grin. "Permit the Prince his slice of theatre. If he wishes to project himself as a man of the people, who am I to stand in his way? But know this, when the time comes for him to choose a bride, he will marry accordingly."

Lord Ricci and Baron Weiss exchanged sceptical glances.

"You can guarantee this?" Baron Weiss pressed.

"I give you my word, Your Lordships. Our future Princess will come from an ennobled household. I will see to it myself. And I will expect you to smile upon the match. We must, after all, in times of great uncertainty, look to one another for support. Must we not?"

The Grand Duke had turned the tables on the delegation. He had given them the reassurances they had sought. Now it was their turn to give him theirs.

"We will hold you to account on this matter, Your Grace. Our loyalty is to the King," Lord Ricci said, reluctantly but earnestly accepting the deal.

"As is mine," the Grand Duke assured them.

The delegation filed out suspecting that they had been bamboozled but not quite sure how. The Grand Duke had no daughters of his own, nor any wards, nieces or cousins of marrying age, therefore, it was unlikely his own family could benefit from this sorry charade. So what was he up to?

Once the nobles were gone, the Grand Duke summoned his son for a special errand.

"Send messengers to the furthest corners of the Kingdom. Every household is to receive word of this King's proclamation. Leave no door unknocked," he told Captain Olivier.

"Very good, Father," Captain Olivier replied with a click of the heels.

"And be sure to include Madame *La Chevalière* Beaufort's château atop *Rue des Roses*. See to this invitation personally," the Grand Duke instructed.

"Madame *La Chevalière*?" Captain Olivier said, as if something didn't quite sit right.

"That is her official title since marrying Monsieur *Le Chevalier*, is it not?" the Grand Duke asked.

"Yes but… they are commoners. I'm not sure his title was hereditary."

"Are you sure it was not?" The Grand Duke asked.

"No Father but…" Captain Olivier started to say but he didn't get very far.

"Then we must give the Beauforts the benefit of the doubt," the Grand Duke confirmed. "I want you to make sure their full title is used in all correspondence and on the final guest list for the Prince's ball. Do you understand me?"

"Of course, Father. Right away," he said with a second click of the heels but he failed to spring into action.

"What?" the Grand Duke asked.

"I don't like them, any of them. There's something not quite right about those women," Captain Olivier said with a narrowing of the eyes.

"Then they and the Prince should have plenty in common," the Grand Duke concluded, shooing his son from his sight.

*

AFTER THREE DAYS OF COLD WEATHER, an early thaw set in to turn the countryside from virginal white to sullied brown, although the Beaufort's château still felt frozen inside.

Captain Olivier arrived a little after midday bringing with him the King's proclamation. Although hand-picked to deliver this particular message, he was instructed to maintain the facade that he was just one of many messengers sent out to every château, farm and homestead beyond the city walls in accordance with the law.

Mother invited him in and showed him through to the parlour so that he could perform his duty. Every courtesy was shown to the Captain despite his obvious antipathy towards the family and Gardenia wondered what he had to do before Mother stopped regarding him as suitable husband material.

"Would you like some broth, Captain? It is bitter outside."

"Er... no thank you. You are very kind but I have many more places I must visit before I am done," he lied.

"Perhaps some to take with you then? It was made by my youngest, Gardenia. She is a wonderful cook."

"What? No. I mean, no thank you. I am warm enough," he replied without so much as a flicker of a smile.

"Just some tea then?"

"Madam please!"

Gardenia felt grateful for his lack of interest but Mother persisted, offering him all sorts of biscuits and buns in Gardenia's name before the Captain protested that he didn't want anything except to do his duty and be gone. He removed a scroll from the inside of his jacket and unrolled it before realising something was amiss.

"The lady Beaufort? Monsieur Beaufort's daughter. Where is she?"

"She is resting. Would you like me to fetch her?"

"She is unwell?"

"She is in perfect health. Do you require to see her?"

But the Captain was in two minds. The house was cold and unwelcoming. The fires hadn't been lit for several days and from what he could see, a great deal of furniture had been sold off since he'd last been here. Oh, how the late Monsieur *Le Chevalier* must have been turning in his grave.

"I am required to see her," the Captain simply answered.

Mother went upstairs and knocked on Ella's door while Marigold and Gardenia attempted to engage the Captain in a little unarmed conversation. Mother knocked again and eventually, footsteps approached from the other side of the door. The lock clicked and the door opened a crack.

"I'm hungry," Ella said glaring out with disdain.

"Captain Olivier is here and he wishes to see you," Mother replied.

A flash of concern passed over Ella's face and Mother saw it before Ella could disguise her reactions.

"Me? He wants to see me? Why?" she asked.

"He waits for you now, downstairs."

Ella dithered in the doorway before following Mother downstairs to the parlour to be greeted by a click of the heels.

"Mademoiselle, you are well, I trust?" he said, noting Ella's somewhat gaunt and pasty appearance. The late Monsieur Beaufort's daughter now resembled his home, a shadow of her former glory.

Ella took a seat next to Marigold, albeit reluctantly, and the Captain returned to his parchment.

"*Ahem-hem-hem*," he coughed to preface his announcement, printed in copperplate text on a lily-white scroll. "Upon the King's instructions, it has been decreed that…" he then rattled through the same proclamation as was pinned up in the town square before ending as he had started, with another, "*ahem-hem-hem.*"

Mission accomplished, he rolled up his scroll and stuffed it away before waiting for Madame *La Chevalière* and her daughters' response. Nothing. In every other household in the Kingdom, eligible maidens had exploded with excitement upon hearing the news, but here in the Beaufort's château, both Madame and her three daughters simply sat and stared at him.

"You're invited to a party," he simplified. "At the Palace. Next Saturday. Eight till late."

The ladies nodded thoughtfully and Mother thanked him for coming all this way out to deliver his message, insisting her daughters stand and curtsey for the good Captain, which they all duly did, even Ella.

"Now, about that broth?" Mother began.

"I must go. Good day to you all," the Captain insisted, bowing with one last click his heels before hurrying out of this mausoleum and into the relative warmth of autumn.

"What could this mean, Mother dear?" Marigold asked as they stood on the front porch and watched their visitor depart.

"I sense the Grand Duke's hand is behind this. Rather clever in a way," she said.

"But what does it mean for us?" Gardenia pressed.

Mother thought on the matter for a few moments, fiddling with her opal ring as she did in times of deliberation.

"Providence," she replied after a time. "If we play along, we should have nothing to fear. In fact, we might even have everything to gain."

"You mean, I might marry the Prince after all?" Ella said to Marigold's obvious amusement.

"I don't think you're his type," Marigold replied, with no word of a lie.

But Mother's ambitions were rather more practical in design. "A great many girls are going to be asking the same question," she said. "And they will all need gowns in the hope of attracting the Prince's attentions. We have much work to do."

Mother hurried off to begin scouring the château for every schilling, livre and cent before gathering up what was left of the family silver.

"But how will we eat, Mother?" Gardenia objected when she saw Mother had left no cutlery in their drawers.

"Rather well, if all goes to plan."

Mother loaded anything of value onto Liquorice's trap while Marigold went upstairs and got dressed into her winter riding gear. She would ride into town and return with every stitch of quality cloth she could lay her hands on. These were her instructions. Time was of the essence and while she was gone, Mother and Gardenia would get on with the work of creating dozens of cutting patterns. The dresses would not be made to measure. They would simply produce as many as they could in a variety of sizes, turning them out quickly and cheaply. Most of the girls invited to the ball were of limited means and would have nothing suitable to wear and no way of affording one of Monsieur Vasseur's creations. This was Mother's big moment. This was her chance. Monsieur Vasseur could keep the aristocracy. Mother would grab the mass market.

"We must labour around the clock," Mother said. "There is a fortune to be had if we all work hard."

"All of us?" Gardenia asked, glancing over to Ella, still wrapped in a thick shawl and staring out of the window towards the woods beyond.

Mother realised Gardenia was right. Every pair of hands, no matter how dainty, needed to be conscripted if they were to make the most of this opportunity.

"Ella, my dear stepdaughter, the ball is upon us once

again. And we have but nine days to remake your father's fortune. This is a golden opportunity. For all of us. Are you with us or are you not?"

Ella continued staring out of the window as she considered her options. Mother had half-expected her to explode in a rage at the suggestion of turning her noble château into a weaver's cottage but Ella was uncharacteristically quiet.

"I will be back shortly," she said, heading upstairs. She returned several minutes later with a small box full of jewellery.

"Take this," she said handing it to Mother. "Get what you can for it."

Mother looked inside and was surprised to discover just how much Ella had been holding out on them. This box could have easily seen them through winter but now it would do more than put mere bread on their table. It would sow the seeds for all their futures. Ella had realised this. Just in time.

"Thank you, my child. This will benefit us all."

Ella had made a sacrifice for the greater good and it wouldn't be forgotten. Sometimes the strongest alliances were forged in the face of adversity.

"Okay, I'm with you," she said.

CHAPTER THIRTY-FIVE

FOLLOWING THE RAID on the bandit camp in Srendizi, the King's Guards returned home in triumph with the Lieutenant leading his men from the front. For once.

Catherine Petit was ordered to accompany their march back to base with an all-conquering drum beat but it sickened her to do so. The last time she'd struck her drum a man had died and she'd seen nothing glorious in that, no matter what he'd been accused of. She couldn't get the way Private Xavier had continued kicking to the end out of her mind, almost as though in the midst of his own execution, he still expected to find a toehold to take the weight from the rope. He hadn't given out meekly. He'd striven to live, right until the end. Three minutes it had taken Private Xavier to die. This might have seemed like an age to him but it had become an eternity to Catherine. She saw him in her sleep and every time she closed her eyes; his final moments played out over and over again until she could barely blink for fear of seeing his struggles. Private Xavier might now be gone but he was far from forgotten and would remain so for a very long time indeed. At least, as far as Catherine was concerned, if no one else.

In overriding contrast, the Lieutenant couldn't have been happier with how the last few days had gone and rode into Andovia with his head held high, like a Roman general of old. Duly, he took a keen interest in Catherine's playing, almost as though he sensed her discomfort and demanded she played louder and louder every time her drum beats trailed off.

By the time the column reached their base, Catherine's hands were in agony and she could barely hold her sticks another beat. The Lieutenant didn't bother to dismiss his men, he was in such a hurry to report back to the Captain, so the Sergeant gave the order and helped Catherine back to the barracks. He dropped her into her cot and she slept in her clothes through lunch, supper and beyond. The Sergeant saved her a chunk of bread and left it by her bedside but it was still sat there in the morning, only marginally more stale than it had been the night before.

"You sleep for another minute and I'll have to report you for desertion," a voice came to her in her dream.

Catherine awoke, with the sounds of Private Xavier's gurgles receding into the night.

It was daylight and the Sergeant was holding a tin of coffee for her. Catherine sat up and tried to accept the hot drink but her hands felt like claws.

"You missed parade," the Sergeant told her, taking a seat opposite.

"Am I in trouble?" Catherine asked, finally taking the tin the only way she could, by cradling it between her wrists.

"I marked you down as wounded-in-action," he said with a shrug. "Think you'll live?"

Catherine sipped her coffee and decided she might, but that it wouldn't be something to boast about.

"What will happen to the rest of the prisoners?" she asked, not sure she could stand the sight of another hanging.

"Dungeons probably, for the lucky ones."

"And for the unlucky ones?"

"Well now, I guess Corporal Samuel will earn his corn," the Sergeant explained with a knowing look.

Catherine thought about the soldier who had carried out Private Xavier's hanging. His hideous leer had burned itself into Catherine's mind almost as much as the Private's death jig but she didn't have to rely on her memory any time she wanted to see him because he was always around, on parade, by the campfires and on the gate. She'd noticed him before. With a face like his, who wouldn't? But now she couldn't get away from him. He repulsed her, both physically and by his actions, yet he intrigued her too.

"How did he mess up his face?" she asked, knowing that it wasn't prudent but feeling compelled all the same.

"His father gave them to him," the Sergeant said. Catherine was horrified until the Sergeant broke into a smile and explained that the Corporal's scars were hereditary, an all too common problem these days, particularly amongst the poor. "But he's one of the lucky ones. He might not be beautiful but at least he's got a full quota of extremities. I've seen some poor critters who were born without a finger or a toe to speak of. And what do you suppose happens to these useless cripples when they grow up? No work for them. And no corn either."

Catherine pondered this as she warmed all ten of her own fully functioning fingers and tried not to think about it.

"Someone has to do what Samuel does," the Sergeant said. "At least until this world learns to get along with itself. And Sam's a good man. He cares. Sounds odd but it's true. As far as he's concerned, he wasn't serving the Lieutenant back in Srendizi, he was serving his old pal Xavi, making sure he didn't suffer unduly, which is more than can be said for you with your four-hour drum roll. What a way to prolong the inevitable."

That hit home and made Catherine feel even worse, if that was even possible, while at the same time re-evaluating Corporal Samuel.

"It's barbaric," she said with a shudder.

"It's soldiering," the Sergeant replied. "Think the other side wouldn't do the same if they got their hands on you? At least here they'll get a proper trial and get to put their side of the story across, which is more than can be said for the Rousseaus."

Catherine tried not to think about the Rousseaus either. The Sergeant would conjure up their names every time her motivation took a dip but she'd never met them. This may have been down to the men they'd captured but how did two wrongs ever make a right? Even at the age of fourteen, Catherine understood that. There was so much hardship in the world, so much suffering, and yet all anyone in power seemed intent on doing was inflicting more of it upon the world. When would it end? The Sergeant read her expression and dug deep into his memory.

"There's an old soldiers' poem I remember from way back. Want to hear it?"

Catherine didn't. She wasn't sure poetry was the answer to the world's troubles but the Sergeant seemed intent on reciting it all the same. He began:

> *"A soldier's life is hard and short,*
> *He takes much land yet keeps but nought.*
> *He kills and kills and kills again,*
> *On different days with different men.*
> *The fighting never truly ends,*
> *The ground turned red with foe and friends.*
> *Until one day his God finds he,*
> *For what will be will surely be.*
> *So worry not these mortal things,*
> *We are but shot in the slings of Kings."*

Catherine let the lines wash over her. She liked the sound of the rhythm but struggled to relate to the message. She didn't feel like a soldier. She felt like an orphan girl posing as a drummer boy in order to trick the army into giving her bread and coffee twice a day. The Sergeant's lines had no meaning for her.

"All of us think that at first," the Sergeant said. "None of us were born to this life and most of us only took up arms for the same reason you did, for food and shelter. And dry socks. And boots. King and country?" he said, shaking his head. "What would I know about that?"

"Hardly makes me feel any better though, your poem. It's like you're saying that we don't matter, that our lives don't matter, and that we should just accept that."

"Ohhh bless," the Sergeant smiled patronisingly. "Did you want to matter then? Now there's a curious concept."

He stood to leave. It was a glorious day outside the grimy barracks windows but Catherine felt grungy thanks to sleeping in her clothes all night; clothes she'd worn to war and back. This sort of thing was acceptable in the field but not in the barracks. But before he bid her good day, he dug into his pocket and pulled out something shiny. It glinted in the light of the new day and Catherine recognised it as his Medal of Valour, the one he'd won at the Battle of Cedar Hill.

"Here, take this," he said, holding it out to her.

"You want me to look after it for you?" Catherine asked in confusion.

"Nope, it's yours," he said.

"But why?"

"That was a brave thing you did back in Srendizi, saving those horses. Without you they would have all been burned to a crisp," he said tossing the medal into her lap when she failed to take it. "Now tell me that you don't matter."

And with that he left, his parting words hanging in the air to give Catherine something else to think about besides the late Private Xavier.

CHAPTER THIRTY-SIX

AS IT TURNED OUT, Mother wasn't the only entrepreneur in town. In the days leading up to the Prince's ball, an entire industry that had never previously existed — or at least, never existed on such a scale — sprang up to cash in on this once-in-a-lifetime event.

Soap, perfume, makeup and dentistry: until now all of these things had been the preserves of the upper classes but suddenly, every girl in town needed a good wash and a few teeth pulling. It was a boom-time for the town's beauticians and, by and large, most were content with the surge in business to take unfair advantage of the situation. Most were. But not all.

"It's so beautiful. I never thought in a month of Sunday's that I'd ever wear anything so lovely. I feel like… like… a lady," Heidi said, swishing this way and that as she looked into the full-length mirror Marigold had leaned against Liquorice's trap. There was nothing vain about the way Heidi admired herself. She was simply startled, such was the effect the dress had on her. Marigold and Gardenia had been doing the rounds for several days now, calling upon girls at their places of work so that they might select a dress for the upcoming ball and try it on for size. Word had quickly spread and the sisters could barely keep pace with demand.

Heidi was a housemaid in service to Lord Ricci. She was eighteen, unmarried and had known only two sets of clothes most of her adult life (which started at twelve for Andovian serving girls); a baggy maid's uniform that had been worked almost as much as Heidi and a dowdy black frock she was obliged to wear to church. So seeing herself in a full-length orange gown that fitted like a glove to accentuate her hourglass figure was, for Heidi, a revelation. It was like seeing a version of herself that she had no idea existed.

"Would you like to try on the red one too?" Marigold asked but Heidi was pushed for time and already smitten with the orange.

"No, this is perfect. I love it. I'll take it," she said, almost in tears at having to swap back into her housemaid's uniform. The sisters had pulled up around the back of Lord Ricci's townhouse, in a narrow alleyway that ran down to the main thoroughfare. They weren't on Lord Ricci's property but his Lordship would take a dim view of the sisters hawking so openly on his doorstep all the same.

Marigold and Gardenia held up a sheet for Heidi to get changed behind and folded the dress up afterwards.

"The price is forty schillings," Marigold told her, which was expensive for a dress but not exorbitantly so. Heidi, like most maids, would've been on around seven schillings a week. After bed and board had been deducted at source and she'd sent a couple of schillings back to her elderly mother in the countryside, she would've had two or three schillings left over each week for herself. But unlike most of the girls who'd bought dresses from them so far, Heidi had no need to pay in instalments. She had the money in full, all forty schillings of it, and still retained another ten for good measure to get her teeth straightened and her pockmarks filled.

"Have you been knocking off his Lordship's silver?" Marigold asked.

"Of course not. Monsieur Guillory loaned me fifty schillings yesterday," Heidi explained, then wondered why Marigold and Gardenia looked concerned. "It's alright, he's helping out a lot of girls this week. It's not just me."

"On what terms?" Marigold asked.

"What?" Heidi asked in confusion.

"How much did he say you needed to pay back?"

"Just a couple of schillings a week," Heidi replied, still none the wiser what the problem was.

"For how long?" Marigold asked.

"I don't know," Heidi shrugged. "Till it's all paid back, I guess."

It was a pretty poor guess by anyone's standards and Marigold was right to be suspicious. Monsieur Guillory had no trade to exploit. He could not make soap, mix perfume, style hair nor design ballgowns but as Lord Ricci's long-time personal valet he did have a considerable nest egg to fall back on and he was intent on tripling his pension before the week was out.

Marigold handed Heidi back her purse.

"Now listen to me; you give Monsieur Guillory back his money, every last schilling you understand, and we shall collect payment from you each week directly until we're all square. We won't take a schilling more. You have our word. And make sure you tell the other girls too."

"But Monsieur Guillory won't like that," Heidi said nervously. "We already shook on it."

"Well, you can just go and unshake on it, can't you," Marigold said. "because if you don't, you'll still be paying him off for this one night in five years time. Or at least trying to."

"One way or the other," Gardenia added, despite not quite understanding how.

Heidi wasn't sure she liked the sound of that. But she took the sisters' advice nevertheless and Marigold and Gardenia went on their merry way happy, their dress shop on wheels rattling over the dusty cobblestones of Andovia.

*

ELLA WAS AS GOOD AS HER WORD and helped out as best she could, although she was pretty hopeless at almost everything. She couldn't sew for toffee, cut cloth for toffee or even make coffee for toffee but she did at least pitch in, which was all anyone had asked of her. However, there was one thing she refused to do. She would not model Mother's cut-priced designs around town as Marigold and Gardenia had been doing. As the daughter of a nobleman, albeit a very minor and a very dead one, she simply couldn't get her head around the concept of touting for business. Mother accepted her objections. This might have ruffled Marigold and Gardenia's feathers but overall, it was hardly a great loss. Ella was a funny shape even for a French girl. She was unnaturally thin and impossibly tall. Nothing fitted her. Certainly nothing that a normal girl might wear, which was Mother's intended market, so she was excused all catwalk duties and instead asked to simply fetch and carry for the cause.

By the morning of the Prince's ball, Mother and the sisters had made almost seventy dresses and, moreover, they had sold every single one of them. They could've easily sold more, twice as many in fact, but they simply ran out of time. They'd worked their fingers to the bone and had burned the midnight oil but they were solvent again. Their prayers had been answered. Perhaps this was because their prayers had been rather more pragmatic than most of those coming out of Andovia this week.

Mother was happy but Marigold insisted they still had a few hours and several rolls of pink and yellow left before the roads around the Palace were clogged again.

"I think we can still make another six dresses at least. Mother, if you get started on the cuts I'll hurry into town and find the buyers," Marigold offered but Mother shook her head.

"Actually, we need only three," she said. "One for each of you. Unless, of course, you have something better to do tonight?"

Marigold had been so focused on making hay while the sun shone that she had forgotten their own invitations. Gardenia too, in light of her last trip to the Palace, had all but given up hope of ever setting foot in there again but Mother was adamant. The Duke had sent his own man to invite them personally. It would be unwise to turn down such an offer.

"But what if it's a trap?" Marigold whispered.

"Then it's a very elaborate one," Mother said. Besides, there were matches to be made and her daughters needed to grasp this opportunity. Who knew when such a chance might come along again.

"You mean I might go to the ball, too?" Ella said in wonder.

"You are my daughter. You have been invited. Of course, you shall go," Mother replied.

The answer seemed to genuinely surprise Ella, almost as though she'd expected to be left at home while the others attended. They might have bitched and bickered since the day they'd met and she might have proved hopeless this week and actually cost them work rather than contributed to it but she was still family and that counted for something. At least, it did with Mother.

"And I might see the Prince?" Ella said, her voice tinged with barely concealed delight.

"You might indeed," Mother confirmed, her voice tinged with completely unconcealed foreboding.

"Then dreams really do come true," Ella said with glee, disappearing behind an enormous smile and giving herself a warm fluffy hug.

Marigold and Gardenia exchanged glances but Mother scowled at them not to say anything. What would be would most certainly be.

"I have prepared dresses for each of you," Mother said now. "Come, let us try them on so that I might make the final adjustments."

Waiting for them in the backroom were three beautiful ballgowns: one blue, one yellow and one maroon. They were similar in design to the dresses they'd been making all week — it wouldn't have been prudent to have worn something too different from those they'd made for everyone else — but the materials were far superior and the cuts and needlework so much more intricate. Mother had taken a great deal of care and attention with these particular dresses. Each had been made with love.

"They are gorgeous," Gardenia squealed with delight, gathering up the yellow gown and holding it to herself as she stepped in front of a mirror. Marigold examined the maroon one and thanked Mother with a warm embrace. But it was Ella's reaction that gratified Mother the most. She'd fully expected a hissy tantrum from her. An outburst of outrage over a dress that, whilst beautiful, simply could not compare with the Prince-snaring dress they'd previously made for her. That would have been impossible. This was the best Mother could manage. Ella would not look out of place amongst the other daughters of the great and the good standing but she would not outshine them either. She would be a rose amongst other roses. Beautiful, if slightly cheaper by the dozen.

"Thank you," Ella said, picking up her blue ballgown to examine it. "It's perfect."

"I have some beads that would work well with your dress," Gardenia said, conscious that Ella had sacrificed her jewellery to help them buy the materials.

"And I have a sash," Marigold offered, wanting to show her gratitude also.

Mother was finally content.

"You'll marry well yet," she declared with pride.

"The Prince?" Ella declared.

"Captain Olivier?" Gardenia groaned inwardly.

Marigold couldn't think of anyone other than Hans or Dirty Didi.

Mother simply shrugged. "That is now up to you."

CHAPTER THIRTY-SEVEN

AS BEFORE, the Prince's ball arrived with much fanfare. Anyone who was anyone — and pretty much everyone else — arrived at the Palace for seven sharp, a full hour before the start of the ball, only to find an enormous crowd already pressed up against the gates. Some had been camped out since the previous evening and many wore strikingly similar dresses but no one seemed to mind. Most were only too excited just to be here in the first place to notice anyone else, even the ones they were stepping on in an effort to get to the front of the queue.

Baron Weiss's coach pulled up at the sight of the frenzied horde and his driver was rocketed for suggesting he and Suzette might like to try walking.

"They should set the Guards on the lot of them!" Baron Weiss thundered before directing his driver to circle the Palace until the King saw fit to either open the gates or the cannons.

Several miles away, waiting on the drive outside the Beaufort's château, Liquorice snorted impatiently. Gardenia shared the sentiment. She, Marigold, Mother and their horse had been stood around for almost half an hour waiting for Ella to join them and still there was no sign of her.

"Shall I go in and see what's keeping her?" Marigold asked. She wasn't bothered about missing the start of the ball but she was quite keen to be there for the end.

"I'll go," Mother told her, handing Liquorice's reins to Gardenia and jumping off the trap. They had a long ride ahead of them and the nights were drawing in. Mother was keen to get to town before it got too dark. She wasn't worried about bandits. Soldiers and militiamen were out in force patrolling all routes into town but these guardians were no defence against a bat in the hair. But before she could take another step, Ella emerged from the château in her undergarments holding what looked like a bundle of blue ribbons.

"Why did you do it?" she cried, her face a mass of tears and smudged makeup. "Why did you let me get my hopes up?"

Three women and the horse looked at the tattered bundle and saw that it was Ella's blue ballgown, the one that Mother had made for her only yesterday.

Mother could scarcely believe her eyes. Hours of work had been slashed in the blink of an eye. She turned to Marigold and Gardenia, still sat upon the trap and looking beautiful in their own elegant (and unblemished) ballgowns, and saw red. She had always known there had been tension between them but she never dreamed they'd do something like this.

"Which of you did this? Out with it. I demand to know who is responsible!" Mother snapped, taking both Marigold and Gardenia by surprise.

"It wasn't me!" Marigold exclaimed, shocked at the insinuation.

"Nor I!" Gardenia insisted, turning pale when she saw all eyes on her.

"This dress did not tear itself apart and I certainly didn't do it so it had to be one of you," Mother reasoned but still her daughters protested their innocence until the whole thing descended into a four-way shouting match.

"You all did it! You're all in it together!" Ella bawled, throwing the ruined dress at Mother's feet and running back inside in floods of tears.

"Please, Mother, on my word of honour, I didn't do this," Marigold swore as earnestly as she could before realising something. "And neither did Gardenia. She's been with me the whole day so she couldn't have. Why on Earth would we?"

"Then who did?" Mother asked, accepting that she may have been a little hasty in her accusations but at a loss to know who else could have done it.

They turned the dress over and saw that the damage had been done not with the hands but with a blade of sorts. If it had been a few torn seams Mother could have repaired it but this was completely ruined. It was no longer a dress. It was only good for dusters now, albeit rather expensive ones.

But who could have done it?

If neither Mother, Marigold nor Gardenia were responsible then it must have been a stranger. But a stranger who had broken into the château, tiptoed up the stairs, cut Ella's dress to pieces and then tiptoed out again, all without stealing anything in the process?

"One of those orphan children perhaps?" Marigold suggested. "I saw them hanging around by the side of the road again yesterday."

But that made even less sense to Mother. Orphans stole food. They didn't damage property for no reason, particularly not the property of someone who had been bringing them cake.

After a little more thinking, it dawned on the women that Ella rarely left the place. In fact, as far as they knew, she'd only ever been into town once, the first time they'd met her, which turned out to be the day she and Monsieur Beaufort had arrived in Andovia. Since then, she had barely set foot outside the grounds, spurning every invitation and living her life as though she were a princess in a tower.

"Waiting to be rescued by the Prince?" Mother suggested.

Marigold had always assumed that this had been Monsieur Beaufort's doing, that he was being overprotective since her mother had died, but he was no longer here to watch over her and Ella had still shunned every opportunity to go into town. Marigold looked at the dress and wondered, was this a deliberate act of sabotage in order to avoid leaving the château?

"But why would she? It makes no sense," Gardenia said, looking for logic where there was only lunacy to be found. "If it's her dream to meet the Prince, then this is her big chance. When else is she going to meet him?"

"She's clearly delusional, pathological even," Mother deduced, having suspected as much but Marigold was not so sure. There seemed to be a method to Ella's madness but she was damned if she could make out what it was.

"I shall put your theory to the test," Mother said, heading back indoors to offer Ella an alternative dress. She had one left over, an early mock-up that she could take in and accessorise with a few ribbons and bows to turn into something lovely but Ella refused to even contemplate it.

"You would make a clown of me for your own amusement?" she wept miserably on the stairs as though her world had just collapsed. "What did I do to deserve such cruelty?"

"You have us wrong, dear child. Please come with us tonight."

Even in a mocked-up frock, Ella was still a rare beauty and would no doubt attract a great many suitors. The Prince might have been all she could think about but there would be plenty of other men in big boots on show tonight. And this could only prove beneficial for all of them. In the first instance, it would help Ella get over her childish infatuation with the Prince. In the second, she could find the love and security she'd lost when her father had died. And in the third, it might ultimately free up their attic room. Which was what Mother was really hoping.

But before Mother could say another word, Ella jumped to her feet and ran up the stairs to her bedroom, bolting the door behind her to stop Mother from following. Fearing that she might be right, and that Ella might indeed be off her rocker, Mother double-bolted her door from the outside and went back downstairs to rejoin her — dare she say it — *real* daughters.

"I don't know what's going on with her but I now know that you're right. She must have done it herself," she told them with a heavy heart.

It saddened Mother that it had come to this. They'd been getting on so well all week that she thought they'd come through the worst of it. But Ella was nothing if not unpredictable, almost like she was several different people locked in the one mind, each conflicting with and blissfully ignorant of the other. Perhaps this was why Monsieur Beaufort had kept her shut away and why, deep down, Ella feared leaving the security of the château?

"Are we not going?" Marigold asked but Mother would not let Ella deprive her daughters of the chance to secure their own futures.

"Ella will be here when we get back," she concluded, climbing into the trap and taking the reins from Gardenia.

"And if she is not?" Marigold asked, climbing into the seat next to her.

"Then I shall try my hardest not to mourn her too long," Mother promised, cracking the reins to drive Liquorice on, over the tattered bundle of rags that lay discarded in the dirt.

And out from under the prying eyes that watched from above.

CHAPTER THIRTY-EIGHT

THE BALL WAS IN FULL SWING by the time Liquorice trotted up the Palace's gravel driveway. The crowd had been admitted and only a few hawkers and gawkers remained beyond the gates to sweeten and sour the air alike with their fare.

Mother circled the Palace's ornate gold leaf fountain and halted at the foot of a sweeping stone staircase. A magnificent red carpet ran all the way down from the Palace doors and uniformed trumpeters lined the route to herald their arrival. It all seemed a bit much to Marigold but then again, what about royalty didn't?

A coach boy took Liquorice's reins from Mother and drove him around the back to park him in the stables, leaving Mother, Marigold and Gardenia to ascend the red carpet on foot. A quick blast from the trumpeters made sure their ears were ringing by the time they reached the top, whereupon a footman bowed and asked to see their invitation.

Mother dug it from her purse and handed it over.

"Your names?" he asked. They were written on the invitation but guests were asked to confirm their names anyway as most people in this town could not read and it prevented their invitations from falling into the wrong hands.

"Madame Beaufort and daughters," Mother replied.

"Just the two of them?" the footman asked, checking their names against his list.

"My stepdaughter has a headache," Mother replied — or rather was one.

"I have corsages for your daughters," the footman said, handing Marigold a white corsage to slip onto her wrist and Gardenia a pink one.

"How lovely. Aren't they lovely, Mother?" Gardenia cooed, showing off her garland to Mother. Mother cautiously agreed but wondered if the flowers were a gift or a tag. She would find out shortly.

"Through the doors and have a lovely evening, Madame," he said, handing Mother her invitation back and bowing graciously.

Mother, Marigold and Gardenia entered the Palace but not before Gardenia thanked the footman and told him she hoped he had a lovely evening too, which irked Mother and confused the footman.

They followed the red carpet through a grand hallway, which was adorned with magnificent paintings and heroic busts, until arriving at a large set of double doors. Here another Palace official, this one a Majordomo, took their invitation, nodded curtly and opened the door to announce their arrival.

"Madame *La Chevalière* Beaufort and daughters, the ladies Marigold and Gardenia," he called out as the doors opened for them.

He called their names as loudly as he could but such was the din from within the Great Hall that Mother hardly heard her own name so what chance did anyone else have? The Majordomo shrugged, handed Mother back her invitation and pointed to the back of the hall, suggesting that was where they should make their way to — if possible. It looked like a daunting task.

Mother had been to a number of balls and Marigold had attended several too but this was Gardenia's first. And it was not quite how she'd imagined it. It looked more like a bunfight than a ball.

The Great Hall was insanely packed, dangerously so. She'd had no idea there were so many eligible maidens in Andovia and the effect on her senses was akin to being shut in a henhouse that had been hosed down with rosewater. Everywhere she looked, girls with painted faces were pushing and shoving each other, ripping each other's corsages off and jostling for position to catch a glimpse of the Prince. Gardenia got a whack in the ribs when they passed too close to an all-out fight and found herself stepping over three girls who'd already fallen foul of the fracas.

Mother used her elbows where needed and struck a path towards the back. The crowd seemed to grow even thicker here but Mother was no stranger to hand-to-hand combat and soon fought her way through to find a line of footmen standing guard in front of another set of double doors.

"Madame, this way if you please," the nearest footman beckoned, inviting Mother and her daughters to pass through a gap in their lines.

The crowd surged forwards as the footmen parted but more footmen hurried in to keep the mob at bay.

"Let me through!"

"Where's the Prince!"

"I wanna see him?"

"I should be in there an' all," came the cries from the crowd as Mother and Gardenia were ushered through the lines but suddenly the footmen closed ranks to leave Marigold outside.

"Wait, what? That's my daughter also. She is with us," Mother objected but the footman simply replied that she had the wrong colour corsage.

"Holders of pink corsages and their chaperones only," she was told and suddenly Mother noticed that pretty much every girl in sight had a white corsage. Only Gardenia's was pink.

"There must be some mistake. Marigold was given the wrong colour. She should've had a pink corsage like her sister," Mother said, a sentiment that was echoed by everyone else within earshot.

"Me too!"

"I had one and it got lost!"

"That thieving trollop nicked mine!"

"Let me in!"

"Where's the Prince?"

"I want to marry him!"

But it was no good. The footmen had their orders and they were clinging onto them for dear life in the face of extreme provocation.

"I'm sorry, Madame *La Chevalière*, but my instructions were explicit," he apologised.

"Marigold, go back and see the first footman. Tell him there's been a mistake," Mother told Marigold but Marigold's reply was lost as she was swallowed up by the surging crowd.

"Please Madame, you have to go in now. I can't keep this door open for much longer. We've almost been overrun three times already," the footman shouted as politely as he could.

"I am not leaving my eldest daughter behind. Let me find her."

"I cannot re-admit you if you go out. I'm sorry, but those are the Grand Duke's instructions."

Mother looked back but she saw no sign of Marigold. There were too many people in here and all of them were fighting to get to the front. Would she even find her again in that crush? And what of Gardenia? Everyone knew that Marigold's chances had come and gone. Reputations, after all, were everything in Andovia. But Gardenia was an altogether different prospect. And the Grand Duke had clearly orchestrated their separation. Mother felt compelled to stay with her youngest daughter; first and foremost to look out for her in case the Grand Duke tried anything sinister, but also to accomplish what she'd set out to do. She might never get this chance again.

"Tell my eldest daughter, should she come back, that I will meet her outside before midnight," Mother told the footman.

"Very good, Madame," he said, willing her inside so that he could shut the doors again. "Get ready to retreat to fall-back positions," he then told the other footmen in the line.

Through a sea of over-curled hairdos, Marigold saw Mother and Gardenia hurrying from the Great Hall as she was jostled further and further back. She gave up trying to resist and let herself be pushed away by the crowd. Too many girls had piled forwards in a desperate attempt to breach the inner sanctum but that room was reserved for very important people — something Marigold was clearly not.

Away from the undignified crush, the Great Hall opened up to a more manageable bustle. There were so many girls and hardly any boys, save for a few frantic footmen and servants who were trying to keep up with the insatiable demand for free fizz and nibbles.

Marigold noticed many of the dresses she had sold and exchanged pleasantries with the wearers. For so many, the reality hadn't lived up to the fairytale. The Prince had briefly appeared on a balcony overlooking the Hall and waved to all the girls. He'd even thrown out one or two pink corsages but these were quickly torn to atoms in the melee below and the Prince was advised against throwing any more, lest they trigger an all-out riot. The Prince had laughed, blown a few kisses then disappeared as quickly as he had appeared. And that was that. That was as close to a royal dance any of the girls in this room were likely to get.

They felt duped. Some felt foolish. Others felt angry. And some, like those in the crush near the doors to the inner sanctum, still believed. But no one went home. Overall, the feeling was that they were here now — and for one night only — so they might as well make the most of it because tomorrow they'd be back to sweeping floors and making candles.

Further back still, the Great Hall opened up to reveal a

large and almost empty dance floor. A line of impatient ladies stood on the edges of the dance floor, desperately sending semaphore with their eyelashes to a handful of 'gentlemen' opposite. Not every man of noble birth had opted to hide away from the hoi polloi with the rest of the VIPs. Some, like the third son of the Earl of Chambrizi or the second cousin of the Count De La Ville, had weighed up their options and seen there was more fun to be had in this Hall.

Marigold noticed one or two of Mother's dresses in here, including Heidi, Lord Ricci's housemaid, but as lovely as they looked, none were as refined as the dress Marigold had worn. In a room full of maidens, she was undoubtedly (and finally) the belle of the ball — but only because the rest of them were house/chamber and/or milk maidens. Marigold frowned. She felt as though she was caught between two worlds: too genteel for this room; not genteel enough for the next.

She decided to move away from the dance floor — the scene of so many prior disappointments — and see the night out as a wallflower, only for the wall she'd chosen to lean against to suddenly disappear. A hidden hatch drew back and a tray of sausages reared up before her.

"Pardon me, but allow me to remove them from the elevator before you try to eat them," a servant said, ushering Marigold to one side so that he could remove the tray from the dumbwaiter. "Please, now take as many as you wish."

"I er... thank you, I'm okay," she replied but a mob of scullery maids who'd known better than most where the free food would be coming from and had no such reservations took the servant for every sausage he had.

Marigold moved off again only to pull up in shock. A gentleman was approaching her. She looked around in case a sausage was caught in her hair but no, his eyes were fairly and squarely on her. Marigold barely had time to breathe before he was upon her. She'd never received such attention before and felt herself turn scarlet beneath his gaze. The gentleman was magnificently handsome: tall, slim and young, with a soft jaw, kind eyes and fair skin. He wore a silver tunic and a blonde hairpiece and looked for all accounts like a proper dandy. Marigold expected him to bowl her off her feet with bluster and bravado but quite the reverse, he seemed coy, almost shy even. It was most unexpected.

He looked down with his kind eyes, smiled awkwardly and then bowed before her.

"Mademoiselle, would you do me the honour of granting me this dance?" he said with almost no conviction at all. Why he should have no confidence in himself when he was a gentleman in a Hall full of commoners? It was a mystery to Marigold but it made him all the more endearing for it.

Marigold remembered to curtsey. Having never been asked to dance before, it had all been theory up until now but suddenly she was stepping out onto the dance floor to put into practice what Mother had prepared her for her whole life.

"May I?" the young man asked, holding his free hand a short way from her shoulder.

"You may," Marigold agreed, shuddering slightly when he placed his gloved hand upon her.

The band struck up with a waltz and the young man led Marigold around the dance floor three steps at a time. He was a good dancer as far as Marigold could tell — although she had only Gardenia to compare him with — but he was clearly uneasy. Perhaps this was his first dance too?

Their eyes met and Marigold smiled but the young man just looked away. He seemed sad, apologetic even, almost as though he was doing something he wasn't supposed to. Marigold wondered what it could have been? Was he promised to another, like Hans?

Hans?

Why had she thought of Hans? Now? When she was in the arms of another?

She'd barely thought of him all week and now she couldn't shake him from her mind. His smile. His touch. His kiss. The memories hit her like a stone but she would not let Hans spoil this moment. This was her magic moment, the one she would take from this night and treasure whenever she felt unhappy. This was her happy ending.

All around the dance floor, girls looked on and tittered. It wasn't quite the reaction Marigold had expected but then again most of these girls had never set foot inside a real ball before and therefore had no idea how to behave. In amongst the sea of faces, Marigold saw Heidi frantically trying to attract her attention. She seemed to be trying to tell her something but Marigold couldn't hear what it was. Several other girls pushed Heidi aside and Marigold gave her no more mind, imagining it was something to do with her dress. As if this was the moment to ask for that sort of advice? Marigold would seek her out and ask her what the problem was after the dance.

"You move well sir. Might I ask your name?" Marigold said, knowing this was a little forward of her.

"Edmund," the young man replied after a moment's hesitation. Marigold waited for him to reveal his family name and title, as was the custom, but none were forthcoming making her wonder if he was illegitimate, which might have explained his presence in this Hall and his painful reserve.

"I'm Marigold," Marigold told him when she realised he wasn't going to reciprocate. "Marigold Beaufort."

"My apologies," he said.

"That's alright," she smiled. "Thank you for asking me to dance." But this just made Edmund sink even deeper into himself.

Marigold was used to coy men. She and Hans — again with Hans! — had guarded their affections for years but there should have been no barriers between her and Edmund. This was a ball, after all. People were permitted to dance. Even if the onlookers didn't think so.

When their waltz came to an end, Marigold and Edmund parted with a curtsey and a bow, prompting all those watching on to hoot in the most unseemly way. Marigold was baffled. Was the spectacle of a lady and gentleman dancing together so amusing to these people? Had they really never seen such a thing before?

Edmund looked mortified and could scarcely look Marigold in the eye. "I'm so sorry. Please, forgive me," he just kept repeating shamefacedly.

From the other side of the dance floor, several gentlemen now strode, friends of Edmund Marigold assumed. But they were no friends. And they were no gentlemen either. They could barely conceal their delight and slapped Edmund on the back for a job well done.

"What is the meaning of this?" Marigold asked only to finally see what everyone else had known.

Edmund slipped out of his silver tunic and handed it back to a jacketless Viscount, along with his blonde hairpiece. The Viscount, in turn, handed Edmund a servant's coat and white hairpiece which Edmund now put on.

Marigold was horrified. She had danced with a servant in front of every girl in town. It had all been a cruel trick. This was why they had all been laughing. And what, no doubt, Heidi had tried to warn her about. She, the girl from the big house, with the titled Mother and the most expensive dress on show, had been brought down a peg or two. And how the other girls had loved it?

Marigold ran from the Great Hall. Her humiliation complete. And one she would take from this night always.

CHAPTER THIRTY-NINE

IN THE UPPER HALL, beyond the thin red line of footmen, the atmosphere was rather more refrained if no less competitive. For in here, on show for all the world to see, stood the ultimate prize — tantalisingly close and yet further away than anyone could've imagined. The Upper Hall was smaller than the Great Hall but just as grand, with herds of stuffed animal heads staring down impassively upon the people who had put them there.

At the far end of the Upper Hall, on a grand stage and surrounded by dignitaries, stood the Prince in his finest regalia and decorated like a cake in a baker shop's window. His uniform was so white that it almost hurt the eyes to gaze upon him for too long and his chest glittered with more medals than there'd been battles in living memory, but the effect was stunning. He looked every inch the epic hero and his people could not tear their eyes away from him — just as the Grand Duke had predicted. Down to the last detail.

But the Prince was forlorn. He looked upon his prospects with a heavy heart. The desperation in so many eyes terrified him. Each girl had been born into a life of privilege and wealth and yet this paled into insignificance next to what the Prince could offer them. At least from a material point of view anyway.

But what would they say if they knew the truth? As one of these girls surely would eventually. What would they think of him then? These were just some of the thoughts going through his mind as he stood before his people looking magnificent but feeling wretched. Why did he have to marry someone anyway? There were plenty of Queens throughout history who'd never married. Why couldn't a Prince exist without a Princess? His father had managed perfectly well since his own dear sweet mother had died. Why did he have to have some sour-faced old trout forced upon him?

"The lady Isabella, only daughter of the Monsieur and Madame Eames," the Palace's senior Majordomo announced, ushering Isabella forwards to be introduced to (and looked over by) the Prince. She hurried along the red carpet and curtseyed as submissively as she could before unleashing her secret weapons upon him. Her eyes, which everyone knew, were the most beautiful in all Andovia. But the Prince barely noticed her. He'd been introduced to so many ladies by now that he could not distinguish one from the other. This one wore a green dress (urgh!). The last one had worn red. How on Earth was he supposed to choose from them when they all looked the same?

Luckily for Prince Carina, he didn't have to.

The King to his right and the Grand Duke to his left coughed in the Prince's ear to remind him to bow, which he did as economically as possible, before snapping his fingers to summon another drink.

"At least try to show some interest, boy. We are doing this for you, you know," the King growled as he watched his son quaff and hand back his third glass of bubbles in almost as many minutes.

"My gratitude knows no bounds, Papa" the Prince grumbled, snapping his fingers once more but finding his line of credit cut off by an angry snarl from the King.

This was hard enough to bear as it was. How on Earth was he meant to get through this ordeal sober?

In the corner of the room, an orchestra quietly fiddled with itself while they waited for the Prince to select a partner. But unbeknown to them (and to the Upper Hall in general), the Prince's card had already been marked. By the Grand Duke no less. And after a couple more minutes of careful stage management, the Grand Duke finally signalled as such to the Prince when the latest in a long line of ladies curtseyed before him.

The Prince looked down and baulked in horror.

"Her?" he whispered over his enormous gold braided shoulder pads. "Are you serious?"

"She is the one," came back the answer.

"Are we looking at the same girl?" he double-checked.

"Just do it," the King commanded.

But the Prince was aghast. There had to be some mistake for the girl before him was a serving maid? Painted though she was, she was a serving maid nevertheless. And what's more, she knew! She knew about him! She was the one from the thing… the one who knew…!

Gardenia waited and waited, vaguely aware of negotiations taking place beyond her but the only signal she could detect was the Prince's repeated and increasingly urgent snapping of the fingers for a drink that was never going to come.

It took a moment for Mother to notice what was going on too. She'd expected her daughter to be seen and dispatched within a moment but suddenly the mood in the room had changed. Mother looked to see Gardenia still curtseying and the Prince and Grand Duke in frantic conversation.

Something wasn't right. Had Marigold been right? Was the Prince about to make a public example out of Gardenia for witnessing something she shouldn't have? This was Mother's instant dread but even as she was thinking it, she knew this didn't make sense.

But then the penny dropped. Far from summoning the guards and having Gardenia hauled away, the Prince was on the verge of asking her for the first dance. And at the King's insistence too. This was beyond Mother's wildest ambitions for her daughters. Could this really be happening?

She had always lectured her daughters on the need for social mobility but she had never dreamed that one of them might rise to the very top of Andovian society. Particularly, after scraping the very bottom but a few short weeks earlier.

Mother fiddled with her opal ring and scarcely dared to breathe. It was enough to make her forget why she'd come here in the first place. Almost.

Behind Gardenia stood a long line of eager maidens, each willing the Prince to dispatch Gardenia to the rejects pile so that they could hurry forth and lash him with their eyelids. But horror of horrors, the Prince seemed to have made up his mind. This was a disaster. Their hopes and dreams were crumbling before their very eyes.

And for one of those terrible ugly sisters too! This couldn't be.

This was very much in tune with the Prince's line of thinking. He'd taken a great deal of convincing to come around to the Grand Duke's plan but had finally acquiesced on the assurance that his marriage would cause him no more inconvenience than the medals on his chest had. But he had never even contemplated such a mismatch. There would be an outcry. It was one thing to enjoy the company of other men, but quite another to enjoy the company of *commoners*. Was that even legal, the Prince pondered?

"Just extend your hand and smile," the Grand Duke instructed, wishing the Prince had strings attached to his limbs so that he could do it for him.

"I will do no such thing!" the Prince snapped. "I will not dance with a peasant."

"She is not a peasant. She now heralds from a titled family," the Grand Duke told him. "No one will object."

"Since when?"

"Since you *defended her honour*, remember? She has done rather well for herself since then," the Grand Duke assured him as every eye in the Upper Hall bore into them.

"Urgh, new money!"

The King snarled. "Do it, boy. Do it now, or so help me I will cut you off without so much a schilling to your name. Just see if I don't."

The Prince wailed inwardly. He was trapped, his choice had been made for him. What if he didn't like her (which seemed highly likely seeing as she was a commoner)? What if she smelled (equally so)? What if she picked her feet and chewed her food with her mouth open? Most girls were dreadful at the best of times but at least rich girls had been brought up properly and came with money and influence. What could this girl bring to their marriage except for ghastly curtains and even ghastlier relatives?

"She is waiting," he heard the King hiss.

At least, the Prince supposed, he could do as he wished with her. That was the one silver lining to marrying someone without people. He could treat her however he wished and the closest she could come to rebelling would be to throw a hairbrush at him, although she would need one hell of an arm to hit him from where he was planning on keeping her.

"She is still waiting!"

There was, of course, the tricky issue of producing an heir. He had no brothers nor sisters so the line would stop with him if he didn't come up with the goods but perhaps they could adopt. In secret. Surely babies weren't that hard to come by in a Kingdom with a childbirth mortality rate such as theirs?

"Guards…!"

The Prince sighed and finally offered Gardenia his hand, drawing a gasp of consternation from his other guests. It was official. She was the one. A girl from peasant stock and modest means? *She* was worthy of his royal attention? Most onlookers wouldn't have even invited her to hold their cloaks and yet here she was being chosen ahead of them. The cream of society being snubbed for a seamstress's daughter.

Gardenia saw a lifeless pink hand appear before her and looked up to see the Prince. His face was soft but his expression hard. There was no love in his eyes. At least, not for anyone but the fizz waiter.

Most girls would have been bowled over by the offer but Gardenia knew that this was a public relations exercise. She may have been the envy of all Andovia but given the choice, Gardenia would have still opted for a gentleman who admired her over a Prince who most certainly didn't.

Traditionally, one or two words were supposed to accompany the gesture, something along the lines of "do me the honour" etc but the Prince was in no mood to go through the whole rigmarole for a serving girl, even if she did now come with pearls and pretensions. It was enough that his father was forcing him to dance with her. He would be damned if he was going to talk to her too. Thus, Gardenia went on staring blankly at the Prince's limp hand without accepting it, only to notice it start to shake. The Prince was growing angry. He may have kept Gardenia waiting while he argued the toss but it was unthinkable that she should now do the same to him. Could he feel any more humiliated at the hands of this girl?

The answer was, of course, yes. There was always room for things to get worse. Always. This was Andovia, after all.

For at that very moment, just as Gardenia realised what was required of her, a flash of white passed by her face and she was beaten to the punch.

By a bird.

CHAPTER FORTY

IT WAS A DOVE

A white dove to be precise, wearing feathers as crisp as the Prince's uniform and an expression to match. She sat grasping the Prince's index finger with her scaly red claws and folded her wings as though it was her regular perch.

"Coooo!" it said by way of a greeting.

"What the bloody hell!" the Prince replied, falling backwards and waving his arms about to ward off the repellent creature. The dove took off and circled the Hall, causing all those below to seek cover for fear of finding themselves on the receiving end of more than a "coo".

It landed once again, on another outstretched hand, but this time the bird was welcomed with affection.

"Good girl," she was told with a stroke and a whisper.

The crowd gawped in astonishment when they saw who'd caught her but they were no longer gawping at the bird. The girl who held her now held everyone's gaze too. Including the Prince.

She was a sight to behold: tall, elegant and beautiful. And wearing a dress the likes of which no one had ever seen. Well, almost no one. Made from blue silk with a white lace trim, low off the shoulders, tiny at the waist and peppered with pearls and gemstones, it sparkled like a fairy princess's most treasured jewellery box and brought the entire Upper Hall to a standstill.

Mother recognised the dress in an instant, even if she could scarcely believe her eyes. It was the same dress she had made for Ella, the one that had been stolen by Franz Grimaldi and that had led to their near-ruin. But Franz Grimaldi hadn't come wearing it (now that really would have brought the Upper Hall to a standstill). Ella had. Together with a pair of the most incredible cut-glass slippers she had ever seen. They were magnificent and made every other girl in the hall look as though they were wearing clogs.

Like Mother, Gardenia stared agog. It appeared their stepsister had found something to wear after all. How convenient!

Of course, all this happened in the blink of an eye. But while the others stood blinking, the Prince stood thinking. He sensed the mood in the Hall swing at this new girl's appearance and saw his chance. The stranger with the bird tricks was the real deal and everyone could see that, even someone with no eye for the ladies, like he.

He may not have wanted to marry at all, but if he had to choose, as was the case, then it would help if she were the most fabulous creature on two legs, if only to bolster his own public standing. The washerwoman (or whatever she was) at his feet hardly fit the bill but this elegant apparition before him most certainly did. And by the looks on the faces of those nearby, the Prince was not alone in his thinking.

Ella walked as though gliding on air, clinking through the crowd on heels of glass and wilting even the stiffest of resolves with her smile. There was a sense of awe about her. And it wasn't just her beauty, which was innocent and yet all-knowing. She was a breed apart. Perhaps even a species apart too. Particularly from smelly serving girls.

"Thank you for returning my bird, Your Highness. I am in your debt," she said with a sweeping curtsey, bowing not just before the Prince but the entire court.

The Prince seized his chance and leapt off the stage. Even his father couldn't blame him for switching horses at this late stage. He would've thought him blind not to. Ergo, in a room full of infinite choices, there was no longer a choice to be made. Such was the effect this girl's entrance had had on him.

"I don't believe we've had the pleasure," the Prince said, hurrying to offer her his hand.

"I surely would have remembered had we done so," Ella said with a fluttering of the eyelashes.

Someone should have probably pointed out to the Prince that it was poor form to offer your hand to one girl while leaving another stranded but no one gave Gardenia a second thought. A collective relief had settled across the assembled aristocracy. It was one thing to be pipped to the post by thoroughbred filly but quite another to be trounced by an old pony. And Ella had fairly and squarely beaten them all. Even Isabella could see that, myopic as she was.

"Would you do me the honour of this dance?" the Prince asked, snapping his fingers in the direction of the orchestra for once and not the fizz waiter.

"I would be delighted," Ella replied, flicking her bird away to take his hand.

The band struck up and the crowd parted to leave the Prince and his jewel-encrusted angel a clear chessboard of tiles across which to negotiate their first dance.

"Who are you?" the Prince asked as they started to waltz, she in step with he. "Where did you come from?"

"I am but a girl looking to dance with a boy," Ella said.

"Who's your family?" the Prince asked, fervently hoping she didn't have six or seven strapping big brothers who were fiercely protective of her. Or, if she did, that one or two of them liked oysters too.

"I have no family, Your Highness. I am all alone in the world," Ella replied, which was music to his ears. As beautiful as she was, she was still not entirely to his tastes. She would play great on his arm and the rest of the time he could do as he pleased with her, shut her away or abandon her for months on end to be with his favourites, all of which would be considerably easier if she had no one to go grizzling to.

"Your dress is incredible. Who made it for you?" the Prince asked, figuring she must've broke — or robbed — a bank to pay for it.

Ella smiled and whispered in his ear. "It was a present. From my Fairy Godmother."

Across the Hall, there were those who knew otherwise. Mother helped Gardenia to her feet after her legs had turned numb and she could no longer climb up off the floor by herself.

"Mother, have you seen?" Gardenia said when she wobbled to her feet.

"Lower your finger, my girl, it is rude to point," Mother told her.

"Rude to point. Let's see how she likes this then," Gardenia said, attempting to switch fingers before Mother could wrestle her arm down.

"Careful, my dear, for not every eye is on your sweet stepsister," Mother advised.

The stage behind them was almost entirely deserted after the King and his assorted dignitaries had hurried forwards to watch the Prince. Only the Grand Duke remained where he was, watching the room as the room watched the Prince. Or rather, as they watched Ella.

The Grand Duke no more recognised Ella than anyone else did. She'd scarcely left the château since arriving in the Kingdom but she was here now. And what an entrance she had made! But who was she and where had she come from? The Grand Duke couldn't think. But what she was after was only too obvious. Of course, in this respect, she was no different from every other girl in here tonight. But what unnerved the Grand Duke was that Ella seemed to have succeeded where all the others had failed — and without his help too. This had not been the plan. So where did that leave him?

Mother and the Grand Duke exchanged looks, Mother concealing her mock modesty behind a lace fan to curtsey. The Grand Duke failed to acknowledge her. He simply glared at Gardenia in disappointment and quietly fumed.

"What are we going to do?" Gardenia asked, still confused at the sight of Ella dancing with the Prince. "She's wearing her dress. How did she get it back?" It wasn't so much that she'd stolen the Prince. That was not what Gardenia was livid about. It was the manner in which she had done it. All her lies and machinations were now laid bare, if only for Gardenia and Mother to see.

"We do nothing," Mother said. "Now is not the time for redress." Besides, Ella was still family. Just about. Where she went, Mother would make sure they all followed. She looked back at the Grand Duke and saw the confusion etched into his ignoble face. This could still work for them.

The Prince swept Ella around the room in time with the glorious music and put on a show. Her dress sparkled like a glittering ball as he twirled her round and round and soon his people were enthralled.

"Everyone's looking at us," Ella whispered as they came together again.

"No," the Prince replied, feeling fabulously giddy as the occasion and adulation swept him off his feet. "Everyone's looking at *me*."

The orchestra reached its finale and the Prince went into overdrive, spinning and flipping Ella as he'd been taught by his former dance master during some of their extracurricular sessions. Ella gave herself to the Prince and ended up on her knees. The effect was stunning, with the Prince standing powerful and proud while Ella knelt pliant at his feet, her beauty tamed by the Prince's grace.

The crowd applauded and now took to the dance floor for the next dance. Several undaunted girls and most of the men planned to cut in on the Prince in order to divide and conquer but Ella had other ideas.

"Why don't we sit this one out?" she suggested as the orchestra struck up again. "I would like to take some air. Perhaps you could show me the rose gardens?"

The Prince was totally on board with that suggestion, but only as an excuse to escape. No one would try to stop him. Not even his father. He'd done as he was charged and was now leaving with the most desirable girl at the ball. More importantly, he would be seen to be leaving with the most desirable girl at the ball. Everyone would watch them leave and ask the same question. Will he? Will she? Well, everyone except his father, of course. And the Grand Duke. And that serving girl. And possibly her sister.

The Duke, Mother and Gardenia hurried across the dance floor, each following the other as they trailed the Prince and Ella out of the Upper Hall. The Prince stopped at the rear doors and looked back with a shrug, as if to say, "hard cheese, girls, but you can't win them all" while Ella cast Mother the merest of glances and winked. And then they were gone, through the double doors and out into the moonlight.

A couple of Guardsmen crossed their ceremonial lances when the Grand Duke arrived.

"No way out I'm afraid, Your Grace. You'll have to find another way around," the Guardsmen said apologetically.

"I trust you know who I am!" the Grand Duke snapped impatiently. This was his chance to go after Ella and find out who she was, for better or for worse.

"I do, Your Grace, just as I know who he is," the Guardsman said, looking over the Duke's shoulder.

The King took his arm and led him away.

"Let's leave them alone for a while, shall we?" he smiled, plotting a course for the bar. "And let nature take its course."

The King was beside himself with relief. He had been confident it would all work out in the end. It had just been a case of the Prince meeting the right girl. Or, as Mother commented to Gardenia as they passed, it was; "more a case of Ella meeting the right Prince."

CHAPTER FORTY-ONE

AS CATHERINE PETIT GREW and became less petit, she found it increasingly difficult to disguise her figure, drum or no drum. At the burgeoning age of sixteen, and at the Sergeant's urging, she took the plunge and changed back into female attire for the first time in three years. Duly, the Sergeant reported to the Captain (formerly the Lieutenant) that the drummer boy known as Calvin couldn't be found and was presumed to have deserted. The Captain ordered up a ten-man search party to scour the countryside, find and hang him, which was a good sign. At least he hadn't overreacted.

"Very good, sir. It will be done," the Sergeant saluted smartly. "Oh, just one other thing, I've taken on a new washerwoman to help with the kit."

"I don't care about your dirty socks. Do whatever you want," the Captain said, no longer listening. He was busy composing a letter to HQ to press for another promotion and camp washerwomen were the least of his concerns. The men paid for them out of their own pockets so what difference did one more scrubber make?

"Thank you, sir," the Sergeant saluted again. You could never salute the Captain enough. Particularly not when he was busy and trying to concentrate.

"What? Oh, yes, get out!" he snapped back irritably.

The Sergeant crossed the base with a smile and stopped outside Catherine's hut. She'd ceased sleeping in the barracks two years earlier and the Sergeant had found Catherine a place of her own. It was dank, draughty and it leaked when it rained but it was all hers and she loved it. Which was more than could be said for her new clothes.

"You can't stay in there all day. Come on out, there's work to be done," he told her.

"But I feel stupid," Catherine replied from inside.

"Why? Because you're finally dressed in something appropriate?"

"It doesn't feel very appropriate. Everyone's going to laugh," Catherine said, refusing to show herself in the light of day. It was Sunday lunchtime and the base was relaxing after a hard week's soldiering. The sun was shining, the pipes were smoking and the men were of good cheer. Sure, Catherine would run the gauntlet. That was inevitable but she had faced worse many times in the face of the enemy so a few choice remarks would do her no harm.

"Let them laugh," the Sergeant said. "You're a girl. You're wearing a dress. If that's the sort of thing they find funny then they must be easily pleased."

But still Catherine refused to come out. She'd been a boy for so long (and an orphan in rags before that) that she couldn't remember the last time she'd worn a dress. And certainly nothing as nice as the dress the Sergeant had bought her.

"I want my old uniform back," Catherine insisted. "Where is it?"

"That's not such a great idea," the Sergeant told her. "Not unless you want to be the first drummer boy in history to drum at his own execution."

Catherine felt trapped. Why had she agreed to this? She could've gone on posing as a boy for a few more years yet, surely? She could march, spit and fart as convincingly as anyone else in the company but the Sergeant had insisted that the time had come. East was east, west was west and Catherine needed to pick a side.

"Do I need to drag you out?" the Sergeant asked, growing impatient at Catherine's stubbornness. How was it, he wondered, that when she'd been a boy, Catherine could pull on her boots, pull on her cap and be on parade in under a minute? Yet the moment she became a girl he found himself standing around waiting for her to get ready?

"That's not even funny," Catherine said with a scowl when she finally emerged to answer the Sergeant's observation. The concept of sexism had yet to be invented but Catherine felt the Sergeant had definitely sewn the seeds with that remark.

The Sergeant, almost without thinking, removed his cap when he saw how Catherine looked. It was remarkable, a true transformation. She wore a long blue skirt with a matching bodice over a loose white cotton blouse. The bodice was pulled tight with laces tied down the middle but it accentuated her figure rather than concealed it, as her strappings had until now. Her clothes were far from refined: the best the Sergeant could find at short notice, intended to be practical rather than pretty, but they brought out a femininity in Catherine that he'd not noticed before. Uncapped and unstrapped, the Sergeant could scarcely believe it. The girl he'd rescued from the forest had become a woman without him realising it.

"Well?" Catherine asked, feeling embarrassed and self-conscious in a way that the Sergeant simply could not appreciate, not without putting on a dress and marching around the base himself.

"It'll do," he shrugged, figuring the less he said the easier this would be on the both of them.

The rest of the company were a little more forthcoming with remarks, and even more forthcoming with their socks, so much so that by the time she got back to her hut she was carrying enough smelly washing to keep her hands in soapy water until the next war broke out.

"I bet that drum doesn't seem so bad now," the Sergeant said with a chuckle when he stopped by a couple of hours later to see how Catherine was settling into her new job.

Catherine looked up from the washboard and wrung out the latest in a never-ending pile of underpants, hanging them up on the clothesline that stretched to the perimeter fence and back. She was nowhere near finished but her water had reached tipping point and was dirtying the clothes more than it was cleansing them.

"Soup's ready," she offered, wiping her face with the back of her hand only to instantly regret it.

"When you're done with that lot, I have something else for you," the Sergeant said, holding out a pair of breeches for her to repair. The seat of his pants was ripped and the seams were coming loose. "A schilling if you can fix them. Two if you can do it invisibly," he offered.

Catherine looked over the damage. She knew how to sew and could mend a popped seam as well as anyone, but to fix these old rags, invisibly, would require a genie, a lamp and twice as many wishes as usual.

"Go and see some of the other washerwomen, they'll show you how to do it. You'll be amazed what's possible with a needle and a thread," the Sergeant told her.

Catherine wasn't sure she wanted to spend the rest of her life on an army base sewing up people's backsides but since her own soldiering career was now over what choice did she have? What choice did any penniless girl in the back of this particular beyond have in this day and age? Outside of the obvious.

The Sergeant sat down and pulled out his penny whistle. He couldn't hold a tune to save his life — his hearing had been shot since the Siege of Mistelbach — but he found it a comfort to chew on since quitting the pipe. Smoking had never agreed with him and Catherine had suggested he tried putting the money he spent on smoking into a pot to help him give up. By the end of the first week, he had enough to buy a shiny new penny whistle. By the end of the second, he found he had enough breath to play it. Since then he'd saved up more money than he'd ever known in his life. He wasn't quite sure what to do with it all. It had come to mean so much more to him than anything he could buy, so instead, he went on adding to his nest egg, a schilling here and a livre there, and figured fate would find a use for it all.

"Do you ever think about the future?" the Sergeant asked.

Catherine did, but like so many former orphans, she had come to regard the future as something to fear. It was a lurking unknown, something to arm oneself against rather than embrace.

The Sergeant could appreciate the mindset. Most soldiers took life one day at a time. It was difficult to plan when Monday could bring bread and beer and Tuesday bullets and bombs. Simple pleasures were all the Sergeant had looked for until now. But man could not live by bread alone — or bombs and bullets for that matter. The Sergeant had felt as though he'd been stood at a crossroads in his life for some time but until today, he'd not known which path to take.

Even though the answer had been under his nose the whole time.

Catherine began unpicking the old threads from the Sergeant's ripped seam and wondered why he was looking at her in such a pensive way. "What's the matter?" she asked. "Something else you want?"

The Sergeant didn't answer. He merely slipped the penny whistle between his lips and began to play.

CHAPTER FORTY-TWO

AFTER SHE'D FLED THE GREAT HALL, Marigold found herself in the same secret passageway that Gardenia had previously explored. She'd tried to leave the conventional way but all the other doors had been barred. The ball finished at one o'clock and the King did not operate an open door policy. Once the guests were in, they stayed in. Until the bitter end. Nobody walked out early on the Prince. The very idea.

Not that anyone wanted to, of course. This was a once-in-a-lifetime event for most of the girls here. When would any cheesemaker's daughter ever see the inside of the Palace again? But Marigold had been here before. Too many times, in fact. The bricks and mortar might have been different but the situation wasn't. Every ball seemed to end in her ritual humiliation and tonight had been no exception. Singled out for separation and shamed for sport, she now burned to get away and no lock nor clock was about to stop her.

Marigold had remembered the corridor and thanked her merciful stars that it was still here, hidden from view behind the giant tapestry that had been returned to the wall since her last visit. Marigold had found her way out.

She slipped through the door and hurried along the dark passageway, without knowing where she was going but trusting her instincts that there had to be a way out down here somewhere. After a time, she found herself in the Palace wine cellar, so favoured for privacy by the Prince. The noise of people clattering on the floorboards above was deafening and Marigold covered her ears as she hurried on through. She'd been stomped on enough for one evening and was pleased to pick up the tunnel on the other side of the dusty cellar.

Cobwebs snared her face and slippery flagstones threatened to slip her up but Marigold sensed the exit was near. A light breeze kissed her cheeks and carried with it the smell of the outdoors. Sure enough, after a few more meters she saw a shard of moonlight illuminating the far end of the tunnel. She had found her exit.

Marigold hurried towards the light and found it pouring through the bars of a little window set in the top of a solid oak door. The door was bolted but fortunately for Marigold, only from the inside. She drew back the bolt and stepped through, happy to be outside but miserable to be an outsider. Why couldn't she take these occasions for what they were and enjoy them like everyone else?

"Why can't I be happy?" she asked the Moon. "Why must I always be the odd one out?" The Moon didn't know, or if it did, wasn't saying. It simply smiled down upon her with indifference and lit up the gardens with its silvery light.

Only a few people were out here. A couple of guards patrolling the walls and some Upper Hall guests taking the air on the balcony above. Marigold kept to the shadows as she searched for the stables. She didn't want to be caught out here and thrown in the cells, although that may have been preferable to being returned to the party, so she moved as stealthily as she could, keeping off the gravel path and stopping at every corner.

The gardens were set out like a beautiful maze with shrubberies, rose bushes and cherry blossoms planted across four acres to offer the King privacy and tranquillity away from the hurly-burly of Palace life. Marigold appreciated the cover, creeping from bush to bush as she headed towards where she assumed the stables were located. She would find Liquorice and wait with him until Mother and Gardenia were done. She'd already decided not to tell them what had happened tonight. They would feel bad enough for leaving her as it was. There was no need to make them feel worse.

As she passed a small row of Juniper trees, Marigold heard voices coming from the other side. Marigold stopped and listened. One was a man and the other a girl. A serving maid perhaps? Or a cook? It seemed unlikely seeing as every serving maid and cook were inside either serving the King or helping themselves, but more than that, Marigold thought she recognised the girl's voice.

"… and you are every bit as handsome as I have been told. We will make a very fine couple," the girl said with steely self-assurance.

"How nice of you to say so but I rather fear you're being a little presumptuous," the man replied. "I am a Prince, and a Prince needs no one's help to make him look fine."

Marigold gave thanks for the Prince's narcism as it helped her identify him, while the other voice sounded as though it belonged to Ella, but this couldn't be, could it? Ella had stayed home. She'd torn up her dress and locked herself in the tower. In which case, how was she here? Marigold peeled back the branches to take a closer look and sure enough, there was Ella, larger than life and looking every inch the Princess-in-waiting. Except Marigold could scarcely believe her eyes. She was wearing Mother's original dress; the jewel-encrusted gown that Franz Grimaldi had stolen. But how could this be? How had Ella recovered it?

That Marigold didn't go tearing through the bushes and launch herself at Ella was a testament to her upbringing. Mother had always drummed into her the need for deportment, even in the face of extreme provocation. And Marigold did indeed feel provoked. Her recent humiliation was instantly forgotten. In its place, pure and unbridled anger. Ella would not get away with this. The moment they got her home, she would face the full wrath of their revenge.

"I presume nothing. I am merely stating a fact," Ella continued to say, "that you, as the Prince and future King of Andovia, should have by his side the fairest maiden in the land. Anything less would reflect poorly upon your standing as a man."

As loathed as the Prince was to agree with her, he had to admit — to himself at least — that they had looked fabulous together. But him knowing this was one thing. Her knowing it was an altogether different kettle of bananas and he wouldn't stand for it. A girl like this ought to know her place, the Prince smarted, taking the decision to clip her wings before she got too far ahead of herself.

"My standing!" the Prince snapped contemptuously. "You, a girl of no account, dare to lecture me on the question of my standing?"

"Who says I am of no account?" Ella said, cocking an eyebrow at the Prince.

"You did. You have no family. You are all alone in the world. Without a family, you are nothing, just a pretty face," the Prince said, repeating her own words back to her.

"And yet pretty enough to entice you, My Lord," she reminded him.

"Don't flatter yourself," he laughed. "You may have dazzled the rest of the guests with your wanton wiles but I am immune to your charms."

"Then it is just as well that I wasn't attempting to charm you," Ella winked.

Through a gap in the leaves, Marigold could see the Prince slouched against a tree while Ella stood before him. His uniform was starched but his posture floppy. He'd spoken of his standing but could barely lean straight after all the fizz he'd sunk. Ella, on the other hand, stood upright and proud, almost defiantly so. She was a tall girl for these parts already, but now she seemed taller still, almost as though she had found an extra couple of inches since Marigold had last seen her. Marigold looked at her feet and saw the most magnificent set of glass slippers she had ever seen. One good flight of stairs and Ella's feet would be reduced to mincemeat but the only kind of climbing she intended to do was the social kind — and across the carcasses of every girl in

Andovia, including her own stepsisters.

"What do you mean, you weren't attempting to charm me?" the Prince snorted indignantly. "If not me, who else?"

But Ella just smiled and swished her skirt to make the jewels glitter in the moonlight. "Your father, of course. His people. Your people. Everyone."

"Everyone?" the Prince repeated, guppy-like.

"Everyone but you," Ella replied with a knowing glint in her eye.

The Prince narrowed his eyes with disdain. The last girl who'd spoken to him this way had been his nursemaid some twenty years earlier and he'd paid her back (and then some) when he'd slapped his own bottom red-raw with a ruler and went running to his papa in tears. He occasionally wondered what had become of poor Margot after her arrest but resisted asking for fear of what he might find out. There was no point in upsetting himself twice over that particular goblet of spilt milk.

Consequently, he was in no mood to truck any insolence from a mere country girl, particularly one who was hoping to use him as a stepping stone to the throne. They were all the same, of course, the girls who fluttered their eyelashes at him. They were all ambitious and greedy and full of fluffy ideas of themselves, which was why it choked him so much that he had to choose one. But choose one he did, though he would be damned if the girl he chose thought she was doing him the favour. All the power and majesty lay with he, the Prince, ordained as he was by God. That any girl should think otherwise was tantamount to insolence.

"You take a great deal for granted, twinkle toes, and that will be your undoing," the Prince told Ella, incensed at her effrontery and yet ever so slightly intimidated too. The Prince didn't like strong women. He didn't much like weaker ones either but at least they were easier to push around.

"Do you know what will be your undoing, Your

Highness?" Ella asked, turning serious to get down to business.

The Prince was so stunned by Ella's impertinence that he forgot to be outraged. Instead, he simply gawped with genuine curiosity: "No, what?"

Ella lifted a foot up onto a small stone bench. She pulled up the lacy hem of her dress to reveal a long slender leg and black garter belt hidden within. From the garter belt, she pulled a small swatch of material, unfurled it and threw it at the Prince.

"What is this?" the Prince asked, catching it with his face before turning it over to examine it.

"It's a number," Ella told him. "From Captain Durand's prison robes."

Sure enough, a row of black copperplate numbers was printed across the dirty strip of material and splattered with flecks of red. Blood, no doubt from…

The Prince recoiled and threw down the strip in disgust.

"What is the meaning of this?" he demanded, ready to drop his breeches and tan his own backside to ribbons should she try anything funny. "Guards! Guards!!"

"I wouldn't do that if I were you," Ella growled, bundling the Prince against the tree and leaning in close enough to kiss him. She was surprisingly strong for a girl. Strong and suddenly really rather frightening. "We have your precious Captain," she said. "He is alive and, as of yet, unharmed."

"What are you talking about? He's rotting in the dungeons and good riddance to him," the Prince said, sticking to the story the Grand Duke had spun despite the sickening guilt that gnawed away at him every time he thought about Durand.

"We will tell him you said hello," Ella laughed. The Prince wondered if Ella was getting ahead of herself again by using the royal "we" prerogative before reluctantly concluding she wasn't.

"Look, if you've got him then you can keep him. He's no concern of mine. The man's an absolute cad. No respecter of women," the Prince said, without the slightest trace of irony.

"Shut up and listen. You are to tell the King that you have made up your mind. That I am to be your bride and that we are to be married a week from today," Ella demanded. And it wasn't even February 29th.

"You must be mad. I'll not be bamboozled like this," the Prince objected, pushing Ella away and ducking around the other side of a shrub to keep her at arm's length. But Ella was not to be denied her fairytale wedding. She'd been planning it her whole life and had gone to too much trouble to let a little thing like the Prince's abject refusal get in the way now.

"You will make me your bride," Ella insisted, stalking the Prince around the shrubbery. "The King wills it. The people will it. And most importantly of all, I will it."

"Well I *won't* it and don't it," the Prince said, moving with her to keep the bush between them at all times. "I might have to marry someone but it won't be you, you old harpy. And I don't care if you've kidnapped Durand. You can do whatever you like with him. It makes no odds to me."

Ella laughed when she realised the Prince's mistake.

"Why he's not our hostage, you silly-billy. He's our honoured and most cooperative guest. And he is eager to tell the Barons the real reason for his imprisonment," Ella said.

"Who would believe him? He's a common criminal," the Prince scoffed, reasonably confident that this would be the case.

"A common criminal who just happens to know the shape of the royal birthmark on your left thigh and the contents of the private and highly scurrilous correspondence you exchanged with him last winter," she said, adding with a grin: "Now also in our possession."

The Prince stopped dead when she mentioned the letters. He'd instructed the Captain to burn them after he'd read them and turned red and white in quick succession when he remembered some of the things he'd written during those long lonely months last winter when the Captain had been away on manoeuvres. These things had been for the Captain's eyes only. The thought of other people reading them — sharing them, publishing them — made him want to be sick.

"… I shall kiss you a thousand times at dusk and a thousand times at dawn…"

"… my love for you burns brighter than the July sun…"

"… the Kingdom could crumble to dust and crush the people beneath it and I would not care a jot just so long as you were by my side…"

"… I really liked those tight breeches you wore yesterday. I could almost tell what you had for breakfast…"

All the fight went out of the Prince upon hearing his former sentiments and his legs turned to jelly. Ella sidled up to him and took him by the arm.

"You know, in some archaic Kingdoms they still lop off a person's head for harbouring such desires," she smiled sweetly. "Amongst other things."

The Prince was only too aware of the dangers. Andovia's own Bishop, that sanctimonious old drunkard, regularly delivered his sermons on the fire and brimstone and lakes full of lava that awaited such sinners whenever he was sober enough to take to the pulpit. Some might've argued he preached a little too much on this subject but the Bishop didn't care, it was a crowd-pleaser and deflected attention away from his own particular shortcomings so he wasn't about to flip the page any time soon. Either way, the Prince would've done well to let God judge him rather than a baying mob of his own people and Ella knew this only too well.

"But fear not *sweet Prince*," she said, deliberately using Captain Durand's pet name for him to ensure she had his full attention, "for I will be a most excellent and dutiful wife. And I shall love and cherish you and shield you from all harm. You need never worry about the Barons or the people ever again. And you shall be free."

"Free?" the Prince said in surprise.

"Free to do as you wish; free to follow your heart; free to live your life safe in the knowledge that you will always be protected by someone who loves you."

"Even though I could never love you in return?" the Prince asked tentatively.

"Matters of the flesh do not concern me. My only desire is that you find happiness. And this is something I can guarantee."

It was a hell of a sales pitch, the Prince had to give her that, but his mind kept returning to her repeated use of the words "us" and "we".

"Who's behind all of this? Who is helping you?"

Ella smiled and said; "Why my Fairy Godmother, of course."

The Prince considered his options. If he refused, the Captain's letters could land him in the mire to the extent that his throne — nay even his life — might be in danger. And yet if he agreed, Ella and her 'Fairy Godmother' would have him over a barrel. But for what? Riches? Jewels? Money? Power? Once he was the King, the Prince would have more than enough of these things to satisfy this craven little gold-digger. And what's more, his position would be secure. After all, one didn't kill the goose that laid the golden eggs, did one? So all in all, it wasn't the worst proposition he'd heard today. And it was certainly more attractive than the thought of marrying that dreadful little commoner girl with the seamstress mother, the Grand Duke had wanted him to.

"It appears you have me at a disadvantage," the Prince conceded.

"No disadvantage intended," Ella said, brushing a loose hair from his forehead. "Ours will be a marriage of true equality."

The Prince wasn't sure he liked the sound of that but one thing at a time. He first had to ensure her cooperation.

"Then I humbly accept," he said, giving Ella a little bow.

Of course, the Prince had no intention of keeping his word and was merely playing for time. Once he'd discovered the identity of her 'Fairy Godmother' and her other cohorts, he would have the lot of them rounded up, wrapped in chains and dropped into the deepest and darkest hole this side of Calcutta. Along with the treacherous Captain Durand. All he had to do was go along with them and bide his time.

"You have made me very happy," Ella assured him.

"I'll bet," he agreed. It suddenly occurred to him that he didn't even know this girl's name, which generally came before pledging one's life and country. "So what do they call you?"

Perhaps it was the way he'd phrased the question but Ella was immediately reminded of the nickname Marigold and Gardenia had given her and it made her smile.

"*Cinderella*," she said but stopped when she heard something crack.

"What is it?" the Prince asked.

"Quiet," she told him, staring intently at the row of Juniper trees a short way away.

Just a few short metres from her, and shielded by a thin wall of foliage, Marigold froze. She'd been trying so hard to hear what the Prince and Ella had been saying that she'd snapped a twig when she'd leaned in too close. To her mind, it had sounded like a gunshot and now Ella was looking in her direction.

Ella approached but Marigold froze. If she moved she would surely be seen but if she stayed where she was there was a chance Ella might miss her in the shadows.

"Come out, come out, whoever you are. We wish to speak with you," Ella said as disarmingly as possible. "Please, don't be afraid."

Marigold wasn't buying it and was very much afraid. Who wouldn't be at someone who'd just successfully bullied a Kingdom out of a Prince? Marigold had always suspected Ella of ruthless opportunism. She had always been so curious about what had happened between the Prince and Gardenia. But Marigold had assumed that she'd been after a little insider information in order to better bait her hook. She never dreamed, for one moment, that she'd be so utterly cutthroat as to use it to blackmail him. And all whilst sailing under a banner of sweetness and light.

"I know you're there somewhere. Come out, come out wherever you are. We just want to talk," Ella said again, this time echoed by the Prince.

"In the name of the King, I command you to show yourself."

But the Prince's authority was shot. If Marigold had learned one thing from this evening it was that the Prince was not so much a man as a marionette. He may have had the ear of his people but Ella had his strings.

Ella continued to stalk her prey, unsure where exactly the interloper was hiding but convinced someone was there. She couldn't afford to let them go blabbing about what they'd seen. She may have kowtowed the Prince but any whiff of controversy at this early stage could ruin her chances. She had to be seen as whiter than white, squeakier than squeaky and so utterly wholesome and innocent that even the Royal College of Surgeons would be astonished to learn that she had private parts just like everyone else.

"Of course, I'll need good people in my service once

I'm the Princess," Ella said, attempting to entice the eavesdropper from their hiding place. "A chief advisor or a lady-in-waiting, say? Someone who understands the importance of discretion."

Ella was now only a metre away but Marigold had buried herself into the foliage so that she and her maroon dress were almost indistinguishable from the autumn leaves, as indeed many of the creatures who lived there could testify. Marigold hated spiders. She loathed and feared and recoiled at the very sight of them but she let the fattest and hairiest spider she'd ever seen crawl across her face and through her hair without moving so much as a muscle. She would flip out the moment Ella was gone but for the time being Marigold and the spider were as one.

"I have all night you know?" Ella said, just as the Palace clock struck midnight.

"Look, you obviously imagined it. Why don't we go inside and I'll... arhhh!" the Prince started to say, only to get the shock of his life when he attempted to lean against the bush and found only Marigold's face.

Marigold leapt out of her hiding place and for one precious moment, she and Ella came face to face. Ella gasped, Marigold scowled, but neither quite knew what to say.

"Let's talk?" Ella suggested.

"Talk to my advisor," Marigold replied, ripping the spider from her hair and flinging it into Ella's face before running off in the other direction.

CHAPTER FORTY-THREE

"HAG!" ELLA SCREAMED after Marigold as she fled the Palace gardens. Ella didn't hesitate, she went straight after her stepsister, determined to stop her before she could go blabbing to the rest of the world.

By contrast, the Prince found himself momentarily forgotten and not sure what to do. On the one hand, Ella had just blackmailed him into marrying her — which was bad enough — but on the other hand, Marigold had just seen him crumbling in the face of Ella's blackmail — which was even worse. It was difficult to know which of these girls posed the greater threat. Ideally, both of them would trip over in the darkness and break their spindly necks but the Prince knew he could never be that fortunate. His was a luckless existence; it was almost as if the very stars were against him. Consequently, he did what he always did in situations like this, he ran to tell his Papa.

Meanwhile, the chase across the gardens was in full fling, or at least as fuller fling as either girl could manage wearing four-inch heels.

"Darn it!" Marigold swore in pain when she went over on her ankle for the second time in quick succession.

She looked over her shoulder and saw Ella was right behind her. There was nothing else for it. Marigold kicked off her shoes, aiming one squarely at Ella's head, before taking to her toes again, this time with considerably more success. She pulled up the hem of her dress to avoid barrelling over in a tangle of silk and ran as fast as her bare feet would carry her, across the ornamental gardens and back towards the Palace to report what she'd just seen.

Ella knew she had no chance of catching Marigold now, not while she was still wearing her precious glass slippers, so she kicked them off to even the odds, but found only one in the darkness when she stooped to pick them up again. After several seconds of searching, she knew she had no choice but to leave it. Time was of the essence.

"Hag!!" she shouted even louder now, blaming Marigold for the loss of her slipper on top of everything else. Did she have any idea, Ella thought, how hard it had been to get glass slippers made in her size? Marigold didn't, or if she did, this wasn't the question at the forefront of her mind. No, having put some distance between her and her stepsister, Marigold was suddenly stumped as to what to do. She'd intended to run into the Palace and tell the first person she met, but this was a stupid plan and one liable to land her in the dungeons. She had no proof. It was her word against theirs; one, the Crown Prince of Andovia and two, the undisputed belle of the ball. Who would ever believe her? She would be regarded as the jealous ugly stepsister intent on spreading sedition. Of course, the King would know she was telling the truth. The Grand Duke too. But how on Earth did she get to them when she couldn't even gain access to the Upper Hall?

"Darn it!" she said again, doubly irked that *Darn it* was the strongest curse word she knew.

She saw Ella coming at her from the other side of the lawn and ducked into the trees once more. That was the one blessing about Ella's dress. She could be seen from a mile away making her easy to avoid. Marigold sunk into the shadows and watched her stepsister run by. Ella had made the same mistake that she had and was heading straight for the Palace but it wouldn't take her long before she realised what Marigold already had, that before Marigold could go to anyone she needed to collect proof. And the obvious place to look for said proof was Ella's bedroom, the one she kept guarded from the rest of the family.

Once Ella had passed, Marigold took off in the opposite direction, back towards the stables and the horse and trap that awaited her. Mother and Gardenia would have to hitch a lift home. Marigold needed to get back as quickly as possible if she was to break in and find anything incriminating. If indeed, there was even anything incriminating to find.

Ella stopped when she saw the Palace all lit up and the party still in full swing. There was no sign of Marigold and there were guards at every entrance. She couldn't have come this way, she concluded, meaning she must have doubled back. But if she couldn't get past the guards on these doors how on Earth was she meant to get to the King? This was when the penny dropped and Ella realised the predicament Marigold was in.

"What are you going to do?" Ella asked herself, putting herself in Marigold's ghastly size tens and grimacing at the very thought. "What could you do?"

The clip-clop of hooves and the clatter of wheels told Ella all she needed to know. From across the gardens, she saw Marigold making her escape down the stone drive, through the Palace gates and out into the night. In that instant, Ella knew where her stepsister was going and why. And she simply couldn't allow that. She had to silence her sisters forever. Both of them.

*

BACK AT THE PALACE, the Prince stumbled out of the darkness and hurried up to a Palace guard.

"Where's Papa? I need to speak with him urgently."

"The Upper Hall, Your High…" the Guard started to reply, only to be pushed aside by the Prince. The Prince hurried through, taking the direct route past the Great Hall and instantly regretted it when this took him by a long line of girls all queuing for the ladies' room. The girls instantly saw him and screeched at the top of their lungs:

"Look, it's the Prince! It's the Prince. I'm here, come back, my lover."

The whole line broke off and gave chase through the Palace and up several flights of stairs but the Prince was able to easily outpace them as he was the only one not currently busting for a pee. He made it to the Upper Hall's service entrance with time to spare and barracked a guard to let him through. On rejoining the party, he looked about in despair, finally locating the King at the bar and rushed to him in an ignoble state.

"Where have you been? I've been looking everywhere for you?" the Prince said despite the King having not moved from this same spot for the last half an hour.

"What's going on? Where's the girl?" the King asked, looking around but finding no one in tow. This was a good question and one the Prince wasn't quite sure how to answer. For unlike Marigold or Ella, he hadn't thought this particular conversation through until it was too late. Now that he was here, he was suddenly lost for words.

"Erm....?"

The Prince was in a spot. If he came clean and told the King everything that had happened since they'd last seen each other, he'd be in more trouble than he knew. It was one thing to be of a poetic leaning (as Captain Durand put it) but another to trade the crown in an attempt to cover it up. And then get caught in the process anyway. What would his father say?

"Well, out with it, boy? Don't tell me you've blown this one too? You really are the most useless little cretin, aren't you? And to think, one day this whole Kingdom will be yours. I feel sorry for them, I do."

"Oh shut up! Shut up! Shut up!" the Prince barked back, causing the cellist in the orchestra to snap several strings and the ball to come to a juddering halt. "She ran away from me, Papa. She ran away!"

It was kind of the truth, and about the best he could do at short notice. But before the King could ask for specifics the clock chimed twelve and the seeds of a legend were sown.

*

"STOP HER! STOP THAT GIRL NOW!" came the cries from the Palace but Ella wasn't stopping for anyone. She'd jumped into her jewel-encrusted carriage and told her coachman to go.

"And don't spare the horses!" she demanded.

Her coachman snapped the reins and they sped off, clattering out of the drive and almost dislodging her footman when they bounced over a rut.

"Close the gates! Close the gates!" the King shouted from the balcony but he was too late. Ella's carriage thundered through and several guards on horseback were unable to give chase when the gates dropped between them.

"No, you fools, open them again! Open them I say!"

Through the streets and out into the countryside, Ella raced like the wind but her coach, much like her dress, could be seen for miles around, and tonight, beneath the pale moonlight, it shone like a beacon. Marigold caught sight of it in the distance and urged Liquorice to go faster but it would do no good. He was one horse and well past his best. Ella's couch was pulled by four strong white stallions, each of them in their prime and galloping like thunder against the repeated cracking of their reins.

"I see her! There! There she is!" Ella called out.

"Come on Liquorice! All the way, get me home," Marigold responded half a mile up the road.

On hearing these words, Liquorice found a strength he'd not felt in more than a dozen years. He put his head to the wind and drove his hooves as fast as he could but still, Ella's coach drew nearer.

Marigold realised the problem. He simply couldn't charge as he used to while tethered to their trap. But on seeing the problem, she also saw the solution.

"Keep going," she urged Liquorice, climbing to her feet

and then jumping onto his back. She caught him around the neck and just about managed to hold on, losing a set of beads in the process that were crushed to dust beneath the heavy clattering wheels.

Marigold set about unbuckling every strap she could reach while Liquorice thundered on. This slowed him up a little and allowed Ella's coachman to close the gap. Almost without warning, Ella was on top of them, breathing down her neck and urging her coachman to get up alongside.

"Go get her!" she shouted at her footman. He duly jumped to it, clambering around her carriage's footplate and in beside the coachman.

"Get us closer," she told the driver as their lead horses charged up the inside of Liquorice and began forcing them off the road. Marigold saw what was happening and knew she had only seconds to spare. She stretched with every muscle to reach the last buckle, splitting her dress down the back and almost joining her beads on the road, but her fingertips felt brass and she began teasing the taut leather strap loose.

"We've got her now! Do it!" Ella demanded, damning the footman for his cowardice and climbing out of her velvet-lined carriage to push him off herself. The footman jumped, his heart missing a beat as he passed from one speeding carriage to the next, but he found the back of the trap, landing squarely on his two feet before tumbling into the vacant seat.

Marigold saw the footman behind her and Ella urging him on. She had the reins between her teeth but the footman was already scrambling to grab her ankle. Without a second to spare, she flicked the final buckle prong and saw the strap fall away. Liquorice felt the weight lift from his shoulders and bucked his legs in order to jump through the tangle of falling harnesses. The trap tipped forwards unseating the footman and then turned over when it slammed into the road.

Marigold and Liquorice were already clear when the two carriages collided, Ella's horses swerving off the road in an effort to avoid the tumbling trap, causing her carriage to go over on its side and crash into a broken heap in the middle of the road.

Ella was thrown headlong into a filthy thicket and her coachman a water-filled ditch, but the footman fared rather worse, ending up on his back and pinned beneath several tons of sparkles and luxury. It wasn't the end for him but he would be left with a permanent lizard-like bulge of the eyes for the rest of his life.

The fading clattering of hooves told Ella that her chances of marrying the Prince now hung by a thread, much like the remaining pearls on her once magnificent dress. Most of her expensive adornments lay lost in the rotting undergrowth and the dress itself had been reduced to ribbons; silk dusters fit for a wannabe Princess. Ella emerged from the thicket in a stinking mood and a stinking state. Her perfect face was scratched, her hands and knees blackened and her hair was caked with a foulness that defied description. This was not how she envisaged her evening ending.

Ella realised she would now have to rethink her whole strategy if she were still to marry the Prince but she would have little chance of that if the King's Guards caught up with them.

"Quick," she told her coachman, wiping some of the sludge from her face with the hem of her skirt. "Lose the carriage and clear the road. And leave the girl to me."

CHAPTER FORTY-FOUR

BACK AT THE PALACE, the King was trying to shake some sense out of his son. He'd deviated from their plan by dancing with a different girl but at least he'd danced with someone. Of course, it had helped that she'd been the most beautiful girl at the ball, but that counted for little the moment he'd let her get away. Had this all been some sort of sordid plan, the King wondered, to get out of their agreement and continue to live the feckless life he'd carved out for himself?

"I promise you, Papa, on my honour as your son, I will marry the girl when we find her," the Prince said on the steps of the Palace, eager to head off the King's increasingly strident line of questioning. He couldn't risk Durand's letters surfacing. He would do whatever it took to keep them out of the public eye, even if that meant placing himself at the mercy of this grasping little witch. For the time being.

The Grand Duke noted the desperation in the Prince's voice and suspected he wasn't telling them everything but he couldn't think what it could have been. Not unless this mysterious girl was yet another Guardsman in disguise. Unlikely, but he wouldn't put anything past the Prince after everything else that had happened tonight.

"Do I have your word on that?" the King demanded.

"You do, I promise, on my word of hon—"

"Enough of that old flannel!" the King snapped, having heard more than enough about the Prince's honour these past few months. "Just you bloody well see you do or I'll pack you off to the colonies, my boy."

"But we don't have any colonies, Your Excellency," the Grand Duke saw fit to remind the King.

"Then he'll have his work cut out starting our first, won't he," the King snorted before heading inside to scour the map for somewhere deep, dark and as yet untouched by human hands.

The Prince slunk away too, eager to renew his acquaintance with the fizz waiter, but the Grand Duke stayed to watch the crowds melt into the night, yet another ball brought to a premature halt thanks to the Prince. Most of the guests went willingly but one or two had to be prised off the fixtures such was their reluctance to accept that the ball was over. He didn't know it now but even after the Great Hall was cleared they'd still be turning up cheesemakers' daughters for weeks to come.

In amongst the departing crowd, the Grand Duke spotted Mother and Gardenia looking lost. Their sister had evidently taken their horse and cart and gone home without them. It was a most undignified ending to a thoroughly undignified evening for the Beaufort party and though he felt no responsibility for their plight, the Grand Duke did at least feel he should see them home — if only to banish them from his sight once and for all. It had been a pitiful plan, pitifully executed and it had all gone pitifully wrong. Never trust a commoner to do an aristocrat's job. That had been his mistake.

With a snap of the fingers, the Grand Duke summoned a Sergeant-at-arms to attend to the ladies and with a sharp salute, he hurried off to do just that.

"If you please, madam, the Grand Duke has placed a carriage at your disposal," the Sergeant said with an introductory click of the heels. Mother viewed the offer with suspicion but Gardenia was more than keen to accept — especially if it meant being taken home by this tall and handsome young Guardsman. Okay so he might not have been a Captain or a gentleman, but his strong jawline and soft brown eyes left Gardenia in a flutter the moment she laid eyes on him.

"I say, that really is most kind of you, Sergeant," she

said with an overeager grin.

"The Grand Duke, Mademoiselle. I am merely following orders," the Sergeant replied.

"And I must say you're doing it rather well," Gardenia told him most sincerely, prompting Mother to note that when Gardenia rebounded she rebounded hard. From a Crown Prince to a lowly Sergeant? Surely that had to be some kind of a record?

The Grand Duke watched them being led away before turning his mind to the continuing problem of the Prince. Tonight, whilst not quite the disaster of the first aborted ball, had still failed in its key objectives. Okay, so the Prince had danced with a girl and pledged to marry her? All well and good but where was she? She'd got away, the Prince had said. Got away? Who on Earth ran out on a Prince? Something fishy was going on here?

It had to be a ruse by the Prince. It had to be. Fairytale Princesses like that didn't just drop out of nowhere and then disappear again the moment they'd had a quick trot around the dance floor. No, the Prince had planned this as a way of getting out of his commitment. It was so obvious. He'd found the girl from somewhere, dressed her to the nines and given her a made-up name, then planned this whole pantomime down to the last detail knowing that the King — the old fool — would swallow it hook, line and sinker.

"So he's promised to marry her, has he?" the Grand Duke mused to himself. "Her and no one else." It was a clever plan, the Grand Duke had to give him that. The Prince would be the talk of the Kingdom. And if they never found this girl again he would go down in history as a tragic hero of love and his renouncement of female company would be seen as a virtue rather than a cause for scurrilous gossip. It was a very good plan indeed. Unfortunately for the Prince, he had overlooked one thing. Namely, that if he could find a beautiful peasant girl to take part in this charade then the

Grand Duke could unearth her too, even if it meant sending his son to scour every inch of the known universe. Then he would have the Prince in the palm of his hand.

At that moment Captain Olivier, came hurrying up to the Grand Duke to make his report.

"Any sign of the girl?" asked the Duke.

"No Father. And nobody seems to know who she was but I'll find her. You have my word on that," he said, without realising he knew her already. But the Ella he'd met before and the Cinderella that had graced the ball were two entirely different creatures and Captain Olivier's assumptions would work against him in the coming days.

"You'd better," the Grand Duke warned him. "Now get to it."

"There's one thing we did find, however," Captain Olivier said, handing his father something they'd found in the ornate gardens. "I believe it was one of hers."

The Grand Duke looked down at the crystal slipper he was holding. It did indeed belong to the girl, he remembered seeing it himself. Surely no other slipper like this existed in the whole of Andovia — but for its pair. The craftsman who'd created this artistry would not be hard to track down.

"Find the other slipper and you will find the girl," the Grand Duke told Captain Olivier.

"It will be done, Your Grace, on thine honour," he promised, pledging the family name and hurrying out into the night.

The Grand Duke smirked. Names, names? This Kingdom was obsessed with names but names were for wannabes. The only thing that truly mattered in this world was blood. And if the Prince's wasn't red enough to fulfil his royal obligations then the Grand Duke's most certainly was.

CHAPTER FORTY-FIVE

MARIGOLD ARRIVED HOME in a clatter of dust and stones. She had no idea how far Ella was behind her but she didn't waste time showing Liquorice to the stables. He knew where his hay and water were kept. He could sort himself out.

Marigold went racing up the steps to the front door. Mother had left it on the latch but Ella must have locked it upon leaving. Marigold rattled the handle fruitlessly before looking for another way in.

All the shutters were closed and every door was barred. Marigold thought of running to the shed to fetch something to break in with but then noticed something fluttering from Ella's window. It was the end of a curtain. Her window must have been open. Marigold wasn't sure how this helped. The attic turret both towered far above and leaned out across the front drive. But a thick tangle of ivy climbed the wall beneath it and several struts bridged the gap between the last few leaves and her overhanging windowsill.

Marigold had no choice. She could either climb up and find what she needed or wait until Ella returned home, at which point any evidence of her conspiracy would be lost forever.

Already shoeless, she now shed her heavy dress too, unlacing her bodice and unbuttoning her petticoats to strip down to her white undergarments. The feeling was curiously liberating and she wondered what Mother would say if she could see her now, half-naked and climbing up the side of their château in full view of the road.

The ivy cracked as she hauled herself up but for the most part it held. In no time at all, she'd made it past the second floor and was reaching out for the struts beneath Ella's attic window. They were just beyond her reach and she made the mistake of choosing this moment to look down, almost losing her footing when she saw how far she'd climbed.

"Please don't let me fall. Please don't let me fall," she whispered to herself, wondering where her own Fairy Godmother was when she needed her. No answer. Like the vast majority of Fairy Godmothers, Marigold's operated a policy of helping those who helped themselves, so Marigold pushed on, reaching up and reluctantly letting go of her safe handhold in order to grab the lowest strut. Her heart skipped a beat when her fingertips slipped but she dug her nails in to find herself all but hanging over the flagstones below.

"What am I doing?" she asked herself and this time she received an answer. A distant clattering of hooves approached from the direction of town and soon a rider came into view. It was Ella. She was unmistakable, even in her tattered ballgown, as she galloped through the gates and up the drive towards the front steps. Before she got there she saw Marigold hanging from the struts below her bedroom window and skidded to a halt.

"You!" she shouted unnecessarily for indeed it was "you", or rather "her", or even "me", as Marigold preferred to think of herself.

Ella jumped off her horse and ran for the front door, stopping only to retrieve the key from beneath the front doormat. Marigold could've kicked herself but figured Ella would be only too happy to do that for her if she didn't get a move on.

A few more struts and a spine of protruding floor beams allowed Marigold to clamber to within touching distance of Ella's windowsill. She thought she was making good progress until she heard the sound of a door opening and slamming somewhere inside the château. Ella was in and hurrying to meet her. Marigold made one last leap and caught hold of a curtain that fluttered in the open window, but the sound of tearing and a snap-snap-snap of curtain rings almost foreshadowed Marigold's quick return to Earth. Only a last-ditch lunge saved her from disaster and for several precarious seconds she wobbled between one life and the next, wrapped in Ella's curtains and clawing desperately at the opening as she fought to find a handhold.

Inch by inch she shifted her weight, drawing nearer to the sanctuary of Ella's room but unable to cross the threshold due to the curtain she was tangled in. Slowly she unwound it from legs and wrestled it aside, snapping more curtain rings and almost bringing the whole lot down on top of herself, but finally she found herself free —

— and face-to-face with her battered, tattered and smoking-mad stepsister.

Marigold had no time to scream. Ella tried to shove her back the way she'd just come but it would take more than that. She had one foot planted inside and wasn't about to be dislodged.

"Get out, you painted old Hag!" Ella hissed, pushing Marigold face-first towards the thin air and kicking at her feet. But Marigold wasn't going anywhere without a fight and yanked on Ella's hair and kneed her in the thigh — and anywhere else she could connect with — as they scuffled half in and half out of the window.

"You're mad! You won't get away with this!" Marigold gasped, forced backwards as Ella brought all her weight to bear.

"You shouldn't have stuck your big fat nose in my business!" Ella seethed, summoning up the last of her might to push her sister from her room — forever.

Marigold regretted sticking her big fat nose anywhere near Ella, especially now. What a smell! What had she been doing?

"They'll arrest you!" Marigold warned her, fighting for her life and holding her breath at the same time.

"Or thank me more like," Ella laughed in reply.

Marigold was hanging out of the window, staring at the stars above and feeling nothing but the wind below. She knew she couldn't hold on forever but there was nothing she could do about it. Her purchase was too flimsy and what little strength she'd had after her climb was failing her. All she could do was take Ella with her.

Which gave her an idea.

With this stroke of inspiration, Marigold stopped pushing and instead yanked on her stepsister. As expected, Ella panicked and lurched backwards, relinquishing her hold on Marigold for just a second, which was all the time she needed to throw herself into her room.

A river of relief washed over Marigold as she rolled across the hard wooden floor. She was inside. She was safe. She would live. She wanted to cry with happiness her reprieve and might well have done had Ella not gone at her with a poker before she could draw breath.

"I told you to stay out!" Ella screaming with fury.

Ella missed by a whisker and the sharp poker barb stuck in the floor to give Marigold a chance to scramble away, knocking over several birdcages and releasing their occupants in the process. The freed doves and pigeons filled the room with their flapping wings as they raced around to find a way out, striking each girl in the face and chirping wildly. Ella fell back to protect her face and Marigold was able for the first time to take a proper look around.

The room was an Aladdin's cave of stocks and provisions. Food, drink, fuel and blankets filled the shelves of one entire wall, while clothes of every kind and for every occasion hung from another. There was a full-length three-side mirror too, so that Ella could view herself from every angle, and so many bottles of perfume that they would smell it in Paris if they got knocked over. And while these items weren't entirely unexpected for a girl's bedroom there was some stuff that most certainly was: a knotted rope that looked long enough to reach the gardens, a spyglass trained on the Royal Palace, a signalling lamp with different filters and a dozen birdcages, most of which were now empty, that had contained carrier pigeons. What modern girl could do without such essentials? There were also several maps, a small fortune in French coins and a flintlock pistol, which was rapidly being loaded and turned in Marigold's direction.

Marigold grabbed the gun and knocked it away just as Ella pulled the trigger, sending a shot into the ceiling and freaking out the remaining birds that were still trapped in the room. The discharge of gunpowder singed Marigold's face and made her eyes weep but through her veil of tears, she could see the desperation in Ella's face: anger, fear, determination and steel. This was a fight to the death but Marigold lacked Ella's ruthlessness. She wanted to live, see her family again and rid herself for once and for all of the lunatic that kept trying to kill her, but when it came down to it, could she do what was necessary?

"Let go you old tart!" Ella demanded, pulling Marigold towards her so that she could bite some part of her.

Marigold yelped when she felt her teeth close around her forearm and she let go of the gun to send them both flailing onto their backsides. Ella scrambled into the corner to quickly reload while Marigold lurched for the exit. Her only thought now was to get away, run back into town and warn the rest of the world that her stepsister was mad.

Outside the door, a precarious wooden staircase ran around the inside of the tower walls and down into near pitch darkness. Marigold could barely see where she was stepping but after hugging the wall and slipping on several steps she reached the bottom. She yanked on the door but the door stayed shut. She tried again and rattled the handle, all to no avail. Ella must've locked it after coming through meaning she was now trapped.

"Oh knickers!" Marigold gasped, going out on a limb with an all-new curse word just for the occasion.

Sure enough, Ella appeared at the top of the stairs holding her freshly reloaded flintlock.

"You should've taken my offer because I meant what I said," Ella said, taking to the rickety staircase to corner Marigold in the gloom. "When I marry the Prince I will need good people around me. People I can trust. People who want the same things as I. And who'll do whatever it takes to help me get them."

Marigold looked for a way out but there was none to be had. The door was locked and there was nothing else down here but for a gap under the stairs in which to cower. If she tried to grab the gun from Ella she would be shot before she could get to within ten steps of her. And if she tried to hide... well, it would be the shortest game of hide and seek in history. About the only thing she hadn't tried so far was bargaining with her.

"You're right," Marigold called up from the bottom of the stairwell. "I should never have run but I didn't know what else to do. I want to help you. Let's be friends. I love you."

Marigold cringed even as she said the words. How could someone who'd spent a lifetime masking her true feelings from all those around her fail to lie convincingly when it was really called upon.

Ella laughed to show Marigold what she thought about that. "Wonderful," she cackled as she approached with her pistol poised. "I shall carry your sweet words with me wherever I go. Now step out where I can see you. It will be easier for you in the end."

This wasn't exactly the bargain Marigold had sought but what else could she do in the circumstances? There was nothing down here to use as a weapon and nowhere left to run. Marigold squeezed under the stairs and awaited the end, damned if she was going to make anything easier for Ella.

The stairs above Marigold creaked as Ella neared the bottom. It was just as well for her that she was so scrawny because the steps were almost falling apart. If only she'd been heavier…?

At that realisation Marigold jumped up and grabbed the step that Ella was passing over and hung on it with all of her might. Sure enough, the step gave way with a crack, snapping in half and pitching Ella headfirst into the darkness. She crashed to the bottom of the stairs with a thump and lost the pistol to the shadows. Marigold was on it in a flash, turning to train the heavy weapon on Ella before her stepsister knew what had happened.

"Nice of you to drop in," Marigold said.

Ella looked up and saw the gun pointed her way.

"You haven't got the guts for it. I've seen it in your eyes," Ella snorted with contempt, testing the waters with a cautious step towards Marigold.

"Keep back," Marigold warned her, fingering the trigger but unable to pull it despite Ella's approach. To do so would've been cold-blooded murder. Ella was right, she didn't have the guts to kill an unarmed girl, even an unarmed girl who, until recently, had been very much armed and intent on killing her, but that was beside the point. Two wrongs didn't make a right.

"Just give me the gun and I'll let you go," Ella promised, forcing Marigold onto the back foot by drawing ever closer.

"Stop right there, I mean it," Marigold warned her, waving the gun to emphasise her point but merely emphasising Ella's.

"You're not going to shoot me and we both know that so why don't you give me the gun and let's talk?" Ella suggested, closing to within touching distance of Marigold. "Please, *sister*."

She reached out for the weapon and Marigold

hesitated. If she pulled the trigger she would splatter Ella's hairdo all over the wall and that was something she could not bring herself to do. Equally, she could not let the gun be taken from her and used by Ella. Thus, Marigold took the middle road and offered it to the top of Ella's head, cracking her over the crown as hard as she could to poleaxe her at her feet.

"If only I was as ruthless as you," Marigold said with a shrug, lowering her weapon and sighing with relief.

CHAPTER FORTY-SIX

MOTHER AND GARDENIA arrived about an hour later, having travelled home at a rather more dignified pace than the rest of the Beaufort family. Gardenia thanked the driver for bringing them home but he didn't reply. They never did. He just cracked his reins and left them standing at the steps of their château as he clattered away into the night.

The first thing Mother noticed was a riderless white horse standing with Liquorice by the stables. The second thing was Marigold's discarded dress. The rest of the house was closed up and in darkness but for the front doors which were open.

"Tether the horses then come right in," Mother told Gardenia adding, "And be careful," when she sensed something wasn't quite right.

Mother walked up the steps and looked in through the open front doors. She didn't call out. She used her eyes and ears to lead the way and duly heard voices coming from upstairs. She couldn't tell to whom they belonged, they were too far away, but they sounded female. Slowly and stealthily she climbed the stairs and followed the voices along the hallway, through Ella's open door and up the stairs to her hitherto off-limits attic room.

A candlelight flickered inside and Mother eased back the door to find Marigold and Ella chatting with as much forced civility as either could muster. Ella was tied to a chair in the centre of the room and Marigold was sat opposite — and wielding a pistol.

"Ah, Mother, you're back," her eldest daughter said as though they'd both been sat drinking tea.

"As are you," Mother said, guessing that much must've happened since she'd last seen either girl.

The Prince's ball had indeed been one hell of a party.

*

IT TOOK ABOUT FIFTEEN MINUTES of explaining to get both Mother and Gardenia up to speed but by the time the clock struck two, everyone knew everything that had happened tonight.

Ella said nothing. She merely sat and watched the candle burn down, neither trying to explain nor deny her role in any of it, not even her attempt on Marigold's life. Gardenia wanted to repay her in kind and shove her out of the window but Mother wouldn't hear of it. As long as they kept Ella alive and in good health they held the upper hand.

"Exact our vengeance and we will all pay the price," she warned them all, having seen far too many bewildered prisoners go to the gallows protesting they'd had right on their side. "We will turn her over to the proper authorities. It's the only thing to do. And it will make a favourable impression on Captain Olivier too," she smiled at Gardenia. This was classic Mother. It didn't matter to her that they'd just stopped a homicidal maniac in her tracks from taking over the Kingdom. All that mattered was impressing Captain Olivier.

"Sergeant Comtois was nice," Gardenia suggested, testing Mother's reaction.

"Let's not go there again, my dear," Mother advised her most sternly. "Captains and above please, if you will."

"I wouldn't do that if I were you," Ella said with supreme confidence. Gardenia thought she was talking to her but Ella was more concerned with her own social advancement.

"Oh? And why not?" Mother asked, happy to indulge Ella while she still had a tongue to wag. Others who'd spread sedition about the ruling family in days gone by had lost theirs along with their liberty.

"Because you would be throwing away a golden opportunity. The Prince has agreed to marry me and I shall be crowned his Princess. Do you really want to spurn the chance to become part of the royal household — albeit by marriage — simply out of spite?"

"Out of spite?" Marigold declared jumping to her feet in outrage. "You tried to kill me."

"And me," echoed Gardenia, now convinced more than ever that Ella had placed that barley snake in her trunk of shawls deliberately.

"Not to mention the dress you stole from us," Mother reminded her, pulling at the tattered remnants of Ella's once eye-wateringly expensive dress, the one that had near-ruined their lives.

"That was not my idea, that was Father's," Ella said as if this explained everything. "It was his idea to come to Andovia and that I marry the Prince. As soon as we learned of the Prince's plans we started making our own."

"What's that got to do with you not paying us for our work?" Marigold demanded.

"Well obviously, I needed the finest costume imaginable if I were to make an impression something that nobody else had ever seen, a dress that was fit for a Princess," Ella said. "There was only one problem. We had no money."

As outrageous as this was, it was nothing compared with the joyous little giggle that accompanied it. Gardenia leapt up to slap her but Mother grabbed her and dragged her back, so Marigold stepped in and slapped Ella for both of them. This wiped the smirk from Ella's face but she looked more angry than hurt.

"Touch me again and you will die first," she seethed, to which Marigold raised her hand and swung it even harder at Ella's cheek. Ella yelped in expectation but Marigold pulled the slap at the last moment, stopping just millimetres from Ella's cheek.

"I'll try to remember that," she said, giving Ella the gentlest of little pats.

"Marigold, step away," Mother ordered, sending her

daughters to the furthest corners of Ella's attic bedroom. She now returned to Ella and smiled politely. "You were saying, my dear?"

Ella went on to explain the whole plot, how she'd always been considered a beauty in her home country but destined to die poor because of her social situation. Her father was not a nobleman. In fact, he was not even her father. He was merely a confidence trickster she'd fallen in with who, like herself, had been hustling on the fringes of Parisian society. They'd been living on borrowed time for a great many months when they heard the news that the Crown Prince of Andovia was throwing a ball with the intention of finding a bride. Sensing a way out of their troubles, they blackmailed and stole every livre they could lay their hands on, reinventing themselves along the way as a widowed French knight and his gentile daughter. Nothing could be left to chance. They had but one shot at the prize so no expense was spared, every line of credit was maxed and Ella was transformed from an attractive but humble French peasant girl and into an Andovian Princess-in-waiting. What red-blooded Prince could resist?

"I know one," Gardenia suggested.

Obviously, once they had secured the Prince's hand their money worries would be at an end but until then they had to be creative when it came to settling their bills, thus they'd struck a deal with a notorious brigand to steal the finished dress and return their payment in return for certain assurances once Ella was in a position of power.

"Franz Grimaldi," Mother shuddered. "What did you promise him?"

"Clemency," Ella replied. "He tires of the death sentence hanging over his head and craves the freedom to enjoy his autumn years."

Everything had gone to plan. The house, the back story and the dress and everything. Ella had been all set to make her grand entrance when disaster had struck and the ball had been unexpectedly cancelled at the last moment. Nobody knew what had happened. The Palace refused to say but rumours were rife that the Prince had injured himself in the defence of a serving girl.

"Attendant," Gardenia corrected her.

"Whatever," Ella puckered.

Suddenly, she and her 'father' were in even more of a pickle. In debt in France, up to the eyeballs in Andovia, and now at the mercy of a notorious Srendizian bandit. Desperate times called for desperate measures.

"Which meant marrying me?" Mother asked.

"We needed to know exactly what had happened because the rumours were obviously a cover story; that whole crock about the Prince getting in a tangle over you."

"Oh, and how would you know?" Gardenia asked.

"A liar can always spot a lie," Mother suggested.

Ella sneered without disputing the sentiment. "So we needed to know what happened but obviously we couldn't just ask you because everyone's so uptight in this servile little backwater that a girl can't even dip her toes in the lake without the whole town going nuts," she said sourly, having almost scuppered her own chances on her first and only ill-advised recce into Andovia. "But as your sister? Well… sisters share everything, don't they?"

"Even shawls?" Marigold reminded her.

Ella's face dropped but not for long. Her supremely satisfied smirk soon returned. She was incredible. Even wrapped in ropes and at the mercy of three women she had robbed, ruined and wronged she still gave off an aura of superiority.

"That was an accident. I didn't mean for Gardenia to get bitten. That was meant for you, Marigold," she smiled.

Gardenia jumped to her feet once more but this time Mother didn't try to stop her. She slapped Ella around the face with such a force that the sting to her own hand almost brought a tear to her eye. Ella likewise reeled and snarled, her face flashing scarlet to match her seething vengeance.

"You will pay for that," she snarled.

"I already did," Gardenia reminded her.

Once the girls had regained their composure, Ella went on to tell them that the incident with the snake had spooked her 'father'. He felt things were getting out of hand and had tried to run but he hadn't bargained on Franz Grimaldi. There was no escaping your fate once you'd struck a deal with the Devil.

"He watches over me like my Fairy Godmother," Ella assured them. "And so, when you still wouldn't tell me what had happened I suggested he secured the only other person in the world who knew the truth. Captain Durand. And what a story he had to tell." Marigold and Gardenia could only imagine.

The Captain's conscription should have signalled an end to the sisters' involvement but then fate's fickle finger compelled Marigold to do what Marigold did best — and bugger everything up.

"Again," she snapped.

"Sorry," Marigold smiled without meaning it.

"Not half as sorry as you're going to be," Ella vowed, glaring at them in a murderous fury.

"That's big talk coming from a girl tied to a chair with a pistol at her head," Marigold pointed out but then a sound from outside pricked her ears.

Gardenia went to the window to investigate. The land was black but the moon was bright. Silver shapes moved about in the darkness, crossing the meadows and slipping over the garden walls. Gardenia counted at least a dozen figures, some of them disappearing into the shadows while others hurried towards the house. Most of them crept under the cover of night but one figure — one immense and hulking figure — carried a flaming torch high above his head. It wasn't for his benefit. The moon provided all the illumination he could've needed but the torch lit up his grizzled leer to warn those inside against trying anything foolish.

It was Franz Grimaldi. Even from this distance, he was unmistakable.

"I told you," Ella smiled like a gambler who held all the aces. "He's my Fairy Godmother. He watches over me."

CHAPTER FORTY-SEVEN

THE KING BARELY SLEPT THAT NIGHT. His son had pushed him to the very limits of his patience and now he felt himself tumbling into a void of uncertainty. And if there was one thing the King hated, it was uncertainty.

Dynasties were built on stone. The Kings of today and the Kings of old should have been — in theory at least — totally interchangeable with barely a chair out of place between monarchs. Why, if good King Sebastian VI himself could have jumped up out of his tomb and joined his great-great-great-great-great-great-grandson for dinner, he should have been able to unbutton his breeches and happily relieve himself without even having to check to see that the pisspot boy was in position.

But he couldn't. Because King Sebastian was long-gone, all of them were, I through VI, and none of them were ever coming back. And as sad as this was, it was also a relief because the King shuddered to think what they would've made of his own sorry excuse for a Prince.

And it wasn't that he was a 'gentile'. Princes came in all shapes and sizes. He wasn't the first and wouldn't be the last. It was simply that he thought this somehow excused him of his normal Princely duties, namely finding himself a Princess and siring as many pups as he could stomach. This particular task may not have been to his liking but damn it, there were no free rides in this world. Not even for Kings. The dynasty came first.

How dare he put his predilections before his obligations! How dare he!

The King hurled the last of his pillows clean across his bed chamber and tried to strangle his mattress into submission, not an easy feat in a bed so big his hands didn't even reach the sides.

"You won't get away with it, you hear me. You won't get away with it!" he snapped, prompting his valet to look in and ask if everything was alright. "No it's bloody not!" the King snapped — of all the damn silly questions.

The valet spotted the King's bedding stripped and strewn all over the room and wondered if he'd had a dog in here with him. But before he had a chance to ask the King was off.

"Your Highness! Your Highness! Your modesty, please!" The valet called after him.

The King didn't like pyjamas, particularly not the ones he was expected to wear. Silk pyjamas on silk sheets? Half the time he ended up on the floor. The Queen (God rest her soul) had left his side twenty years earlier so he'd dispensed with wearing anything but a moustache to bed shortly afterwards. It made for a more comfortable night and it turned the chambermaids an agreeable shade of scarlet when they came in for his pot in the morning so he wasn't about to start now.

"To hell with my modesty. I am the King and upon my command, you can all bloody well imagine I'm wearing a suit of armour, and to hell with you too."

And with that, he stormed off up the corridor in his pink and floppy armour to have it out with his conniving feckless son once and for all.

The Prince was sleeping like a log. It took a lot to deprive him of his beauty sleep and this evening's shenanigans hadn't even made it into his dreams. There he was, standing in the middle of a battlefield, drenched in sweat and stripped to the waist, waving his mighty sword at an enemy who was on his knees begging for forgiveness when a door was kicked open and he felt himself tumbling out of bed.

"I'll not stand for it, you hear me! I'll not stand for it. You'll marry who I say, when I say, where I say and do whatever else I say, do you hear me, boy?"

"But Papa, the girl who wore the glass slipper. I've already said I'll marry her. What more do you want from me?" the Prince told his father — the stupid old goat. It was then that he noticed, to his horror, that the King had neglected to wear his crown — amongst other things. "Oh sweet mercy, pluck out my eyes," he pleaded.

"I'll do worse than that if I have any more of your nonsense," the King roared, towering over his son with his legs akimbo and his hands on his hips. It was dark, thank God, but not dark enough. An outline was clearly visible and it had burned itself into the Prince's mind before he'd known to look away. "Your wedding is set for next Saturday at three o'clock sharp. At the cathedral."

"But Papa, what if we can't find her before then?"

"That's your problem. You gave your word that upon your honour you would marry the girl who wore the glass slipper. Well, I'll find you someone who'll wear it even if you can't. So chew on that," he snapped, making the Prince baulk at the thought of chewing on anything before adding, "and congratulations."

The King stormed out to see the Grand Duke and would've no doubt done so in his altogether had the Palace staff not conspired to ambush him at the bottom of the stairs with an overcoat and some tactical breeches.

The King's ultimatum left the Prince in a perilous position. Okay, so he had agreed to marry the girl who had worn the glass slipper but he hadn't agreed to marry any old strumpet who fitted it. That would be ridiculous, like saying, okay, first silly cow with size five feet to report to the Palace shall be the Princess. Who did that?

But the King's patience had snapped and he was no longer thinking clearly. This was nothing new but the danger posed by the Prince's scheming bride-to-be most certainly was. The Prince could not allow himself to be bamboozled into marrying just anyone else. There was more at stake than his happiness now. He had to make sure that he married his blackmailer and his blackmailer alone. This was the only way of guaranteeing her silence — in the short term at least.

But how?

A thought now occurred to the Prince. Something his father had said — that great drunken old oaf. The Prince leapt from his bed and summoned his valet to get him dressed.

"One day, I must learn to do this for myself," he chided whilst waiting.

*

IT WAS AROUND FOUR in the morning when Otis, the town's pre-eminent glassblower, was roused from his slumber. The urgent knocking sounded like thunder against his door and didn't abate until he pulled back the bolt. What terrible set of circumstance could possibly require the services of a craftsman at this ungodly hour?

If his early morning wake up call had unnerved Otis, this was nothing compared to the surprise he got when he saw who had called upon him.

"Your Highness?" Otis gawped, dropping to his knees and almost causing the Prince to tumble over his head when he hurried in before anyone saw.

"Get up. Get up," the Prince demanded, bundling Otis back into his hovel and throwing the door closed once inside.

Otis, like many craftsmen, lived in a small cottage that clung to the side of his workshop like an overgrown carbuncle. It was dark, cramped and doubled as his stockroom, as the Prince soon discovered when he pitched over an entire table full of bottles in his hurry to come inside.

"Who put that there?" the Prince said as the sound of smashing glass rang out as more and more bottles rolled over the side to join the rest in bits on the floor.

"Your Highness, have a care!" cried Otis without

thinking, causing the Prince to step back and put his boot through six panes of glass that had been carefully stowed to one side.

"Don't worry about that. They were already like that," the Prince reassured him, lifting a foot to examine his boot, only to knock over Doctor Guillot's new leech jar that had been awaiting collection since last Wednesday. "What was that?"

"Please, Your Highness, I implore you, allow me to light a lamp."

It was only once a wick had been lit that the two men saw the extent of the damage.

"You'll have that lot swept up in no time," the Prince told him, as if this was the problem. "In the meantime, we've far more pressing matters to discuss."

Otis couldn't think what was more pressing than seeing the fruits of a month's work cast onto the flagstones but then the Prince produced what Otis could only describe as a piece of artistry unlike any he'd ever seen in his life.

"A slipper, sir?"

"Indeed. One of your creations?" the Prince asked.

Alas, it wasn't. Otis was a craftsman but this hadn't been crafted, this had been conjured surely.

"It is real?"

"As real as the girl who wore it," the Prince confirmed, handing it to Otis to examine. The slipper hadn't simply been blown from glass, it had been sculpted and cooled using a technique akin to the Prince Rupert drop method. This had created a compressive stress glass moulding that had given the slipper its strength. Impressive and yet reckless. One false step and the slipper would have shattered into a million murderously shards. What sort of a fool would have thought to take such a desperate gamble?

"I need you to remodel it," the Prince told Otis.

"Remodel it?"

"Change the inside, leave the outside, and make sure this slipper fits no person on Earth."

"I'm not quite sure I understand, Your Highness," Otis gawped.

"Look you imbecile, it's perfectly simple; restrict the inside of the shoe by adding a little more glass or warping what's there to make it so that no one can get their foot inside; at least, not without causing themselves considerable discomfort. Can you do that?"

Otis inspected the slipper and said he could.

"And it must be completely seamless. No one must know that the slipper has been tampered with."

"Very good your Highness," Otis said, already seeing where he could layer in a small amount of molten glass to restrict the heel. "I will see what I can do."

"I would be most obliged," the Prince said, tossing Otis a small purse of silver schillings, more than enough to pay for the work and almost enough to cover the breakages. "One last thing," he then said. "You are not to breathe a word of this to anyone. Ever. If you do…"

The Prince took a bottle off the shelf and dropped it on the floor to demonstrate his point. This time, bizarrely, the bottle didn't break, it merely bounced on the stones and rolled harmlessly into the corner but the Prince had made his point.

Except, it wouldn't be bottles the Prince would be breaking next time.

CHAPTER FORTY-EIGHT

IF THE OLD GENERAL who'd previously lived in the Beaufort's château had been alive today, Mother would have spat the nails from her teeth and given him a big sloppy kiss. The rest of the town might have dismissed him as an old eccentric for attempting to shore up his home against the demons of his past, but it was his DIY fortifications that were now holding Franz Grimaldi and his murderous hordes at bay.

Monsieur Beaufort had prettied up the place but many of the General's bars and bolts remained in place and Marigold and Gardenia hurried from window to door to lock them before the intruders outside knew what obstacles were being thrown in their way.

Mother followed them around nailing up the shutters and stacking anything she could in front of the exterior doors. Fortunately, there were rather fewer doors than usual for a château of this size. The General had bricked up all the extraneous exits and ensured he had a clear line of sight on those that remained. As a result, after just seven minutes of urgent reinforcing, the downstairs was near impenetrable — or at least, as near impenetrable as any place could be with Franz Grimaldi at the door.

"Tie this off," Mother told Marigold, laying trip wires between the shadows should their defences be breached. Having seen several sieges first-hand, Mother knew all the tricks. She doused the stove to prevent the intruders from covering the chimneys to smoke them out and fetched the mops and buckets from the kitchen to use as beaters should their attackers attempt to start fires of their own. But Mother didn't think it would come to that. Grimaldi had come here to rescue Ella, not burn her to a crisp.

"There's a musket in the basement. Go and fetch it,"

Mother told Marigold. Marigold couldn't ever recall seeing any weapons before but this was because Monsieur Beaufort had removed them all from the walls and placed them into storage before the girls had moved in. Mother had come across them during the big sell-off and had decided to keep the musket for hunting should the girls ever tire of cabbage soup.

Marigold returned with an unwieldy antique musket and a second stubby flintlock pistol to go with the one Ella had gifted them. Mother inspected both to make sure they wouldn't explode the first time anyone touched the trigger and concluded they were still fully functioning. God bless the General's ghosts. There was also a bag of shot and a pouch of gunpowder. Mother armed and primed both weapons with the practised ease of a seasoned campaigner and noticed her daughters looking at her with surprise.

"Dressmaking wasn't the first thing I learned when I was your age," she said, answering their unasked question.

They hunkered down and waited for the first hammer blow to sound but no such assault came. This was more unnerving than anything. At least while the enemy was making noise you knew where they were and what they were doing. But all was eerily quiet. Almost as though the invaders outside were also waiting to see what the opposition did.

Franz Grimaldi, for once, was unsure of the situation. He'd raised his lantern to give Ella the signal but she hadn't responded. This was most unlike her. He signalled her again but still no light had appeared in the window of her ivy-clad tower. And yet he knew she was up there so why wasn't she responding?

"Something's not right," he deduced, thoughtfully teasing the flesh from the black olive between his teeth. So many things had gone wrong with Ella's plan already that he could scarcely believe it. First there was the aborted ball, then Monsieur Beaufort's attempted flight, then the Prince's disappearance from public life, Captain Durand's prison break and now this, Ella's midnight flight the moment everything had seemed to come together. Again and again they'd had to improvise and adapt just to stay one step ahead of the game. If this was what it took to seize a Kingdom, no wonder the nobility were all barking mad.

But finally Grimaldi's patience had worn thin. He'd backed a beauty to woo a Prince and vanquish the noose that hung over his head and yet here he was five months on and still living like an outlaw in the wilderness. This wasn't what he'd come to Andovia for. And it wasn't what he was used to either. Sneaking around. One way or the other, Franz Grimaldi had done all the skulking he was prepared to do.

"Take the château," he barked at his men, spitting the pip from his mouth before selecting another. "And find me the girl. This ends tonight."

Grimaldi's men hurried to the doors and tried the handles. The doors were locked. They usually were but it was always worth checking as you never knew. Andreas, still dressed in his coachman's coat, started whacking the lock with a hammer in an attempt to prise it off while the rest of the gang set about the windows. They made no effort to cover the noise. The château was miles from anywhere and there were only women inside. Taking the house wouldn't be the hard part. Finding where they were quaking once they were inside would be. And yet after ten minutes of hacking Andreas was no nearer to gaining entry than when he'd started. The lock was formidable, more so than he'd ever seen on any private residence. This could take all night by hand. Better to blow the thing with black powder and be done with it.

It was at this moment, almost as though fate were waiting for its cue, that a loud crack rang out in the night. Every man in Grimaldi's gang heard it but Andreas was the only one to feel it. A shot tore away his left instep and dumped him on the front step in a pool of his own humility.

"Shooter," someone shouted unnecessarily and all looked up to see a cloud of smoke hanging in front of Ella's own window to indicate that the shot had come from there.

Grimaldi doffed his cap, metaphorically at least, and spit out another olive pip. That was some sixty metres to Andreas's position and had involved hanging out of the window to get a clear line of sight. This one, precise and admirable shot had served notice on his boys that no women were quaking inside. And if they wanted to take this château, they would have to do just that — take it.

"C'est bon," Grimaldi said with a crooked smile.

As much as Grimaldi admired Ella's duplicity, this was more his kind of deal. He cracked his fingers and reached for the crossbow that was slung across his shoulders, firing up at the window with a steel-tipped bolt to reply to whoever had opened the dialogue. A pane of glass was the only casualty but those inside now knew they'd shaken the wasp's nest. Grimaldi's men took their lead from him and began peppering the château with their own bolts and arrows, forcing Grimaldi to remind them to watch who they were aiming and not to kill "the golden goose", his pet name for Ella.

Inside, and well away from the thud of bolts, Gardenia tried to be brave. She'd always hated thunderstorms as a child and used to seek solace in the arms of her sister, under the stairs and with a book for distraction. But her sister was too busy learning how to reload Mother's musket and the storm outside wasn't about to blow itself out. Gardenia crawled out from beneath the bed and asked what she could do.

Ella, in the corner, screamed at her from behind her gag to untie her and let her go. "Or you'll be sorry," she added as a muffled threat. Gardenia may have been frightened but she wasn't a child anymore. She knew that lightning could not be bargained with.

"Make an ally of gravity," Mother suggested as an alternative. "You too Marigold. I will keep a watch over your stepsister."

The sisters hurried from Ella's room, taking care not to linger in the doorways or open hallways lest a stray bolt find its way through their defences. Next to their bedroom was a hatchway up into the main loft. Marigold pulled on the cord to release the steps and she and Gardenia climbed up. Unlike Ella's attic room, this loft was structural only; a long narrow space that ran the length of the house that was crisscrossed with cantilevers and cobwebs. Above their heads were the roof slates and they were able to push them apart to peek out at those below.

Marigold figured she was more or less directly over the kitchen entrance. She could not see it due to the slope of the roof but she could hear the axehead biting at the door below. Marigold now did as Mother had suggested, pulling a tile loose and sending it on its way down the roof.

After an initial rattle, there was a moment of silence before a sudden crash prompted a torrent of vitriol. The language was unlike any that Marigold had ever heard — or indeed understood — but for a time at least the axehead was silenced.

"Let me have a go," Gardenia said, picking a spot over the drawing-room and sending another roof slate down to those below.

A howl this time followed the crunch to tell Gardenia she'd scored a bullseye but there was little time to celebrate. All at once they were showered with shards as every crossbow in the garden now aimed high. Marigold and Gardenia hurried across the rafters and ducked behind the brick chimney stack at the centre of the house. The men below couldn't see them inside the loft but it didn't stop them from trying to shoot them anyway as they dragged their injured man away. The sisters hugged the brickwork as bolts crashed through the slates to skewer the roofing beams, but suddenly a second musket shot rang out and another of Grimaldi's men was felled.

Mother had been waiting for her moment. She only had a few musket balls and needed to make every shot count. Still, even with only a handful of shots, a skilled sniper could hold back an entire company if need be, and having scored two for two, no one was in a hurry to offer themselves up as another easy target.

Ella's attic room whipped and snapped with a dozen ripostes but Mother paid them no mind. She had retreated to cover and now sat safely in the bottom of Ella's oak wardrobe along with her stepdaughter as her room was raked with death.

Ella said something behind her gag, something Mother couldn't make out, so she pulled the gag from her mouth and warned her against shouting for help.

"How long do you think you can hold them off?" Ella asked.

"As long as I need to," Mother replied.

"You've only the one musket," Ella said.

"And a pistol too," Mother reminded her.

"You're not going to hit much with that thing," Ella said, knowing only too well that flintlock pistols were useless at anything more than about ten metres.

"Don't be so sure," Mother replied in no uncertain terms. Grimaldi needed Ella alive if he was to get his pardon. And Ella was a lot closer than ten metres.

The axeheads had fallen silent and the men were taking cover. Two of Grimaldi's gang lay bleeding, another concussed, and this was after only ten minutes of laying siege to a house of women. Girls even.

"Get back there you floundering dogs! Get into the fight!" Grimaldi roared, charging headlong at the front door and with his crossbow cocked and ready.

Mother was out of the wardrobe and saw him running. She brought the musket to bear and took a breath. Grimaldi was moving quickly but Mother anticipated his run, tracing him across the moonlit garden and firing just before he disappeared from her sights. The musket ball raced across the night, skimming his face to leave him with yet another scar but missing anything that might've otherwise slowed him down — just as scores of shots before it had.

Grimaldi slammed into the door and knew exactly how long he had before Mother could reload and was ready to fire again. He picked up the hammer Andreas had dropped and began smacking the lock as hard as he could, not to smash it off. He knew he wouldn't be able to do that before she was ready to shoot again. But he just needed to loosen it, just a little, to create a crack into which he could pour black powder.

"This is a fine night's, boys, a fine night's work!"

His men ran across the gardens to his aid and kept up a constant quiver of arrows raining up onto the roof. More slates now began to reply, poleaxing another of Grimaldi's gang and causing the rest to run around like a swarm of angry ants but nothing could slow their assault. Not this time. Grimaldi was determined to get inside one way or the other.

"Powder," he growled, having finally knocked enough of a gap behind the lock. But before he could pour the powder into the mechanism a shout went up from his lookout on the gate.

"Riders!"

Grimaldi stopped dead and called back.

"Who?" he demanded.

"Guardsmen. Two of them."

Grimaldi reached for an olive. He'd waited five months already. Another five minutes wouldn't make any difference.

"Then we'd best make them welcome," he suggested with a leer before hurrying away to take cover.

Corporals Babin and Deniau slowed as they approached the main gates. Babin thought he'd heard something but it was nigh on impossible to hear anything over the clatter of hooves on gravel. They stopped at the end of the drive and saw the château in darkness. Nothing stirred.

"The house sleeps," Deniau noted.

"Maybe they heard someone pass this way," Babin replied. It made no odds, they had to call in anyway just to be able to report to their superior officer that they had swept the entire area. The King had ordered his men to find the jewel-encrusted carriage after Ella had fled but it had vanished into the night. The King's Guards had fanned out in order to search the countryside but still they found no sign of it. It was as though it had disappeared into thin air — as if by magic.

Babin and Deniau clip-clopped up the main drive and dismounted at the front door. Neither man noticed the bloodstain on the front step nor realised the damage the door wore had occurred only moments earlier. Some châteaus were well-maintained, some lay in utter ruins. This place obviously fell into the latter. And as all of Grimaldi's bolts had been aimed high, none lingered in the local woodwork to invite awkward questions.

Babin rapped on the large brass knocker and awaited the sound of footsteps. He didn't like waking people in the small wee hours but he had no choice. The King had ordered that the carriage be found and so the carriage had to be found, even if it meant waking up every household in the Kingdom.

Mother heard the door and peered down from the top window to see the soldiers below. Grimaldi and his men were gone, or at least no longer visible. But they were still out there somewhere, in the shadows or behind the gates, waiting to see what Mother did next. But why didn't Grimaldi just kill them? They were sitting ducks and no one would know.

Perhaps he was serious about his pardon. It was one thing to be pardoned for past crimes from yesteryear but another to be forgiven for killing two of His Majesty's Own in the pursuit of his very pardon.

"Just open the door and let me go. It's the only way you're going to get out of here alive," Ella said in the corner.

It was then that Mother realised that this must've been what Grimaldi was thinking too. These soldiers had obviously come from the Palace in search of Ella and Grimaldi was giving them a way out. Let her go and live. Refuse and… well, what chance did three women have against Franz Grimaldi?

"Wait here," Mother told Ella, hurrying downstairs to where Babin and Deniau were knocking. "I'll just be a moment," she called through the door, pulling out nails with a hammer and dismantling the barricades as quickly as she could. The door had stood up well. It bore a few cracks and a couple of creaks but otherwise, it had stood firm against the relentless onslaught. The General would have been proud.

Mother yanked open the door and stared aghast when she heard something rattling on the roof above.

"Ah, Madame, I trust we haven't…" Babin got as far as before Mother grabbed him and Deniau and dragged them out of the way just as a slate exploded on the steps behind them.

"My goodness!" Deniau exclaimed. This place really was falling apart.

Mother slammed the door and set to rebuilding the barricades. Grimaldi had shown his hand but it wasn't a mistake he was likely to make twice. Ordinarily, a soldier's duties were sacrosanct. The King had ordered them to find and bring Ella back and nothing else should have prevented them from doing this. In this respect, the soldiers, by default, should have been on Grimaldi's side.

Except he hadn't bargained on one thing.

"Gentlemen, I am Catherine Roche, widow of Sergeant

Armand Roche, once of the King's Guards, and I beseech you; in the name of the *King's Men*, I need your help."

The hairs on the back of Babin's neck stood to attention. He'd heard the name, Sergeant Armand Roche. Who in the regiment hadn't? But as to the myths that surrounded the *King's Men* and the debacle of Widows' Ridge? He'd never given them any credence. To consider such things was akin to treason. And yet as a Guardsman, Babin knew better than most what had happened to his brothers on that fateful mountainside. What rank and file trooper didn't?

Deniau was equally dumbfounded. This was Sergeant Roche's widow? In the flesh? He'd always assumed that she was either dead or in a faraway place or a composite of several real people and yet here she was, very much alive and speaking the unspoken oath in the name of the fallen. It was rather a lot to take in.

But neither man got the chance to express their astonishment, for at that moment a volley of arrows slammed into the door as Grimaldi expressed his frustration. Both Babin and Deniau stumbled back but Mother simply went on swinging her hammer to shore up the château before things got serious.

"I'll tell you what is going on in a moment," Mother promised, poking her flintlock through a hole in the door and firing out into the night.

"Mother!" came a yell from the top of the stairs.

Babin and Deniau looked up to see Marigold and Gardenia in their white and dirty undergarments holding what looked like roof slates ready to throw at them.

"It's quite alright girls, these gentlemen are here to help," Mother assured them.

"You are here alone? It is but the three of you?" Babin asked as the sound of men charging suddenly came from outside.

Mother thought on that and frowned. "Not quite."

CHAPTER FORTY-NINE

"YOU WANT MY PERMISSION TO DO WHAT?"

"Marry sir. One of our seamstresses," the Sergeant said as he stood before the Major in his office. The Major shrugged with indifference. It was the same indifferent shrug he'd developed as a young Lieutenant and then perfected as a Captain during his meteoric rise through the officer ranks, but now it seemed even more pointed, as though the very act of bringing such trifling matters to his attention merited contempt. And yet Heaven help any soldier in his company unwise enough to try marrying without his express permission.

"A seamstress?" the Major said, as though the words themselves disagreed with his nostrils. A good seamstress should've been like a good seam, invisible, and yet the barracks were full of them, chattering and gossiping and thinking they didn't have to salute him like the rest of his men just because they weren't in the army. The Major didn't like seamstresses. But then again, there were very few things the Major did like.

Catherine Petit wasn't a gossip or a chatterbox. In fact, very few of the seamstresses were. Most had too much work to do for that sort of nonsense. She had served the company diligently for three years now, first as a washerwoman and then she had trained as a seamstress. She had a natural touch with a needle and her skills soon surpassed those who had tutored her. Where some woman could mend invisibly, Catherine could mend almost magically, fixing not just the tear but improving the garment's overall fit. Within six months, she was doing half the company's repairs. After another six, she was doing them all and subcontracting half a dozen other seamstresses to repair each garment to her exacting specifications. She'd even helped adjust the Major's new tunic after it had arrived slightly tight around the waist although he'd been as indifferent to Catherine's fine work as he was to the Sergeant's impending nuptials. She'd been with the company in one form or another for over six years now, first as an intruder, then as a drummer boy, a washerwoman and a seamstress and still, the Major couldn't have picked her out of a line up of one. His eye was reserved for Colonels and above. Drummer boys and washerwomen all looked the same to him.

"She is a very respectable girl, sir. Upstanding and pure of heart. I should be glad to take her for my wife," the Sergeant said.

The Major snorted as though the Sergeant had just slapped a saddle on a cow and put in a request to join the cavalry. Barracks girls were scrubbers, plain and simple. Any girl that handled the dirty underpants of enlisted men for money could not, in any sense, be regarded as upstanding and respectable. Why the very thought of his own wife up to her elbows in grotty crackers filled him with revulsion. Such occupations were beneath respectable girls. And to suggest otherwise was plain insulting to his own dear Elspeth.

"Is she a Christian girl?" the Major asked.

"Blessed by the Bishop himself, I believe, sir."

"Does she have a family?"

"Not as yet, sir, no."

"She will be taking your name?"

"That is the intention, sir, yes."

"And she is free of the pox?"

"I... er yes sir. As I say, she is a good girl sir, God-fearing, no less."

"Good, because I'll not have some pox-ridden trollop deprive me of one of my ablest Sergeants."

There was a compliment in there somewhere, the Sergeant felt, but he was damned if he could make it out.

"Thank you, sir," he simply replied, wondering if he

should ask after the Major's own wife in this regard.

"Very well then, go and marry the wretched girl and be done with it but I'll expect you at roll call as usual in the morning. You'll not get a twenty-four-hour pass out of me if that's the big idea."

Twenty-four hours of freedom for a lifetime of commitment? It would've been a slightly weighted trade-off had it been a gambit. Still, the Sergeant didn't take the insinuation to heart, or indeed anything the Major said. He was simply flexing his authority because this was what the Major did. And neither the Major nor the Sergeant knew any different.

"Of course not, sir. You can rely on me, sir," the Sergeant saluted.

The Major wafted the Sergeant away, which was as close to a salute as he came since winning his latest promotion but the Sergeant refused to be wafted.

"What? What is it now?" the Major asked irritably.

"I thought, sir, that you might grant us the honour of marrying us yourself, sir?"

The Major blinked and wondered why he was still having this conversation. "Get out, Sergeant," he simply barked.

"Yes sir. Thank you, sir," the Sergeant saluted again (just to annoy the Major) then left.

Of course, the Sergeant knew there was no chance of the Major conducting the ceremony himself, but he had to ask, just for protocol's sake and to stop this from being used against him at some later unspecified date. The Major had a short memory when everything was fine and dandy but a very long and selective one when things weren't. And he could get upset about just about anything if he put his mind to it.

The Sergeant checked his pocket watch. He was late. He'd left seeking permission until the very last minute and now needed to beat his feet to be at the church on time. The parade ground was empty and the whole base was quiet. It was a Saturday morning so this was not unusual, but today everything was even quieter than normal. At least, until he arrived at the regimental chapel. This small and nondescript building tucked away behind the arsenal normally attracted barely a dozen pilgrims a day. But this morning almost everyone in the company had squeezed in and around it, such was the occasion.

A cheer went up when they saw the Sergeant sprinting around the corner and he was jostled and ruffled as he fought his way through to the front, into the chapel and towards the Padre at the altar.

"Nice of you to make it, Sarge!" went up the cheers.

"She came and went, got bored of waiting!"

"She slipped through the wire, same way she came in!"

"I'll marry you if you like, Armand!"

The Sergeant took it all in good humour, or at least he didn't retort. He couldn't. His mouth was too dry and his breathing short, and not just from the run. He felt something he'd not felt since Cedar Hill — nerves. They surprised him and yet brought him comfort too. Some of the numbness that had followed him around for the last ten long years had gone. It was almost as though he had awoken after a lifetime of sleeping to find he was more than just a soldier of the King's Guards. He was Armand once again, Armand Roche.

"Stand aside!" a voice cried out at the back of the church and all at once, the massed congregation parted to reveal Catherine stood at the door dressed in a flowing white dress of her own making.

She had two seamstresses to serve as her bridesmaids but no father to give her away. This was the reason so many had crammed in and around the chapel today. The entire company had stepped in to give her away. She was every man's daughter, adopted by the company and truly beloved. And it wasn't just because she was good with a needle or young and beautiful either; most of these craggy old men still saw her as a drummer boy in drag, such had been her lasting impression. But she had proved herself to everyone a hundred times over, as a girl, a boy, a soldier and a person. She was ingrained in the company's soul. She was Catherine Petit. And she was loved by all.

Corporal Jacques was the first to offer his arm, which Catherine accepted with a smile. But no sooner had she taken a step than Sergeant Santin stepped in to offer his. Catherine thanked Corporal Jacques and accepted Sergeant Santin's only to be immediately offered Corporal Samuel's. This steady procession of arms slowed Catherine's progress a little but every man that lined the route wanted to be able to say that he had walked her down the aisle, albeit for just a step.

By the time Catherine reached the front, the Sergeant had lost his nerves. She was so beautiful, more so than ever before, with her hair pinned back, her eyes sparkling like jewels and her huge round belly now fit to burst. This had been the reason the Sergeant had been forced to wait until the very last moment to ask for the Major's permission. Pregnant seamstresses were ten-a-penny on the base. Pregnant wives were likewise nothing unusual. But pregnant brides-to-be? This sort of thing offended the sensibilities of the officers of the King's Guards. It smacked of indisciplined and cocked a snook at formality. Had the Major laid eyes on Catherine between permission being sought and their vows being spoken, he might well have delayed their wedding until after she'd given birth simply out of spite to give their baby that most unfortunate and unshakable of tags. If there was one thing the Major did not like, it was impropriety being passed off as respectability.

But the wedding had been planned with military precision. Every man present had been sworn to secrecy, look-outs had been posted and a time had been chosen when the Major would be busy with his precious reports. Nothing would disturb the happy couple now. Or at least, so they thought.

The Padre urged Catherine and the Sergeant to take each other's hands.

"This is a happy occasion. This service brings me great pleasure. And I see from the faces of those gathered here to witness this union today that I am not alone. This is a good day, a blessed day, and one on which God smiles upon us all."

The Sergeant would've agreed but he scarcely heard a word of it. Catherine was before him and that was all that mattered. He remembered to say "I do" when someone prompted him with a nudge but for the most part all he wanted to do was stare into the face of his wife. His wife? He couldn't quite believe it. Catherine was his wife? The way she looked up at him, with such love and devotion, was the memory he would take with him always. She accepted him with her eyes. The words the Padre spoke, as noble in sentiment as they were, were a secondary consideration. Catherine felt equally distracted although her concerns were somewhat less flowery.

"Catherine Petit, do you take this man, Armand Roche, to be your wedded husband? Do you promise to be faithful to him in all things, as a woman should her husband, in accordance with the commands of God?"

Catherine didn't answer but unlike the Sergeant, it wasn't because she needed a nudge. Something wasn't right and it wasn't the wording of their marriage vows either.

"Catherine? Catherine?" the Padre asked.

The Sergeant snapped out of his romantic trance and realised something was wrong.

"What is it?" he asked, almost too afraid to ask.

Catherine looked at her feet and the Sergeant's eyes followed hers. Immediately he saw the problem. Catherine was now stood in a puddle of amniotic fluid and it wasn't getting any smaller.

"My waters have just broken," she told her new husband in case he thought that she hadn't managed to contain her excitement at the thought of marrying him.

"It certainly looks that way," the Sergeant agreed before turning to the Padre and asking, "Do you want to throw in a Christening too, seeing as we're here?"

CHAPTER FIFTY

DULY, THE MORNING AFTER the Prince's restaged ball, the King summoned a dozen suitable maidens to the Palace to try on Ella's discarded slipper. The Grand Duke urged caution but the King was having none of it. His feckless son had tried his patience once too often, so now he would compel him to marry. And if the Prince didn't like any of the girls the King selected then that was just tough titty and would serve him right for not getting on with it when he'd had the chance. In fact, the King went out of his way to choose a few girls he knew would be sure to get up the Prince's nose. The niece of the Earl of Beaumont-St-Bruyère. God, she was annoying. Or the eldest daughter of those ghastly Eames merchants. The one with the boss eyes. That would teach him.

    The Grand Duke looked on with consternation as the usual suspects were trotted up to the Palace. They were the same old damsels and dilettantes the Prince had been baulking at for the last decade. Events were moving beyond his control. The King was in a hurry to resolve this particular royal crisis even if it meant laying the seeds of another somewhere down the line. As such, the opportunity was slipping from the Duke's grasping hands. He'd hoped to have found the Prince's mystery girl before now but it seemed his son was almost as useless as the King's. This lottery was rigged. And the Grand Duke held none of the balls, metaphorically or otherwise.

    The girls themselves were stunned yet ecstatic at being given one last crack at the Prince. Everyone had assumed all hope was lost. Therefore, to wake up the next morning and be told, "it might still be you" was perplexing enough, only to then hear the proposed method of selection. Half the girls leapt out of bed and into their crumpled ballgowns without a thought in their minds while the other half got dressed more cautiously, some wondering what kind of skullduggery was afoot — literally. Surely there should be more to a Princess of Andovia than the size of her feet? Moreover what had happened to the original wearer? It seemed a curious way to select a bride, let alone a national figurehead, but who were they to argue? Stranger methods had been used. That boy who plucked a sword from a stone in England, for example. Or that barmy notion in the New World in which the great unwashed were asked to choose from a list of ordinary men. Such foolishness could only lead to the coronation of charlatans and clowns.

"This is it, Claudia. This is your moment," Lady Ricci assured her daughter on the coach ride into town. "The crown sits within your grasp. Do not fail me now."

"No, Mother," Claudia pledged.

Suzette was likewise undergoing a last-minute pep-talk as she pulled up to the Palace steps. "Whatever else happens today, you must pull on that glass slipper, no matter how uncomfortable it might be. Do you understand me, daughter?"

"Yes, Mother," Suzette vowed.

"Dear sweet Isabella," Madame Eames said as they too trundled along, through the town square and towards the Palace. "I always swore I would never hurt you but today, my darling, I am afraid I must break that promise."

"Mother?"

"Your feet are too long and your toenails will prove your undoing. We must not allow such things to stand in our way," she explained, producing a pair of scissors from her bag and banging on the carriage roof to tell her driver to pull over.

Poor Isabella, such striking eyes but seriously big feet.

Nina Laurent had no such worries. Her feet had stopped growing at age 13 and she was known for having the daintiest toes in all the Kingdom — according to the boy in the shoe shop who fancied her. But would this be enough to see her crowned a Princess? What if someone else had size two feet? It wasn't exactly outside the realms of possibility. Perhaps this was just the first of many hurdles and eventually, after another dozen trials, she would find herself desperately trying to suck a golf ball through a length of garden hose while various Palace officials threw buckets of water over her?

"If that's what it takes, precious Nina, then that's what you must do. It is what your father would have wanted," her mother assured her.

"Then I will do it for him," Nina promised, looking up at the Palace balcony and picturing herself stepping out to the rapture of her people.

Throughout it all, while the girls were arriving at the Palace, the Prince was uncharacteristically tranquil, as though the notion of marrying the first silly cow to have the right-sized feet held no horrors for him. The King took this as a good sign, his son had finally been brought to book, but the Grand Duke was not so sure. The Prince was too temperate — merry even — like he was actually looking forward to this whole sorry charade.

They'd assembled in the Great Throne Room for the initiation, as seemed fitting. The King was sat on his throne with the Prince stood by his side. The Grand Duke was stationed a short way from the bottom of the steps with the glass slipper on a velvet cushion and a footman on hand to do the huffing and puffing. While the girls themselves awaited their destiny at the far end of the room, staring longingly not at the Prince they hoped to marry but at the glass slipper that stood in their way.

"The Lady Isabella," the Majordomo announced, ushering in the final candidate. Isabella limped in, grimacing with every step and clinging onto the wall for support to stop herself from keeling over. Mother had given her nails a very thorough trimming indeed.

"Is that everyone? Can we get started now?" the King asked.

"Yes, Your Majesty," he was told, so the King jumped to his feet and pointed to the first girl he liked the look of.

"You. Yes, you there. Come forward and try on the glass slipper."

"Me?" Isabella wavered, so faint from the pain that she neglected to add, "Your Majesty," "Royal Highness" or "catch my shoes" as might have been expected.

"Yes, come come, let's get on with it."

Isabella stumbled into Claudia, who gave her a shove in the right direction and she hobbled over to where the footman was waiting.

Something was amiss with this girl and everyone could see it yet still the Prince didn't seem phased. If she was to be his wife, then it was a case of indifference-at-first-sight.

When the footman slipped Isabella's shoe off he almost scrambled away in disgust again. Her toes were red-raw and a couple encrusted in blood. It hurt his eyes just looking at them so what they must've felt like to poor Isabella he could only imagine. He looked to the Grand Duke for instructions and the Grand Duke pulled his hands from his pockets and took a step back. What on Earth had happened to this wretched floozy's foot?

"I am ready, Your Highness," Isabella spluttered, swaying to and fro and turning lily-white as the blood drained from her face and onto the carpet via her toenails. The Grand Duke signalled the footman to get on with it before she left a puddle and accordingly the footman picked up the slipper and slipped it over Isabella's toes. It barely got past her third little piggy before becoming wedged. Isabella yelped in despair as she tried to grind the rest of her foot inside but all she did was bloody the slipper and leave herself feeling even fainter than before.

"I think I need to sit down," she said moments before falling flat onto her face and vomiting at the Grand Duke's feet.

"Such a great pity," the Prince ventured cockily. "I liked her too."

There was a brief intermission while the Palace maids were summoned to mop up Isabella and her contributions but soon the line was moving again, first with Claudia Ricci and then Suzette Weiss fighting over the slipper and each refusing to accept that it didn't fit. The girl who'd originally worn it to the ball had been about their age and, if anything, taller than both of them, and yet neither's feet even came close to fitting. How could this be?

"Thank you, you may go," the Grand Duke declared, pulling the slipper from their hands and almost calling in the guards when they tried to snatch it back.

"Please, Your Grace, one last try," Claudia pleaded.

"I was trying it on the wrong way," Suzette said.

"You may go!" the Grand Duke insisted.

"And try not to trip over the furniture on the way out with your big feet," the Prince sniggered as they were ushered from the room.

"Wait wait," the King called, prompting Suzette to look back in hope.

"Yes, Your Royal Highness?"

"What size do you wear?" he asked.

"Size six," Suzette replied eagerly, as though this would explain the mix-up and allow her some other way of proving herself.

"Size five," Claudia quickly lied in an attempt to trump her rival.

"Anyone with size five or over may go," the King said to the disappointment of both. Suzette and Claudia were unceremoniously booted out along with several other

Sasquatches who were trying to hide at the back.

"I am a size two, Your Grace," Nina audaciously declared, gambling her petit feet against her impertinence in order to jump the queue. The Grand Duke wasn't sure he liked girls who spoke out of turn, even those with size two feet, and he was about to disqualify her from proceedings when the King signalled him to not be such a tool and ushered Nina forwards.

"If the shoe fits, she's our girl," he declared in no uncertain terms.

"Absolutely Papa," the Prince agreed as he leaned against the throne. "After all, I'm not fussy."

And with these fine words of encouragement ringing in her ears, Nina kicked off her shoes and sunk her foot into the slipper, heel and all. The King leaned forwards, the Grand Duke dropped his monocle and the remaining girls at the back let out a wail of despair.

"It fits!" the room declared with wildly mixed emotions.

Nina's heart leapt. The Prince was hers. She, a humble girl from the baker's shop, was to be a Princess. Her dreams had come true. The good Lord had guided her. Praise be.

Despite his future now laid bare for all to see, the Prince barely reacted. He simply raised an eyebrow, cleared his throat and invited his gleeful new fiancée to come towards him. Nina willingly obeyed, eager to take her rightful place by her Prince's side, only to go over on her heel with her first step and then shed the slipper with her second. Nina was mortified and looked around the room to see all eyes staring at her intently. She pulled on the slipper once more but barely made it two steps before kicking it off again. See, while the slipper fitted the length of her foot it was too wide by far and caused her foot to slip around inside as though she was wearing the shoe box rather than the shoe.

"It doesn't fit!" one of the girls at the back yelped in

hope and all at once everyone could see. Nina was not the one, after all.

In a panic, she tried to hurry to the Prince's side, convinced that he represented some kind of a finishing line, but after only three more clomping steps she turned her ankle and went down in a flash of searing pain.

"My Lady," the Grand Duke urged but Nina wasn't for dissuading. She'd come too far to give up now, she was almost to within touching distance of her destiny.

"I can make it," she cried, crawling up the steps towards the Prince on her hands and knees.

"I must say, I am so looking forward to our first dance," the Prince declared with a jolly chuckle.

The King now finally twigged what the Grand Duke already had, that some jiggery-pokery had taken place and that he'd walked right into the Prince's trap. He'd tried to use his son's promise against him by posting an official proclamation stating that the Prince "had vowed to marry the girl who fitted the glass slipper" and yet all he'd done was create a loophole through which he could wriggle.

"This is your doing," the King snapped, jumping to his feet and turning on the Prince in a fit of eye-popping rage.

"Of course not," the Prince lied. "But did you really expect me to marry just anyone, Papa? Love is not a one-size-fits-all emotion. My heart belongs to one girl alone, Cinderella. You saw her. You all saw her. I shall marry her and her alone."

"By God, you will keep your word, boy!" the King thundered, shocking everyone inside the throne room. His beetroot face looked set to explode and his fist was clenched so hard that he almost fired off the emeralds from his official ring in all directions. "Scour the land! Bring in every freak-footed maiden you can find, even if you have to drag the swamps. For I will find you someone who fits that accursed glass slipper! I will hold you to your pledge — unless you can produce your conveniently disappearing Cinderella."

And with that, the King stormed from the room before he lost his temper entirely.

The Prince looked down at Nina Laurent, now just a step from the throne, and smiled.

"So close, and yet so far," he said before stepping over her and walking away in amusement.

CHAPTER FIFTY-ONE

MOTHER WAS RUNNING PERILOUSLY LOW on ammunition. The old General had left quite a cache but he hadn't reckoned on keeping an army of bandits at bay for an entire night and day.

Corporals Babin and Deniau had fought valiantly but now both lay injured. Deniau was the more seriously hurt of the two, having taken a bolt to the shoulder but both men were still in the fight, just about, each taking up key positions overlooking the approaches to the front and back doors.

Marigold hurried to Babin's side with more shot, crawling past the shattered windows as powder charges were hurled at the front of the château to reduce the timbers to matchwood.

"Here, they're still warm," she said, handing Babin two dozen newly-minted musket balls.

She and Gardenia had melted down every scrap of lead they could lay their hands on, including the General's prized collection of model soldiers, painstakingly sculpted and painted over many solitary evenings, now boiled down and recast as ammunition. The General would have approved. Mother had shown them how to create basic lead shot by dipping pearls into molten lead and letting them cool. Ella provided the pearls, or rather her precious ballgown had, but unlike the General, she'd been rather cooler on the whole enterprise.

"They're mine. Take your hands off them at once," she hissed as she watched Mother harvest her dress for baubles.

"They are Grimaldi's," Mother corrected her. "And we're giving them back to him."

Crouched behind the front door, Babin fed his weapon with the improvised ammunition and hung it through a blast hole, shielding his face as he pulled the trigger in case the new shot blew his flintlock to pieces. The ball not only fired well but winged one of Grimaldi's men who was lurking behind the steps of the veranda. The bandit rolled around on the ground and hollered in agony, unconcerned that he was now one pearl the richer, almost to the point of ingratitude.

The inevitable angry response soon followed and the walls seemed to explode all around them. Babin dived on Marigold to protect her from the blast, only to receive a searing shard of shrapnel to the hand. He cried out in agony and dropped his weapon, so Marigold returned the favour, dragging him through the smoke and flames and across the tiles until they found shelter behind the heavy oak bannisters.

"Show me," Marigold demanded, ripping part of her undergarments away to use as a tourniquet on Babin's shattered hand. "Hold it high to slow the bleeding," she told him before hurrying back across the floor to reload his fallen weapon and shoot. She didn't hit anyone but she sent out a clear message to those outside that they were still here and still a force to be reckoned with.

Corporal Babin, though pained as he was, felt buoyed. He'd never known a girl like Marigold. She was dressed in rags, her hair was haywire and her face was a mass of powder burns and blood and yet she was undoubtedly the most beautiful girl he'd ever seen. If he were to die today, he could not have been prouder to have fought and died alongside such a person.

Gardenia was receiving equally favourable dispatches at the back of the château from Corporal Deniau. The Corporal had felt the full force of one of Grimaldi's grenades and was now blind in one eye and blurred in the other but Gardenia had cleaned his wounds and made him as comfortable as she could. But Deniau was unable to enjoy Gardenia's attentions, the enemy was at the gates and there was no time to convalesce. He couldn't see to shoot but Gardenia was able to aim for him, guiding his arm and telling him when to pull the trigger as she became his eyes. They'd not hit anything for all their efforts but once again they packed enough of a punch to keep Grimaldi's men at bay.

"Mother will be disappointed with me," Gardenia said. "She always told me to aim for a Captain or higher."

The Corporal didn't get the joke but he appreciated the admission, not least of all when Gardenia pressed her lips to his in a moment of unrequited urgency and kissed him with all the pent-up passions of sixteen starchy years.

"I will be with you until the end," she told him when their lips finally parted.

"And I with you," he vowed in return.

A crossbow bolt ripped through the wall and passed between them to remind them this might come sooner rather than later but neither flinched. Deniau reloaded his flintlock, Gardenia took his arm and together they returned the enemy's fire, undaunted and unafraid.

This was something of a first for Franz Grimaldi. He was so used to people throwing their weapons aside and dropping to their knees at the very sight of him that he was still using scare tactics to try to break the siege, unwilling to believe he'd found three women who refused to be scared. But he was learning fast.

"We need more powder," Durand said as he and Grimaldi watched from the treeline. Since being rescued from the dungeons, Durand had become a fully paid-up member of Grimaldi's gang. Torture wasn't needed to extract his confession. He willingly traded every scrap of information on the Prince for something more valuable — revenge. And not just against the Prince, but against Marigold, Gardenia and this whole pitiful Kingdom. When Ella was back on the throne and he was restored to his rightful rank, the people would rue the day they'd ever heard of Captain Durand.

If Grimaldi had wanted, he could have reduced the chateau to cinders but the chateau wasn't what he'd come for.

And way up in Ella's attic room, overlooking the drama, Mother knew this only too well. This was why she hadn't left Ella's side since the first shots had been fired. Marigold and Gardenia may have been closer to the firing line downstairs but only Mother had the steel to do what was necessary should the inevitable come to pass. Grimaldi couldn't have known this for sure but he wasn't prepared to take any chances. Not after all he'd been through. So he watched and waited and bided his time knowing that eventually, Mother would make a mistake. Everyone always did. It was only a matter of time.

"Ladders," he told Durand with a grin. "Get to the woods and make me a ladder. And be back by dark."

At the heart of the drama was Ella herself, still tied to a chair after twelve long hours and the only one out of everyone unable to affect current events — which, seeing as she was the catalyst behind them, proved frustration in spades.

"He's never going to give up on me. When are you going to understand that?" she said, struggling against her bonds until her wrists were red-raw.

"When he understands that neither will we," Mother replied all matter-of-fact, as though they were discussing the weather.

"You are a stubborn and wicked old woman, to sacrifice your daughters needlessly like this."

"My daughters are born of Sergeant Armand Roche of the King's Guards. They carry his spirit in their blood. They do not know how to give up."

"Ha ha ha!" Ella howled, throwing back her head to laugh. "And we all know what happened to him, don't we?"

As evil as she was, Mother had to admire Ella's gumption. Even at the point of a gun, she was still full of herself. But a foot against the back of her chair and a quick trip to the floor soon put paid to her bravado.

"Witch!" she hollered, landing full-weight on her shoulder when she turned to protect her precious face.

"Now now, is that any way to speak to your mother?"

"You're nothing to me. You're not my mother, my stepmother or even my biggest concern. You're a stepping stone, that's all. One of many and not the last by any means."

"You talk tough for a pretty Princess," Mother said as she kept watch at the window. There was a little movement down there but not much. She'd been here before, the calm before the storm, and she was ready for the endgame even if Ella wasn't.

"Don't fool yourself. It's not the pearls around a girl's neck that makes a Princess. It's the steel in one's gut. I've had to fight for this. No one's handed me anything."

Mother had heard these words before. She'd used them, or words to this effect, on many occasions to prepare her own girls for what was to come, but she had never coached them to murder. Ella looked up at Mother from the floor and could almost read her thoughts. She pursed her lips and shrugged, almost apologetically, the mask slipping a little. Perhaps there was a person behind her aspirations after all.

"No one was supposed to get hurt, especially not Marigold or Gardenia. But needs must. And they were in my way. That's the truth."

"The sad thing is you truly believe this justified your actions, don't you?"

"History remembers the winners. There are no portraits of seamstresses hanging in the palaces of Europe," Ella pointed out.

"More pity on the palaces of Europe," Mother replied to Ella's bewilderment.

A stray bolt came through the window and chipped the brickwork to momentarily suspend their hostilities. Ella growled in annoyance as she was showered with grit and Mother replied with a shot towards the woods. She couldn't see anyone down there but she adjudged the position of the shooter from the angle of the bolt.

No cry. She'd either missed by a mile or hit a bullseye.

The sun was sinking in the west. An orange hue hung over the chateau. This time of the evening was beautiful but it wouldn't last. The night was fast approaching and Grimaldi would no doubt go for broke. Mother would in his shoes. They wouldn't last until morning. Any of them. As tough as Mother was, this was a sobering thought. Despite Ella accusations, she loved her daughters deeply and would do anything to protect them. This was why she could not allow Franz Grimaldi across her threshold. She wasn't being stubborn. She just knew the man. And what he was capable of.

"It's getting cold," Ella said with a shudder.

This wasn't a complaint, just an observation, a sign that their relationships were normalising between them in spite of the situation. Even the most ardent of enemies made small talk occasionally. Hate was energy sapping. And no one could keep it up forever.

Mother righted Ella's chair and dragged her into the far corner away from the path of any errant arrows. She plucked a blanket off the bed and threw it over Ella's legs but stopped short of tucking her in and reading her a bedtime story.

She'd save that for when she heard Grimaldi's boots on the stairs outside.

The sun sank further behind the trees to blot out the day. Grimaldi's men kept the shooting up but only sporadically. They were going through the motions and everyone knew it. The darkness would cover Grimaldi's final assault. He had to get the jump on Mother. He couldn't allow her to snuff out the prize before he'd made it up into the attic otherwise all of this would have been for nothing.

Durand came back from the woods carrying the siege ladder he'd spent the evening making. It was a flimsy-looking creation but long enough to reach the upper windows. Durand was the leanest of Grimaldi's men, helped no doubt by his stint in the dungeons, so it would also be his job to breach their defences.

Grimaldi spat out an olive pip as he looked over Durand's work.

"Now get me more powder," he said. "All of it."

The first explosion blew out what remained of the front porch and roused Babin from his slumber. He'd succumbed to his injuries and had allowed the bandits to get the drop on him. Smoke filled the hallway and Marigold could barely see when she tried running to his aid.

"Get down!" Babin shouted to her just as another explosion blew the shutters from the parlour windows. Marigold was knocked sideways and hit her head. Dizzy and momentarily confused, she fired her pistol at what she thought was the towering figure of Franz Grimaldi only to kill Monsieur Beaufort's grandfather clock with a shot to the pendulum.

"Here! To me!" Babin urged as another powder charge ripped through the night, this one towards the rear of the house.

Gardenia dragged Deniau through the debris just as the rear of the house was peppered with crossbow fire. Even after all the fighting, she'd been though nothing could have prepared her for the ferocity of this assault. Deniau was no longer capable of loading or firing his weapon so Gardenia took over his duties for him, returning a single musket shot in reply to more than a dozen bolts. It seemed like a feeble retort but it was all she had.

"Fall back!" beckoned Mother from upstairs. "Back to me!"

Marigold and Gardenia heard the instruction and knew what to do. Each helped their wounded partner to their feet and led them through the chateau as it was systematically blown apart around their ears. Mother hurried to the top of the stairs and covered their retreat, firing at the newly created hole in the wall as the smoke began to stir.

Deniau slumped onto the stairs. He couldn't go on. His legs were like string and his body quivered with pain.

"Go!" he urged Gardenia. "Save yourself."

"I'm not leaving you," she protested, but Mother raced down to drag her away as crossbow bolts starting darting through the blast holes.

"We have to go!"

"No!" Gardenia screamed, refusing to relinquish his arm despite Deniau pushing her in one direction and Mother pulling on her from the other.

"Gardenia, listen to me, child. Do not dishonour his sacrifice by making a gift of yourself to the enemy. We have to go," Mother told her.

Deniau looked up at Gardenia and pleaded with her to go and Gardenia did not have the heart to refuse him, no matter how much it hurt. She let go of his hand and felt herself plucked from his touch as Mother dragged her up the stairs. Marigold was already there, helping Babin across the landing and up the attic stairs before he too dropped to his knees.

"Leave me my weapon and go. I will hold them off for as long as I can but lock your door and do not open it again for anything."

Marigold too was dismayed by Babin's request but unlike her sister, she knew it was the logical thing to do. Babin could not run and there was scant room in Ella's bedroom to fight. The stairs offered him his best hope of holding the enemy at bay until... until... until there was no longer any hope. At which point she would see her brave Corporal again. If not in this life then the next.

Mother loaded Babin's pistol for him and left him a handful of melted down toy soldiers.

"For the *King's Men*," she said, placing a hand on his shoulder to show her gratitude for all he had given.

"For the *King's Men*," he replied, before turning his eyes to Marigold. He was only young, scarcely out of his teens and he was afraid, but he was also resolute. Marigold tried to fight back the tears but failed. "Go," he told her. "And thank you."

Marigold was confused. She didn't understand why Babin had thanked her and Mother didn't have time to explain. The first arrows whipped across the landing door to tell them Grimaldi's men had made it into the chateau and were now closing in fast. Babin returned fire and quickly reloaded, stealing one last look at Marigold as she made it to the top of the stairs and into Ella's room before the door closed between them.

He had vowed to protect them and protect them he would. He would fight on until the bitter end. No one would get past him while he held a breath in his body and a sword in his hands. Some things were worth dying for.

But unbeknown to Babin, he was already too late. The door to Ella's bedroom had not been shut by Marigold. Ella stood waiting for their return, finally free of her bonds, and aching to pull the trigger of the mini-crossbow Durand had brought her.

Mother went for her own weapon when she saw Ella free but Ella already had the drop on her. She wouldn't make it in time and would've no doubt died trying but she wasn't given the chance. A large dirty hand came out of nowhere and swatted the gun away before she could take aim.

"Do not do that, madam," growled a voice that turned her blood to ice. "For I would hate for us to start off on a sour note."

CHAPTER FIFTY-TWO

FRANZ GRIMALDI STEPPED OUT of the shadows dragging some of the gloom with him. His face seemed permanently steeped in darkness, almost as if the candles were afraid of him. His murderous cutlass was drawn, its jagged blade bridging the air between his over-sized hand and Mother's slender arm. One shot. That's all she'd get, one shot, before falling foul of either Ella's crossbow or Grimaldi's evil sword. But who did she take with her? Beauty or the beast?

"I can hear you thinking, Madam. Tick-tock tick-tock," Grimaldi leered, spitting an olive pip onto the floor as if to tempt Mother his way.

Durand had scaled his improvised ladder and scrambled up the ivy while Mother had been distracted with the girls, but neither would've taken Grimaldi's weight. He'd climbed the rope that Durand had subsequently lowered, one end tied to a ceiling beam that now bowed perilously, but he'd made it just in time, heaving himself through the window before Mother could get back.

"Mother no!" Gardenia cried when she saw Mother tensing to fire. She attempted to throw herself in between them all but found herself pulled back by Marigold. It seemed like nothing could stop the inevitable and yet Gardenia's outburst pricked something inside Grimaldi. Remembering his objective, he unknitted his brow and lowered his sword.

"Perhaps we should listen to your daughter, madame?" he suggested, throwing Durand and Ella a look to do likewise. Ella was less willing and had to be barked at before she complied, leaving Mother as the only antagonist still waving a weapon.

"Put the gun down, old woman, and let's talk," Ella said impatiently. As much as she wanted to make her beloved family suffer for the indignity of the last eighteen hours, Ella also was a pragmatist and knew she stood nothing to gain from petty revenge and everything to lose. And like Grimaldi, she had not come through all this for nothing. The prize was still within her grasp.

But Mother refused to be kowtowed.

"My ears work fine even with my arm raised. Say your piece," she told them, backing away towards the far wall where Marigold was wrestling with Gardenia. The corner of Grimaldi's crooked mouth curled upwards. He had hobnail boots that weren't as tough as this old bird. She was something to behold.

"I have no wish to kill you," Grimaldi announced. "You nor your daughters."

"The lies fall easily from your lips. Do not expect me to stoop to pick them up," Mother hissed.

"Oh please," Ella scoffed. "If I am to marry the Prince, I need a lily-white backstory. How do you think it'll look if my whole extended family lies butchered while I walk away scot-free?"

"Every Princess needs a little tragedy in her life. I'm sure you'll spin it to your advantage."

"Tragedy yes. But a massacre of all remaining witnesses to my upbringing? After already losing my mother and father? That's not a tragedy, that's a curse. And do you really think the Kingdom wants someone like that, with the harbinger of death at her elbow, for their Princess and future Queen?"

She had a point, Mother had to give her that. It was not unnatural to lose one parent or even unheard of to lose both, but to lose whole branches of the family would've looked "a shameful business". Heads had ended up decorating city gates for far less.

"I need you. All of you. You are citizens and known in this Kingdom. You must corroborate my story."

"I will not lie for a duplicitous harpy like you," Mother

said, leaning towards Ella as the one most worthy of the contents of her barrel.

"Then lie for the lives of your daughters, madame," Grimaldi suggested. "Lie for yourself. Lie for the soldiers we now have in our charge. Death before dishonour is not honour. It is merely death."

"Forget our aims, just think of yourselves," Ella echoed. "Everyone else in Andovia does."

Durand smiled with complicity. Never a truer word had been spoken in this God-forsaken Kingdom, as he above all others could testify. Out of the corner of his eye, he noticed Gardenia staring at him. Despite everything that had happened, she was still drawn to him by his looks but the former Guardsman soon put paid to that when he returned her stare with a snarl.

"I made a mistake," Ella continued. "I underestimated you. I see that now, but it's not too late. Join us. Help me take the crown and I will see to it that your daughters marry beyond their wildest dreams."

Mother could scarcely argue with Ella's sentiment but she didn't trust any of them to practice what they'd preached the moment she set aside her pistol. Liars lied, end of story.

"And the soldiers? What of them?" Mother said, asking after Babin and Deniau.

"Do not worry about them…" Ella began to say, only to be talked over by Grimaldi.

"What would you have us do with them, Madam?" he asked, getting the measure of Mother as the negotiations progressed.

"Their lives are indebted to me. I require you to hand them over. As a sign of good faith."

Ella scowled at the thought of that. These men had seen too much. They couldn't be allowed to live and Grimaldi should've known this better than most. So she was stunned when he asked:

"You can guarantee their silence?"

"By the oath of the *King's Men* I can," Mother confirmed.

Durand tensed but Ella just shrugged.

"Who the hell are the *King's Men*?" she said, ready to shoot the old lady for even suggesting such idiocy. Grimaldi's eyes narrowed. Even if Ella hadn't heard of the *King's men*, it was clear he had. And his opinion of Mother rose further. No wonder Ella had underestimated her.

"And what would you know of such treason?" Grimaldi asked with genuine curiosity.

"Enough to see my head on a pike alongside yours I'll wager."

The old outlaw laughed. His was a big, angry, booming laugh and it sent several extra roof slates crashing to the ground before he'd regained his composure.

"What? What's the big secret?" Ella demanded.

"You are a fool, little girl. This woman is a bigger brigand than I," Grimaldi said, without feeling the need to embellish any further.

Marigold and Gardenia were equally perplexed. They knew those words carried danger but they couldn't have dreamed they'd be enough to placate Franz Grimaldi.

"I still don't trust you," Mother said, turning her pistol on the hulking Bandit King.

Grimaldi grinned, his gnarled features distorted into ugly shadows in the dim of the candlelight.

"And neither should you, madame. All I ask is that you hear me out."

Grimaldi sheathed his cutlass and looked around for a chair. Durand offered him one but he brushed it aside and instead flopped onto Ella's bed, the frame creaking beneath his weight and his gargantuan feet dangling off the end.

"You know what I am after?" he asked with his eyes closed. "What I desire?"

"A pardon, I am told. And yet not even God could pardon you for your sins," Mother said tersely.

"Then it is just as well I'm not petitioning Him, isn't it," Grimaldi reasoned, unruffled by Mother's assessment. "When Ella is crowned she can arrange me this favour. Then I can walk out in daylight like a normal gentleman, without looking over my shoulder and without killing all those I fancy have come for my reward. I am changed, Madame. And I wish the world to change with me."

"Poppycock. Leopards do not change their spots," Mother said.

"So true, madame, so true, but they do stop killing antelopes when fresh meat is left for them on a silver platter," he argued, debating for a moment whether to kick off his shoes or not. Fortunately for all concerned, he elected to leave them on. "Like I say, I can hear you thinking. Ella might need you and your daughters to corroborate her story but she does not need the soldiers. They are an inconvenience. A danger. But madame, I ask you, from my perspective, what chance have I of acquiring a royal pardon if I have killed two of His Majesty's Own in the commission of this pursuit? Oh no, your soldiers will be well taken care of, as though they were my very own men. Captain Durand can testify to that fact, can't you?" he said, eliciting a snort of derision from Durand. "And should they keep their own counsel about the events of tonight, they should be well rewarded too."

Ella winked. "Well, I'm not trying to marry the imbecile because I fancy myself in a crown, am I?"

Gardenia blanched. The notion of marrying a man for anything other than love shocked her sensibilities. Mother had spent years trying to drum the facts of life into her, that in a world of men a girl's only method of advancement was at the altar, but it was no use, Gardenia was a hopeless romantic. So whenever Mother had talked up Captain Olivier in the past, Gardenia had tried to convince herself that this was because he was a kind and chivalrous gentleman (despite all evidence to the contrary) and not, as it would seem, because of the fortune he stood to inherit when his own odious father fell off the perch.

"Oh sweetheart, look at your face," Durand smirked. "You're in for one hell of a surprise on your wedding night. That is if you ever manage to find anyone desperate enough to have you." The barb felt all the crueler coming from Durand because of how Gardenia had once felt about him but Mother just glared.

"Talk to my daughter that way again and you'll receive one hell of a surprise yourself," Mother advised the former gentleman, aiming her pistol between his eyes.

Ella sought to intervene before the situation spiralled beyond her control. "Gardenia darling, I was merely stating that once I am the Princess none of us will ever eat cabbage soup again."

Marigold took note. Now she was talking.

Ella continued. "I'm not that different from you, you know. Any of you. All I want is what every little girl wants: love, security and comfort, and of course, to be kept in a style of luxury to which I have no Earthly right to expect. I'm just prepared to go a little further than most in order to achieve these dreams."

"You are not like us," Marigold said, unable to hold her tongue a moment longer. "You're ugly."

"Ha!" Ella laughed. "You're calling *me* ugly? You should hear what they say about you two around town."

"Enough of this," Grimaldi snapped, sitting up and dropping his legs off the side of the bed. "You have our offer. Your lives, the lives of your soldiers and riches beyond your wildest imaginations. It's a good deal, the best you'll receive tonight, and all you have to do is let your stepdaughter walk out of that door and smile at her wedding. Leave the rest to us."

"I'll even set Gardenia up with Captain Olivier if that's what you'd like. Personally, I'd aim a little higher but if that's who you two have had your eye on, who am I to judge?" Ella said with a smug and self-assured smirk.

Gardenia said nothing. It probably wouldn't have helped the situation to point out that, in her heart, she now felt betrothed to Corporal Deniau. Likewise Marigold kept her counsel. She wanted to live and she wanted her own Corporal returned to her safely. If she had to sup with the devil in order to do this then she would, but as the proverb went, she would use a very long spoon.

Mother kept the pistol on Ella the whole time but relaxed her eye a little.

"Then go. Marry your Prince and live happily ever after. We will not stand in your way," she said.

"And you'll come to the wedding? As my honoured guests? My family?" Ella pressed.

"We will… we will be there," Mother confirmed hesitantly.

"With a pistol pointing at me throughout the whole service?" Ella joked.

"We'll see," was about the best Mother could promise.

"Then we're friends again," Ella said sweetly. "See you Saturday."

Ella dropped her mini-crossbow with a thud and headed for the door, stopping at the last moment when she remembered something. She walked back to her wardrobe and parted the wall of silk dresses hanging up inside it to reveal several things stacked up at the back. One was a wicker basket that looked suspiciously like a snake trap, the other was a small trunk, the type used to lock away personal correspondence. This was the thing she took with her, the thing that Marigold had scaled the side of the house to find.

Ella noticed Marigold's quizzical eye.

"My vanity case," she said, omitting to mention that the

case was hers but the vanity was the Prince's. Inside, were his love letters to Durand, prints of the Prince's official likeness, cuttings from *La Gazette* and other such European news sheets on the Prince's comings and goings and an introductory guide to Andovian culture (not the biggest booklet in the world). More tellingly, there were several plans of the Palace and other royal residences and a wanted poster featuring the face of a rather haunted-looking Monsieur Beaufort, only his name was listed as Larue. His crime? Deception and theft. His punishment? To have fallen foul of Ella before he'd fallen foul of the investigating magistrate.

"Best not to leave this behind," Ella reasoned, carrying the case with her.

"Just one thing," Mother said before she left. "Who's doing your dress for the wedding?"

Ella almost laughed. Almost. "Someone else, old woman. Someone else," and then she was gone, without so much as a backward glance. She couldn't get away from this place quick enough.

Mother now turned the pistol to Grimaldi but he didn't so much as blink.

"Good day to you, Madame. Ladies?" he said, tipping his cap and spitting out an olive pip as he followed Ella out. Durand went too, stopping momentarily in the door to deliver one final barb.

"You're welcome," he said with a malicious smile, echoing Marigold's own words the last time they had seen each other after the first Prince's ball. And then they were gone. Mother watched from the window as the marauders pulled out and finally the women were alone.

"Do you believe them?" Marigold asked.

"Not a bit of it," Mother replied, at last able to lower her aching arm.

"Then what should we do?"

"Pack," Mother replied. "And quickly. We're leaving."

"For where?" Gardenia asked.

"Anywhere, just as long as it's a long way from here. I have a feeling this Kingdom is about to go to the dogs." Mother thought about what she'd just said and added: "Literally."

CHAPTER FIFTY-THREE

GRIMALDI ACCOMPANIED ELLA for most of the way but said his farewells just short of the city gates, for obvious reasons. Ella took a horse and trotted through Andovia's winding streets, past the main square, beneath the towering cathedral and on to the sprawling Palace beyond.

The streets were quieter than normal and when Ella reached the Palace she saw why. Everyone was here, or at least every young maiden was, which naturally attracted every young master too — each wistfully eyeing the long line and wondering what it must be like to be the Prince for a day.

Most of the girls had thrown on their finest frocks for the occasion but Ella wore rags. This was hardly surprising. She had just come through an eighteen-hour siege and had been in such a rush to get to the Palace and claim her prize that she hadn't thought to do much more than wipe some of the dirt from her face. Not even all of it. Just some. But then again why should she? The deal had been done. The Prince was hers. A life of silks and pearls awaited her. All she had to do was turn up, knock on his door and order the Prince to run her a bath of ass's milk. Or so she thought.

Ella found the back of the line and asked the girl in front, almost in trepidation, what on Earth was going on.

"Where have you been?" the girl asked, before seeing the state of Ella and deciding she didn't want to know. "We're here to try on the glass slipper."

"The glass slipper?" Ella asked in confusion. Her glass slipper?

"Of course. The Prince has vowed to marry whomever it fits," she replied, looking Ella up and down. "Within reason, of course."

This revelation hit Ella like a brick. The notion was as bizarre as it was unexpected, unreal even, so much so that she had to check whether she'd heard right.

"The Prince? Prince Carina? My Prince?"

"Yes, the girl who fits the slipper will be his," she confirmed, crosslegged with excitement.

Ella peered past her and looked up and down the long line of others, counting maybe a hundred girls of all shapes and sizes.

"When do the doors open?"

"They opened this morning. Scores of girls have gone in but they've all come out again. None have been worthy."

This confused Ella even further. Setting aside the fact that the Prince had decided to call her bluff by marrying someone else, he'd now elected to find Andovia's future Princess by her shoe size (presumably to match her IQ). But most bizarre of all was that no one had fit her slipper yet. How was this even possible? After all, Ella was a size five. Surely this wasn't such an unusual size? Was she really the only girl in this God-forsaken backwater with size-five feet?

"They say it's enchanted," the girl explained with a knowing look.

"Do *they*?" Ella nodded politely, 'they' being the types of people who still peeped around the backs of mirrors. As puzzling a mystery as this was, Ella wasn't prepared to take her chances by waiting in line. She had to get to the Prince and quick before he went and did something silly, like marrying someone because she was clever or nice.

Unfortunately, the line wasn't keen on the idea of 'cuts', especially by someone the cat hadn't so much dragged in as coughed up, so Ella came up with another plan. She went back to her horse, grabbed the canvas bag that hung from her saddle and made her way around to the side entrance, away from the glare of the main gates, and approached the sentry stationed there.

"I wish to speak with Captain Olivier," she demanded.

"The Captain's busy," the sentry replied, smelling Ella

before he saw her. Ella was the sixteenth girl who'd asked to see the Captain but the first who'd slept in a pigsty.

"I think he'll make time for me," Ella said.

"I seriously doubt that," the sentry said, caught in two minds over whether to turn his nose up at her or simply pinch it closed.

Ella slid the canvas bag off her shoulder and opened it to show the sentry what was inside. His face fell open and his disdain was soon forgotten.

"I'll go and get him right away. Stay there! Don't move!" he insisted, almost tripping over his feet as he dashed to get the Captain.

*

INSIDE THE PALACE, the Prince was enjoying the spectacle of a great many girls hurting their feet in his name. He wasn't a sadist but given the chance, he'd take a slice of other people's pain in the name of amusement. The King had long since given up on the whole charade and had gone off to research the family shield. He'd finally come to the conclusion that the Prince had won the day. He would not marry and he would not produce an heir, legitimate or otherwise. His intention, as always, had been to simply make hay while the sun shone, and not worry about what came next. Life was one long party to the Prince. What did it matter who cleared up the mess after he'd turned in? The Prince had no sense of history. The King had no sense of fun. They were never destined to get along. But as the King's stable master had once told him, sometimes even the most magnificent of stallions would not mate, regardless of how long you tethered them alongside the prettiest of fillies. It was just the way it was. Win all the races you can while they were still running because that was all you were going to get out of them. That and dog food.

The Grand Duke remained on hand to oversee the whole slipper-fitting process. He had men scouring the land looking for the Prince's mystery girl but he himself refused to let the slipper out of his sight. No one was going to play switcheroo with him and saddle him with some old sow.

The latest in a long line of chambermaids was wincing in agony and declaring (through a veil of tears) that "it fits" when Captain Olivier burst in dragging Ella with him by the elbow. Neither the Prince nor the Grand Duke recognised her as Cinderella. She was just a girl, that much was discernible, but the timeless beauty she'd radiated at the ball was hidden beneath several festering layers of rags and grime.

"I have found her, Your Highness. This is she," Captain Olivier declared, attempting to grab the credit for himself. Ella let the Captain have that one. Every dog got a bone today and the narrative played better if she had been found rather than had come looking.

"Who?" the Grand Duke asked, surprising his son. Just how many girls was the Prince looking for today?

"The girl from the ball, Cinderella," he said, remembering not to call the Grand Duke "dad" while he was at work. "*Your Grace.* As you see before you."

All eyes turned to Ella but still, they couldn't see it. The girl from the ball was a creature of unrivalled grace and sophistication. This filthy trog would struggle to get a job as an outhouse cleaner during a dysentery epidemic.

The Prince didn't know whether to laugh or roar at the insinuation but realising that others would hear of this incident, he decided to take it as ungracefully as he could.

"Do you have a hankering to see the insides of your own dungeons, Captain Olivier?" the Prince asked to make the Grand Duke seethe at his son's incompetence.

"Your Highness, on thine honour..." the Captain protested but he wasn't allowed to elaborate.

"Thine honour?" the Grand Duke bellowed, figuring it was better that he bawled out his son than anyone else did. "Exactly what honour do you show your Prince with this...

this… insult? And watch where you're pointing that thing, who knows what we all might catch."

This hadn't been the introduction to royal life that Ella had been hoping for and sensing the Captain's stock was now on the wane, she pulled free and took a step towards the Prince.

"I admit, Your Highness, that my silks are not quite as silky as the night we first met, nor my gemstones as shiny, but the girl beneath the grime is the same that yearns to *kiss you a thousand times at dusk and a thousand times at dawn*," Ella said, quoting directly from the Prince's own correspondence. Now he recognised her; the voice, the mannerisms, the steel in her eye and the hint of barely concealed menace whenever she smiled at him, which she was doing right now. He recognised her, but could scarcely believe it was the same girl.

Ella continued: "*My love for you burns brighter than the July sun. The Kingdom could crumble to dust and crush the people beneath it and I would not care a jot just so long as you were by my side.*" She could've also added; "*nice breeches*" with a wink but she could see from the Prince's horrified expression that she'd got her point across.

"You impudent little wretch. Captain!" the Grand Duke bellowed. "Take this hag out into the courtyard and flog her to within an inch of her life. And then, when she's had all she can take, flog her some more."

"But Your Grace…" Captain Olivier objected, having made the same mistake his father was now making. In the last twelve hours, the one place he hadn't visited had been the Beaufort's château because he knew all the women who lived there and none could've possibly been Cinderella. What a fool he had been!

But before he could explain this, the Prince interjected with a cry of "No!"

To universal astonishment, Prince Carina now leapt from the royal stage and hurried to Ella's side, bowing before her as though she were Aphrodite herself. "My darling, how wonderful to see you again. How have you been?" he asked, and not just to be polite either, he was genuinely curious.

"All the better for seeing you, My Prince" she replied with a curtsey that emptied dirt on the floor from the folds of what was left of her skirt. The Prince took her hand, kissed it and considered spitting or retching at what now flavoured her but managing to maintain his composure.

"Gentlemen, your search is over," the Prince announced. "I give you our new Princess."

For the time being, only the Captain let out a solitary "Hoorah". Everyone else was still waiting for the punchline, including the glass slipper's current wearer who felt free to say what everyone else was only thinking.

"Her? That stinking trollop!"

Few could take issue with this observation, not even the Prince, whose eyes certainly weren't watering out of happiness.

"You must forgive the condition I now come in. For I have been held prisoner these last few hours in the most frightful of circumstances."

"Prisoner? By whom?" the Prince demanded, fearing his letters had fallen into the hands of a rival faction.

"Why, by my wicked stepmother, of course," she explained. "And her daughters, my horrid stepsisters." It was less a lie than a variation on the truth and, more importantly, it cast her in that most feminine of lights — a victim. What true Prince could resist?

"I knew it," the Captain declared. "I knew they were up to no good. I will have them arrested forthwith."

But his father was still struggling to make the connection. "Your stepmother?" he baulked. "What kind of hogwash is this? Who are you? And who is your family?"

"Why I am… *Cinderella*," Ella said with a sly smile, already working to lay the seeds of her tragic backstory. "And as far as I am aware, you are well acquainted with my family, Your Grace. The Beauforts, of *Rue des Rose*."

The Grand Duke's brain went into a spin. This was Madame Beaufort's stepdaughter? His son had told him there was another girl living at the château, a ward from her short-lived marriage to Monsieur *Le Chevalier*, but he'd described her as some backward French girl of no consequence. What was he doing presenting her to the Prince now?

"I found her," he simply kept saying. "I found her, Your Highness," as though he only had to hand her in to collect another promotion.

"She's a charlatan," the Grand Duke objected, loathed to undermine his own son in front of everyone but left with no alternative. He was making a fool of himself and the Prince with this grubby peasant girl. "Your Highness, do not let this trickster deceive you. She is obviously not worthy of your royal affections."

"Oh no, she's the one, alright. I would know her anywhere, even without her clothes on," the Prince replied, prompting several of those in the room to choke with laughter.

"I must disagree with you most earnestly, Your Highness. Your entire future and that of your Kingdom depends upon you making the right decision."

The Grand Duke might've added "and mine too" when it dawned on him that he'd not only backed the wrong horse, he'd backed the "wicked and horrid" family who had kept Ella a prisoner. And by the way Ella was glaring at him now, he could tell that this was something that would linger long in the memory of the Kingdom's new 'Princess'.

"I am grateful for your concern, Your Grace, but she is the one. I would know her anywhere," the Prince insisted.

"She's a witch, Your Highness. She has you in a spell," the Grand Duke said, grasping at straws.

"What the blue blazes are you talking about?" the

Prince said, genuinely flummoxed by the Grand Duke's reaction. It was clear the Grand Duke was trying to put the squeeze on him but for what reason, he wasn't sure. Ella, on the other hand, had put the squeeze on him already and he knew only too well what leverage she could bring to bear so whatever the Duke was flogging, he would have to find another buyer. Besides, wasn't it enough that he'd finally picked someone? If his old man — the bombastic old buffoon — had insisted he married the first girl who fitted some discarded old shoe, then how could they start objecting to his choice of tart now?

The door flew open and suddenly the King was standing there.

"What's all this I hear? We've got a winner?" he cheered, looking around the room and almost stumbling backwards at the sight of Ella. "Well, he can't say I didn't warn him," he concluded with a blow of the cheeks.

"She is not the girl, Your Majesty," the Grand Duke protested. "She is an imposter."

The King looked at Ella.

"And such a cunning disguise," he said. "I would never have guessed she wasn't a Princess."

"I meant merely that she was not the girl from the ball. And as the Prince has vowed to marry that girl and that girl alone, I cannot permit him to break his sacred vow."

It was a fair argument. You had to give the Grand Duke that. But he'd overlooked just one tiny thing.

"There is only one way to settle the matter, is there not?" the King suggested. "She must try on the glass slipper and we shall see for ourselves."

Almost in unison, the Prince and the Grand Duke both hollered, "No!" then looked at each other quizzically and wondered what each other's objection could be. But Ella was already striding towards the slipper, unaware that it now fitted nobody, least of all her.

Likewise, the Grand Duke was unaware of the slipper's recent remodelling. Once Ella had slipped it on and shown everyone that it fitted, as surely it would if it was truly hers, then she would be untouchable — an enchanted Princess ordained by magic. The Grand Duke could not allow this to happen, not when he had championed her subjugators.

Even as the Prince was racing after Ella, in what everyone assumed was his great desire to slip it onto her foot himself, the Grand Duke saw his chance. If the shoe was never seen to fit, there would always be a question mark against Ella. And this was something the Grand Duke could work with.

So, before anyone else got their hands on the slipper, the Duke tipped the current wearer out of it, spilling her across the tiles with a shove, and tossed it to the Prince.

"Here you go, Your Highness, all yours!"

The Prince, having never played ball as a child (he had a boy from the village who was flogged to do this sort of thing for him), missed it and looked on helplessly as it sailed past his face, turning through the air and crashing to the ground to smash into a million pieces, such as this method of glassware had a tendency to do.

The tinkering crash rang out across the Palace, if not the entire Kingdom, as the shards of glass fanned out like ice.

Ella's fury was matched only by that of the King but the Prince seemed almost relieved. Once again, the Grand Duke couldn't help but wonder why.

"My apologies, Your Highness. I fear we shall never now know for sure if the slipper fitted," the Grand Duke declared supremely.

"Oh contraire, Your Grace," Ella said, slipping the canvas bag from her shoulder and producing the broken slipper's twin. "Perhaps I could try this one on instead?" And before the Grand Duke could come up with a convincing argument why not, Ella had slipped the slipper on to her foot reveal it fitted perfectly — as indeed, it would have fitted anyone with a size five foot.

"It's a miracle," the chambermaid gasped and all at once, every Palace official in the Great Throne Room dropped to their knees to hail the new Princess.

"Let the bells peel out, I have found my bride," the Prince declared with a sigh of relief, having cleared one hurdle and keen to start negotiating the next. Namely, ridding himself of his new Princess with a minimum of scrutiny. "Gentlemen, if you'll excuse me, I would like to show my... my... *Cinderella*, where she might shed some of her cinders."

The King laughed, Captain Olivier "Hoorahed" and the assorted chambermaids dropped to their knees and sobbed at the steps of the royal throne. The Grand Duke, however, just stared at the broken glass that stretched out before him. It seemed like a portent of things to come. As if to underline his fears, just as Ella was leaving, she looked at him, still on his knees and lost to despair, and said with a stare that filled him with foreboding.

"Please, Your Grace, don't get up on my account."

CHAPTER FIFTY-FOUR

THE DAY OF THE WEDDING ARRIVED with much fanfare but very little notice. Five days was not a lot of time in which to plan a royal wedding but the King had decreed that his son should marry within a week therefore marry they would. Happily, neither Ella nor the Prince objected, both seemed keen to get the deed done and get on with their lives as quickly as possible, albeit for rather different reasons. Ella had promised to return the Prince his letters the moment they were wed and once she had, he would rid himself of this avaricious banshee once and for all.

For her part, Ella had yet to make good on her pledge to Grimaldi. As the Prince's bride, she could ask the King for a wedding day favour for which, as tradition decreed, he could not refuse. Grimaldi had always assumed that she would seek his pardon on this day but Ella decided otherwise. What would the Andovian people say if the first act of their new fairytale Princess was to ask for forgiveness for the most notorious marauder the Kingdom had ever known? No, Instead, she asked the King to bankroll the biggest street party the Kingdom had ever known. And indeed, the first. Everyone would be invited; young or old, rich or poor, labourer or Lord. This would be a day for everyone. Even Ella's "wicked and horrid" family would be in attendance.

In point of fact, the Princess-to-be's first request had not been a bar of soap, but a detachment of men to ride out to *Rue des Roses* and collect her errant family. Captain Olivier took charge of this personally and intercepted Mother, Marigold and Gardenia just as they were loading up Liquorice to skip the Kingdom.

"Going somewhere?" he said with a grin.

The three women were escorted back to the Palace and put in the guest quarters under armed guard, comfortable but prisoners all the same. The Captain had wanted to throw them in the dungeons but Ella would hear none of it. They were her family, no matter what, and she insisted they be treated as such, albeit a family who required guarding around the clock.

"Captain, might I be able to speak with my stepdaughter, the lady Ella?" Mother asked Captain Olivier as he was about to lock the door to their quarters.

"The Princess is not to see anyone until the day of the wedding," he replied coldly, using Ella's royal title before he needed to and glaring at Mother as though she were worse than a common criminal.

Mother discovered the full and unabridged reason for the Captain's hostility shortly afterwards. Ella might not have been seeing anyone until her wedding day but that hadn't stopped her from talking to *everyone*. The rumours had spread around the Kingdom like wildfire; at how Ella's 'ugly' stepsisters had been so hell-bent on marrying the Prince that they'd torn up her best dress in a jealous rage and left her at home alone to do their chores and cry herself to sleep.

"She does chores?" Marigold asked upon hearing the rumour.

And yet true love could not be denied. Because that night, when Ella had given up all hope of going to the ball, she had been visited by her Fairy Godmother.

"Her what?"

A kindly spirit guardian had transformed her rags into a ballgown, turned a pumpkin into a carriage, some mice into horses, lizards into coachmen and Ella herself? Into the belle of the ball. There was only one problem.

"It was all codswallop?" Marigold suggested.

The spell would wear off at midnight and Ella's dress would return to rags, hence her sudden departure at the stroke of twelve. But she left behind a clue to her identity, an enchanted glass slipper that only she could fit into. And thus, the Prince had dedicated his life (or at least, the last couple of days) to searching for his mystery girl, inviting every maiden in the land to try on the slipper until eventually, he found the one it fitted.

"Why didn't the slipper turn back into a shoe like her dress and the horses?" Gardenia asked, picking holes in the burgeoning legend.

"And what did she do with the mice? Eat them?" Marigold further speculated.

"That'll do girls," Mother chided. Walls had ears.

If the Beaufort's popularity had been prone to the odd downturn before these rumours circulated, this was nothing compared to how they were viewed afterwards. An angry gathering formed outside the gates of the Palace to petition the King to place the women in the stocks but they were soon confronted by the Captain of the Guards.

"It is for the Princess Cinderella to decide how best she deals with her family, not the will of the mob. That such a thing should happen in Andovia is nothing short of shameful. Could you imagine anything so egregious happening in France?"

The crowd dispersed but the Beaufort's sins were not quickly forgotten.

Mother knew it would do no good to counter these lies. All they could do was go along with the plan, act contrite and trust Ella to hold up her side of the bargain. If not for their sakes, for the sakes of Corporals Babin and Deniau.

The next five days were the longest of Marigold and Gardenia's lives.

*

AND FINALLY THE WAITING WAS OVER.

Monsieur Vasseur had fashioned three beautiful dresses for Mother and her two daughters on Ella's instructions. Mother's was grey (cold and austere), Marigold's was green (the colour of envy) and Gardenia's was scarlet (for obvious reasons). They would not be able to hide from the mob today.

Once ready, the women were collected by Captain Olivier and driven out of the Palace and delivered to the steps of the cathedral, the same ones upon which Mother had been left as an unwanted baby all those years earlier. The crowds were already out in force, jostling for a decent vantage point for when Ella arrived, and so her stepfamily's arrival did not go unnoticed.

"Boo!" rang out the crowd. "Shame on you!"

"Ugly Marigold! Ugly Gardenia! Wicked... er... what's the mum's name?"

But Captain Olivier had stationed his Guards all around the cathedral so the women were in no physical danger but the abuse they endured was almost unendurable. To be the object of so much hatred was beyond humiliating. It was monstrous, devastating, crushing and terrifying. The crowd's love for Ella seemed almost multiplied by their hatred for her sisters. Gardenia fought to hold back the tears but she could not stop them from running down her face as she stood trembling like a leaf before the angry rabble. Marigold felt for her sister's hand and took it to reassure her that she wasn't alone. They had come through so much in the last few months but they were not invulnerable.

"Heads up, girls. Do not give them the satisfaction," Mother whispered to her daughters, turning to face the mob with a glare so icy that it momentarily silenced the jeers.

At last, the clatter of hooves drew near and a joyful cheer rippled through the Square. A gilded carriage followed arrived and stopped in front of the cathedral and there, bedecked in a wedding dress so white that it almost dazzled the crowd, was Ella looking every inch a fairytale Princess and not a cinder to be seen. The people cheered uproariously, with a little undercurrent of sobbing from some of the girls who'd unsuccessfully tried on Ella's slipper. Ella stood, looking out across the sea of smiling faces and milked the moment for all it was worth. She nodded approvingly, waved and then produced a small purse of schillings which she threw into the crowd like confetti. The crowd cheered, jostled and crushed each other underfoot in the resultant mayhem but Ella just laughed. These were her people. And she held them in the palm of her hand.

A coachman opened the door and Ella stepped down. This particular coachman seemed to be a regular person, not a lizard transformed, but everyone looked closely anyway, just to be sure.

As Ella had no father to walk her down the aisle, a small child had been dressed in traditional Andovian folk dress and selected to represent the people. That the boy was the son of Baron Weiss and not an ordinary child rather missed the point but the crowd loved the spectacle all the same.

Everyone bowed their heads as Ella glided up the red carpet towards the doors of the cathedral, her long train still tumbling out of the carriage with the end nowhere in sight. Three steps short of the doors she passed Mother, Marigold and Gardenia. She stopped and beckoned them to look up. The women lifted their eyes and braced themselves for whatever their 'stepblister' had planned for them.

Ella turned to face the crowd and waited for absolute silence, which she duly got.

"Mother," she announced in a voice loud enough for those in row Z to hear. "Marigold and Gardenia, my dear family, I… forgive you. I forgive you all."

The crowd wept, such was Ella's kindness, and Mother played along and bowed, which seemed to go down well with everyone but Captain Olivier. A snake could shed its skin as many times as it liked but it was still a snake, as far as he was concerned. Marigold and Gardenia did likewise and suddenly all were pardoned. Unlike Franz Grimaldi.

Ella then went one step further and embraced her

newly absolved stepsisters, assuring Marigold that she was so happy that they were a family once more and telling Gardenia where to stand in order to catch the bridal bouquet after the wedding.

"They will be expecting me to throw it out to the crowd but I won't," she told her quietly. "There is a bookshop on the other side of the square. Wait for me on the upstairs balcony and I will instruct my driver to stop below so that I might toss it up to you."

It was an incredible offer. In catching the Princess's bouquet, Gardenia would be the envy of every girl in Andovia, even after everything that had happened. That was how great the honour would be. It was something she'd always dreamed of but for the first time in her life, Gardenia would have rather remained a bridesmaid and let everyone else fight over becoming the next bride.

"It means you could marry anyone of your choosing, even a particular Corporal should you so desire. And no one, and I do mean no one, would be able to insist otherwise," Ella said, glancing towards Mother to underline her point.

Ella gave one final wave to the crowd and then went into the cathedral, a flock of scrubbed-up orphan children suddenly appearing out of nowhere to carry her magnificent train.

Mother, Marigold and Gardenia were ordered to follow the procession and issued an order of service once through the towering oak doors. The crowds outside would have to wait for several hours before they caught a glimpse of the Princess again, for the service was a long and self-indulgent affair, with dozens of solemn pledges and a couple of unbreakable oaths to be sworn. Likewise, Mother, Marigold and Gardenia would see precious little of their sister despite their invitations for they would sit out the hallowed ceremony in the very back row. Behind a sandstone pillar.

And alongside the once all-powerful Grand Duke.

WHEN AT LAST THE SERVICE was over and the happy couple were proclaimed, Gardenia felt a tap on the shoulder. It was one of the children who had carried in Ella's train.

"I am to give you this, my lady, from the Princess," the child said, handing Gardenia a note. Gardenia opened it and there was a rough sketch of the bookshop balcony and Ella's carriage, with a dotted line between the two in case she failed to recognise the significance.

"Go now, out the back," the child urged, pointing towards a side door that was situated close by.

As tepid as Gardenia was towards the idea of catching Ella's bouquet, she went anyway, if only to escape the confines of her claustrophobic pew.

"Go with her," Mother told Marigold. "Make sure she gets into no mischief." Memories of Gardenia's jaunt through the Palace still lingered in the memory.

Gardenia and Marigold left, excusing themselves and slipping out of the side entrance. The Grand Duke watched them go and caught Mother's eye. She stared at him in a way that both insulted and unnerved him, as though she were somehow his equal now that they had found themselves sitting on the same back row.

"Madame," he snorted in barely disguised contempt, making a mental note to remember her impertinence but strangely aware that he knew her from somewhere.

"Your Grace," Mother replied without fear or intimidation. She merely returned his glare and fiddled with her large opal ring, the one given to her by her first, and most beloved, of husbands.

The Grand Duke blinked and finally looked away. But Mother went on staring. At the Grand Duke. At the power behind the throne. And at the architect of so many of Andovia's most glorious episodes.

Both present. And past.

CHAPTER FIFTY-FIVE

GARDENIA AND MARIGOLD were able to slip by the crowds unnoticed. The vast majority of people were gathered in front of the cathedral, hoping to catch a glimpse of the Prince and Princess when they emerged as man and wife. Also, and this was not to be underestimated, there was considerable and mounting excitement over the imminent street party that was being set up in the Square by an army of Palace staff. At least five huge hogs were roasting on spits, chickens and lambs were sharing the fire pits beside them; bread was being baked, cakes were being iced and bottle upon bottle was being uncorked, all in the name of Andovia's new Princess. The royal wedding breakfast was set to eclipse even the Prince's ball in terms of splendour and extravagance. Both of them.

Gardenia reached the front door of the bookshop and tried the handle. The door opened and Gardenia looked in.

"Hello?" she called inside but nobody answered. "Should I just go in?"

"I guess so," Marigold said, hearing a huge cheer and looking back to see the doors of the cathedral open and the congregation begin to emerge. "You'd better hurry and find the balcony."

"Do you think we'll be able to leave the city afterwards?"

"I imagine *Cinders* will positively encourage it," Marigold replied with a hopeful shrug.

Gardenia went inside but Marigold didn't follow.

"Aren't you coming?" Gardenia asked.

"I'm going to get some air," Marigold replied, walking off to slip into the first alleyway she came to and away from the crowds. Marigold had no desire to stay and see Ella revered as though she were virtue incarnate. She yearned to get away from the Square, from the people and the events of the past. Her life, and those of her mother and sister, had been turned upside down and inside out by that wretched girl's machinations. All Marigold wanted to do was leave Andovia, travel far away and live the quiet sort of life where nobody snubbed her in the street, tried to push her out of windows, ambushed her on horseback or left barley snakes in her delicates. Was this really so much to ask?

More cheering and now whistling too. Either Ella has emerged to the delight of the crowd or they'd opened the bar. But there was no telling which from the back street Marigold now found herself in. All was quiet here. There were just a couple of cats chasing the odd rat, a few birds nesting in the gables and a tiny little stone that tinkered on the tiles above and dropped off the roof to land by Marigold's feet.

Marigold looked at what it was and couldn't make it out at first. But then she recognised it for what it was and realised where she'd seen stones such as this before. The blood drained from her face when she looked to the roof above.

For at her feet was a pip. From a black olive.

*

WHEN AT LAST, the happy couple emerged onto the warm autumnal sunshine, all eyes were on Ella. Few had ever seen a bride looking so beautiful, with hair spun from gold, features of delicate porcelain and a smile that filled her people's hearts with hope and joy. A shower of confetti was now released from above, blowing through the Square and touching each and every onlooker as though the Princess herself were bestowing kisses upon them. The real kiss though, was saved for her Prince, and she turned to him now, still clutching her bouquet and closed her eyes.

The Prince took a deep breath, leaned in and pressed his lips to hers. He found her lipstick greasy and her hairless chin made him feel like he was kissing a prepubescent boy. Nevertheless, the Prince held their kiss for as long as he could and allowed Ella to part first, just as they had rehearsed the evening before, and these efforts were duly rewarded with the hugest cheer of the day.

"The people love you," she reassured him with a whisper, and indeed they did. The Prince had always been admired — this was only natural — but now he felt truly adored as he stood before his people in full military uniform, with shiny knee-high boots, a chest full of medals and a trophy Princess on his arm. He was unquestionably the envy of every man. And now that he had his letters back too, he could finally enjoy married life — while it lasted.

"After you, my Princess," he invited, steering Ella down the steps and towards the waiting open-topped carriage.

All eyes watched as the Prince helped his Princess into her seat and then held the door open while a pack of children bundled her enormous train in around her feet to her great amusement. The King followed his son and shook him manfully by the hand. It was staged just as the Prince and Princess's kiss had been but the crowds lapped it up all the same, even cheering enthusiastically when the Prince saluted his father, something they hadn't rehearsed, which caught the King off-guard and made him look old and doddery in front of everyone. Just as the Prince had intended.

The bridal carriage departed and the Prince and Princess headed back to the Palace for their first change of the day. They had four outfits in all; one to get married in and three more to eat, meet, dance and retire in. Each had been lovingly designed by Monsieur Vasseur and each allowed the Prince and Princess to disappear at strategic points throughout the day in order to milk the crowds for another grand entrance an hour or so later.

A second carriage took the place of the first and Captain Olivier helped the King in. He too was heading back to the Palace but not to change his outfit, just to use the loo.

The rest of the guests were left to please themselves.

The celebrations were just beginning and the first of a small army of waiters and waitresses had appeared with tall flutes of much-needed champagne. Mother relieved a waiter of two glasses and slipped through the assorted dignitaries to look for the Grand Duke.

"Your Grace," she smiled, offering him one of the flutes. But the Grand Duke, thirsty as he was, rebuffed Mother's offer and turned away.

"You think I'd share a toast with you?" he snorted without looking, his hands firmly behind his back and staying there.

"You do not wish to drink to the Prince and Princess's happiness?" Mother asked.

"Pah!" he replied as he watched the royal carriages creep slowly through the parting crowds. "You would do well to remember your place, Madame. Your assumptions do you much discredit."

"My place?" Mother said, raising an eyebrow. "And where exactly is my place? I am the stepmother of the royal Princess, future grandmother to a future King and the guardian of many secrets."

"Then I suggest, Madame, that you go on guarding them and remove yourself from my company forthwith," the Grand Duke advised, knowing only too well as to what Mother was alluding to. Or so he thought. The Prince's disposition would be less of a problem now that he was safely married. And once there was a baby for the Kingdom to coo over, he would be able to indulge himself at will, ironclad against even the most salacious of tittle-tattle.

Mother saw Captain Olivier striding about the crowd like the town rooster, ordering his men this way and that and barking at ordinary townsfolk to the Grand Duke's obvious approval.

"The Captain seems destined for great things, Your Grace. You must be very proud," Mother persisted, refusing to take her leave now that she had him in her sights. She'd waited too long and had come too far to give up now.

"Yes... he is a fine officer. Reminds me in many ways of myself," he said wistfully.

"He will make a fine match one day, I predict," Mother ventured.

"Not with either of your heifers, Madame, if that's your game," the Grand Duke scoffed.

"I would not presume to look to your Grace's son for my daughters' happiness. Besides, I suspect his duties to the Princess will keep him well occupied in the coming months."

The Grand Duke turned to face Mother and once again caught a flicker of recognition, as though he knew her from somewhere, before dismissing the idea as ridiculous.

"His duties?" he pondered. Was the old crow getting at what he thought she was getting at? With a worldly twinkle in her hoary grey eye and her thin lips cocked into a crooked half-smile he guessed that she was. "Indeed," he merely concurred, wondering if his blood might sit upon the throne yet, one way or the other. With the right sort of encouragement and a bit of fair weather, it wasn't yet out of the question. And as everyone knew, all daughters turned to their mothers for advice on their wedding nights, did they not? Even stepdaughters?

"Let us drink to your son and wish him bon voyage in *all his duties*," Mother said, once more offering the old soldier the champagne she'd brought *especially* for him.

"You are nothing if not a tenacious old bird, Madame. I will give you that," he reluctantly said, finally taking the glass from her outstretched hand.

"His health and yours," Mother said, about to lift the champagne to her lips when the large opal ring on her finger swung open to reveal an empty chamber inside.

"Broken heirloom?" the Grand Duke snorted with amusement.

"It was a most special gift," Mother glared, with a tear forming in her eye. "From my late husband."

*

THE TWO ROYAL CARRIAGES had edged their way through the crowds before coming to a stop outside the bookshop on the far side of the Square. Ella whispered something in the Prince's ear then stood up to look out over the sea of faces. This was the moment every maiden in the Kingdom had been waiting for. This was the moment the Princess would toss her bouquet. Duly, all the menfolk made way and every eligible girl with three fingers or more surged forwards to do battle.

Ella smiled and taunted the girls with her bouquet, feeding off their excitement and their desperation, and tickled with the certain knowledge that none of these appalling wenches would receive her precious bouquet.

But for that matter neither would Gardenia. She'd made her way upstairs alright but once there found that the shutters to the balcony were securely fastened. Try as she might she could not open them. Next to the shutters was a small window. She was able to open it but the window was no bigger than her head. She'd struggle to catch a ray of sunshine through here, let alone a hefty bouquet.

Gardenia looked for another way out but to her confusion found the door she'd entered by was now locked. She heard the sound of a child scampering away and realised she'd succumbed to another of Ella's slippery schemes. In fear, she turned to face the room, horrified at the thought of what might be lurking between the shelves. She grabbed a nearby broom, ready to start whacking its bristles should anything strike out at her and pushed over an ominous-looking stack of books to reveal that something had indeed been hidden here. But it wasn't a snake, as she feared, or a rat or a bat or anything else that might jump out at her.

It was a crossbow.

"What on Earth?" she said to herself.

*

ON THE ROOF ABOVE the bookshop was a second crossbow. But this one wasn't waiting to be found. This one was in the hands of a skilled marksman, loaded and ready to fire. Grimaldi squinted down the weapon's sights and picked out his target. The carriages were so close that he could scarcely miss. Ella stood before him and waved her bouquet backwards and forwards as she whipped up the crowd into a frenzy. She would toss it at any second and the moment she did, he would fire and be gone before anyone knew what had happened.

"Are you ready?" Ella asked the field of distressed damsels before her.

"Yes," they pleaded in turn.

"I can't hear you!" Ella taunted further. The Prince rolled his eyes and grumbled at her to throw the bloody thing and be done with it.

"Here it comes," she announced with aplomb, turning away from the scuffling crowd and throwing her bouquet high over her shoulder and into the forest of arms that stretched out before her.

It was the moment Grimaldi had been waiting for and without further ado, he squeezed the trigger. The latch released and the wire set the poison-tipped bolt free but at the very last moment, a clattering weight smacked into the side of Grimaldi's head to skew his aim and send his arrow flying wide.

Ella gasped as the shard raced past her face, missing by an atom and thunking into the red velvet seats of the carriage behind, just a stitch and an itch from where the King was happily sitting.

The crowd screamed in horror, but not at the attempted murder, Instead, their horror was reserved for the sight of a boss-eyed merchant's daughter called Isabella clutching the bouquet and deliriously declaring, "I got it! I got it!"

The Prince almost fell out of his seat and pointed up towards the first floor of the bookshop. "Assassins!" he shouted, and all at once the festivities were checked and the crossbow bolt in the King's seat spotted.

Across the Square, the Captain saw the unfolding crisis and blew a whistle to alert his Guards. "To the King!" he screamed. "Protect the royal party!"

The crowd surged away, attempting to flee the murderous arrows that were expected to come at any moment, and the panic quickly spread to the steps of the cathedral, bowling into the assorted dignitaries like a wave to knock the Grand Duke over before he'd taken so much as a sip of his champagne.

Mother stared at him aghast, sprawled out at her feet and rolling in spilt fizz with his hand stretched upwards.

"Well, help me up, you old crow! Help me now!" he hollered as people started to tumble over him from all sides.

*

MARIGOLD SAW NONE OF THIS. She was running for her life, across the slate ridge tiles and leaping between rooftops as Grimaldi gave chase. Twice already he'd stopped to load his crossbow and fire, but twice she'd managed to seek shelter behind a chimney stack.

She had no idea if she'd managed to stop the assassination or not. She'd simply grabbed the first thing that had come to hand and thrown it with all of her might the moment she'd seen him fixing to fire. She had found a way up onto the roof via next door's skylight and had caught him in the act. Why she had done this, she had no idea. She was terrified of Grimaldi. Even the thought of crossing his path filled her heart with dread but it had been an instinctive reaction, like shouting at a bear as it was about to grab a bunny.

Grimaldi's reaction had been predictably bad-tempered. He'd jumped from his vantage point and immediately given chase. Marigold had tried to flee the way she'd come, but the skylight slammed closed and her only escape was across the maze of rooftops that fanned out before her.

Marigold lost her footing and dislodged several slates as she slid. The cold hard flagstones loomed up from below but her dress snagged on a nail and the cartwright's backyard was spared an unscheduled scrubbing.

"I'll have your guts for garters," Grimaldi roared indignantly, sending scores of tiles crashing off the roof to leave a trail of destruction in his wake. Marigold could barely keep her footing across the slender ridge tiles and yet Grimaldi seemed almost impervious to disaster, like a boulder that rolled over ice, breaking all that it touched but moving too fast to actually sink.

She came to the end of the terrace and looked down in alarm. A two-metre gap stood between her and the next roof and certain death lay in between. Marigold saw Grimaldi crouching to reload. She had no choice but to jump. But there was no way she would make it in her shoes and dress. Quick as a flash, she kicked off her heels and ripped her dress apart.

Grimaldi took aim, Marigold took two steps back and then both of them went for it. Grimaldi missed his target by a slither but Marigold made hers, crashing painfully across the terracotta tiles and rolling down to end up hanging by her fingernails. Marigold kicked out, finding a toehold in the brickwork and kicking as though the Devil himself were snapping at her heels. She hauled herself back onto the roof and looked up in horror to see Grimaldi running across the other roof to make the leap himself. Just above was a crumbling old chimney stack that almost sent Marigold tumbling back when one of the bricks came out in her hand. But Marigold was able to arrest her slide and scramble to take shelter behind the stack, fearing a bolt in the back should she try to run.

But it was too late to run. Grimaldi had caught up with her and was leaping across the span to land a few short metres from where she was. She couldn't escape him on foot and she couldn't outrun his arrows. She had but one hope to evade the murderous fiend.

When Grimaldi landed with a crunch, Marigold pushed against the crumbling brick stack with all of her might until it pitched forwards and fell. Grimaldi saw it but was too late to run. He swore in anger as it smashed through the tiles at his feet, caving in the entire roof to sweep him down into a dusty abyss.

But Marigold didn't have time to savour her victory because the roof kept on crumbling, the destruction fanning out faster than her battered legs could carry her. And all at once, she was running on air, tumbling and turning through a cloud of devastation until she slammed into a wall of pain.

And then, in the blink of an eye, everything went black.

CHAPTER FIFTY-SIX

WHEN MARIGOLD AWOKE the pain was still there, only more evenly spread. Her whole body felt racked and bruised and a spongy lump on the top of her head made her nauseous when she touched it.

Despite the pain, she sat up and looked around. The room was small but dark and warm. She was in a small cot bed with clean sheets and a soft pillow. Nearby was a smokeless tin stove that vented up through a low-lying ceiling via pipework made from tin cans. A copper kettle sat atop a stovetop and blew steam into the air to further warm the room.

The door opened and a large man looked in. The sun was at his back and his face was caught in shadows so at first Marigold let out a gasp. But as the man entered, kicking off his boots as he went, Marigold realised it was not Franz Grimaldi but someone quite different.

"You're awake?" Didi said when he saw Marigold sitting up. "How do you feel? Are you in discomfort?"

Marigold felt weak and weary but her confusion was more disconcerting. "Where am I? How did I get here?"

This was Didi's home. Everyone in Andovia assumed, not unnaturally, that Didi was homeless because he spent every day loafing around in the park and on the city's streets. But in fact, Didi had collected enough bits of discarded timber over the years to build himself a bijou little residence in the nearby forest. Each morning he would wander into town to take up his pitch in the park, sit in front of his hat and panhandle passers-by for pennies and pity and then, when everyone went home after work, he would do the same.

Much to Marigold's surprise — and at first, alarm — Didi now took off his disgustingly filthy rags and hung them up outside. This was just his uniform. He didn't wear it indoors. In its place, he donned a clean nightgown and robe and even slippers for his feet. A wash in a bowl of hot water further transformed Didi from deadbeat to dandy and suddenly a different man stood before the astonished Marigold.

"The dirtier I am, the more pity I elicit," *Dirty Didi* said with an embarrassed roll of the shoulders. "It's a living."

"And a fair one, I see," Marigold concluded as she looked around. The place might have been small but Didi wanted for nothing. Blankets, cooking pots, winter fuel and books. There were even flowers, fresh cut from the woods, in homemade earthenware pots that hung from the ceiling to lend the place a rustic charm. Didi must've been very happy here, far away from the intrigues of town, where he could simply relax and be himself.

"How did I get here?" Marigold asked.

"I pulled you from the rubble," Didi told her. "You were in a bad way." It seemed that Didi had been one of the few Andovians not in the Town Square for the wedding.

"I don't go down well in crowds," he said to put it mildly.

He'd been wandering the back streets of the city when he'd heard the building collapse and went to see what had happened. Finding Marigold buried beneath a heap of debris and unresponsive, he'd dug her out, patched her up and brought her back here to convalesce.

"You've been out for almost three days," he said.

Marigold was grateful but still confused. "Why here?" she asked.

"The Guards are looking for you," he explained. "Everyone's looking for you. There's a reward out for your capture."

"What! What on Earth for?" Marigold said in disbelief, despite having wilfully demolished several candlemakers' shops in her rampage. But this hadn't been her major crime.

"Treason," Didi said soberly.

Didi went on to explain that while she had been busy endearing herself to the roofers of Andovia, Captain Olivier had surrounded the bookshop from where the assassin's arrow had been fired and found Gardenia banged to rights upstairs, with a crossbow in her possession.

"Tried to kill her stepsister, the Princess, that's what they're all saying. Tried but missed," Didi said. "And you? You were the lookout but you upped and legged it to leave Gardenia to carry the can."

"But that's absurd. It was Grimaldi, Franz Grimaldi. Didn't you find him in the rubble too?" Marigold said, sitting up too quickly so that she was overcome with dizziness.

"Franz Grimaldi!" Didi exclaimed in surprise to illustrate that he hadn't. "In Andovia! He wouldn't dare show his face in the Kingdom, surely."

"I've got to tell the King. Please, help me find my clothes. I must go to the Palace."

Marigold swung out of bed and almost baulked at the sight of her legs. Both were a patchwork of gashes and bruises and four of her toenails had been ripped off, but at least they were still in one piece. "My petticoat?" she demanded.

"You don't understand. If you set foot out the door you'll surely be thrown into the dungeons. The Guards are swarming all over the city and your sister and your mother have been banged up since they were arrested. They're only holding on to them still because they want to punish you all together. Everyone's after you."

"Then how come you're helping me?" Marigold asked, wondering if Didi had one eye on the reward himself.

"I know how this Kingdom works. It's all flimflam and skullduggery. I saw enough of it myself when I was part of the system. I don't believe a word of anything I hear these days. If you and your sister are assassins then I must be the

Queen of Sheba," said the one-time Burgermeister of Andovia as he lamented on his own brief time in office. "You're a scapegoat. Either because they don't know who pulled the trigger," Didi speculated. "Or more likely, because they do."

"Then there's even more important that I see the King. Ella brought Grimaldi back to Andovia. She made a deal with the Devil and it was he who tried to kill her," Marigold said. She didn't understand why he'd made an attempt on Ella's life — or even if she had been the target — but she reasoned crooks fell out with each other all the time. It was only natural that Grimaldi should go after Ella if he thought he'd been double-crossed.

But Didi just shook his head. "There's been a trial," he said ominously. "The day after it happened. The King himself presided. The facts were indisputable. And Gardenia was found guilty. You too, in absentia."

This revelation rocked Marigold backwards. How could they possibly believe Gardenia was capable of anything like that? It was preposterous. But Didi went on to explain how it had all come out in court; how it was said that Mother had squandered Monsieur Beaufort's money after his death; how Ella had been forced to work as a skivvy and fed only leftovers. How she had been banished to the cold and draughty attic room and how they'd fitted her door with a bolt to keep her locked up at night; how she'd been forced to sleep huddled close to her fire for warmth while her lazy sisters had stayed in bed all day long. And how they'd dressed her in rags and called her *Cinderella* because of the filth she'd ended up covered in as a result of her various hardships. Everyone remembered the terrible state she was in when Captain Olivier found her.

Marigold listened astonished and even recognised some of the incidents that Didi was referring to: the pumpkin stew incident when they'd set some stew aside for her and watched it grow cold when she'd refused to touch it; the freezing cold days that she and Gardenia had spent in bed because it was too cold to heat the house; and Cinders' secret stash of firewood that she had kept in the attic while the rest of the household froze.

Ella had been very clever with her accusations because every lie had a grain of truth contained within it. Mother and Gardenia must've come across as craven miscreants at the trial when they'd tried to refute the allegation.

"Not really," Didi said sadly. "They were never given the chance. Who needed two sides of a story when the first was told by a Princess?"

"What's going to happen to them?" Marigold asked, wobbling to her feet despite the pain in her shins. Didi looked away, too afraid to say. "Didi, tell me," she insisted, turning him back to look her in the eye.

"Your Mother is to see out her days in the dungeons and your sister…" his voice began to crack but Marigold now shook him by the shoulders. "Your sister is to be executed in the morning."

Marigold stepped back and then her legs failed her. She crumpled to the floor and wondered if she was still dreaming. She had to be because this couldn't be true, could it? This had to be a nightmare. Nothing this terrible could have really happened, could it?

Marigold tried to wake herself by screaming but her cries were stifled by Didi.

"Hush my little darling. We're in the woods but you never know who might be passing. Don't let them find you. Don't end up like your poor sweet sister," Didi urged her, hugging her close until her screams had abated to sobs. Marigold didn't know what to do. She felt helpless as she pictured her poor Gardenia all alone and afraid, awaiting a terrible fate. That was the worst thing. To not be able to do anything for her. To have failed Mother when she'd told her to go with Gardenia and look out for her. And to not be there to hold her hand when she needed her the most.

The irony of the whole case was that the King had come down doubly hard on Gardenia because of Ella's great public spectacle of 'forgiveness' a week earlier. Well, the same mistake would not be made again. Gardenia would be made to pay the ultimate price. And when they caught her, Marigold would too.

"I'm not going to let them do this," Marigold eventually said. "I don't know how but I'm going to go to my sister. I have to."

"It's impossible," Didi insisted. "The Guards are all over town. You wouldn't get to within a dozen blocks of the dungeons. And even if you did, what then?"

Marigold didn't have an answer but neither did she have a choice. Doing nothing wasn't an option. Doing nothing would see Gardenia dead and her Mother condemned to rot in the cells forever. Doing nothing was death.

"She's my little sister," Marigold said solemnly. "And it's my job to see that she gets into no mischief."

CHAPTER FIFTY-SEVEN

FAR FROM BECOMING HIS OWN MAN, Hans found that since taking charge of Stefano's Ice Cream Kiosk, he now had two bosses rather than one: Monsieur Stefano, who had stepped down on paper but still ran the whole operation from the comfort of his front porch, and Cynthia, his patron's favourite niece and Hans's new wife. This meant a lot more work for Hans but very little extra money, especially now that he was married to someone with Cynthia's aspirations. She was an impossibly small lady who could barely see over her own countertop but what she lacked in legs, she more than made up for in conceit. Cynthia may have married the bucket boy but this didn't mean she now saw herself as the wife of the bucket boy. Far from it. Hans was now the legal proprietor of Stefano's Ice Kiosk (if not the primary beneficiary) therefore he was no longer a bucket boy, but a restauranteur, and as such he was required to maintain a certain standard of living, for both he and, more importantly, his wife.

And it was never less than a daily battle to remind him of this fact, Cynthia found.

"At last, they have come!" Cynthia exclaimed in excitement when she saw Otis's boy standing outside their front serving hatch with three wooden crates atop his pull cart.

"What's come? What is this now?" Hans asked nervously, looking down at the cart and feeling the ground opening up beneath him when he saw the word's "Finest Crystal" emblazoned across the side of the crates.

"I ordered some new serving dishes."

"What! Why? What's wrong with the ones we've got?" Hans objected.

"Everyone in Andovia has eaten out of them. They

needed replacing," Cynthia said, hurrying out of the side door to take receipt of her new cut-glass sorbet dishes.

"They're fine. I wash up, don't I?"

"You can't expect the type of clientele we should be attracting to lick their desserts out of someone else's dish, for Heaven's sake!" Cynthia said, failing to explain how these new dishes would differ in this respect, unless of course, they were made of disposable cut-glass crystal.

Otis's lad opened one of the boxes and handed Cynthia a dish. It was a beautiful piece of tableware, sparkling and ornately carved. It would not have looked out of place on the King's own table. An ice cream kiosk in the park? Perhaps. But not the King's own table.

"How many did you get?" Hans asked, gulping in trepidation.

"Sixty," Cynthia replied with glee.

"Sixty? But we seldom get more than fifteen customers at a time, even on the hottest of afternoons."

"Hans, you need to think bigger. You're not a bucket boy anymore," Cynthia reminded him for the third time today which, in fairness, was partially true in that collecting ice was now only one aspect of his working life, not the whole shebang. They had tried in vain to take on a new bucket boy but after weeks of trying found no takers, a situation that was unlikely to change unless Cynthia relented and was prepared to offer wages for the position.

"And how much did they cost?" Hans asked of the crystal dishes.

"I didn't ask," was Cynthia's surprising reply.

"You didn't?"

"And look like a cheapskate in front of the glassmaker? Does my reputation mean nothing to you?" she said indignantly, hurrying back into the kiosk to begin clearing their shelves of their old dishes.

Hans fought hard to control his bottom lip as he

watched Cynthia at work. Eventually, he turned to Otis's boy and asked: "How much?"

Otis's boy just shook his head and replied: "Don't ask," with a superfluous puff of the cheeks.

While all this was going on, Didi took the chance to wander up and appeared at Hans's elbow.

"Begging your pardon, Monsieur Hans, but I bring a message from a friend," he said out of earshot of the boy.

"A friend?" Hans said without really listening.

"Of long-standing. You are to accompany me for instructions."

"Now? I can't go with you now, I've a business to run," Hans squawked irritably.

"She understands that but it is imperative you come with me now. It's a matter of life and death. And you will be handsomely rewarded for your time," Didi promised, finally catching Hans's attention.

"She?"

Didi handed Hans a lady's glove which bore the initials, *MB* and gave the overgrown bucket boy a conspiratorial wink. "She," he confirmed.

*

HANS AND MARIGOLD renewed each other's acquaintance in the woods a short way from Didi's shack. The ice cream vendor had slipped away before Cynthia noticed and felt like a fugitive himself the moment he laid eyes on Marigold.

"Mademoiselle Beaufort," he said with a semi-bow, not entirely sure if this was the proper etiquette for meeting wanted terrorists but taking no chances either way. Treason was one thing. Decorum was quite another.

"Hans, thank you for coming," Marigold replied formally, the memory of their last brutal meeting still lingering in both their minds. Marigold had said some cruel things on that occasion but nothing Hans felt he hadn't deserved. And seeing her now, up close and alone, and knowing that she was beyond his reach once and for all was more torturous than he could bear. Not least of all because he knew he had no one to blame but himself.

"You are well?" he asked, seeing her legs wrapped in makeshift bandages and her clothes tattered and torn.

"As well as can be expected," Marigold replied unconvincingly. "You have heard about my sister, no doubt?"

Hans had. Of course. Everyone in Andovia had heard about the assassination attempt, regardless of whether they'd been there or not. In actual fact, Hans and Cynthia had been in the Square at the time, quite close to where it had happened. They had been commissioned by the Palace to supply desserts to the masses and had made all the necessary preparations with a bumper batch of ice and several urns of fresh milk, only to see the whole lot go to waste when the King's Guards cleared the Square. Naturally, they wouldn't see a schilling for their troubles and Cynthia wouldn't dream of submitting an invoice to the Palace. Not after everything the poor Princess had been through.

"My sister is innocent. In this and in every other respect," Marigold assured Hans.

"It's hard to know what to think. People are talking. The things they are saying are… unkind."

"People talk. And they are unkind. This is Andovia. This is what we do here," Marigold reminded him and such was undeniable. Reputations may have been everything in this Kingdom. But seeing one crumble was so much more fun.

"I believe you," Hans finally ventured before diluting this statement with an all-important caveat. "I *want* to believe you."

"I have never lied to you, Hans, and I never will."

Marigold moved towards Hans and took him by the hand. She wanted to embrace him, to feel his body against hers one last time, but she knew this was impossible. Hans was married. To hold him now would be akin to admitting the lies were true, that she really was a wretched harlot of deplorable morality, capable of all manner of wickedness. Hans felt the same and burned to take Marigold in his arms but likewise, he couldn't any more than he could unmarry Cynthia. That part of him was gone, like a man who had lost a hand, unable to touch anything with it even if he could still feel his fingers.

"You are my biggest regret," Marigold said. "You are a pain that never leaves me. But tomorrow I will have another, and that one will numb all before it."

"I know," Hans said. "But what can I do? The Guards are after you. Everyone is after you. You must leave Andovia and never return. For your sake, my lady."

"I intend to but before I go, I ask one final service of you. Something only you can do."

Hans swallowed hard. He wasn't sure what "only he could do" but he resolved to accommodate her anyway, fingers or no fingers. He may have denied himself a lifetime of happiness but he couldn't deny Marigold her final wish, even if it went against the very grain of God's sacred laws. She had risked everything to see him one last time, her love had burned that brightly. It was the least he could do for her, especially now that Didi had wandered off to give them both some privacy.

"I want you..." Marigold whispered in his ear.

"Yes," Hans trembled.

"I want you... to take my sister some ice cream."

*

GARDENIA SAT ALONE on the cold stone floor of her dark and dank cell, frightened and confused. Her only comfort was an old straw mattress provided to her by a loathsome individual who shuffled around the place and called himself Hooky. But the mattress was alive with lice and rotten with damp, much like Hooky himself. Having it in the cell was worse than not.

For three straight days she had agonised over her fate and wondered how she could have been so stupid; to have given Ella the benefit of the doubt — again, and to have fallen into one of her traps — again. Gardenia didn't know how Ella had done it or even why she'd done it. All she knew was that she'd signed her own death warrant by going into that bookshop. And Ella had blown on the ink with her lies at their subsequent trial. None of it made sense. What did Ella have to gain from seeing her stepsister put to death? Petty revenge? Sadistic pleasure? Both?

On more than one occasion, Gardenia's courage failed her and she found herself crying with fear and screaming with rage at the same time, but neither had done her any good. Only hoots of derision and howls of abuse had echoed back from the dungeons below. She had no friends down here. No sympathisers. Mother was elsewhere, presumably going out of her mind over the thought of what was about to happen. Gardenia was all alone.

Her only relief was the knowledge that Marigold had got away. It would have been more than she could've borne if her folly had cost Marigold her life also. She wondered where she was right now; riding across the mountains or sailing out to sea? She hoped so. It made her smile to think of Marigold unfettered and free. Ella must have been kicking the furniture upstairs as the search parties came back empty-handed. This made Gardenia smile even more.

But not for long.

Gardenia didn't know if it was day or night. Very little light penetrated down here and every minute felt like an hour. Her only sense of time came with the bringing of her meals, mostly gruel with the occasional lump of stale bread. Hooky had asked her what she had wanted for her final meal, as was customary in these circumstances, but the very idea of a final meal robbed her of her appetite. This was precisely the point of this custom. It wasn't to give the condemned prisoners a nice treat to go out on but to cause them further unnecessary anguish as they prepared to meet their makers. It was psychological torture at its cruelest and the King had insisted the tradition be honoured for Gardenia. Accordingly, Hooky had urged her to ask for lamb cutlets or beef steak or bratwurst and sauerkraut or anything else that he liked knowing full well that very little of it would be eaten — by Gardenia at any rate — but she had baulked at every suggestion, robbing Hooky of one of the few perks of his position.

And so it came as something of a surprise — and in Hooky's case, great delight — when a large earthenware bowl of ice cream was delivered to the dungeons on the eve of Gardenia's execution. Protocol dictated the prisoner be given first refusal, something Gardenia almost did, until Hooky let slip the message it had been delivered with.

"From Stefano's Ice Kiosk, the young man himself who runs the place brought it himself, can't remember his name, gormless-looking cretin. Said he was a friend of the family and instructed me to tell you 'Snap'," he chortled through the bars of her cell door, a pernicious piece of taunting if ever he'd heard one.

"What did you say?" Gardenia said, jumping to her feet and hurrying to the cell door.

"'Snap'," he repeated, watching her face keenly. He'd passed on hundreds of secret messages to hundreds of prisoners in his time, most of which had consisted of malicious gloating from the victors of whatever squabble had landed them here in the first place and it always tickled him to see the prisoners' reactions. Gardenia looked shocked but not in the way he'd expected. Far from breaking down in tears and demanding he take her accursed pudding away, Gardenia seemed to regain her composure.

"That's very kind of you, thank you," she smiled,

reaching up to the small window in her cell door for him to pass it through.

"You want it?" Hooky said in surprise.

"Was that not the intention?"

"Well yeah but… what are you going to do with it?" he demanded, almost incensed at the thought of Gardenia robbing him of such a rare treat.

"Eat it would it surprise you to learn?"

"On the day before you die! You're a cold fish, you are, and no mistake. I don't know how you've got the nerve, I really don't."

"Then allow me to write to my stepsister, the Princess, informing her of how you denied me my final meal and I dare say you'll discover for yourself," Gardenia suggested, turning Hooky's face pastier than it already was. Hooky was no fool. He'd seen men, women and children locked up for far less in his time and he wasn't about to try anything that might upset a real bonafide Princess.

"I hope you choke on it," he simply sneered as he passed it through.

"I hope so too," Gardenia agreed. It seemed a preferable way to die to the one they had in mind for her tomorrow.

Gardenia waited until Hooky had shuffled off before examining the ice cream. No spoon had been provided so she was forced to use her fingers, first to taste it and then to poke around inside in case something had been hidden within.

It was the word "Snap" that had fired her hopes. It had been the first word she had spoken to Marigold after coming around from her snake bite and only she knew of its significance. Gardenia had been so sure that Marigold had sent her the pudding with a secret message inside it or a tool for escaping with but there was nothing, just ice cream, cold and wet, all the way to the bottom.

"Why did you do this?" Gardenia fumed, even more

crestfallen than before. Had her sister — the person who was closest to her in the whole wide world — really thought that a bowl of ice cream would bring her some comfort at a time like this? Gardenia lashed out, launching the bowl at the wall to smash to pieces on the black slimy bricks. She slid down to the floor and sobbed into her knees at the hopelessness of it all and was about to scream in despair when she noticed something glinting amongst the scattered fragments. It was buried in one of the larger pieces, half in, half out, and made of some sort of metal. Gardenia scrambled across her cell and grabbed the largely still intact piece, cracking it open to reveal the object had been baked into the clay.

She recognised it immediately but she had no idea why her sister had sent it to her. It was her late father's medal. Marigold carried it everywhere with her. The word "Valour" was inscribed onto the front of the silver disk and "Cedar Hill" onto the back, along with the dates of the battle, but it was the extra word that caught Gardenia's eye, the one written in ink across the medal's blue ribbon. It said simply this:

"Payment".

CHAPTER FIFTY-EIGHT

MONSIEUR SAMUEL SHARPENED HIS AXE with a heavy heart. He had a job to do and he would do it to the best of his abilities but never before had his official duties pained him so. As Andovia's official executioner, he had dispatched scores of criminals in his time; murderers, bandits, traitors and thieves. He pruned and weeded the Kingdom on the last day of each month just as he pruned and weeded the Eames's garden the rest of the year-round. It was a service he had first performed whilst serving in the Guards and, so adept at it was he, that the Grand Duke had invited him to stay on as the Kingdom's official executioner when he retired from campaigning. Part-time, of course. Andovia didn't have enough knaves to keep Samuel in full-time employment the Duke was sorry to say.

Inevitably, over the course of his long career, he had encountered people of his acquaintance — Private Xavier sprang to mind — but he had always done his duty towards them, even if it had pained him to do so. The way Samuel saw it, once a person was condemned to death, the execution would go ahead with or without him. If he didn't do the job, someone else would. But unlike a lot of executioners, Samuel was a humanitarian. He may have claimed more victims than the last Typhus outbreak but that didn't mean he didn't care. And he regarded it as his duty towards the prisoners in his charge to see that they left this life and entered the next as quickly and as painlessly as possible.

This was something he was very very *very* good at.

And as such, when informed of the sentence against Mademoiselle Beaufort, the youngest daughter of his finest friend, the late great Sergeant Armand Roche, there was no way he was prepared to leave her final moments to some other ham-handed butcher. He would see to their blessed reunion himself. This, Samuel swore, upon all that he held sacred.

Fortunately, as a member of the newly crowned Princess's extended family, it was decreed that Gardenia was to be extended the honour of a noble person's death. This may have brought scant comfort to Gardenia but Samuel was well aware of the suffering she would be spared and he was grateful for small mercies. The axe was far quicker than the rope.

And so this quiet old gardener spent his morning behind the woodshed, sharpening his blade and practicing his swing until he was absolutely sure he could dispatch the young maiden in the blink of an eye.

The axe would fly and the crowd would gasp.

But Gardenia herself would never know what had hit her.

*

THE CROWDS HAD BEGUN GATHERING since before dawn. Most executions were poorly attended. A few morbid gawkers stood around on their tiptoes at the back of the dungeons to watch the condemned dance their last jig at the end of a rope. But the execution of Gardenia Beaufort, stepsister and failed assassin to a Princess of Andovia, promised to be an event of historical proportions and nobody wanted to miss it.

The last nobleman to lose his head was the Comte de Aardmas, an imperious old blackguard who, on occasions, would run his servants through with a sabre whenever they displeased him. But it wasn't for this that he finished his days staring into a basket full of sawdust, but rather a duel he'd fought with the Marquis de Roque after the Comte had run through his host's favourite footman. The Marquis was a more considerate employer than the Comte and insisted that his friend compensate the footman's nearest and dearest for the loss of the family breadwinner, a suggestion the Comte took great personal exception to.

He, after all, had been the one who had been insulted when the footman had laughed at a quip the Marquis had made at the Comte's expense. The Comte was the victim in all of this, at least as far as the Comte was concerned.

A quarrel broke out and the gauntlet was thrown down but it wasn't picked up until a few more bottles of Marquis's cognac had been decanted and even then only with great reluctance. And so it was, with wigs askew and the Marquis rapidly sobering up, that the two noblemen found themselves out on the foggy lawn the next morning, back to back and with pistols drawn. The Comte de Aardmas won the day easily, shooting the Marquis stone dead before he'd even got a shot off. In fact, it was subsequently found that the Marquis's pistol was unloaded. The cocksure Comte had shot an unarmed man. The Captain of the Guards was called and witnesses were questioned but none vouched for the legality of the duel. Not even the Comte's own people. All were certain that the Comte had knowingly handed the Marquis an unloaded pistol. Thus, the Comte was found guilty of murdering a peer of the realm and sentenced to die.

And so it was, four days later and with his head on the block, that the Comte de Aardmas looked out into the crowd to see his own valet produce a pistol from below his tunic, drop the shot from its barrel and blow the powder from the flash pan to disarm the weapon — just as he had a few days earlier while the Comte had been busy savouring victory. It was said that only the axe dropped faster than the Comte's jaw.

But even that momentous spectacle, which had been greatly attended by a huge number of domestic servants, promised to pale into insignificance next to the execution of Gardenia Beaufort. In fact, it was said that her execution would be almost as well attended as her stepsister's wedding, a notion the Grand Duke found positively vulgar despite reserving his own seat as soon as the arrangements were announced.

In light of the expected crowds, it was deemed that there wouldn't be enough room for her topping in the usual spot around the back of the dungeons, so a scaffold was built in the town square, around which the fun-seekers could safely cluster. Moreover, the Prince and Princess were said to be keen to personally oversee justice was done and so the whole thing was positioned in front of the Palace to gift them a prime vantage point in their balcony on high. The King hardly approved, not least of all because of the other murderous stepsister who was still running around on the loose, but the Prince assured his tiresome father that the Princess was perfectly safe. A bodyguard — or *Honour Watch*, as she called it — had been handpicked especially to protect her and would go everywhere with the Princess wherever she went until both sisters had been dealt with accordingly. The King still didn't like it but then again the old codger didn't like anything these days — the miserable old windbag — the Prince reasoned. It mattered not. The King's tide was ebbing, the Prince's was coming in. The balance of power was shifting in their little corner of the world.

At midday exactly, the gates of the dungeons were opened and a prison wagon driven out. The bars of the cage in which Gardenia was chained did little to protect her from the barrage of rotten vegetables that were hurled her way as she journeyed through the town. Neither did the cavalry officers who rode alongside her or the King's Guards who fought to hold back the mob at key intersections. Gardenia simply had to run the gauntlet until she reached the Town Square, in which a better class of ghoul had gathered to watch her die.

"Here she is. The prisoner is here!" the cry went up and all at once every face in Andovia turned her way as she was driven through the Square. Despite wearing a robe, Gardenia felt naked without so much as a smudge of makeup on. And in front of so many people too. This was the disjointed thought that occurred to her despite her more immediate concerns.

Gardenia picked out several faces she recognised from the crowd. Isabella Eames waved to her frantically from the steps of the cathedral while Claudia Ricci and Suzette Weiss cast scornful looks upon her from the bookshop balcony itself, having paid a King's ransom to watch the spectacle from this infamous location. Nina Laurent was here too, sitting atop her new stepfather's shoulders and eating a tart until her face was sticky with jam. And even Didi had broken his own rules and braved the crowds, stinking worse than high heaven in his filthy hat and overcoat and waiting by the side of the scaffold to stop anyone from getting close except the hardiest of bluebottles. Everyone was in fine fettle and making the most of this historic occasion but now came the main event.

A bugler sounded his horn and all turned to the Palace to see the balcony doors open and the Princess emerged to take her seat for the show. With her were the Prince and the King and several of her *Honour Watchmen*, unmistakable in their distinctive bright white tunics.

Gardenia looked up and almost choked on her anger. Shoved out onto the balcony alongside the Prince and Princess was her Mother, dressed in prison robes and flanked by blue-coated King's Guards, their rifles at the ready. Ella's cruelty knew no bounds, forcing Mother to watch her own daughter's execution. Neither Mother nor Gardenia reacted when they saw each other. They just swapped helpless stares and yearned to be able to comfort one another. This would be the last time they laid eyes on each other. And every difference and disagreement was forgotten. Only their love burned now. As it would do for both of them always.

The wagon pulled alongside the scaffold and a

Guardsman unlocked the prisoner's cage. Gardenia, hungry and afraid, was weak and wobbly on her feet so the Guardsman helped her down from the back of the cart and up the newly built scaffold steps. Another Guardsman was there to help her the last few steps and Gardenia now saw the small party waiting for her on the scaffold; the Bishop, who was there to lead her in one last prayer, a drummer boy to play her out and Monsieur Samuel, whose grizzled old face was hidden behind a black executioner's mask. The two men bowed deferentially and Gardenia replied with a curtsey, not really knowing what else to do in this situation. It was all rather new to her.

Samuel held out his hand and, not wishing to give offence, Gardenia, took it as if being introduced to an old friend at a social function.

Samuel smiled politely but this was a different sort of custom he was observing. The Bishop whispered in Gardenia's ear when he realised she hadn't been properly briefed:

"No mademoiselle, you are required to pay him," he said and it was then that she noticed the Guardsman behind offering her a small purse of schillings, for few prisoners carried cash with them for this sort of occasion.

"Oh," she realised, briefly wondering what would happen if she refused to pay. Would they let her go? It seemed unlikely so Gardenia was about to take the coins when she remembered she already had her executioner's "payment".

"Would you accept this, Monsieur?" she said, producing her father's Medal of Valour from her pocket and offering it to Samuel instead. When he saw what it was, he almost dropped it again in surprise. "For your services," she explained, hoping that this might mean something to him because it surely didn't to her. She had been wondering, right until this moment, if she was going to be able to use it to buy or bribe her way off the block but whatever Marigold's intention had been in sending the medal to her, it would remain a mystery for all time. As Gardenia's final moments had now come.

Samuel continued to stare at the medal in disbelief before remembering himself and muttering, "Thank you, my lady". Inwardly, he was dying but outwardly he couldn't allow himself to react. He had to stay strong for his friend's daughter. He owed her that much. If there was anything he could've done for her, anything — even if it meant trading places with her — then he would've gladly done so and to hell with the consequences. As an executioner of thirty years standing and one of the few surviving veterans of Widows' Ridge, death held no fear for him. It was all just one big cycle of planting and rebirth anyway.

But unfortunately…

… no one was asking.

The scaffold was surrounded on four sides, Guardsmen controlled every point in and out of the Square and marksmen lined the rooftops. To have tried anything now would have been to invite certain failure, and worse still, lead to a more cruel and unusual punishment for all concerned. If there was one thing the judiciary in this backwater Kingdom despised, it was a lack of etiquette from their condemned, especially when a merciful punishment had been prescribed.

Gardenia took a moment to kneel with the Bishop while he said a few words in Latin. She didn't understand any of them but got the general gist (penitence, remorse, sins and atonement, etc), then when all was said and done, the Bishop went on to bless the King, the Prince, the Princess, the people and "everyone else who knows me" to dilute the condemned's prayer entirely.

Gardenia's moment had almost come. Just one thing remained. Her final words. It was generally agreed that the most dignified thing a prisoner could do just before they were beheaded for the crime of treason was seek forgiveness from — and reaffirm their loyalty to — the King. This sort of contrition was seen to demonstrate great personal courage and always went down well with the crowd. Moreover, it usually stopped the King from tarring the rest of the prisoner's family with the same brush and bunging them into the clink to rot, so this moment had been eagerly anticipated.

The crowd fell deathly silent and Ella leaned into the wind to crane her ears. Not a baby cried nor a beggar coughed, such was the people's appetite to hear the heinous traitor's pleas for forgiveness.

Gardenia approached the edge of the scaffold and looked out across the sea of expectant faces. As was tradition, she now turned to the royal box and to the person she needed to seek contrition from. To the rest of the Kingdom, Ella was beautiful with her white flowing gown, diamond crown and a glittering array of jewels but to Gardenia she was grotesque; an abomination of cold, hard cruelty concealed in clover.

"Your Majesty," Gardenia declared, addressing Ella by her proper title and almost choking on the words as she did so. "I have but one thing to say to you." And with that, she blew the biggest fattest raspberry the Kingdom had ever seen. Her Mother was already sentenced to life in the dungeons and her sister was riding for the hills. What more could they do to her?

The crowd gasped and the King squawked. The Bishop crossed himself and the Grand Duke lost a monocle. Such insolence! Such disrespect! "They should have the wretched tart flogged to within an inch of her life!" he declared but only to himself, as he had been forced to watch the whole affair from a different window from the rest of the royal party. As for Mother? She had never seen a more wanton and unladylike display from her daughter before. And she had never felt prouder.

Still smarting, Ella caught sight of Mother smirking.

"Let's see who's smiling in a minute, shall we, old woman?" she said, signalling the Guards to move the prisoner into place.

A Guardsman dragged Gardenia into the middle of the scaffold and pushed her head onto the block. There was no need to be so rough as Gardenia wasn't resisting but he did so anyway, just to teach her a lesson, albeit one that would not linger in the mind for long.

Monsieur Samuel now moved into position and hoisted his axe. Such a slender neck, such a big axe, he could barely miss. But such slips had happened in the past — not by him, of course, but by others — to cause the object of the exercise much unnecessary suffering, not least of all when a second blow was required to finish what the first had merely started. Samuel couldn't let that happen now. He had to focus. He had to stay strong. The Guardsman relinquished his hold and Samuel had a clear line of sight.

The drummer boy began to play.

And for one terrible moment, nobody moved.

Nobody breathed.

And nobody blinked.

Almost.

As if on cue, Didi threw off his filthy hat and coat to reveal that he was a changed man beneath. And not just metaphorically either. But literally. For *he* was now a *she*. A dirty wig, a fake beard and generous helping of rotting fish guts had helped Marigold transform. And standing at the scaffold with her head hung low no one had given her a second look — particularly when she had been accompanied by such a noxious stench. The long overcoat had helped also. It concealed something she'd smuggled into the city and it was this that she now hurled at Monsieur Samuel, screaming as she did so with a cry to wake the dead.

"FOR THE KING'S MEN!"

CHAPTER FIFTY-NINE

CATHERINE AND ARMAND had been married for barely two years when war came to Andovia, or more accurately, Andovia went looking for war. Seven years of bloodshed was drawing to a barbarous conclusion across Europe and victory for the British and her allies now looked assured. A peace conference had been announced and the last few salvos were being exchanged in the latest conflict between the superpowers.

This, the King adjudged, was the perfect time to show his hand and so, eight days before the Treaty of Paris was signed, rather to everyone's surprise, the tiny Kingdom of Andovia declared war on the combined forces of France and the Holy Roman Empire.

Of course, it had all just been a cynical ploy to snatch a few crumbs from the peace table and everyone saw the manoeuvre for what it was worth, but the King wasn't proud, unlike his own father from whom he'd taken over just a few months earlier — the supercilious old soak. A little glory went a long way in a place like Andovia, especially when it came with reparations.

Fortunately for the French, they had very few soldiers camped in the area and Saxony and Bavaria had even fewer, but there was a small detachment of Austrians garrisoned in the mountain passes just east of Srendizi. These troops may have been stationed here to stop Srendizi bandits from raiding Austrian settlements but they were allied to the French just the same.

The King called in his commanders for a conference.

*

"WE'RE MOVING OUT," the Sergeant told Catherine when he came for her in the barracks.

"Where to?" Catherine whispered, having only just got

Marigold to sleep after some thirty minutes of walking around with her.

"East, that's all I know, but Sam says we're at war."

"At war? With who?"

"Sam didn't know. I guess we'll find out once the shooting starts."

This news could not have come at a worse time for Catherine. Not only did she have a one-year-old on the hip, she had another growing heavy in her belly. Her feet ached, her back was sore and her morning sickness seemed to go on all day. And as Marigold was still on the breast, Catherine was having to eat for three and having huge difficulties keeping any of it down.

And now they were going on campaign.

"Not we. Me. You stay here, my love, rent a cottage and look after yourself. I've enough saved up and we'll be back in a month or two, you'll see," the Sergeant said, looking in on Marigold sleeping peacefully in her cot and placing the gentlest of kisses on her forehead.

"No, we're coming with you, all of us. Who'll take care of you otherwise?" Catherine said, knowing that other wives, washerwomen and seamstresses, would be making the trek eastwards. War was a family affair in the eighteenth century, more so than it would be in the years to come. The camp worked as one and as such, where the soldiers went, the women and their children followed, if only because there was very little to stay back for unless a woman had the means to support herself in her husband's absence. Few did, but Catherine was one of the lucky ones.

"It'll be cold in the mountains. Think of our daughter," the Sergeant said before correcting himself. "Daughters even."

"It might not be a girl," Catherine reminded him, and not for the first time either.

"She's a girl," the Sergeant insisted, having already met

Gardenia in his dreams and refusing to countenance any other thought.

"No," Catherine replied sternly. "We are a family, Armand. Where you go we follow."

"Stubborn to the end," he said shaking his head.

"Stubborn to the end," she confirmed.

"And that's why I love you," he smiled, pulling her close — or at least as close as Gardenia would allow — to kiss his wife. "Heavens above, with you as their mother, my girls are going to be a force to be reckoned with."

"And you'll play your part as well, I should say," Catherine replied, holding her husband close. "Just promise me one thing."

"Anything."

"Don't start them off as drummer boys."

The Sergeant laughed. "I wouldn't hear of it. My girls are going to wear only the finest clothes. And eat only the finest foods. And they are going to be ladies. And learned. And beautiful. And they are going to marry better than their mother ever did."

"Impossible," Catherine replied, straightening the Sergeant's collar.

"I'm serious," he said, giving Catherine one of those looks he always gave her when he was speaking from the heart. "I've been thinking about this a lot. It's their one shot."

"At happiness?" Catherine asked.

"Of course, I'll not see them married to a cad or a wife-whooper but neither will I see them married to the kindliest beggar in the Kingdom. Marriage is a girl's opportunity, like a ladder. Most girls stay on the same rung generation after generation but beauty and grace can give them a leg up, just as the battlefield can for a man. Kings have fallen for concubines before and nations have changed."

"Every father fancies his daughter a Princess," Catherine mocked, something which rankled the Sergeant.

"I don't expect them to become Princesses but it is important that they marry well. How else are they going to secure their futures? Through work?" the Sergeant said, looking down at Marigold in her cot and feeling the impulse to pick her up, something he knew Catherine would kill him for, having only just got her to sleep.

"One step at a time, my love, they're not even walking yet and you're already looking to marry them off," Catherine said, leading the Sergeant away from Marigold's cot in case his impulses got the better of him.

"One step at a time is right but we need to look at the long road in front of us too. If Marigold marries well and her daughter does even better, who knows, maybe in a hundred years time, her great-great-granddaughter might be a wife of someone with real power."

"For all the good that would do us, my love," Catherine laughed, unsure just how serious her husband was being. But then he reminded her once more of the soldiers' poem:

> *"A soldier's life is hard and short,*
> *He takes much land yet keeps but nought.*
> *He kills and kills and kills again,*
> *On different days with different men.*
> *The fighting never truly ends,*
> *The ground turned red with foe and friends.*
> *Until one day his God finds he,*
> *For what will be will surely be.*
> *So worry not these mortal things,*
> *We are but shot in the slings of Kings."*

These words were never spoken lightly, by any of the rank and file, they were sacrosanct and Catherine felt a sudden chill blowing in from the East.

"It's not about us as individuals. Silks and jewels are just medals for the rich and idle, as meaningless as the one I'm required to wear for the King's parade. What matters is the power to change the world. For the better. And not just for a pampered few but for everyone. And that can only happen from the top down."

Catherine took the Sergeant by the hand to stop him pacing the room as though it had no door and took hold of him.

"I will do my best by them," she promised him. "And I will prepare them accordingly."

The Sergeant was an idealist and it weighed on him in times of turmoil. Most of the time he was able to hide his ideals behind his usual bluff and bluster but something was different about today, almost as if he knew something that no one else did. And this worried Catherine more than anything.

"Let's get packing then," he said. "We have a long journey ahead of us."

*

THE FIVE-DAY MARCH across Srendizi was hard going. Most went on foot but the Sergeant had bought a small cart and a horse from a cavalry Sergeant to help Catherine and their young daughter keep pace with the rest of the column. The horse was jet-black, the colour of liquorice, and a luxury for a couple on an army income. But the Sergeant had assured his wife that this wouldn't always be the case.

Besides, "who else is going to look after my girls when I can't be there?" he'd said.

After five days on the road, word reached the Colonel that the peace conference was underway and he knew that time was against him. In order to justify Andovia's place at the table, he needed to have at least sighted the enemy and fired off a couple of shots. This was his mission and he was determined not to disappoint. His reputation, and that of the King's, was on the line. And, as everybody knew, in Andovia, reputations were everything.

The Colonel was new to the post. Only a month earlier

he'd been a modest Major and before that a humble Captain and lowly Lieutenant. But family connections and an insatiable ambition had seen him win rapid promotions and the omens looked good for this mission too. He'd campaigned before, of course, many moons ago, when his platoon had cleared out a bandit camp in the forests of Srendizi. That joyous victory had helped him on the way to his first promotion and the Colonel wasn't about to squander this chance either. Especially not against a real enemy in a real war.

After another day of marching, the Colonel's scouts located a detachment of Austrian troops camped high on a peak above a pass that ran between Srendizi and the Austrian border. They were quite a way inside Srendizi so the King could not be accused of attacking a foreign power in their own backyard. This would simply be a skirmish fought over neutral territory in lawless land but it would show the world whose side the Andovians were on — and just in time for the share-out too.

The Colonel crouched in the rocks on the other side of the pass and surveyed the enemy's fortifications through his spyglass.

"How many do you suppose are up there?" he asked his officers as they stood behind him awaiting their orders.

"Initial reports suggest not more than a platoon, sir," his Captain replied, eager to be noticed ahead of the other officers. The Colonel had to look at the Captain twice before he recognised the face. He'd been a Lieutenant a few weeks earlier and now he was a Captain. The Colonel didn't like having a high-flyer snapping at his heels. It made him feel uncomfortable.

"Excellent," the Colonel said and heartily declared: "Then we shall have no problems in taking it."

"Taking it, sir?" the Captain said, wondering if he'd misheard his commanding officer.

"Of course. What do you think we're here to do?" the Colonel asked.

The Captain looked up the snow-lined slopes and towards the gun emplacements above and could only guess at the castle-in-the-sky the Colonel was constructing inside his head. In spite of the enormous risks involved, the Captain felt duty-bound to share his thoughts on the impending operation.

"Begging your pardon sir, but I was under the impression the King merely wanted us to fire off a few volleys at the enemy, not take their position by force," he said, earning the ire of his Colonel.

"Fire off a few volleys!" he thundered. "Are you a soldier or not, Captain?"

"Yes sir. Of course, sir," the Captain warbled, attempting to salute his way out of trouble. "Forgive me, Colonel."

"You said it yourself, there's barely a platoon up there and we're a whole company. I want to see our flag planted on that ridge before this day is out, do you understand me?" the Colonel fumed, half-considering having the Captain flogged for his insubordination before a better idea occurred to him. "You will lead the charge personally."

"Yes sir. Thank you, sir," was all the Captain was able to say about the honour.

"For the King," the Colonel reminded him in no uncertain terms.

"For the King," the Captain echoed, so numb with shock that he neglected to give three cheers when he turned and trudged away, which the Colonel decided to take as another act of disrespect from a thoroughly disagreeable young man.

CHAPTER SIXTY

WHAT FOLLOWED WAS A SLAUGHTER.

The Captain led from the front and was cut down before he'd finished hollering "For the Ki…!". The rest of the company clawed and fought their way up the frozen slopes and into a hailstorm of musket-fire, returning the occasional shot when they could but doing little to dent the Austrian's resolve. The whole company had been committed to the assault, some two hundred men in all, against thirty. But those thirty men had been dug in all winter and commanded the high ground with a clear field of fire. The terrain was so remote that it would have been easy to isolate and starved them out but the Colonel didn't have the luxury of time. He had a day in which to grab a slice of glory. An impasse of stalemate would do nothing for Andovia's place in the history books.

The Sergeant was climbing the steeper slopes to the west when his advance came under fire. He'd not been seen before now as the Austrians had assumed that no fool would attempt to climb the near-vertical western slopes. But in light of the insanity they saw unfolding before them, suddenly nothing surprised them.

"Take cover!" he cried, dropping behind an overhang as the snows around him were peppered with blood. Corporal Jacques had taken a musket shot to the chest and left a scarlet trail as he slid down the mountain. Private Collier was next, losing his footing against the ice and presenting an easy target as he flailed between the boulders. The Austrians above were crack shots and picked off their attackers with ease. Corporal Samuel took a ball through the knee and fell screaming face-first into the snow. The Sergeant dragged him out of the line of fire before he could be finished off and did what he could to patch up his leg but Samuel's fight was over. He was going nowhere now except for the surgeon's table.

"Get him down," the Sergeant shouted at Private Henri, a young recruit who'd only been with the Guards a couple of months and who was huddled behind a rocky outcrop unable to move. The Private grabbed the lifeline with both hands and hauled the Corporal from rock to rock as those few men still standing were able to give him covering fire.

Henri and Samuel made it down but a great many others wouldn't be so lucky. The Sergeant looked out along the slopes and saw other brave men slipping between the boulders as enemy fire and ice conspired to sweep them from the mountainside.

"We're going to die out here," Sergeant Santin shouted from a shallow dug-out in which he was taking shelter, or at least attempting to. They'd barely made it halfway to their objective and they'd lost over half their number already. If they went on like this there wouldn't be a man amongst them left standing by the end of the day. And yet still the order to disengage hadn't sounded. What the hell were the officers playing at?

*

FAR BELOW, beyond the range of the guns, the Colonel followed his company's progress through the lens of his spyglass. For reasons he couldn't fathom a great many of his men seemed to have made it halfway up but were now sat around deliberating instead of finishing the job. It was positively infuriating. Couldn't these imbeciles be trusted to follow a simple order? Alright, so some of them had fallen in the course of their duties but that didn't matter because they had the numbers on their side. If they stopped worrying about their own skins and thought more of the regiment they could've taken the Austrians by now.

"FOR THE KING! FOR THE KING!" the Colonel bellowed over and over again in an effort to inspire his men, unaware that he could neither be seen nor heard where he was standing by anyone but his fellow officers and a rapidly swelling troupe of wives who'd raced up once the wounded had started coming down.

"Oh my God!" was the collective assessment as the tragedy played out before them on brightly lit slopes. Even through the palls of smoke that drifted over the snows they could see the scores of dead that now littered the mountainside. These were men they knew, had lived alongside and in many cases, committed their lives to. And now they were seeing them being flung into the grinder for reasons none of them could understand. Even the Austrians were willing their enemy to fall back, not for their own sakes but to halt the senseless slaughter. There was nothing to be gained from any of this.

"No!" several of the women screamed when they saw the tiny figure of a Guardsman shot through and fall from a great height.

The Colonel looked up from his spyglass and ordered his adjutant to do something about "those women".

"Get them out of here," he demanded, but the women rushed forwards, past the Colonel and his officers and into the battle to help the wounded.

Catherine now appeared with Marigold strapped to her back and Gardenia sitting low in her belly. She'd tethered Liquorice when she'd heard the first shots and hurried forwards towards the mountain, but it was hard going over the rugged terrain so she was slower than most

She got there just as the first of the wives and washerwomen reached the bottom of the slopes and was shocked by what she saw. The women tore at the rocks, clambering hand over fist to reach those who had fallen, oblivious of the musket shots that whipped past them with a crack. Many men lay dead but many more were injured and it was to these that the women went, dragging them from the jaws of death and applying field dressings to stem the bleeding.

Catherine, already a deathly pale because of her condition, went whiter still. She was close enough that snows around her were being peppered with stray shots but not close enough to pick out individuals still moving about on the mountainside. The continuous *crack crack crack* of musket fire rained down on all those now taking to the slopes, men and women alike. In years gone by, Catherine would've not hesitated from running into the fray but she couldn't today. She had more than her own life to consider and couldn't risk putting her girls in the line of fire, even for their father. She was stuck between worlds, unable to move forwards and unable to turn back, helpless in the face of this unfolding nightmare.

*

THE SERGEANT SAW their unexpected reinforcements taking to the slopes and prayed that his own wife would stay back. Several of the women now lay wounded alongside their menfolk, either from bullets or boulders as the fighting knocked rocks onto those coming to their aid. The Sergeant couldn't let this happen, either to Catherine or to anyone else. He couldn't cower below this overhang forever and watch his whole world being torn apart. He had to do something and he had to do it now. But not for the King. The King was not here clinging to these rocks. He would do it for his men, and for the women and girls who were now digging in alongside their husbands, lovers, fathers and friends.

"The flag! Give me the flag!" he called to his company, ordering all to halt until the flag bearer was found, already dead, with the accursed piece of cloth tucked inside his tunic. Private Lopez was relieved of his duties and the flag was tossed from rock to rock until it reached the Sergeant's outstretched hand.

There was no need to take the ridge, he concluded. It

was a rock, politically unimportant and strategically worthless. The only reason they were here was because of the Austrians. But the Colonel had wanted to see his flag flying from the ridge before this day was out and so that's what he would see. It may have been an empty gesture but if it saved the lives of his brothers he had to try.

"On three, cover me with everything you've got!" the Sergeant shouted, tucking the flag into his own tunic as he braced himself to go.

In the gulley below, all became acutely aware that something was about to happen. No one had fired or moved an inch from the Andovian side and this always foreshadowed a coordinated attack. But when it came only one man surged forwards. The rest of the mountainside opened up on the enemy positions as one, freed of the need to push forwards and now charged with the simple duty of keeping a single man alive as he took on the running of the entire company.

Catherine dropped to her knees when she realised who that man was. The fool! The damn fool!

The Sergeant leapt from lip to ledge, scrambling up the side of the ridge for most of it on his hands and knees and running between cover when it presented itself. Every musket ball was now gunning for him but this allowed his comrades to lift their eyes a little higher as they took aim on the enemy. The crack shots amongst the Andovians now started to tell, forcing the Austrians onto the back foot for the first time today and opening the way clear for the Sergeant.

Most of the Austrians were strung along a craggy ridge overlooking the pass but the Sergeant wouldn't have got to within ten metres of this position. Instead, he was aiming for a small peak some way to the left. This was unmanned and even more militarily meaningless than the ridge itself, but crucially it was ever so slightly higher. And in the mind of the Colonel, the Sergeant estimated, this would undoubtedly count for something.

Far below, all the company was now willing the Sergeant on, so much so that one or two of the officers forgot themselves entirely.

"Go on, man, go!" Major Leclercq cheered, earning himself a rebuke from the Colonel in the process. It didn't do to make a display of oneself, especially when cheering on someone other than the person whose plan this had been in the first place. The Colonel struck a big mental mark against the Leclercq's copybook and went back to tracking the Sergeant through his spyglass.

The higher the Sergeant climbed the harder it became for the Austrians to see him. The ridge was curved and the rocky brow now shielded him from view. The Austrian Lieutenant sent two of his men to intercept the Sergeant but they found to their cost that he couldn't just climb, he could shoot too, having armed himself with a pair of flintlocks before he'd set off.

"Bravo!" muttered Leclercq, this time under his breath.

The way to the top now clear, the Sergeant clawed, kicked and threw himself up the last few metres until by sheer force of will he reached the snow-covered summit. It was a hell of a view from up here, but it had been bought and paid for at a terrible cost. The bodies of friends and foe littered the ground. Even the Austrians had paid a hefty price for this desolate patch of ground and now ceased fire when it became obvious that the assault on their position was off. The Austrian Lieutenant urged his troops to keep fighting but enough men had died today. Few had the appetite for continued bloodshed.

Just below the summit to the west, the Sergeant loaded his pistols and waited for the Austrians to come but none did. The musket fire had stopped and an eery silence settled across the mountains. Ordinarily, a person can not hear silence but after a battle there are few more beautiful sounds.

Keeping watch, the Sergeant set down his pistols and

blew on his frozen fingers to get them working. When he was sure no one was coming he popped open his tunic and pulled out the flag. The royal crest had a little more colour to it than usual, courtesy of Private Lopez, but it was unmistakable all the same and the Sergeant held it aloft to proclaim victory over this nameless ridge in a forgotten corner of a lawless land. The Colonel saw the flag flying through his spyglass and allowed himself a moment of pride. He'd done it. He'd taken the ridge. His officers gathered around to offer him their heartiest congratulations and the Colonel despatched a messenger to ride hard for Andovia and report the glorious news back to the King.

But on the mountainside itself, there was very little glory to be had. Scores of wives now wept over the scores of dead and the surviving Guardsman began to trudge back down to the bottom, their orders to abandon it as fast as they had taken it. And yet they hadn't taken it. The Austrians still held it. And the Austrian Lieutenant believed in King and country and flags and glory every bit as much as his Andovian counterpart did. So he grabbed a musket from his own Sergeant, took careful aim and, with the final action of the final battle of seven long years of unremitting slaughter —

— fired.

CHAPTER SIXTY-ONE

"FOR THE KING'S MEN!"

The crowd could scarcely believe what they'd heard. Everyone knew it was treason to even utter these words in private let alone shout them out in public. In front of all Andovia? And the King himself?

The words harked back to the Battle of Widows' Ridge, where it was said that over a hundred men had been sacrificed needlessly in the name of the King. Their loss had become a rallying cry for insurrectionists and mutineers everywhere, people who maintained that the King and his kind should be shown the same kind of loyalty he'd shown his men. To speak these words was to renounce the King. To even think them to was to condone revolution. But to shout them out in public? That was nothing less than terrorism.

But no one had time to ponder these implications because of what else Marigold had brought with her today. It was an earthenware pot, the size and shape of a large vase and sealed with a gauze at one end. She'd hurled it straight at Monsieur Samuel, knowing full well that he'd turn and fend it off with the only thing at his disposal, his axe. Duly, he swung the fearsome blade, smashing the pot to pieces and unwittingly unleashing hell upon the crowd. The wasps inside had been confined all day, having been first subdued with smoke and then encased in clay. It was hot in the pot and the sweet cider that had been dripped through the gauze got made them drunk and aggressive. But now they were free. Free to exact their revenge upon anyone and everyone they saw for their egregious incarceration.

Five thousand wasps in all.

The swarm filled the Square and panic quickly followed. The crowd broke and the Guardsmen flailed but their weapons were no match for this particular enemy.

Within moments there was pandemonium as people ran. Everyone shoved everyone, people were trampled underfoot and even the Princess was hurried inside, her diamonds glinting enticingly in the sunlight to attract the swarm's attention as much as Nina Laurent's jam-covered face.

Marigold threw her hand up to Gardenia, who still had her head on the block, and urged her to come.

"Let's go!" she said, dragging her sister off the scaffold and fleeing with her into the crowd. Monsieur Samuel, in his executioner's mask, was better protected against the stings than most and able to watch the sisters as they fled. They were their father's daughters alright. Even if she hadn't thrown the pot straight at him, he would have known what to do the moment he'd heard the cry. But this way no one could blame him for defending himself. No one could hold him to account. And in rescuing her sister, Marigold had rescued Samuel too, and for that, he thanked her with all of his heart.

"*Bonne chance, les fillies,*" he said with a smile, slamming his axe into the block for the last time and heading on home.

Such was the chaos below that the sharpshooters on the rooftops immediately lost the sisters to the crowd and dared not open fire for fear of hitting innocent bystanders.

Marigold, with her rotten fish stench, went relatively unmolested by the wasps but they attacked everyone else, including Gardenia, although she scarcely felt it. The sting she had been anticipating had been far greater and besides, once a person had been bitten by a barley snake, a wasp sting barely merited consideration. Marigold rubbed some of her stench into Gardenia's face and the attacks stopped immediately.

"How do we get out of here?" she asked, holding onto her sister's hand for all she was worth and not daring to let go. Every route in and out of the city would be blocked and Marigold was now out of insects to throw at people.

"We're not," Marigold cryptically explained, pushing her way through the crowd until a gap opened up and they saw the Palace before them. "Come on."

The wasps had cleared the guards off the gates and the stone driveway stretched out ahead. Marigold figured that most people would expect them to flee the other way, so by heading into the lion's den they might be able to find somewhere to hole up for a time. At least, this had been her intention. But then, just before Gardenia had been brought to the scaffold, Marigold had seen her Mother on the balcony alongside Ella and under armed guard. She didn't know if they could find Mother in the enormous Palace or even what they might do if they could, but she had to try. In the confusion, an opportunity might just present itself.

The girls headed off the main drive and took to the gardens. Marigold remembered them from after the ball although they looked different in the daylight. The greenery looked less green and the lawns less crimped. It was as though the Palace had lost some of its lustre in the intervening days.

Several guards ran through the gardens but most seemed more intent on getting back to the barracks to douse their faces with vinegar than apprehending trespassers and so the girls were able to avoid them. After a quick search of the ivy that covered the rear of the Palace, Marigold found the concealed exit she had previously left by. The door was locked but Marigold had planned for that. She remembered the bolt on the other side and produced a small length of rope that was tied into a lasso. She dangled it through the barred window and after a little fishing, caught hold of the catch. Carefully, she tightened the lasso and yanked. The bolt clicked back and the door creaked open. They were in.

"I must say, it does feel rather like we're returning to the scene of the crime," Gardenia said.

"We've committed no crime," Marigold reminded her. "Not yet anyway."

The corridor was dark and deserted. They followed it

through to the wine cellar where Marigold and Gardenia stopped to rest.

"I need to get out of these things and wash. The smell will give us away before anyone lays eyes on me," she said.

Marigold stripped out of Didi's rags and scraped off what filth she could but there was only so much she could do. Fish guts are nothing if not a resilient odour so she opened a bottle of Cognac to tame the stench and soothe her stings.

"Put some of this on your face," Marigold said, handing Gardenia the bottle. After treating their stings as best they could and wiping themselves down with a cloth, Marigold untied a small parcel she had tied to her waist. It was a maid's uniform. Didi had pinched it off a washing line for her yesterday.

"There's one for you also," Marigold said, handing her sister a second set of clothes.

Gardenia held it against herself and concluded: "Looks like Captain Durand was right. I guess we are just a couple of common serving girls after all."

"That we should aspire to such heights," Marigold replied.

They inched their way along the dark and winding passageway and soon found themselves in the corridor that sloped up to the Great Hall. Halfway along, Gardenia remembered the spy holes she'd encountered and stopped to take a peak.

"What do you see?" Marigold asked but Gardenia was unable to say, too great was her shock. "What is it?"

A stony-faced Gardenia climbed down, took Marigold by the hand and led her onwards, up the gentle sloping corridor and out through the hidden entrance behind the tapestry, first making sure to check that the coast was clear. It was, but it wouldn't remain so for long. The Great Hall was ready and waiting for company.

Marigold now saw what Gardenia had seen and

understood her reaction. The stage was set for a magnificent banquet. Indeed, not just any banquet but the Prince and Princess's belated wedding breakfast. Three huge tables filled the hall in a horseshoe arrangement and were set out with the King's finest crystal and silver. Food of all descriptions had been prepared for the feast with game birds, venison, smoked salmon and lobsters set out of silver serving platters and several whole sweet suckling pigs complete with apples in their mouths awaiting the knife. But the pièce de resistance, the wonderment that dominated the room, was the wedding cake set before the head table. Atop this five-tier marvel, decorated with the finest white chocolate, succulent cherries, edible gold and a small cluster of fizzy candles, stood figurines of the happy couple themselves. They'd been carved out of icing sugar and sculpted so meticulously that Marigold could scarcely tell them from the real thing. Even their smiles were painted on, just as they were on the full-sized versions.

"They were going to sit down and eat after I had been executed," Gardenia said, her voice shaking with anger. "I was to be part of their celebrations."

It was all too much for the younger sister. She thought she'd seen the worst of people in the course of her short life but to discover that her death had been scheduled as the pre-dinner entertainment to a joyous feast was the final insult. That they could eat an apple, let alone the pig that was sucking it, after witnessing her decapitation spoke volumes for their humanity. The bandits in Srendizi had more honour than these people. If she'd had a bottle of arsenic she would have flavoured every dish but it was too late to do anything. For the doors at the far end of the Great Hall were suddenly flung open and an all-too-familiar voice bid them a warm welcome.

"Why, my sweet stepsisters. How happy I am to see you again," Ella laughed as the Prince, the King and half a dozen *Watchmen* led by Captain Olivier, fanned out behind her.

CHAPTER SIXTY-TWO

"AH-HA, AND SO THE TRAITORS have returned for a second crack, have they?" the Prince deduced from the sisters' presence. "Well, we'll not stand on ceremony this time. Captain, off with their heads and let's not make a great song and dance about it, huh!"

The Grand Duke hurried in with a detachment of King's Guards just as his son was about to seize the sisters. Mother arrived next, escorted at the point of a bayonet by yet more Guardsmen and she cried out when she saw her girls cornered and with no way out.

"Go girls, go!"

Marigold and Gardenia didn't need telling twice. They may have been surrounded and certain for the chop but that didn't mean they were ready to give in without a fight. Marigold leapt up onto the table and Gardenia quickly followed. Goblets were tossed and the fine china dispatched as they threw everything they could at Captain Olivier and the oncoming Guards.

"Lock the doors," ordered the King.

"This ends now," agreed the Prince.

But it was Ella who put it most succinctly.

"Get those old trollops down from there before they ruin everything," she cried, apoplectic at the scale of destruction her barge-footed sisters were causing.

"Run for it, sis', run!" Marigold urged Gardenia as they tore up the table cloth, trod trout into trifle and trampled through a selection of cheeses as they strove to evade their captors. One of the suckling pigs ended up on the floor, spitting out his apple as he fell, as did the salmon, dozens of swan eggs, a nest of spare ribs and anything else that got in their way. At one point, the spread had been fit for a King. Now it was strewn everywhere, violated and inedible to all except possibly Didi, although even he would have had his misgivings about the pâté.

"Stop them! No!" Ella screamed in horror, pulling out her hair and imploring her *Watchmen* to shoot before the girls could get anywhere near her cake but it was too late, Gardenia tripped in the Taleggio and stumbled forwards, windmilling helplessly as she fell face-first through the fourth tier of Ella's magnificent pièce de resistance.

The fairytale Princess could scarcely look as the whole thing came crashing down. It had taken two days to make, three chefs to bake and four men to carry but only one girl to destroy it, sprinkles and all. Tier after tier burst open on impact to send infused fruits across the Great Hall, icing turned to dust, gold leaf fluttered on the breeze and the miniature couple lay broken on the floor. But finally, Gardenia was wrestled into submission by the Captain of the Guards.

Marigold too was soon captured but for one moment neither girl held sway. For the final tier had done something rather peculiar to catch everyone's attention. Far from breaking open when it fell, it had hit the floor with a clunk and the icing broke apart to reveal something unexpected inside. It looked like a tin on first inspection: a large black metal canister with markings on the side and twin candles still lodged into the top like a pair of antennae.

"What the devil is that?" the Prince asked non-plussed, stepping forwards to take a look at the curious object. Had Ella arranged for a pair of doves to burst forth from out of their cake as a show-stopping finale? If so, all seemed quiet inside now. "What is that?"

Ella turned scarlet at the sight of it but this was nothing compared to the colour the Grand Duke turned when he saw the strange object for what it was.

"Heavens above, it's a bomb!"

Everyone stumbled back in shock and panicked. The

bomb had taken one hell of a dent when it had fallen so who knew if it was about to go off but the Grand Duke assured everyone that it was perfectly safe.

"The device appears to be powder-ignited rather than contact," he said, realising that the attached candles were actually the devise's fuses. They would have been indistinguishable from the rest of the candles on the cake, the only difference was that their flames would have been seen from the other side of the city, never mind the Hall.

"Well where the bloody hell did it come from?" roared the King. "And how the hell did it get into our cake?"

Ella turned an accusatory finger at the sisters and hissed: "They did it. They must have planned it from the start. They intended to kill us all," to almost universal incredulity. But where before Ella's word had been taken as gospel, her explanation this time didn't make sense and the stony silence it was met with reflected that.

"How could they?" Mother said, pointing out. "Gardenia and I have been languishing in the dungeons these past four days and every guard in the land has been searching for Marigold. What did she do, break into the Palace and bake the wretched thing without anyone seeing?"

"Her accomplices then. She is in cahoots with our enemies. The plot is as clear as day," Ella said all too desperately but the Prince just looked at the cake and back at Ella in confusion.

"But the cake was made to your designs," he said. "You took charge of it personally."

Ella recoiled, as if this was the most ludicrous thing she'd ever heard and she shook her head. "Darling, think logically. Why would I plant a bomb next to my own place setting? I mean, seriously!"

It was a fair point but one that was easily pulled apart, this time by the head waiter who had been stood in the corner minding his own business until such a time as someone needed a refill or an explanation.

"The illuminations were to be lit once the guests had been seated but before Your Royal Highness had made her entrance, as you'll recall, Your Highness," he said with a smile, only too pleased to be of service, as was his remit.

"Upon your instructions," Ella told the Prince, backing herself into a corner both literally and metaphorically.

The Prince took exception to this and swore he'd had no such hand in the preparations. "It was you," he insisted. "It was all you."

"Me?" Ella shrugged with a simper. "How could I? I'm just a girl."

"As indeed are they," replied the Prince, glancing at Marigold and Gardenia with a little more sympathy than previously.

The sounds of weapons being cocked did little to reassure Ella that her charms were disarming her accusers. Instead, the wind seemed to have dropped altogether as the final piece of gold leaf fluttered unceremoniously to the floor. Between Ella and the locked doors were several *Watchmen*, each now holding their rifles unslung and cocked and each eyeing the Princess intently. The tables had been turned and not just by Marigold and Gardenia's size sevens. Where only moments earlier the sisters had found themselves cornered and alone, Ella now conspired to usurp them.

"But this is ridiculous," she laughed unconvincingly, moving slowly to avoid making any sudden movements. "They're assassins, for Heaven's sake. That old bag was caught red-handed in case you've all forgotten."

"On your bidding," Gardenia shouted. She had been denied the chance to speak at her own trial but would not be silenced a moment longer. "I was only there to catch your bridal bouquet. You set me up."

"Set you up?" Ella spluttered theatrically. "To do what, to shoot me with a crossbow?"

But the congregation were inclined to give Ella's stepsisters a fairer hearing in light of recent events. Even Captain Oliver had begun to ease up on Gardenia, not releasing her entirely but no longer seeing the need to push her head into the table quite so determinedly.

"No," said a voice towards the other side of the room. The King was still staring at the bomb when a moment of clarity took hold of him. "The bolt was intended for me. Just as this contraption was."

"You couldn't be more wrong," Ella insisted.

"Grimaldi! It was Grimaldi who fired the crossbow. She is in league with him," Marigold shouted in an attempt to hammer the final nail into Ella's coffin. This almost drew a contemptuous snark from Captain Olivier but then he thought better of it. If Ella were proved to be in league with the biggest marauder this side of the Alps, it would do his career prospects few favours if it became known that he had dismissed earlier reports of his return. And from these same witnesses too.

"Your Majesty, please, I beseech you," Ella said, throwing herself to the floor in an act of contrition but the King had heard enough.

"Beseech yourself you treasonous tart. Guards, seize the Princess."

But in that instant, Marigold caught sight of the glint in Ella's eye. She was not done with her tricks just yet. Just as she was not prostrate on the floor in an attempt to petition the King for mercy. She was ducking out of the line of fire with her henchmen getting ready to take aim.

"Oh hell!" said Marigold already too late.

Ella's face contorted into vengeance and now shouted at the top of her lungs: "*WATCHMEN*, PURGE!"

CHAPTER SIXTY-THREE

A THUNDERCLAP OF MUSKET FIRE filled the Great Hall. The King's Guards were the first to fall, shot down almost at point-blank range by the Princess's handpicked *Honour Watch* — handpicked from Grimaldi's best men to watch over her.

Such was the surprise that hardly a Guardsman got a shot off in reply. The King saw what was happening but he was powerless to act. All around his own troops were falling as the trap was sprung. He turned to flee he was already dead and he knew it.

Durand had him fixed in his sights. The turncoat looked resplendent in his crisp *Honour Watch* tunic but barely recognisable with his dyed hair and new set of whiskers. He'd drilled Grimaldi's men and helped them pass off as soldiers, but they'd needed no schooling in the art of killing. In this respect, they were in a league of their own. But in taking aim at the King, Durand would trump them all.

The King drew a breath to bark one last indignant scream but when the shot came he felt nothing. He touched his chest and found all was as it should be. Durand, on the other hand, was reeling into the furniture. A musket ball had struck his breech and his own weapon had exploded in his face. He staggered away screaming, his hands to his eyes and his beard on fire, no longer the possessor of the most exquisitely delightful features in all Andovia.

The King looked across the room and saw to his astonishment Mother, kneeling on the floor with a musket at her shoulder.

"Get a rifle!" she shouted at the King, tossing the empty weapon aside to grab another from the shoulder of a dead Guardsman.

Captain Olivier was in shock. The *Watchmen* under his

THE UGLY SISTERS

command had gone mad. They were killing everyone.

"Cease fire! Cease fire!" he demanded, jumping to his feet only to feel a punch to the back that knocked the wind from his sails. He reached up to touch his tunic and it felt wet. He tried to walk but had no strength. Without warning, he felt himself buckling as all hell let loose around him but he was now powerless to do anything about it. Gardenia jumped from the table and tried dragging him away to safety but his life was already forfeit. "Forgive me..." he whispered, picturing his name in granite and not minding it as much as he thought he might. The Captain fell silent but the rest of the room still raged around them like a thunderstorm. Gardenia pulled the Captain's pistol from his belt, took aim and fired at the nearest white tunic.

Marigold had likewise taken shelter behind a heavy table and had pulled a musket from a dead man's hand. The weapon was bulky and unwieldy but the enemy so close that she could scarcely miss, blasting one of Ella's infiltrators as he came charging with his sabre unsheathed.

Chaos and confusion reigned wherever the petrified Prince looked; the Hall hung thick with smoke, bodies lay everywhere and white and blue tunics grappled in the blood of others. After the initial round of musket fire, the *Honour Watch* attempted to finish the job with their bayonets. But one or two Guardsmen had clung on to repel their attack with Mother and the sisters caught in the middle.

The Grand Duke was distraught at the sight of his son stretched out in the middle of all this chaos. The King pulled him back behind an upturned table and told him to get a grip.

"Retribution is the best kind of medicine," he said, thrusting a pistol at the Duke and directing him towards the enemy. The Grand Duke fired, finishing off the last suckling pig but feeling better for it all the same. The King now handed him another.

"I'll load, you fire, and we'll get these blaggards yet."

Ella's coup hadn't quite gone to plan. The King and Prince still lived, albeit with the King fighting back and the Prince having disappeared. All the doors were locked so he must've been in here somewhere but Ella had no time to look. More soldiers would soon be on their way and if they weren't both dead by then, Ella most certainly would be. The Grand Duke and the last few Guardsmen too. There could be no witnesses to her treason otherwise she would not have been able to take the throne — and not as a Princess either, but as the sole and rightful Queen of Andovia.

"Kill them all. Leave no one alive," she said, urging her Srendizian murderers to finish the job but try as they might they had lost the initiative and now the lines were drawn, with the King's men on one side and Ella's on the other. Mother, Marigold and Gardenia found themselves in the middle and were loathed to pick a side. Both parties had been less than merciful toward them over the last few weeks, but necessity being the mother of all evil, they saw no choice but to throw their lot in with the King, if only because of the enemy they both shared.

Marigold scoured the Hall looking for Ella. With her dead, all of this would be over, but Marigold's shot went wide and Ella scrambled away, over the debris of her wedding breakfast and to where her cake lay in bits.

Gardenia took advantage of a brief lull and dashed across the Hall to join Marigold.

"We need to go. Let's get out of here!"

"Not before I put that little cow on her back," Marigold replied, pouring powder into her musket barrel and ramming home another shot as the upturned tabletop splintered around them both. Gardenia peered out and saw several white tunics move through the smoke. A shot from the King's table made them duck for cover but it was clear they were making their way around to room.

"Forget about her. We've got to go," she implored but

Marigold was of a mind to neither forget nor forgive. She took aim towards her stepsister's position and waited for her to pop out her head.

"Throw something. Make her look around," Marigold said. Gardenia looked around for things to throw and started hurling knives and forks, goblets and glasses until one of Ella's cronies took a shot in their direction.

"I really don't like this," Gardenia said, growing short with her sister.

Marigold glanced at her from her gunsights for a moment and cocked an eyebrow. "Let's not lose our heads over it, shall we."

"That's not even funny!" Gardenia said, punching Marigold on the arm just as Ella chose to appear. She was only there for a moment and then she was gone again, dashing away having done what she'd set out to do and running for the tapestry.

Gardenia saw Marigold's face fall. "What is it?" she asked, looking out to see the problem before her sister could say. Something cylindrical was rolling across the Hall towards where the King was sheltering. It was large and round and had two candles fizzing in its lid as it rolled.

Ella had lit the bomb and was now making good her escape.

"Oh, crumbs!"

Gardenia reacted instinctively, running out from behind the table and dashing through all hell to intercept the smoking canister. She hardly knew what she was doing and didn't have a chance to think. All she knew was that this thing wouldn't discriminate. It would kill everyone in the Great Hall and Ella would be victorious. And while the thought of death might not have appealed, the idea of Ella escaping was even more unpalatable. She had no choice. She had to get that bomb.

Marigold saw what she was doing but was too late to

stop her. Instead, she took aim and shot at the last of the *Honour Watch* who were fleeing through the secret door. Likewise, Mother was powerless to prevent her daughter's folly. All she could do was watch in horror.

"Gardenia, get away from it!" she cried but it was too late. Gardenia had caught the bomb halfway to its target and had hoisted it about her shoulders. The fuses were almost burned out. There was no time to act. Gardenia pirouetted like a ballerina, building up speed with every turn, before launching it in the direction of the open French windows.

"Down!" she shouted, dropping to her face the moment it left her fingers.

No sooner had the bomb dropped out of sight than it exploded like a thunderclap, knocking every last table onto its back and raking the Great Hall with broken glass. The dust and smoke made it feel like the world had come to an end and for the thousands of wasps roaming the skies outside it was, killed in the shock wave to put a stop to their short but spectacular reign of terror.

With his ears still ringing and his face white with dust, the King looked out from behind his table to see Gardenia standing in the middle of the Great Hall, brushing herself down.

"Heavens above, girl, what possessed you to do that?" he asked.

Gardenia looked at the King and smiled sweetly. "She told me to catch her bouquet," she shrugged, "so I caught it."

Marigold now looked around the room. It had been almost entirely demolished with the tapestry in tatters and oak-panels peppered with shot. If Ella's plan had come to fruition, it would have doubtlessly killed everyone in the Great Hall, all the rich and the powerful, the great and the good. There would have been a power vacuum like no other. Lawlessness would have followed, all overseen by the new Queen and her Srendizian sponsors. But this was something to ponder later at their leisure. For now, the sisters had work to do. And a family squabble to resolve once and for all.

"Come on, let's go!" Marigold demanded, making for the tapestry and grabbing two pistols as she went. Gardenia followed despite the King's protestations.

"Wait a minute, where are you going? Come back here! Come back, I say!" he shouted but his cries were to no avail. Marigold and Gardenia left by the way they had come in and the banquet was over. There was just one course left to be served and it was Mother who would be serving it.

Cold — just as vengeance should be served.

"Alone at last, Your Grace," she said, staring down the barrel of her musket at the man she'd spent the last sixteen years plotting to kill.

CHAPTER SIXTY-FOUR

MARIGOLD AND GARDENIA had spent so much time in this subterranean side passage that it almost felt like a home away from home. Marigold was racing on ahead but Gardenia quickly caught up to ask what she was doing.

"We can't let Ella get away or we'll never see the Corporals again," Marigold replied, meaning Babin and Deniau. They may have been dead already, murdered the moment Grimaldi carted them away, but there was just a chance that they were not and with Ella in their care, they might be able to get them back.

Voices ahead compelled the sisters to slow up and listen. In the wine cellar around the corner, Ella had met more of her *Watchmen* and they had a nasty surprise for her.

"What do you mean he's not dead?" she said, scarcely believing what she'd just heard.

"It is true, Your Majesty, both the King and the Prince have been sighted at the windows of the Great Hall. They escaped the blast unharmed," she was told.

"But that's impossible. That bomb was big enough to destroy everything in that room," she said, unwilling to accept she'd failed in her second bid to assassinate the King.

"And so it would had it not been thrown from the window. The Palace facade has been destroyed but his Majesty lives. We have to go."

This was appalling news. Ella's plans were now in ruins and a swift and merciful reckoning would surely follow. All she could do was flee, escape the Kingdom and disappear. Grimaldi wouldn't be happy after all he'd invested but this was no fault of Ella's. If he'd been able to shoot straight in the first place she wouldn't have had to resort to such extreme measures. The King would be dead, she would be Queen and Marigold and Gardenia would have carried the can for it. Ella cursed the day she'd ever heard of Andovia. Or moreover, laid eyes on her dour stepsisters.

"Damn them to hell!" she hissed, hurling a bottle of cognac at the far wall.

Crouched behind the furthermost wine rack, Marigold felt a warm glow of delight at Ella's frustration, only to realise that it was actually the heat from the fire she had just started. This was to be Ella's parting gift to her soon-to-be ex-husband and father-in-law. A bottle of cognac and a naked flame. It quickly spread and engulfed an entire wall. Ella and her *Watchmen* left, taking advantage of the diversion in order to slip out of the Palace grounds but Marigold and Gardenia were stuck, unable to follow because of the flames and unwilling to give up the chase.

"That spoilt little brat," Marigold commented, dashing towards the fire to see what could be done. A great many of the spirits were flammable but the wines were not so the girls set about hurling bottle after bottle into the flames until they eventually brought the fire under control. A couple of crates of the King's finest champagne extinguished the last of the flames and the girls congratulated themselves on becoming the first female firefighters in Andovian history and definitely the most expensive.

"Somehow, I don't think the King's going to thank us for this," Gardenia ruminated, standing in several million schillings worth of booze. Marigold agreed and led off, hoping to never see this terrible ghastly wine cellar ever again.

The grounds were deserted when they emerged into daylight. Everyone had run to the front of the Palace following the explosion to see what had happened. Voices were shouting, Guards were responding and whistles were blowing but Marigold and Gardenia were no longer the main focus of the commotion. Ella and her *Watchmen* had got away.

"Come on, we can still catch them," Marigold urged.

"How? We don't even know where they're going,"

Gardenia replied but Marigold did. It was so obvious that she didn't know why she hadn't thought of it.

Shortly after Ella had come to Andovia, Hans had told her that he'd seen tracks in the mountains. Riders from the north. This also explained Grimaldi's use of crossbows, silent weapons best suited to a place unsympathetic to loud noises.

In normal circumstances, the girls might've reported their suspicions to the authorities, but given that the authorities had tried to stick Gardenia's head on a spike barely twenty minutes earlier, neither was inclined to put their faith in the system so soon afterwards.

"I know how to get there. If we set off now we'll be able to follow their tracks in the snows," Marigold said.

"But it's miles away. How will we get there?"

At the far end of the Palace gardens stood the royal stables. Most of the horses inside were still twitchy and unsettled from the noise of the explosion but there was one horse with his face in the food bag who seemed indifferent to it all. When Mother and the girls had been brought to the Palace by Captain Olivier, Liquorice had come too; a grizzled old warhorse stabled alongside the King's thoroughbred fillies. How apt.

He perked up the moment he saw Marigold and greeted her with a snort.

"Good to see you too, boy," she replied, stroking his nose. "Want to go for a ride?"

*

BACK AT THE PALACE, a newly arrived detachment of King's Guards started pounding on the doors of the Great Hall but no one was available to answer. Mother had the King, the Prince and the Grand Duke at the end of her musket sights and she was in no mood for company.

"Order your men away," she told the King, pointing the barrel at the bead of sweat that was caught on the bridge of his nose. "Do it now."

"Madam, have you taken leave of your senses? Put that weapon down immediately and let's have no more of this," he demanded, albeit none too convincingly. But Mother had waited a long time for her vengeance and she wasn't about to be denied now.

"One…" she began counting. "Two… Three…"

"THIS IS YOUR KING SPEAKING," he shouted at the door, having already guessed that there wouldn't be a four. "I ORDER YOU TO… TO… GO AWAY."

"But Your Majesty, are you alright in there?" a junior Lieutenant called back.

"I SAID BUGGER OFF!" the King replied. "THIS INSTANT."

There was a short pause while the King's Guards deliberated their orders before complying. "Very good, Your Majesty. As you wish." And with that, there was a *stomp stomp stomp* of departing bootsteps and Mother and the royal party were alone again.

"Now Madam, what's all this about?" the King asked anxiously.

"Widows' Ridge," she uttered, barely able to speak its accursed name.

"Widows' Ridge?" the King asked in confusion.

Mother shifted the musket from the King's head to the Grand Duke's and scowled down at him in contempt. "Yes, Widows' Ridge. You remember that, don't you, Your Grace?"

As indeed he should. The Grand Duke had commanded the King's Guards during that glorious final chapter of the Seven Years War. He'd joined the regiment years earlier and had served as a young Lieutenant before winning quick promotions to Captain, Major and Colonel before his exploits in Srendizi had won him Andovia's highest military medal and the rank of Supreme Commander, a rank he still held today despite having left the army to assume his duties as Grand Duke.

"You don't recognise me, do you?" Mother said, yearning to pull the trigger but not before the Grand Duke knew why.

"Of course I know who you are. You're that ghastly Princess's stepmother. We talked at the wedding," he said, scarcely scratching the surface of their shared history.

"Oh, but I'm so much more than that," she said, retreating a few steps to tear open the back of her dress. "Look again," she told him, turning to show him a crisscross of discoloured welts across her back. "You remember me now?"

The Grand Duke looked long and hard into the past. He'd seen dozens of people flogged in his time; men, women and children alike, but only one of a feral little forest child with the brazen attitude had left an indelible impression on him. He may not have been able to recall the face but the enmity was unmistakable and here, years later, as inconceivable as it could be, he saw her in the woman before him.

"The girl?" he said, almost incredulous.

"The rat," she corrected him, giving him the same steely glare she'd given him while strapped to the cannon to await justice. The Grand Duke turned white, as though he'd seen a ghost, and shrank before her.

"You mean to say you actually know this woman?" the King asked, astonished. The circles some people moved in beggared belief.

"It wasn't my fault. I was only following regulations," the Grand Duke insisted, still scarcely able to believe that the forest girl had come back for her pound of flesh after all these years. "It was the Captain, in fact. He ordered me to have you shot. I insisted we let you off with a flogging."

But Mother wasn't interested in hearing any of his lies. She'd long forgotten her lashes and bore the Grand Duke no malice for them. If anything they'd performed a service, joining her life with Armand's. No, it was her husband she was here for. Sergeant Armand Roche and the King's Men. They were unable to speak for themselves and so Mother would speak for them. And exact the vengeance she'd spent half a lifetime seeking.

"You know what the curious thing is? There was an assassination attempt on the day of the royal wedding. But it was not aimed at the King, or Princess or even the Prince," Mother told the Grand Duke. "It was aimed at you, Your Grace."

"Me?" he gawped, not understanding what Mother meant.

"And if you'd just drunk your glass of champagne like a good little boy we wouldn't have to do this the hard way now."

"Wait! Wait!" the Grand Duke implored. "Your blood is up, Madam. Do not act in haste or else you will repent at leisure."

"Act in haste?" she almost laughed. "I've spent years trying to get close enough to you to poison you. I have clawed my way up through society, ingratiated myself to the worst of people and even exploited my own daughters in the hope of receiving a moment's grace from you. All for one reason and one reason only: restitution."

"Restitution?" said the King. "For whom?"

"For my husband, Your Majesty. And for the King's Men."

"The King's Men!" the King gasped.

It is said that history is written by the winners and so it was following Widows' Ridge. The official version of events, based on the report that the Grand Duke sent the King, bore little comparison to what had actually happened on that fateful day but it had won the Grand Duke the Andovian Cross and a few stitches on a Palace tapestry. His glory had reflected upon the King and the King's glory had reflected upon all Andovia, so no one ever thought to question the account. To do so would have been tantamount to disrespect. Thus, the official account read as such: after a five-day march through hostile territory, the King's Guard came under heavy attack from an Austrian ambush. The enemy numbered several hundred and had them pinned down on both sides. The King's Guards would have been wiped out had it not been for the quick thinking of their commanding officer, Colonel Olivier, who directed his men to capture the high ground overlooking the enemy and repel their attack. After several bloody assaults and a good deal of encouragement from their unwavering commander, the Andovian flag eventually flew over the Austrian position, forcing the enemy to withdraw and saving the Andovians from complete annihilation. The battle barely merited a footnote in the margins of the Treaty of Paris but it was enough to earn the King a tiny slice of the spoils. There was only one problem.

"It was all a lie," Mother told him.

The King had no idea and was staggered to learn the shameful truth, that so many men had been sacrificed so needlessly in the pursuit of the Grand Duke's personal ambition — and in his name too.

"The King's men," he said, finally seeing the significance of this seditious call to arms.

"I was with the Guards when they took the Ridge. My husband, Sergeant Armand Roche, the finest and most loyal man to ever serve in any army, gave his life to save his men. He climbed the ridge and waved your precious flag and yet lies forgotten in a mass grave along with a hundred others, Andovian and Austrian alike," Mother said through a veil of bitter tears. "And this is why I must avenge him. This is why I must avenge them all. In the name of the King's men, His Grace must die."

But just as she was about to pull the trigger, the musket barrel was snatched from her and the shot went wide, blasting a hole just inches from where the Grand Duke's head had been.

Mother turned to see Captain Olivier back from the dead and just in the nick of time too. His chest was bleeding and one arm hung limp but he'd found enough just strength to save his father from this mad old hag.

"By God, we have you now," the Grand Duke roared as he jumped to his feet and wrestled Mother to the wall, his strength reborn in the face of extreme provocation. "Open the doors and call in the Guards. We have a flogging to administer. And I intend to see to this one myself. Just like old times, hey rat!"

CHAPTER SIXTY-FIVE

MARIGOLD AND GARDENIA had grabbed more than just Liquorice when they came away from the Palace stables. They also borrowed riding boots and winter coats for the long trek north. It would be cold where they were going — cold and inhospitable — away from the city and into the clouds of *Mont Magie*. The snows were lower in the mountains than the last time Marigold had been here, a sure sign that winter was on its way, so they picked up Ella's trail easily. Fresh tracks led up through the pass, around the winding trails and into the deeper snows of the precarious north face. Permanently steeped in shadows and potted with drifts that could swallow a person whole, the north face was a dangerous place to traverse even without being on the trail of a murderous lunatic. Marigold eased back on Liquorice's reins and slid from his saddle.

"We should go on foot from here."

Marigold led the way with Gardenia and Liquorice following in single file behind. The sun was setting and fresh snows began to fall. In no time at all Ella's tracks were gone and they'd lost the trail. Liquorice seemed to favour one direction over another so they followed his lead, eventually coming to a small valley that was sheltered from the worst of the weather. Here, at the entrance of this valley, stood a rustic winter stable that had been partially built into the rock, probably what Liquorice had sensed. Further on, and nestled in the shadows of *Mont Magie*'s most desolate slope, was a dilapidated old hunting lodge and a few ramshackled outhouses — all that was left of Ella's realm. It must have been one hell of a comedown for a girl who'd almost been Queen.

They approached with care, keeping low and moving slowly before arriving at the side of the stable. Inside, the bandits' horses acknowledged their presence with a snort but no one was with them to raise the alarm. It was too cold out here and the light was fading fast. The snows were getting deeper and the wind was baring its teeth. Night was almost upon them.

"Let's see if they're in there. Come on, keep quiet," said Marigold, putting a gloved finger to her chapped lips.

"I'm so glad I have you to keep reminding me," Gardenia replied from inside her hood, her feet near-frozen despite her fur-lined boots.

Marigold stabled Liquorice with the other horses and gave him a bucket of oats to keep him out of trouble. The last thing she needed was to have him wandering off. Chances were, when it came time to leave, they would need to leave in a hurry.

The sisters edged their way around the valley, sticking to the shadows and approaching the lodge from the side. Candles burned within and the chimney belched smoke but no one looked out. There was no point. There was nothing to see out here but snow and more snow.

Marigold and Gardenia crouched by a small side window and peeped inside. Through the dirty glass, they could make out a dozen people, either huddled around an open hearth or pacing restlessly. On her feet and lambasting anyone who'd listen to her was Ella, unmistakable even in her heavy winter gear. Neither Marigold nor Gardenia could make out the particulars of her tirade but they recognised the rhetoric and sympathised with those on the receiving end. Durand sat to one side, with bandages wrapped around his face and his fingers around a bottle of schnapps. Even beneath his dressings, Marigold could make out his expression, angry and snarling, and now fixed that way for keeps.

Likewise, in the opposite corner, skulked Grimaldi, silent and brooding. He had much on his mind, not least of all what he should do with his paper Princess. He and his men were used to living with a price on their heads but how would this delicate snowflake react? Hardship and discomfort drove people to act rashly. He would have to keep a close eye on Ella from now on. Or come up with a — beneficial — way of dissolving their partnership.

"Our best shooters. That's all we need. We line the routes around the Palace and I could be crowned Queen yet," Ella was demanding of her cold and indifferent collaborators. "Hello! I'm talking to you here."

But Grimaldi just grunted and spat an olive pip into the fire in front of him.

"I am next in line after Prince. By law. Nothing has changed. And those dopey Andovians are nothing if not sticklers for tradition."

"We ride north," Grimaldi said instead. "We move out tomorrow, burn the lodge and cover our tracks. The clock has struck twelve. And this party is over."

"That wasn't our agreement," Ella snapped, causing one or two of Grimaldi's men to raise an eyebrow. "You vowed to make me Queen and I'm not the Queen of anything yet so get off your backsides and go and do what you said."

Grimaldi jumped to his feet with an agility that startled Ella. He glowered down at her menacingly before baring his crooked teeth and removing his hat.

"Your Majesty," he said with a theatrical bow, much to the amusement of his men.

"So that is it, is it?" Ella asked when he flopped back into his chair and popped another olive into his mouth. "You're just going to give up?"

"It was over a long time ago," Grimaldi said, spitting the pip into the fire to watch it crackle. "You're just having trouble accepting that fact." Ella looked around the lodge and was met by the same surly expressions on every face. They'd been promised riches beyond their wildest dreams and yet had nothing to show for their endeavours except the loss of half their comrades. As bandits, there were none better. But as subjects loyal to a cause, their indifference knew no bounds. Particularly when that cause was lost. And the only thing on offer anymore was the snap of a noose. Only Durand thirsted for vengeance as much as Ella, but he was shrewd enough to keep this thought to himself.

But Ella refused to let the dream die. She'd come so close, worn the crown and been feted by the people. Her people. Surely, if she went to them now they would rise up in support of her out of love.

Grimaldi burst out laughing and almost choked on his olive. It was an evil sadistic laugh that few people heard. And lived to tell the tale.

"I wouldn't count on it," he said when his amusement had ebbed. "Fear is what drives men's hearts, not love. Grab them by the balls and their hearts will follow."

"And what of women? What of girls?" Ella asked pointedly.

Grimaldi stared at her and rasped his lips. "What of them?" he replied with disdain, lifting two feet into the grate and closing his eyes.

The girls outside might have taken issue with Grimaldi but they were no longer listening. Instead, having seen no signs of Babin and Deniau in the lodge, they were now searching the outhouses. The first was a frozen toilet that looked like it was going to cause the cleaners a lot of problems come Spring. The second was an arms cache of crossbows, bolts and swords. While the last was a provisions store filled with grain, cheap schnapps and a half-empty barrel of black olives. Marigold almost missed Babin when she first searched the place. He was bundled up and buried beneath a stack of blankets against the cold and almost too weak to open his eyes. Deniau was alongside him, white as the snows that lay about and scarcely breathing. Both men's hands and feet were tied but there was little need. Neither could have made it to the door unaided let alone down the mountain.

Marigold cut Babin's bonds and handed Gardenia the knife. "Corporal. Corporal," she whispered into Babin's ear, shaking him awake but ready to cover his mouth in the event he cried out. Babin opened his eyes and looked up at Marigold dreamily.

"Are you real?" he asked with some effort.

Marigold kissed him to prove that she was before pulling him to his feet. "Come on, we're getting you out of here."

The sisters dressed the Corporals as best they could. Time was not on their side. Anyone could wander in at any moment looking for a bottle of schnapps or a handful of olives so they knew they had to get out of here as quickly as possible.

Gardenia covered a couple of grain sacks with blankets to make it look as though the prisoners were still there but it wouldn't fool anyone who leaned in for a closer inspection. "It'll have to do," she told herself, hoisting Deniau to his feet and helping him towards the door.

Outside the winds had dropped and the heavy snows fell to settle with scarcely a sound. Marigold led Babin towards the mountain trail, grimacing with every step as their boots crunched into the fresh snows to break the deathly silence. Gardenia followed in their tracks, struggling after the others with Deniau leaning on her for support. He tumbled onto his face and only found the strength to climb to his feet when Gardenia got angry with him.

"I've not come all this way for you to give up now, so get on your feet and move it, Corporal!" she scolded him, half-carrying half-dragging him towards the stables to where Marigold was already helping Babin into Liquorice's saddle.

She slipped his boots into the stirrups and handed him the reins, then saddled up a second horse for Gardenia and Deniau.

"Release the others," Babin suggested. "It'll make it harder for them to come after us." The sisters did as he said, opening up the rest of the pens and shooing Grimaldi's horses out. A few were reluctant to leave but a little encouragement soon saw them heading out into the cold to leave Grimaldi with a long walk back to Srendizi.

"Let's get going," she told Babin, leading Liquorice out of the stable with Gardenia and Deniau following.

"And where exactly do you think you're going?" said a voice when she stepped outside.

Marigold froze. The sudden shock of being confronted almost made her legs give way. She couldn't tell where the voice had come from but it had been close. She looked around, peering through the veil of snows, and saw, to her dismay, Durand stepping forth with a crossbow in his hands. The Captain no longer needed to go seeking vengeance. Vengeance had sought him out.

"Nice and easy," said a second voice, aimed not at the girls but at the former Captain. All at once, the shadows stirred and more of Grimaldi's men stepped forth from the night. Durand glowered, aching to pull the trigger but restrained enough to know that his life would be forfeit if he did. Like an overgrown cat, Grimaldi liked to toy with his prey before dispatching it, but the Captain would get his chance. Even if it was just as a spectator, Durand would see these ugly harlots pay for his precious face.

Gardenia was too angry to be disconsolate. They'd come so far and had got so close, how could this be? Another minute and they would have been clean away. What had they done wrong?

"Delicious, isn't it?" said Ella as she drew back her hood. Her hair was quickly drenched with snow but Ella didn't flinch. She was as cold as ice already.

"What is?" asked Marigold, taking the bait.

"Seeing someone else's hopes and dreams fall at the final hurdle," Ella said vindictively, her own bleak and wretched future not looking nearly so bleak and wretched next to their uninvited — but very welcome — guests.

Marigold steadied Liquorice and looked up at Corporal Babin. One good slap and they might break free but neither of them would abandon her and she knew it. Darn honour and all that.

"We're not here for you," Marigold explained. "We just want our friends back. Let us go and you'll never see us again."

"Sisters. How could you say such a thing? After all we've been through," Ella simpered, taking a step towards Marigold with her arms outstretched.

Marigold drew her flintlock and warned her to get back.

"Any of you try anything and I'll kill her," she said, directing her warning at Grimaldi in particular who was watching closely. The hulking bandit smirked as though daring Marigold to do her worst. He had little use for Ella anymore and she'd all but worn out her welcome. She might have fetched a good price where he was going but that was four days from here and four more days of listening to her bellyaching didn't appeal.

"Do what you have to do, mademoiselle," Grimaldi replied, intrigued to see if Marigold had the courage of her convictions. Most people didn't.

Ella sneered. "Do you see the esteem I'm held in?" she said bitterly. "And it's all your fault."

"Our fault?" Gardenia said, now also with pistol drawn, for all the good it would do.

"It was so perfect. I had the Prince right where I wanted him. The Kingdom was mine. All the days and weeks of planning. All the thousands of schillings invested. All the lives that were lost. And you ruined everything," Ella vented, glad to finally have a target for her frustrations.

"Because we wouldn't roll over and die?" Marigold almost laughed.

"Everyone dies," Ella replied. "What's your problem?"

"You first," Marigold invited.

"You still don't get it, do you? You're pawns in a game far greater than you could ever imagine. And pawns sacrifice themselves for their Queen. That's what pawns are for." Ella was nothing if not committed to the concept of her own glory. As she'd once pointed out, there were no paintings of seamstresses hanging in the palaces of Europe. The annals of history were reserved for Kings and Queens alone. Those who had risen to the very top and left their mark upon this world. There was only one problem.

"You're not a Queen," Marigold said. "And you never will be."

Ella's face turned to thunder. "Enough of this," she snapped, knowing that her stepsisters didn't have it in them to shoot her, even with their own lives in jeopardy. "Seize them." Unfortunately for Ella, what she failed to realise was that her authority counted for even less with Grimaldi than it did with her own stepsisters. When nobody moved Ella ordered them again, only to invoke a few merciless chuckles — and a snarl from Durand.

"What's wrong with you all?" she said. "Didn't you hear what I said?"

"They heard," Grimaldi said with a growl. "But they don't take orders from the dead."

Ella turned and glared at the blackhearted fiend. She knew he was a snake but until now she had held him in the palm of her hand, just as she had the Prince. Alas, such was her single-minded self-involvement that it hadn't occurred to her that the moment the prize was gone, so was her value.

"Wait," she said, backing away. "We had a deal."

"And so we did," Grimaldi confirmed with a flash of evil in his eye. "And as you know, us outlaws always keep our word."

His lackeys laughed and Ella finally snapped out of her conceit to see that her predicament was no laughing matter. Before she could take another step, she found herself beside her stepsisters and saw that their pistols were no longer trained on her.

"Step to it, boys," Grimaldi now roared. "Kill the soldiers and bring the mademoiselles. All three of them."

This was the moment Durand had been waiting for. His beef with the sister was finally to be slaked. And he was more than happy to start with their precious Corporals.

Even with two pistols, the girls were hopelessly outnumbered. They might've been able to drop a couple of them but they couldn't drop them all and Grimaldi would make them pay for their defiance. Not that he wouldn't anyway. But Marigold had one last card to play. And one that the old bandit had clean forgotten about.

"Make an ally of gravity!" Marigold told her sister and together they fired as one to send a deafening crack racing up the snow-covered mountainside. Durand ducked but quickly realised that the sisters had not only missed, they had missed by a mile.

"You even shoot like girls," he sneered, at least until he heard distant popping sound followed by an ominous rumbling that seemed to grow by the second. He turned to look up the slopes and sure enough, *Mont Magie* had awoken and was now racing towards them in a cascade of fury.

"Away!" Grimaldi hollered but it was too late. His winter lodge was quickly buried beneath a wall of snow as the avalanche surged over them.

Marigold slapped Liquorice on the hind and he didn't need telling twice. He charged away with Babin on his back and Deniau's horse on his heels, heading back down the mountain as though the Devil himself were thundering after him.

Grimaldi and his men tried to scatter but there was no way they could outrun death. Marigold knew better than to try and had gambled accordingly, albeit with little to lose.

"In here," she shouted, bundling Gardenia and Ella into the stables just as *Mont Magie*'s wrath swept all before them. The structure had been built into the granite for added support but it splintered like matchwood beneath the weight of the cascade, quickly filling with snow and slamming the girls against the rocks at the back of the pens. The roar was like nothing they'd ever heard, louder than a hundred thunderstorms at once, and just when it all seemed like it would never end, everything turned black and the mountain fell silent.

Mont Magie slept once more.

As did the souls of those who had once walked upon her.

CHAPTER SIXTY-SIX

IT WAS DAYBREAK when Marigold came to. Her world was still dark but she could sense light coming in from somewhere. It took her a moment to remember the events of the previous evening but when she did she realised where she was. Her legs were trapped beneath a great weight and her body felt cold and sore. A few bits of straw tickled her face and invaded her clothing to leave her racked with discomfort. She tried to free her arms to scratch her nose but they were pinned to her sides by something heavy. After a little probing, she found it was another person. She could barely turn her head but she knew it was her sister. She'd shared a room with Gardenia long enough to recognise her breathing and nudged her until she began to stir.

"Five more minutes," Gardenia muttered before noticing where she was. "Oh!"

"Can you move your hands?" Marigold asked.

Gardenia could and, what's more, felt someone on the other side of her — Ella.

"She's alive," she confirmed and once they'd roused her the three sisters began the painstaking process of clawing their way out, inch by inch, up through the ice pack and into the blue skies above.

The girls had ridden their luck and no mistake. They'd been buried in a small air pocket at the back of the stables, protected by the fallen roof and kept warm through shared heat and straw. Some might have said it was a miracle. Others that it was science. But Marigold had a better explanation.

"It was our Fairy Godmother," she told Gardenia as they took stock of their position. The mountain had been wiped clean. Grimaldi, Durand and the others were gone. All they found to suggest that anyone had ever been here was a handful of black olives dotted around in the snow.

Everything else had simply vanished. As if by magic.

"Come on," Marigold said, "let's go home."

Ella was reluctant to follow and the girls were reluctant to have her along but they put their hostilities aside while they walked off the mountain. Ella told them of her determination to head north once they got to the pass and said she was prepared to fight to the death if they tried to drag her back to Andovia but neither Marigold nor Gardenia were of a mood to fight anyone to the death this morning, least of all their stepsister. Not after the night they'd had.

"You're free to go anytime you like," Marigold said.

"On one condition," Gardenia agreed. "We don't ever want to see your ugly face again."

Ella laughed and almost embraced her stepsisters. "At last, we can agree upon something."

Unfortunately, it wasn't to be. Waiting for them at the pass was a detachment of King's Guards, sent to search for the sisters after Babin and Deniau had been found at the foot of the mountain, still clinging onto their horses, alive but only just. It had been Hans who'd found them. He'd been here with his bucket as usual, gathering ice for another day's trading. The Kingdom might be in chaos, the Palace half-destroyed and the Princess on the run but the people still needed their ice pops. Some things were too important to let politics get in the way of.

"Your Highness, if you please," a Guardsman said, inviting Ella to take a seat in the waiting carriage. Though heartening as it was to still be referred to as "Your Highness", Ella decided not to read too much into it seeing as the invitation had been made at the point of a bayonet. Marigold and Gardenia were placed in the carriage too and the three Beaufort girls trundled off the mountain, through golden fields of spun wheat and verdant orchards, and back to the city they'd fled, and to the uncertain futures that awaited them.

The crowds turned out in their droves as word spread of their return. None could quite believe their eyes at seeing the three sisters together; the Princess, the assassin and the insurrectionist. How could three girls have caused so much turmoil?

For their part, the sisters couldn't get over how grotesque the people all appeared. The wasps had really gone to town on everyone and their faces had swelled accordingly. It was as if the whole of Andovia had turned ugly overnight. Everyone except the three sisters, of course. They'd escaped unscathed. But not for long.

Nobody cheered as they drove on by. Nobody jeered and nobody even leered. The crowds just watched in silence as the girls were escorted back to the Palace, unsure of what this meant or what tomorrow might bring.

Ella looked across at Marigold and Gardenia and saw they were holding hands as the carriage clattered up the final straight. It occurred to her that for a time she and her stepsisters had been close. It hadn't lasted long and, from her point of view, it had simply served as a means to an end. But now that it was all over she wondered if she had spurned one set of riches in pursuit of another. It was a thought that unsettled her but, try as she might, she couldn't escape it.

The scaffold that Gardenia had ascended still stood in the Square. All stared at it warily and wondered which of them, if any, would tread its boards. If indeed, they would be let off so lightly this time.

The Palace loomed large before them and, much like its people, looked to have suffered miserably, with its front windows blown in, the balconies destroyed, part of the roof missing and huge ugly scar scorched across its lily-white facade. If nothing else, Ella had written her name into the history books with this act alone. For as briefly as it had lasted, her reign as Andovia's fairytale Princess would surely be remembered for centuries to come.

"I hope with time they remember me kindly," Ella said before turning to her sisters and declaring: "There's nothing so reviled in this world as a girl who shows ambition."

Waiting for them on the steps of the Palace stood another girl who'd harboured similar ambitions to Ella. Mother had clung onto her hatred for so long that she could scarcely remember a day of sun. Everything she had done and everything she had striven for since Widows' Ridge had been fuelled by one intention. But now, and in the most unexpected of circumstances, her reckoning had been served. The clouds had parted and her wrath dispelled. The *King's Men* had been laid to rest. And Mother was finally free.

The carriage pulled up to the steps and Mother helped her daughters down.

"What's going on? What's happening?" Marigold asked in surprise, looking around and noticing that for the first time in days that no one was pointing a rifle at them. The Guards had shouldered the muskets and the staff were stood to attention. It was most unexpected.

"Fear not my dears, it is perfectly safe. For we have friends in high places," she said, indicating up to the shattered windows above to where the King stood looking out.

She embraced her daughters and held them close, the tears spilling down her cheeks. In days gone by Mother would never have dreamed of making such a public exhibition of herself but now she had no such reservations.

"I am proud of you both," she told Marigold and Gardenia. "My big, brave and beautiful girls."

Finally, she looked up to see Ella still sat in her seat and nervously looking around for her own welcoming party. Mother parted from her daughters and extended a hand.

"Fear not," she said, enticing her stepdaughter down from the carriage with a little cajoling. Ella, as reluctant as she was, had no choice but to accept. They may have been mortal enemies until recently and she may have tried to kill all three of them in various ways but they were still her family. Everyone else on the planet was a stranger.

Mother smiled to put her at her ease.

"Come," she told them, turning to lead her three daughters up the stone steps and into the once-magnificent Palace. "I fancy we have much to discuss."

CHAPTER SIXTY-SEVEN

THE GRAND DUKE NEVER got to administer his flogging. He might have overpowered Mother and called in the Guards but she wasn't the one they arrested. The King had heard enough. The Grand Duke's treachery was a revelation to him. The lies he'd told, the men he'd sacrificed and the families he'd destroyed, all in the pursuit of personal ambition were unforgivable. He and his ineffectual son were clapped in irons and carted off to the dungeons forthwith; his titles revoked, his lands confiscated and his riches used to compensate those he had wronged.

Finally, the King had come riding to the defence of those who had given all in his name.

Mother was key in advising the King on the things that had been kept from him. And what the people really felt. Not the Lords or the Barons or the Dukes or the Viscounts but the people. Those he regarded as his loyal subjects. Needless to say, the King was appalled to hear the truth but hear it he did, and without interruption too. Mother and her daughters had saved the Kingdom, not to mention his and his only son's lives. She had earned the right to speak freely.

"Go on," he would say, urging her to continue until she had lifted the veil on forty years of fawning.

And while the King might not have liked what he heard, he appreciated it all the same. Not because it was refreshing to hear Mother rattling off some of the funnier songs the town's sewing circles sang about him but because knowing the truth at least gave him a sense of perspective as to his own place in history. And he had no desire to end up being mocked for all eternity like Ethelred the Unready or John the Careless. These vain and feckless Kings, who had no doubt thought very highly of themselves during their own lifetimes, had become the objects of ridicule for generations to come. Their lives and misdeeds summed up with one single unflattering word. It was a bitter pill for the King to swallow but at least it gave him a chance to do something about it. Few rulers got the chance to rewrite their own epitaphs before it was too late.

"Of course, once the truth gets out about this whole hullabaloo we're finished, both me and the boy. That'll be us for all time," he lamented, seeing no way out of the corner he'd painted himself into. The history students of the future would need a special dictionary to look up the adjectives he'd reserved for himself. Him and his foolish scheme to bully the Prince into marriage.

"Not necessarily," Mother had suggested. She knew the King would be finished when the truth came out. The Barons would take the opportunity to rise up, his throne would be usurped and like would change for like at the top, while nothing would change for anyone else at the bottom. Life would still be tough. And brutal. And short. But there was an opportunity to be had if the King was courageous enough to take it. It wouldn't be easy and it might even be dangerous but if the King was amenable, maybe just maybe, history might remember him as the most benevolent ruler of all time. And Sergeant Roche's great-great-granddaughters might grow up in a very different Kingdom indeed.

"There is another way?" Mother suggested.

The plan depended on Ella's cooperation but, given her options, Ella was open to offers.

And so a story was concocted and a legend was born. Ella — or Cinderella as she was to be dubbed — was confirmed to be the simple country girl she had claimed to be who went on to become a Princess. And while the stories of her tumultuous relationship with her stepfamily were true (because it was too complicated to rewrite them now) the plot against her had been none of her sisters' doing. That dastardly betrayal had been engineered by the Grand Duke,

THE UGLY SISTERS

with the help of the *Bandit King*, Franz Grimaldi. The Prince had used Marigold and Gardenia as bait to help smoke the traitors out and disaster had been averted when a bomb had been discovered in the Princess's cake. The sisters were cleared of all wrongdoing and had "even helped in some small way" lead the authorities to the real perpetrators. And in doing so, they had absolved themselves of their misdeeds and all was forgiven between them and the girl they once fed their leftovers to.

The sisters and the Princess didn't see much of each other after that. The sisters dropped out of the spotlight and the Princess had a busy schedule of appearances to keep up. At twelve o'clock each day she would appear at the windows of the Palace and then again at six, always in a different outfit and always smiling and waving to her people. It was said that a person could set their pocket watch by her and a great many people did just that. Occasionally, she would be seated at official banquets — but always on a special table reserved for her alone and always with several Guards in close attendance — but Cinderella was never heard to speak in public again. The Prince took care of this sort of thing for her. He was, after all, a man. And who knew a woman's mind better than her husband?

Besides, it was generally agreed that Cinderella's greatest attributes were her grace and beauty. She was a fairytale Princess, just as she'd always dreamed of being. What more could any girl wish for?

Unfortunately, as Marigold had predicted, she would never become Queen. For the King had made the momentous decision to break with the past and drive Andovia into the future, whether it was ready for it or not.

"Therefore," the King announced to his people from his newly rebuilt balcony with the Prince and Princess by his side, "we have decided to create a new kind of Kingdom — one without a King."

There were gasps of consternation. A Kingdom without a King? Who had ever heard of such a thing? The King appealed for silence and went on to explain how it would all work.

"As such, I shall step down with immediate effect and resign from my royal duties. I will forthwith vacate the Palace and retire to the countryside to tend a smallholding, an ordinary citizen of Andovia," he smiled, and not disingenuously either. The thought of getting away from the pressure cooker of power and tending to a few chickens genuinely appealed to the King. He might have enjoyed a lifetime of unrivalled privilege and had more money than he could have spent in a thousand years but he was getting old. And a lot sooner than he planned. The weight of history had borne down on him for far too long. Surely, he had earned the right to live out the last few years of his life for himself?

That said, his smallholding wouldn't be *that* small. And he might keep back one or two servants to tend to the chickens whenever he didn't feel like doing it himself. But it would still be a considerable step down from all he had known. A simple, and yet comfortable, country life.

"Your Prince has given his full support to my decision. Indeed, he himself has opted to follow his heart and pursue a career in the Guards, as an officer and a gentleman."

Again there were murmurs from the crowd but on the whole, they sounded positive and one or two even let fly with a half-hearted "Hoorah!". The Prince puffed out his chest and tried to milk the moment for all it was worth, stepping forward and saluting the crowd enthusiastically, but the stony silence resumed, broken only by a few distant coughs.

The King muttered something under his breath for the Prince's ears only and continued with the announcements. "Likewise the Princess has asked to step down from her official duties and surrender any and all claims to the throne, for both herself and any child born to her — on pain of death," the King chuckled, as if an entirely unnecessary clause had been inserted into her abdication contract for a joke. Ella looked into the wind and chewed her lip. "Indeed, the Prince and Princess have elected to make the ultimate sacrifice and bear no heirs lest it led to struggles and bloodshed in the future. A clean break must be made. Instead, they have decided to adopt you, the people, as their rightful heirs and bequeath the Kingdom to one and all."

This confused everyone with some thinking that they were going to move into the Palace while others wondering if this was some sort of gag that only Kings understood.

"Therefore, from this day forth, you will all have a say in the running of the King…" he started before correcting himself. "… in the running of the country, from the richest in the land to the poorest, you will each have a voice. And the right to exercise it however you wish, as enshrined in law."

The concept of 'rights' was foreign to the people of Andovia. Indeed most had never even heard of democracy or elections but with the first ballot in only three weeks they would learn fast. And once they had, there would be no turning back.

"My loyal subjects, my people, my friends, I look back upon our glorious past with a great sense of pride, but I look forward to our wondrous future with something far greater — hope," the King said with a benevolent smile. "I go now, but before I do, I want to wish you the very best of luck. And say that I know that you, the people, will make Andovia truly great. For *everyone*. Farewell."

And with that, the King removed his crown, twisted it a few times to snap it in two and then held up both halves to show the people. It was the last act of the last King of Andovia — King Alexander the Magnanimous, as he would come to be known by students of history in years to come.

EPILOGUE

IT WAS A GLORIOUSLY CRISP autumn day some weeks later when Marigold and Gardenia were out taking the air. Their 'sins' against the Princess were long forgotten and their slate wiped clean, they were, at last, free to live the lives they had always wanted — without obligations or expectations. They didn't even have to wear their Mother's latest fashions. She sold more than enough designs without her daughters having to model them anymore. Today, they were dressed against the weather in elegant and yet simple clothing, and with just a touch of rouge to colour their lips rather than the layers of cake they had previously been unable to step out without donning.

"What a beautiful day," Gardenia said, looking out across the frost-covered park.

Marigold smiled. It didn't matter if it had been hailstones or hurricanes, Gardenia would have said it was a beautiful day regardless, such was the rejuvenating effect of escaping the block with her head still attached to her body.

It was the day of Andovia's first Presidential elections and the people were out in their droves to cast their votes. Five candidates in all had stood, four of whom had, somewhat predictably, come from the ranks of the aristocracy, but it was a complete outsider who had caught the public's imagination — a former Burgermeister who had apparently helped thwart a plot against the King. At least, this was the rumour that had spread around town shortly after the bomb plot had been uncovered. Such was Didi's dedication to the cause that he had spent the last thirty years living undercover as a down-and-out, stinking to high heaven and being universally shunned by all, all in the name of the King until finally, his actions had come to light on that fateful day of Gardenia's execution. Now, with his cover blown, he had no choice but to retire from his secret agent work with his head held high and the Andovian Cross on his chest.

It was an incredible story to say the least, scarcely credible in fact, but as most people in this Kingdom still believed in magic slippers and pumpkins that turned into carriages, few thought to question it.

Of course, some of the other candidates didn't give Didi much of a chance. He was, after all, still a commoner as Lord Ricci was quick to point out, and as such, unsuited to the responsibilities of high office. But what Lord Ricci failed to grasp was that the vast majority of the electorate were also commoners and the winds of change were blowing through Andovia like a gale, sweeping away the old to make way for the new.

"Good afternoon," smiled Heidi, Lord Ricci's housemaid as she passed them by in the avenue.

"Good afternoon," Marigold and Gardenia replied as one.

Heidi, like every other person in the land, had the day off work to vote, much to the consternation of his Lordship. She still could not quite believe that she — a humble serving girl — was being allowed a say in who ruled their Kingdom. Of all the strange turns of fate that had befallen the Kingdom in the last few months, none could compare to this. Heidi crossed her fingers into the sign of good luck and touched the 'DD' lapel button she was wearing, one of thousands worn by chambermaids, shop assistants and farmhands across the land — again, much to the consternation of their wealthy employers.

The park was busy with people taking to the lawns after casting their votes. Marigold and Gardenia had arranged to meet Corporals Babin and Deniau at Hans' Ice Kiosk (as it had since been renamed) just after twelve.

The two Guardsmen were convalescing after being treated for their injuries. Neither could fully explain how or where they had come to be wounded but the outgoing King had assured their commanding officer that it had been in the defence of the Princess and as such, both were awarded the Medal of Valour.

A few days earlier, Corporal Babin had taken Marigold to one side, got down on one knee and, with a little effort, proposed but to his surprise and disappointment Marigold had declined.

"It's not that I don't feel for you," she had told him as she helped him back to his feet. "It's just that, well, the siege asides, I don't even know you." This was true. All in all, they'd barely spent twenty-four hours in each other's company. The siege had thrown them together and their feelings had been forged in the intensity that had followed but it had still only been twenty-four hours regardless. "Let's take our time, shall we, and see if we like each other when people aren't trying to kill us?"

It sounded like a wonderful idea to Corporal Babin. He liked the idea of getting to know Marigold and would take each day as it came. They did, after all, have their whole lives in front of them.

Gardenia had a similar conversation with Corporal Deniau. They were still both so young. She'd barely been regarded as a woman for more than a few weeks after a lifetime of being a mere girl. She wanted to wear the label a little longer before swapping it again to become a wife. Corporal Deniau didn't fully understand but he vowed he would wait for her whatever she decided. She was, after all, the most desirable woman in the Kingdom. Some girls were worth waiting for.

The Corporals were at Hans's Ice Kiosk when Marigold and Gardenia arrived. As it transpired, so was pretty much everyone else in town. It seemed like the entire population had decided to buy an ice cream today to commemorate the end of one era and the start of the next. Hans and Cynthia had never been so busy. It was all down to the new cut-glass serving dishes, Cynthia was adamant.

Babin and Deniau were about a quarter of the way down the line, with their uniforms helping them past the ranks of unfeted shopkeepers and unwashed farmhands, but still with a long way to go before reaching the kiosk. A great many courting couples, married couples, widows, spinsters, children and maidens held prominence before them and the line was growing longer all the time. But they had promised the sisters an ice cream and so an ice cream they would have. Besides, once the girls arrived they would be able to leapfrog a few places and join the echelons of courting couples before them. After that, it shouldn't take more than another hour to get served. If they were lucky. Deniau gave his Medal of Valour a quick polish and stuck out his chest. Every little bit helped.

Babin was the first to spot the girls arriving at the back of the line. He waved to them and several others also noted Marigold and Gardenia's arrival. The Moreau boys were the first to jump aside. By rights, they should have been further forward but since turning ten, the older Moreau boy simply refused to stand with the rest of the children and insisted on being with the men at the very back of the line. The younger Moreau boy always went where his brother went which meant neither had tasted ice cream in weeks. But some things were more important than ice cream.

"Mademoiselle," Jacob Moreau said, doffing his cap and bowing like a Lord. Wilhelm copied and the boys were rewarded, not with a glance as was customary, but a full-on curtsey from both sisters.

"Messieurs," Marigold said, acknowledging the boys to their obvious delight. They'd finally made it. They were finally men.

In amongst it all, Mademoiselle Renard turned and trudged off home. She'd had enough of this nonsense and after years of getting nowhere had decided to stick to fruit from now on. Apples were abundant. Red and juicy. For making pies with. That was what made the menfolks' mouths water anyway.

Others in the line now turned and saw the sisters. Only a few short weeks ago neither could have shown their face in public for fear of reprisals but much had happened since the King's abdication. Few official details had been made public — in the interests of national security — but curious whispers had begun to circulate that Marigold and Gardenia may have played more of a role in recent events than they were ready to admit. The rumours were rife, and the speculation wild, but some had heard that the sisters were far from the unwitting innocents they had claimed to be.

The line stood before them and stared. It was the first time either had been out in weeks and they had expected such a reaction. Gardenia was set to flee. What would the Corporals think of them when they saw this response? She was about to turn when the farmhands stood aside with their caps in their hands and their heads bowed low. The shopkeepers were next, each seeming to compete with each other over who could make more room for the sisters.

Marigold and Gardenia joined the Corporals when, to their great surprise, the line continued to step aside. First, the courting couples, which Deniau had thought was because of his and Babin's medals, but then the married couples too, which wasn't proper etiquette at all and everyone knew it.

Marigold immediately declined, as was only proper, but the married couples would not accept her refusal and continued to stand aside.

"Please, you are most kind but I insist," Marigold said again in case there had been some sort of misunderstanding, as indeed there had been, but the misunderstanding was all hers. The Perrins, the Legrands, the Eames, the Viponds and all. Husbands and wives alike. None would put themselves before the sisters. All were immoveable.

And still it didn't stop. The widows and spinsters now followed suit, making way with a curtsey and inviting Marigold and Gardenia to take their place. The young maidens were next, shop girls and maids of all kinds, stepping aside for the perplexed sisters. And none seemed to mind either. Indeed, most sought to catch Marigold and Gardenia's eye with a grateful smile, only too happy to give the sisters their proper accord.

Finally, at the front of the line, came the girls of good standing. Claudia Ricci, Suzette Weiss, Isabella Eames and at least half a dozen others. Daughters of the rich and the powerful. The Lords and the landed. The titled and the entitled. Every single one of them now stepped aside without hesitation to make way for Marigold and Gardenia.

Hans looked out from his serving hatch and could not for the life of himself work out what was happening. That was until he laid eyes on Marigold and Gardenia, still stood towards the back of the line and too confounded to move.

"Ah," he said with a knowing smile, inviting the sisters to take their rightful place at the head of the line. "I believe you are next?"

There may still be few portraits of seamstresses and their daughters hanging in the Palaces of Europe. And the annals of history may, to this day, be reserved for Kings and Queens alone. But in some small corners of the world, such things told only part of the story.

One such place was the Kingdom of Andovia.

A tiny fairytale land.

Where reputations were everything.

The End

ACKNOWLEDGEMENTS

MY SINCERE THANKS to Jeannie King, Jon Evans, Tony Wilson and Iain Morrison for all their invaluable feedback and help, especially with the editing of the text. Also, to Giambattista Basile (1566-1632), Charles Perrault (1628-1703) and the Brothers Grimm – Jacob (1785-1863) and Wilhelm (1766-1859) – for allowing me to play with some of their wonderful and timeless characters.

19th May 2021

ABOUT THE AUTHOR

DANNY KING was born in Slough in 1969 and later grew up in Yateley, Hampshire. He has worked as a hod carrier, a supermarket shelf-stacker, a painter & decorator, a postman and a magazine editor and he has performed all of these tasks to the best of his limited abilities. He lives in Chichester with wife, Jeannie, and four children and today writes books and screenplays.

*

Find and follow him on Facebook at 'Danny King books' and Instagram at 'dannyking_books'.

If you enjoyed *The Ugly Sisters*
please consider posting a review or telling a friend as that
sort of thing can really help independent authors like myself.

Thank you.

BY THE SAME AUTHOR

BOOKS
The Burglar Diaries
The Bank Robber Diaries
The Hitman Diaries
The Pornographer Diaries
Milo's Marauders
Milo's Run
School for Scumbags
Blue Collar
More Burglar Diaries
The Henchmen's Book Club
Infidelity for Beginners
The Executioners
The No.1 Zombie Detective Agency
Eat Locals
The Monster Man of Horror House
The Monster Man of Horror House Returns
Curse of the Monster Man of Horror House

YOUNG ADULT BOOKS
Amy X and The Great Race
Amy X and The Prim and Proper Princess School
Amy X and The Terrible Typhoon

TELEVISION & FILM
Thieves Like Us (2007)
Wild Bill (2012)
Eat Locals (2017)
The Hitman Diaries (2010) – short
Run Run As Fast As You Can (2017) – short
Little Monsters (2018) – short
Seven Sharp (2017) – short
Romantic (2019) – short (Russia)

STAGE
The Pornographer Diaries: the play (2007)
Killera Dienasgramata (Latvia) (2007-12)

Printed in Great Britain
by Amazon